The Dead Sagas

Volume I

A Ritual of Bone

LEE C CONLEY

Wolves of Valour Publications

Written by Lee C Conley
Second Edition 2019

ISBN:
978-1-9993750-2-7

Cover art by Cloud Quinot
and
Cover layout by Lee Conley

ACKNOWLEDGMENTS

Thank you to everyone who believed in me and who pushed me to finish this. Thank you to all those who didn't believe I could do it, you drove me onwards.

Thank you to my wife Laura and my daughter Luna for your patience and insight. Thanks to my family, to Mum, Dad and Nan for all your support. Thanks to my editor Tim Marquitz for your critical eye and hard work. Thanks to Cloud Quinot for your fantastic artwork on the cover.

Thank you to Alan and to Morag for the proofing, and to Nigel for your wise thoughts on plot and for teaching me the noble art of swordsmanship.

Thanks to everyone who has helped me this year and those who gave your valued opinions on the cover that's you, Dyrk Ashton, Michael Baker (and for the map advice & good chats, thanks dude), Kareem Mahfouz, Sadir Samir, Rob Hayes. Thanks to Timy Takacs for hosting my cover reveal and everything else. Thanks to Graham Austin-King for the publishing advice.

Thanks to all the reviewers who have taken the time and the folks in the online writing community and also to the fellow authors I met through SPFBO not listed above, to Phil Parker, Jacob Sannox, Scott Kaelen, Aidan Walsh, Nick Borrelli, Jesse and Rebekah Teller, Dave Woolliscroft, Paul Torr, David Humphrey, Jennifer at Bunnyreads, Steven McKinnon, Paul Lavender, J.P. Ashman and Alicia Wanstall-Burke - You guys all rock! There are so many great authors and other folks I've met this year if I've missed any of you I'm sorry. Also, thanks to Pete, Katie, Nina, Fox and all the guys at Wolfshead, and all my other friends and followers for all the support and likes.

For my girls.
Laura, Luna, and baby Anya.

A Ritual of Bone

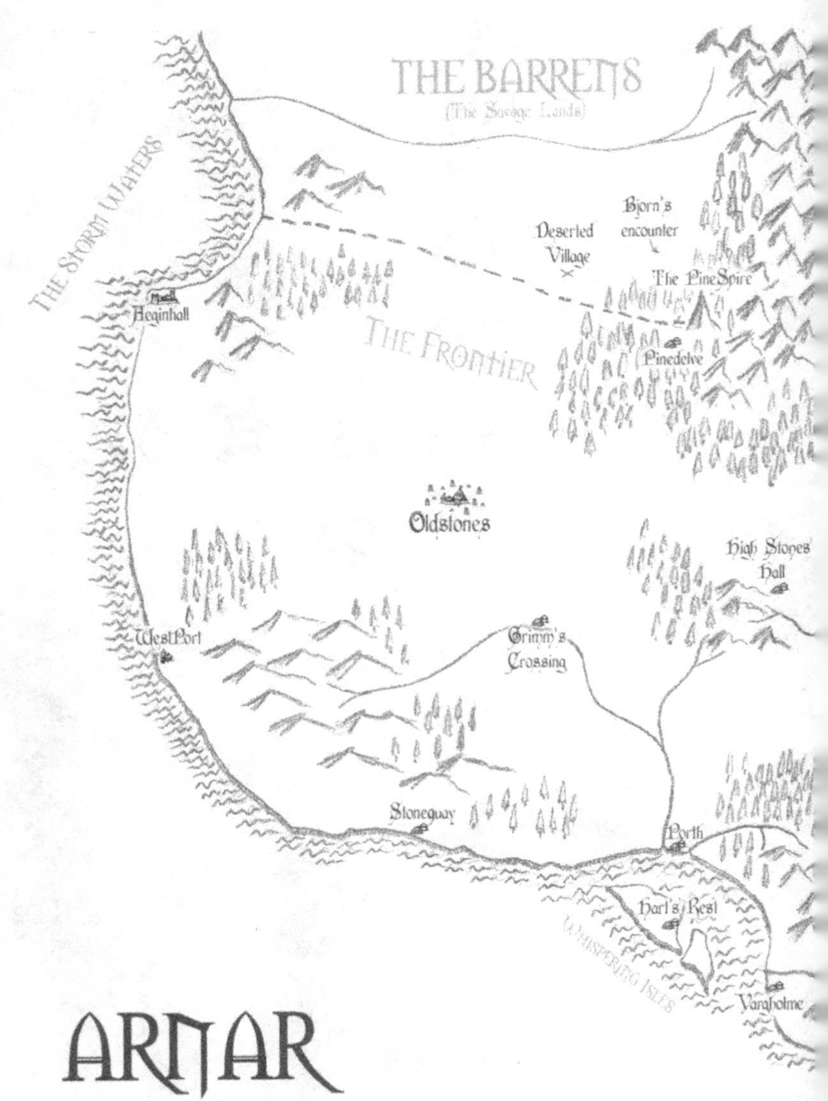

ARNAR

From the archives of the College of Arn

By Master Areion
Master Cartographer and Scholar of Charts

CYDOR
Three Bridges
The High Passes
Arnulf's Watchpost
Dunholme
Ravenshold
Weirdell
THE BORDERS
Hammer Motte
Peren
THE OLD LANDS
Eymsford
ARN'S PASS
THE SEA OF SPIRES
Wayfell Harbour
Barrowford
Stoneshore
ARN
Anchorage
Cairnholme
Ironfell
Flint Hall
Havenholme
THE GREAT SEA

CHAPTER ONE

The Apprentice

A great sense of fear and dread came over him as he stepped into the dim moonlight. He glanced up at the rising sliver of moon through the trees. The faint light silhouetted the branches, which clawed the sky like black twisted fingers grasping the moon's crescent.

He was being watched. A cold shiver ran over him, and he stared into the darkness.

Nothing.

He lowered his hood and turned to look down the track, which led through a gap in the crumbling wall and off into the dark tree line. The darkness seemed to close in around him. His mind let his eyes see dark shapes staring at him through the shadows. The feeling of being watched grew stronger.

He absently clutched at the idol hung around his neck, a totem for the gods of his fathers. Not generally a follower of the old ways, yet he sought any protection against the night and its watching shadows.

Still looking into the trees, he kissed the wooden carving and tucked it under his shirt. He shook himself—he should know better about such things. It was just this place, old and full of spirits. He glanced up at the thin sliver of moon rising through the trees, the object of his study, and the reason for his venture out into the ruins this night.

The young apprentice ducked back inside the marquee and returned with a small glowing lantern. After a long searching look back off into the trees, he made his way out from the crumbling stone enclosure, picking his path carefully so as not to stumble in the dark. He followed a track that cut through the rock-strewn undergrowth, leading up a short distance to a high place on the hillside it overlooked the small cluster of crumbling ruins in which they had made camp.

The track led on to another path, older and worn. Still rocky in places, it wound up the hill he now ascended. He could still sense that strange feeling of unfriendly eyes as he climbed. He glanced about nervously. He was exposed, with nothing but grass and the dark trees below. The thought of a dark shape staring at him through the shadows made him uneasy. The lantern light just seemed to bring the darkness even closer.

He hurried on. The top of the path came out into a square space. If natural or cut into the rock, the apprentice was not sure, but at some point in the past, someone had laid stones to make a low wall on the two outward sides, creating a small open room on the hillside. If it ever had a roof there was no sign. It was ancient, a grass and moss-covered ruin, akin to those it stood watch over. To one side was a large flat stone and upon it was a clay bowl. Beside the stone, a large bronze bell set in a wooden frame.

His master had ordered the bell brought with them and the bowl was theirs also. He remembered it took two mules to haul the great bell up the hill when they first came to this accursed place. He still had no idea why his master had insisted on bringing the damn pointless thing. They seemed to have brought so many strange and seemingly useless things, but who was he to question his master's wisdom? Just a lowly apprentice from the College, it was not his place to challenge such things.

Shrugging to himself, the apprentice approached the bowl on the stone and filled it with water from a skin he took from his bag. He then placed a small piece of ironwood in the water. The wood floated in the bowl but spun round and round, finally coming to rest in one direction as if pulled by some unseen force. He looked up at the rising moon. The slim waning crescent had now risen above the trees and was framed by the clouds in its pale light. He thought perhaps two, maybe three nights until the black moon. From his bag, he produced a strange measuring device. He then measured the moon's height and position in the sky compared to the direction of the floating wood. He took out a piece of slate and chalk and noted down his findings, then hastily put his equipment back into the bag hung at his side.

He looked out over the low wall at the gloom of the ruins below. He could make out little but vague shadows, not even the glow of fire from the campsite. The wind picked up and whistled through the stony bluffs, blowing out the candle in his lantern. He cursed, and turned to make his way back down the path. He half-feared to see some fell creature standing in his path as he turned, but the way was clear. All he could see was the dark path down to the shadow of the trees.

The sense of dread again filled him as he made his way down the hill, carrying the extinguished lantern. He neared the dark trees and quickened his pace. The wind had brought the trees to life. They creaked and groaned, bending to the will of the wind.

There was a loud *crack*. He froze—just a branch falling. Then another *crack* came from the darkness, followed by the sound of tumbling of rocks. There was something out there.

A sudden panic clutched his heart, and he ran. He had no desire to meet whatever evil was stalking him in the darkness of this ancient place. His terror and panic overcame his judgment. He ran recklessly back down the track, hardly looking. He was waiting for some terrible hand to seize him or to be felled from a blow from behind as he ran. Ahead, through the gap in the crumbling wall, he could make out the warm glow of the fire from the campsite. In his blind panic, his shin struck a hidden branch. In pain, he stumbled. The extinguished lantern flew from his hands and sailed off into the gloom. His foot found some hole or gap and he tripped, his foot remaining lodged as he went over.

He cried out at a flash of pain from his trapped ankle. He tried to dislodge his foot and get up. The pain flashed up his leg again. He realised he couldn't.

He cried out again. Was something chasing him? Well, it had him now. He lay in agony, terrified. And then, blackness descended upon him. He must have fallen unconscious, for the next thing he remembered was the sound of voices and a great dog looming above him.

The hound towered over the fallen apprentice, howling into the night. It was a great grey shaggy beast with long matted hair and a thin, pointed face. The apprentice lay dazed. The great hound licked the apprentice's face with a rough slobbery tongue, and continued howling and barking towards the sound of the approaching voices.

He became aware of a nearing light, and then, of two figures standing over him.

'Good dog,' said a low, aged voice. He recognised it as his master's voice.

'See, I told you I heard something,' spoke another voice.

His master replied, 'The dog certainly did.'

The lantern light only half-illuminated their faces from below, but the apprentice knew the other figure to be the large frame of Master Logan.

'Are you okay down there, lad?' asked Logan.

The apprentice, relieved at the familiar voices,

then realised his pursuer had not manifested into hard reality.

'My foot's stuck, I can't walk,' whimpered the apprentice.

He cried out at a sudden burst of pain from his leg as a heavy weight was lifted away, and his leg freed.

'You're a mess, boy. How did you manage this?' demanded his master in a stern tone.

'There was something out there, in the woods.'

The master's tone softened with interest. 'What did you see?'

'Well, nothing…but I could feel its eyes hunting me for some time. Then I heard something in the trees, and as I hurried back, I must have tripped. It was chasing me, I swear.'

The master, not satisfied, persisted, 'But did you *see* anything? Or just running from shadows?'

'Well, no, Master. I saw nothing, but…' The apprentice suddenly felt very foolish under their gaze.

His master, Eldrick, just looked at him with a stern frown. Although, he did then look off into the night, searching. Master Logan raised his lantern and also looked into the shadowy tree line. Nothing.

Logan turned to the stricken apprentice. 'If there was something out there, the dog would have caught wind of it and would have been barking all over the place long before you saw anything.' He bent and stroked the great hound's ears.

'Well, old boy? What do you think? Anybody out there?' The hound nuzzled at Master Logan's hands and continued to sit there, staring up at his master.

'See, he don't think anything's about.'

Logan laughed. 'Perhaps you were just spooked by the shadows in the darkness. This is a fell place after all.'

The two masters helped the young apprentice up and, supporting him on either side, bore him back to the warmth and safety of the campfire.

They came through the gap in the crumbling wall and back into the campsite. The light of the campfire came from the hearth inside a large tent, giving it a flickering glow.

The hound ran on to reclaim its spot by the fire as the masters helped the apprentice through the heavy canvas flap, which served as an entrance to the great marquee. Inside, it was quite large and lavishly decorated, not something set up for a night or two.

It was held up by a thick wooden pole set deep into the ground and was covered by a thick canvas which was pegged closely to the earth. The marquee housed several other smaller tents, all clustered around the fire, and had various provisions and equipment stored in the corners. There was a hole in the roof at the central point above the fire through which the smoke escaped. The flickering firelight sent shadows dancing across the canvas overhead.

They laid him down in his own open tent.

'This leg needs tending. You will not be wandering about in the dark for some time, boy,' said his master gravely.

Master Eldrick had, among the many things in his time with the College, studied healing and herbcraft and his abilities were more than apt. However, this did not lessen the pain for the apprentice as his master first reset, and then bound his leg in splints.

Master Logan brought the apprentice some tea brewed from strange herbs and a bitter tasting root to chew on.

'For the pain, lad,' he said. The pain was great but the tea and foul-tasting root, obviously medicinal, did seem to ease the throbbing in his ankle.

As he lay there, staring up at the roof, he felt the fear slowly ebb away, leaving him instead with the growing feeling of foolishness.

This camp had been his home for some weeks now. It was, in fact, the second moon that he had recorded since they arrived, a moon now waning and nearly black. The tea and root were starting to take effect and make him feel drowsy. As he drifted towards sleep in the safety of the campsite, he felt it again.

He was being watched. He glanced around. The hound was asleep on his side near the fire outside Logan's tent. The master himself was presumably seated inside with a drink. Master Eldrick's tent was now closed, but he would, no doubt, be in there, studying some ancient lore or far off text—ever reading to guide him in some of the research they had come here to conduct.

He dreaded some of the research of the coming days, but he would not think of that, even if his master was now in his tent planning so. Not with this terrible sense watching him from some hidden corner.

He looked up. He could see the moon through the centre hole above. Its crescent had risen high, still framed by the clouds. He clutched at the wooden idol hung around his neck. He hoped that if any of the many gods were watching, they would protect him. His mind had been playing tricks on him of late. He lay watching the moon and eventually fell into an uneasy sleep.

CHAPTER TWO

The Tracker

The village was deserted. The surrounding trees were motionless and the air was quiet and still. The lone rider passed amongst the small huddle of crude buildings. One had been set ablaze, the charred timbers lay blackened, the embers still smoking.

The buildings were round but still little more than primitive hovels, low walls made from mud and woven bracken with turf packed over the roofs. The ground seemed well trodden—the local folk had lived here some time.

There were many tracks laid across each other. He could make out little from the confusion around the buildings. The animal pens lay open and empty. Possessions and tools littered the floor. The folk who lived here either seemed to have left in great haste, or been caught unawares.

Strange? If they had moved on, they would have taken more with them, and if they had been attacked, would more not have been taken? Granted, much had been looted, the food stores empty, no sign of any animals and weapons, but still, valuable tools and trinkets had been abandoned. *If there had been an attack, where are the dead?* The mystery deepened.

He was a huntsman, tracking the wild creatures that haunted the hills and deep forests of Arnar. If it were man or beast, he could hunt them, he was Bjorn.

He had hunted many great beasts across the realm and his skills as a great huntsman and tracker had soon earned him renown far and wide. The lords of the local villages and towns paid him to hunt with them, or to hunt down troublesome beasts that attacked villages or took livestock. Even on occasion to track down men who fled into the wilds for refuge from their crimes, but Bjorn always found them. Lord Archeon had recently sought him out and hired him to ride to the northern borders and investigate the disappearances.

There had been many tales of these strange disappearances. Folk had been reported missing, and outlying farmsteads had been found mysteriously deserted. Fear and rumour had spread amongst the local folk. There was whispered talk of an evil beast stalking the land and rumours of attacks coming from the Barrens in the north, a place known as the Savage Lands.

Lord Archeon served as the king's warden of the west, and he ruled over these north-western frontier territories. It was he who had summoned Bjorn. Word of his deeds had indeed spread far and wide to catch the attention of such a powerful lord. The hunter had sworn to track down this beast—if it even existed. More likely, he thought, he would end up finding some foolish outlaws responsible.

He had searched and talked to all who would speak of the matter. He spent much time in the taverns here and there listening to the local talk, hoping for some word or news to aid his search, but so far nothing but rumour.

Yet Bjorn had found farms and homesteads deserted, their buildings left dark and empty. Some days past, while searching one such place, he picked up an odd trail leading from one of the strangely deserted farmsteads out along the border, and had followed it north into the Barrens.

The Barrens, despite the name, were not empty. Many had settled the lands there. Beyond Arnar's northern borders, small defended villages were dotted here and there. Exiles and outlaws came to these lawless lands to evade capture. The primitive savages, who once gave the lands their name, had long ago fled north when the armies of Arn marched west from Cydor and forged the realms now known as Arnar.

He followed the trail for leagues across the border deep into these savage lands. It was this morning when he had seen the smoke rising above the trees. Bjorn followed it to the small hamlet nestled in the wooded hills.

The burnt-out house had been smoking at least a day, maybe two. He searched the floor around the houses. There was no hope. There were too many tracks, old and new, all laid over each other. He moved his search to the surrounding ground, there were still tracks but they were clearer. He took in every bent blade of grass, every broken twig and footprint until he found something.

He could see where people had knelt a while under the trees. *Yes, they knelt for some time, watching.* He touched the imprints of feet and depressions left by knees in the mud.

His eyes then followed the tracks through the grass as they split up towards the houses. He followed. Studying a footprint, it looked like they were running.

Bjorn walked back in amongst the houses, following the tracks until they were lost in the trampled markings of the villagers.

There were some other tracks, a single set of prints here and there, leading off into the woods, perhaps fleeing to safety. But each one he followed, all ended abruptly in the woods and disappeared with no trace. *Were they attacked?*

Bjorn made his way back to the buildings and checked inside each hut for anything of value, finding just tools and belongings scattered about at random. Things seemed to have just been dropped and the houses searched and ransacked. He led his horse out and away from the eerie darkened doorways of the huts. It was too quiet. This place was dead.

He returned to the mass of tracks that seemed to also lead away from the village where they arrived.

He followed them east beneath the trees. The tracks were clear now. He had them.

He followed the trail deeper into the trees, leading his horse by the reins. Some of the signs in the disturbed leaves of the forest floor were easy to follow. It looked like some were dragging their feet as they stumbled through the undergrowth. *Prisoners perhaps?*

Bjorn smiled. Not a beast after all then, but men. Perhaps a war chief amongst the border clans needed slaves. He must find the truth and bring the high lord an answer.

He tracked them over three days through a silent pine forest. The lack of sound was eerie, perforated only by the occasional startled bird and the soft *crunch* of last year's pine needles beneath his feet.

He followed cautiously. He found their campsites, the fires cold but fresh. He tracked them from hearth to hearth, moving only in daylight as to not miss sign of their trail. They were close.

As the sun lowered behind him Bjorn found himself heading up into high ground. The trees thinned away as he got higher, giving way to grassy scrub and rocky gullies. The trail became harder to follow amongst the rocks and seemed to disappear altogether in parts, but he hoped to pick up more signs as he moved further east. He could not afford to lose them now, he had come so far.

He tethered his horse amongst a copse of trees and took a steep rocky slope up to the top of a ridge. He found the summit covered in low twisted trees and small bushes, clawing out an existence in the thin soil. The climb was a hard effort. As the tracker caught his breath, he looked east to get the lay of the land he was venturing into.

He saw the great mountains to the east. He looked to be moving into a bleak rocky pass heading up through high cliffs and up towards the hills that marked the foot of the distant mountains. There were patches of woods on the slopes of the pass ahead. Thickets of small twisted trees and bushes grew amongst the rocky heathland. He was hopeful he could pick up the trail amongst the undergrowth. He searched for signs of movement in the dying light or the glow of a fire somewhere ahead, but the pass looked deserted.

He noticed he seemed to be getting steadily closer each day to the great snow-capped peaks that dominated the eastern sky, the Spine of the World. The great mountain range ran from the furthest known peaks of the far north and ran down hundreds of leagues to the Great Sea in the south, a vast immeasurable barrier of mountains and stone which cleaved through the lands of men.

He would have to stop soon and make camp for the night but stayed up on the ridge until the sun had set. Still no signs of a fire in the darkening pass ahead. When it was too dark to make out anymore from the ridge, Bjorn carefully made his way back down the dark slope. He tended his horse and made a small camp amongst the bushes. He would sleep on the ground and could not risk a fire, not with his mysterious quarry possibly so close.

The huntsman took a rolled-up bundle from his horse's saddle and unfurled the skin onto the fallen leaves and soft damp mosses that grew on the floor beneath the trees. He unrolled a woollen blanket and pulled it over himself as he lay on the soft fur of the skin. It was surprisingly comfortable. He probably slept outside more than in a bed these days, he mused. Bjorn looked up into the dark branches spread out above him. He lay listening to the familiar sounds of the wilderness and to the wind in the trees until he drifted off into an easy sleep.

He awoke with the sunrise. The light streamed down through the trees, the green leaves giving way to the reds and oranges of autumn. The huntsman made ready to continue his pursuit. As he made his way around the ridge and into the pass, Bjorn was hopeful he would pick up the trail again in the pleasant morning light.

As he rode around a small grassy hillock, Bjorn noticed something in the grass. He reined in his horse and rode back to look again. The grass seemed to catch the light differently and seemed a slightly different colour. The hunter dismounted to look closer. The grass was indeed bent and flattened, and as he moved back and forth, he noticed from a certain angle a definite trail could be seen heading off into the trees. He found no footprints. *Perhaps a game trail?* But with no other tracks, he once again followed the trail into the trees.

Bjorn searched carefully for any signs of someone having passed this way. He stopped as his eyes fell onto something that made him smile. There was no print, but to Bjorn, the sign was obvious. A broken twig lay in the trail. It had been broken twice perhaps a hand's span apart. Bjorn recognised the sign, breaks most likely made by a man's foot.

Bjorn followed the trail up towards a cluster of large rocks. It looked as though in some time past the rocks had crashed down the slopes from the cliffs above and now lay huddled together where they finally came to rest, overgrown and covered in moss. What he found there amongst the rocks would later haunt his dreams in the dark hours of the night.

He was no stranger to blood, skinning and carving a kill was part of his trade, but what he found there chilled his heart. It looked like it had once been a man. He had been mutilated and dismembered, his arms and legs cut off. The torso lay on a large flat stone which was thick with sticky congealing blood. The chest had been cut open and the heart torn out.

Bjorn walked amongst the blood splattered rocks, the scene of some ritual sacrifice he thought. There were strange markings daubed in blood on the surrounding rocks. Perhaps one of the rumoured forbidden cults had done this? He had heard of such, those who fled across the border to perform their dark rites in the lawless wilds of the north.

The man's head had been flayed, sliced along the scalp and the hair torn away. His mouth gaped open, tongue cut out. His eyes had been pecked out by the carrion birds, and the bloody sockets stared blankly up off into the sky. Despite this, Bjorn didn't think he had been here long. The birds were always swift to feast on the fallen dead.

The sudden force of a blow threw Bjorn against the rocks. A piercing pain shot through his shoulder. Something had struck him hard from behind. The pain was intense.

An arrow *thumped* into ground beside him. Then another clattered off a nearby rock splintering as it struck the hard stone. Bjorn peered from between the rocks before ducking back as a hail of rocks and arrows whistled overhead and crashed around him. There was a flicker of movement amongst the trees.

Bjorn was dismayed. How could he let this happen? Now, it appeared he was the one being hunted. He cursed as he broke from cover and ran.

His horse, it was still tethered by the rocks. There was no time. He plunged into the trees and turned to look. There was movement now amongst the rocks. He ran on into the depths of the trees.

His shoulder burned with a hot pain that seemed to spread down his arms. He stopped and leant against a tree, resting his head on his arm. It was hard to breathe and his vision was blurring. He reached around his back and felt the wooden shaft of an arrow buried deep in his shoulder. Bjorn grimaced from the stab of pain as he snapped the shaft, leaving its buried point and part of the short, splintered arrow protruding from his back.

He could hear the sounds of pursuit drawing closer through the undergrowth. There was no time. Bjorn tried to run on but his limbs felt heavy, he stumbled. He crashed against another tree and fell.

The hunter lay sprawled face down in the fallen autumn leaves. He could smell the earthy fragrance of the forest floor. His head was spinning. As his vision faded out into dark unconsciousness, he became aware of someone standing over him.

CHAPTER THREE

A Scholar of Ruins

As he awoke, the pain returned to his ankle. The sunlight beamed in through the top of the marquee. The apprentice swung his legs out from the furs he slept under. The splints were cumbersome, and a sharp pain shot up his leg as he tried to move it.

Seeing the apprentice stir, the hound got up and padded over to greet him. As he sat and idly scratched the great dog's head, Master Logan ducked into the tent.

'Morning, lad. We let you sleep. It's been a while since sunrise.' He laughed, always quick to laugh.

Master Logan was a big man, broad and tall, not the average academic physique. His long black hair tied behind his head and with a gruff bushy beard, both streaked with the silver of years passed. He wore the long loose hooded robe currently in fashion with the scholars of the College. Master Logan's robes were not frayed and dirty like his own, but were of a fine looking dark green weave and intricately embroidered with gold and bronze knot patterns around the hems and sleeves.

'You'll not be going far, but I have something for you.' He went and fetched a walking staff. 'For all the walking about in the wilderness, good to have a firm stick to walk with, you know.' He paused and studied the staff before handing it down to the apprentice. 'I got it from a place I know near the College. Consider it a loan. Should do you fine to get about if you really have need, but I would stay off that leg if you can.'

The apprentice took the staff gratefully. It was about five foot long, slender and sturdy—a fine walking staff. Far too fine for a young apprentice such as himself.

'Thank you, master,' said the apprentice, smiling through the pain. The master nodded and turned to leave, then paused. 'Don't be going far. You had best rest that leg. You broke it you know. I think Old Eld has some tasks for you though. The sitting type, of course, but tasks nonetheless.'

'Yes, master,' replied the apprentice. Logan left and went about his own tasks. The great grey hound followed, trailing along at his heels.

The apprentice managed to painfully get to his feet, using Logan's staff to lean on, and laboriously made his way to a bench by the fire. The entrance to the marquee had been pulled wide open, spilling in the morning light. He was seated at the large table where they ate, or often read and worked. The apprentice could see out to the track through the crumbling wall, to the ruins and trees beyond. The daylight brought colours to the old stone and illuminated the shadowy tree line, the twisted old trees could now be seen clearly amongst the rocks. The apprentice could see far into the wooded tree line, which eventually sunk into shadows some distance in. Not at all as menacing in the daylight.

There was a low mist hanging over the place. Not much grew except the thin grass and the mosses that hung from the trees or clung to the ancient stones. The grey rocks and stonework were mottled in the yellows and greens of lichens, and worn smooth by the years and elements. These ruins, left by a people now long forgotten, the only legacy of an untold age.

His master, Eldrick, approached him. 'Good morning, my boy.' The apprentice turned. His master was an elderly man, he was balding with age and what was left of his hair had long lost its colour, faded into a silver white. His face had many lines and his eyes were wise and stern.

Master Eldrick was wearing the old worn cloak he often wore, perhaps once black but like his hair, had faded and was now a dirty grey. He had it wrapped tightly around him. He had often grumbled at the cold since their arrival.

'I hope your leg is not in too much pain, it did not look pleasant. It will be some weeks before it is healed, at least a moon's passing. The next will be waning before you will be walking unaided. Such a shame.'

'I am sorry master, it was foolish.'

'Indeed.' The master looked sternly upon his apprentice. 'I have given it much thought, and spoken with Master Logan upon the matter'. He paused before continuing. 'I have decided to send for someone to take you back,' he said finally.

'Back?' the apprentice gasped.

'Indeed, my boy, back to the College. It will give you time to recover and allow you to continue your studies. There is also much to report. The council will want to hear our findings.'

'But, master, there is still much I can do here, still much to learn.'

Master Eldrick frowned. 'Alas, I fear you will be of little use to me up here in such condition. Indeed, a shame. There will be more you can't do than can. I feel you will serve me better back at the College. But take comfort in the knowledge that I plan not to remain here much longer as we have nearly completed our work. You will be missed, but your reports and continued work back in the scriptorium will be of much use to me.'

'But, master…' pleaded the apprentice.

Eldrick cut him short. 'It has been decided, I will hear not another word on it.'

The apprentice didn't quite know what to say, torn between the hurt of being sent from his studies with the shame of injury. On the other hand, he would be glad to leave this cold haunted old ruin and return to a warm bed and rest his foot. He could feel the pain throbbing even now.

Eldrick continued, 'Still, it will take a day to

summon the wagon to take you back. Logan has gone to send one of those hired rogues off to acquire another wagon from the town to the east, but it is some miles, a good day's ride. Hopefully he should arrive sometime after dark and be back before sunset the next day or maybe even morning if he comes straight back. But I doubt he would, not with the ale houses and lure of a warm bed.'

The master did not hold their hirelings in high regard. Master Logan mostly dealt with them; he had experience with their type.

'Anyway, I still have need of you for the time being. There is much to do before I conduct the final rites we have been preparing.'

A shiver ran through the apprentice. If they were again successful, he did not dare to think of the sights he would witness before its end. He had already seen so much, things to haunt his sleep for years to come, things that had chilled his heart. Even now he wondered if it had not just all been a terrible dream, yet so incredible. He could not help his curiosity in another glimpse. Had they unlocked some dark eldritch secret? He had to know.

The master gave him his instructions. It turned out he intended to try variations of the ritual over the next several nights. Eldrick had only been awaiting the return of Truda, the apprentice of Master Logan, before continuing.

The apprentice had the task of preparing not only his final notes in his grimoire, but also the various reports and findings of their venture. He had to prepare all which was to be taken back to the College for proper recording in the *Great Histories*—a task that would take some time upon his return. The master brought him his writing tools and many books and scrolls, including Eldrick's own great book, from which the apprentice could transcribe to add to his own grimoire.

Before turning to leave Eldrick suddenly turned to the apprentice, 'You should have been more careful, boy,' snapped Eldrick, 'but this place is watchful, it almost…whispers.' The master now seemed distant as he spoke. 'We have delved in many places, and disturbed many bones, performed the rites and rituals of many gods, and we noted and recorded all we found as best we could, but who knows what evils may have noticed us?' He paused, 'Are now watching us.'

His tone softened and his gaze fell upon the apprentice once more. 'I do not blame you wholly for last night, lad. Fear comes easy here after dark.' Then he turned and went to his work saying nothing more.

The master had seemed strange of late, despite many successful studies in this place. Perhaps it was just the creeping, watching nights and the guilt on some imbedded beliefs that they had disturbed old spirits and performed deeds, although in pursuit of knowledge and truth, still dark and chilling to behold. The fear of them having meddled in something that has indeed taken notice of them had been in the back of the apprentice's mind, and seemingly, also his master's. He tried to put it out of his thoughts and get to his study. So, he got to work preparing the many reports and hastily recorded much in his own grimoire.

Every member of the College generally kept a great book of all research and study, an accumulation of their collected knowledge. Areas of study and expertise could make up large volumes in a grimoire, some of the masters had amassed several tomes.

The apprentice had been given his by the master, shortly before they had set off to this place, a deserved gift given on the anniversary of three long year's servitude in the master's service. It was an honour for an apprentice, to then be permitted to begin his own studies under the guidance of his master.

He had been busy since, filling its pages with the studies and findings of his past few years. He desired to transcribe much from his master's writings into his own before he left and now had little time. So, he busied himself, first organising the master's reports and findings from the venture at hand.

Master Logan had been conducting a survey of the ruins to ascertain its origins or anything of interest. He had delved into many mounds and made many excavations, from which he had amassed a large collection of historical finds and surveys of the land and rocks here about. There were also studies on the local wildlife and plants, his eyes passed across the pictures and diagrams of anatomy from the many specimens of the beasts they had caught roaming these parts.

There were also, of course, Master Eldrick's reports. He looked over the many new drawings and diagrams from his master's studies. The study of the anatomy of man, a taboo study his master had been conducting. Some of this work however, although no doubt brilliant, was at times gruesome. He shuddered at the drawings of organs and body parts. The apprentice had no taste for blood but he had his duties to perform, and each one of the gory specimens depicted brought back the memories of the blood and entrails. He had done his best but the master soon realised his apprentice had no stomach for the more practical examinations, and with Master Logan's apprentice, Truda, seeming far more willing, the apprentice had gladly stepped aside to just watch and document.

The master had, of course, chosen their remote location with this gruesome study in mind, the study of the human body through dissection. It has been a study of the dead and indeed of death itself, in both its medical and also spiritual sense. The old master had said, "If we were to understand death, we can perhaps prolong life itself and advance our healing ways and lore. Who knows, even command death itself one day?"

And so, his curiosity and, perhaps fear of his encroaching age, led to a great study of the anatomy of both man and animal and the ways and beliefs of peoples old and far, seeking the secrets of life and death.

His master had amassed quite an agenda of reports. Other than the anatomical work, there were also his mystic studies, from the chilling Bone Ritual, to various religious ceremonies and rituals concerning death rites, and the invocation of the gods and spirits of many peoples.

The apprentice looked over the catalogue of all

the studies and findings he was to deliver, for they had found much in their various fields, and also dismissed much as myth. Surely the council would be satisfied with approving the venture.

He paused, placing his large quill down on the table and looked out over the ruins. The mist was lifting as the day wore on, leaving a clouded sky above the old stones and twisted trees. He looked at the path winding down through the ruin, casting his mind back over his time spent in this old place and his long journey here. He thought of his return back to the great College with this terrible throbbing pain in his foot.

The apprentice sighed and again scribbled with his quill, recording his time on the expedition and making his own report.

The apprentice turned to his master's weathered tome and began to leaf through. He desired greatly to transcribe as much from his master's grimoire into his own as his time allowed.

Master Eldrick's herb lore contained detailed pictures of the plants and trees produced with far more skill than the apprentice was able to replicate. His mystic studies of gods and lore contained many strange eldritch texts and arcane symbols.

He knew what he desired the most, the notes of the Bone Ritual. As he leafed through the pages, his eyes passed over strange texts and symbols. He had seldom had such access to his master's work.

Then his eyes then fell upon glyphs that gave him a sudden chill. He remembered these markings, *the Bone Ritual*. He began hastily scribbling much of the various recreations of the rite into his own grimoire.

The apprentice had witnessed the rites firsthand now. For after many failed attempts, the masters had been finally successful only this past moon, yet, after trying it again only three nights past, nothing.

This recent failure greatly troubled the master. He could not risk making the claim of success at the College without proof or the ability to do it again. At least the master had done it once before and now, the apprentice knew, he sought to do it again. The apprentice knew this for certain, for Eldrick had, often of late, been closed away alone in his tent, at work on the mystic symbols, searching for further secrets of the ritual. The apprentice suspected this was truly an ancient and powerful rite, of that he had no doubt, and he was certain few men had ever, let alone living now, known its secrets. He saw the great intellectual power one wielding this knowledge could achieve.

As he turned the pages, his eyes fell upon obscure texts he could not decipher but was sure were related to the ritual, perhaps some ancient sources from which the master was drawing from. He did his best to transcribe them, but the scripts were written in a strange hand, which was hard to replicate.

He came to the arcane symbols and notes of the most recent Bone Rituals. He felt that cold shiver and, again, as he stared long at the page before him, that strange sense of watchfulness came upon him once more.

Out of the corner of his eye, he saw a flicker of shadow amongst the ruins, just out of the edge of his view. He looked up quickly from his work. The surrounding ruins outside the marquee still looked pleasant in the sunlight. He searched the grassy, moss strewn masonry and the clawing trees. Nothing.

The feeling passed. Last night was still playing tricks on his mind. He went back to his work. There was much to be done, and the afternoon was upon him. Tonight's ritual was approaching, and he wanted to transcribe as much as he could from his master's writings before the daylight failed him. Then later in the darkness of night, he would observe another attempt at his master's latest work.

It must have been late in the afternoon when the apprentice heard the sound of a wagon accompanied by horsemen, clattering up the stony path towards the camp. He looked up from his writing. The cart was drawn by an old and overworked pack horse, its head hung low and weary. A hooded figure sat upon the cart, swaying back and forth as the wheels clattered over the rocks and uneven ground. It was Truda, Master Logan's apprentice. She had returned from her errand.

Two weathered roan horses slowly trailed the cart. Their riders were cloaked but glimpses of worn leather and rusting mail could be seen below. Their faces stern and grim, as weather beaten as the mounts they rode. Hired blades. Truda raised her hand in greeting. The cart came to a stop outside the marquee.

'It went well?' called the apprentice as she clambered down.

'Just a girl, her two guards, searching for her fallen loved ones,' replied Truda. Lowering her hood, she flashed him a wry look. 'Perhaps a father, a brother…a fallen lover,' she said, leaning close with the latter as she sauntered up to him. 'There were a few close moments when my heart was in my mouth, but we made it through okay. Could have gone a lot worse. It's a nasty business going on up there.'

'What happened?' asked the apprentice, curious of the missed adventure. 'I was going to ask you the same,' replied Truda, glancing at his leg. 'Master said you were injured?'

The apprentice tried to hide his embarrassment. It seemed everyone now knew. He looked down at his work before him. 'Aye, I fell in the ruin last night. My leg's in agony.'

She laughed. 'I heard. Master is at the lower camp drinking with the hired-swords. He told me just now. "Running from something" he said?'

'Aye, something like that,' replied the apprentice ruefully. 'Anyway, you're avoiding my question. What happened?' asked the apprentice, desperately trying to change the subject.

She grinned. 'Well, we heard word of a skirmish over the border between Jarlson's men and the crown troops, not a big one, out near Dunholme Tower, so we set off.' She leant provocatively on the table and continued. 'Jarlson's raiders hit them hard and fled before more crown troops showed up. They don't even bother burying the dead anymore, you know? Anyway, a Cydor patrol stopped us near the field. Fortunately, they didn't just kill us as looters. They bought our story. We didn't have anything but a few stripped bodies, no valuables or loot from the dead, so they believed us and went off scavenging themselves. My heart nearly stopped...' She trailed off as her gaze shifted to the tents behind him.

Master Eldrick emerged and hurried towards them. He looked down at the apprentice, noting his work but continuing out to the cart without word.

'You're late,' he snapped at Truda as he examined the cart's load. 'Yes, good,' he muttered to himself. 'Come quickly, take them straight to the cave.'

He dismissed the still waiting guards with a gesture and waved the wagon up the track further. The silent horsemen slowly wheeled and began a slow trot back down the track. No doubt to join Master Logan and their comrades for a drink.

'Now, apprentice,' he snapped at Truda. 'Get a move on.' He then hurried back inside his tent. Truda shrugged, and with a sigh, turned and climbed back onto her cart. She called thanks to the hired-swords as they slowly trotted off. The lead rider turned in the saddle and with a slight grin, raised his hand to clutch his hood in some kind of casual salute. The apprentice caught a smile on Truda's face as she flicked the reins, lurching the cart into motion. His gaze returned to the riders as they slowly trotted back down the track. An unexpected pang of jealously hit him, followed by a sudden dislike for their sell-sword protectors, in particular that lead rider, the rider his gaze now rested upon as they disappeared through the twisted trees. Perhaps the master was right in his mistrust of them?

The cart rolled past, and as it moved away, the apprentice's gaze fell upon the linen bound cargo stacked in the back, some blood-stained. More bodies for the master's work.

The master came back out of his tent in a hurry and came to the apprentice. 'I am sorry, boy, I will need my grimoire for now.' He scooped up his large book and hurried off after the clattering wagon. Obviously, he could not resist the immediate dissection of Truda's latest finds.

The apprentice watched Truda depart until the cart passed out of view from his seat by the entrance of the marquee. He knew where she was going, heading up to the small cave set into the rocky crags a little away across the ruin. The cave in which the master had been conducting his gruesome studies on the specimen corpses of Cydor. He shuddered.

The apprentice had thought that the master's anatomical work seemed fairly complete from the writings he had read that afternoon, but who was he to judge such things? He watched as the master hurried away, his robes flapping until he slipped from view into the decayed ruin. The apprentice was glad he was missing this one and didn't want to think of the blood and the macabre scene soon to be unfolding.

The hour was late in the day, the light would soon fail him, and he did not like to work by torch or lantern light if he could avoid it. He did what more he could until the dusk came upon him. The campsite was empty, and the cold night was drawing in.

Master Logan had not returned to the camp, he had been gone since the morning. The apprentice now found himself the lone occupant of the camp.

He painfully rose to his feet and made the short way to the hearth using his walking staff. He reached for the flints and tinder to start the evening's campfire. There was wood stacked next to the fire, but it was running low. It was his job to collect the firewood and keep the wood pile stocked, but he had not done so today, and with Truda off on her errand, no one had done the chore. There was enough wood to get the fire going at least. He scraped the flint with his knife in a smooth firm motion, and the tinder took first time, a skill he had mastered in his time here.

Once the fire was going to his liking, the apprentice examined the remaining wood pile. A little kindling remained and, anyway, over the weeks past, he had collected more to dry, and it was piled on the other side of the marquee. Someone would have to fetch it later. He was sure the masters would not mind in his incapacity.

His foot throbbed with pain. He wished for a little more of Logan's tea and root. Perhaps later, he would allow him, but for now, he had to endure. He rose to make his way back to his tent but sank back down at a burst of pain. He sighed heavily. And so, sat watching the darkening ruins about, pondering the coming night's ritual observation.

The thought of witnessing another Bone Ritual made him uneasy. The feeling grew as the moment came creeping closer by the hour. It had haunted him for weeks now since he first saw it, and although he could not take part, he still hoped he could watch. He sat there trying to divert his thoughts, his leg in pain. He was not able to relax, he had much on his mind. What if they were successful this night? He could not miss another chance to look into the dark abyss, incredible but so very terrible. Such eldritch power totally awe-inspiring to behold.

He was drawn by the morbid desire to see the Bone Ritual again. The apprentice remembered the strange droning chanting, the macabre altar, the strange arcane symbols and writings on the floor, which they also marked on the bones themselves. The skeleton of a warrior buried long ago, ancient bones from a tomb found inside a large burial mound at the ruin. As the evening darkened and the time approached, he couldn't put the memories out of his head. He remembered the cold dark presence that came upon them, stunning them with terror and wonder. As he sat there trying in vain to keep the cold at bay, he couldn't stop himself thinking of it. He remembered the way suddenly, it moved. The memory chilled him every time it came to him. It had now haunted his dreams for weeks. Like a twisted puppet suspended on invisible strings, it moved. The bones moved.

CHAPTER FOUR

The Hunted

The first thing he remembered was the smell. His mouth watered at the smell of roasting meat over a fire. Bjorn's shoulder burned, and his head was pounding as his vision slowly cleared. He was starving, his stomach aching for food, for some of that meat. Bjorn tried to raise his hands to his head but found he couldn't. His hands were bound. So were his legs. He panicked as he realised the truth of his capture.

Bjorn fought to release himself, but it was no use. As he struggled, pain lanced through his back. He remembered; he had been hit by an arrow and it was still half-buried in his shoulder. A numbing pain had crept across his back and down his arm. He found he was bound tightly, his arms behind him.

'Poison,' he muttered. The arrow must have been poisoned for him to fall into unconsciousness so quickly.

Bjorn cursed under his breath and carefully tried to look about at his surroundings. He appeared to be bound to a roughly trimmed branch and lay on his side with his face in the earth. As he looked around, his shoulder lancing pain with every movement, the hunter became aware he was not alone. There were others around him and, like himself, they were trussed to branches like game from a hunt. None of them moved. They all lay limp and motionless. The missing villagers perhaps? Some looked to be from Arnar, although their clothes were ragged and filthy. He could make out the sound of men nearby, there was smoke and that alluring smell of food floating through the trees. Bjorn listened to the raised voices and talking nearby. He listened but could not make out the words.

He rolled over painfully and his eyes met a fierce gaze staring through a mat of wiry dark hair. The man's face dirty and his beard wild. They stared at each other for a long moment.

'Where are we, friend?' whispered Bjorn after a while.

The man said nothing just merely returned him an icy stare.

'Do you understand me?'

Still, the man said nothing and just closed his eyes. Bjorn studied him for a few moments. He was dressed in crude skins, and his features were strange. He was not a man of Arnar. Perhaps one of the clan folk, or a wild man descended from the savages of old. The man opened his eyes after some time to find Bjorn still watching him and closed them again.

Bjorn checked himself. They had taken his belt upon which were hung the sheaths of his hunting knifes and his woods-blade. There was no sign of any of his gear or of his horse. They must have taken his horse. He left the poor beast tethered up near the rocks as he fled. Only a fool would have left such a valuable prize.

Bjorn still had his boots on, had they found it? He slowly tried to bring his bound legs up towards his hands. He pulled and struggled at the bindings on the branch and slowly slid them up till he could reach his boot. He slid his fingers inside. It was still there, they hadn't found it. Bjorn smiled and slowly took the small blade from its hiding place in his boot. He fumbled with it, trying to cut his bindings. He dropped it. He rolled over and searched the floor with his bound hands frantically till he had it again.

Bjorn tried again and again until he suddenly became aware of the man watching him once more. He had seen the knife and was bobbing his head up and down. He stopped when Bjorn looked over at him, and then suddenly, snatched at the knife. He missed. The man's hands were bound in front of him so he had the advantage. He lunged again and seized the knife by the blade and cried out as it cut into his hand as he snatched it away.

Bjorn rolled over to face him, ignoring the pain shooting through his back. The man stared at the knife wide-eyed and looked at his hands as the blood trickled between his dirty fingers. He held it fearfully as if it were some animal and could attack him and gazed in wonder at its shiny steel blade as though he had not seen such like before.

The man's cry had been noticed, and a growing sound of approaching footsteps reached the bound pair. A sudden look of terror came over the man's face, and he dropped the knife to the floor. He then closed his eyes and fell limp to the floor, lying perfectly still. Bjorn rolled over to face the sound and as it drew near, he closed his eyes also. He was aware of someone standing close by and looking over them. Bjorn could hear the sound of chewing and the smell of food grew stronger.

He peeked out from under his closed eyelids to behold his captor. He could not see his face but he was barefoot. He wore crude clothing fashioned from skins and adorned with bones and skulls of animals. Bjorn could see in one hand he held a half-eaten bone of the cooked meat. Bjorn was ravenous.

The man stooped low over the captives and moved out of view behind him. Bjorn didn't dare move, he was hardly breathing. The man's feet came back into view again, and then he appeared to move away back through the trees. Bjorn opened his eyes. As his captor moved away, Bjorn saw his long dark hair matted with mud, or paint, and a quick glimpse of the back of a mask before he disappeared into the forest.

Once he had gone, Bjorn slowly moved to feel around behind him for his small knife. He had it. He rolled over to keep the blade from the reach of the man beside him. As he turned to face him, Bjorn was met with an icy stare as he began to blindly hack and slice at his bindings. It took some time, but then his hands were free.

Bjorn quickly sat up and began to cut away at the bindings around his waist and legs. He was restrained with thin twisted strips of some kind of tree bark, but now he could see what he was doing it didn't take long before he was free.

The Wildman looked on in wonder. He began to bob his head up and down and was making a low whooping sound. Bjorn gestured to be quiet, but whether the man understood or not, he wasn't sure. He continued his strange, low whooping as Bjorn checked the motionless captive who lay beside him. As he rolled the figure over, he saw it was a man. From his clothes, a man of Arnar. He was dead.

Bjorn shrank from the corpse and its cold pallid skin, rolling it away from him. The hunter rose to his feet, but still crouching low, he took a look around him. There were others laid nearby. There was no signs of life amongst them. A deer and other small game were trussed up on a branch nearby, no different from the prisoners, all spoils of the hunt.

He could hear the sound of his captors through the trees. They were close. He made to move against a tree to peer in the direction of the sounds, but the strange Wildman's whooping became louder. They would hear him. Bjorn frantically tried to hush the man, and as Bjorn drew closer again, he quietened down and raised his bound wrists to the hunter in a wordless plea.

Bjorn looked about. Even if the other captives were alive, he had no hope of escape with them, they would be run down before they had gone a league. His only hope was to slip away and disappear into the forests and hills alone. He thought a moment. If his escape was soon discovered, this strange man could provide enough distraction to let him slip away unseen. Yet, if he left him, the Wildman would call out and his captors would be on him in seconds. He had little choice.

The man looked at Bjorn with his wrists raised towards him. The hunter put a hand over his own mouth, a gesture of silence he hoped, and slowly moved the knife towards the man's bonds. He became silent, his eyes transfixed on the blade. Bjorn cut his hands free and moved back. The Wildman instantly began to pull and untie his legs.

Fighting the throbbing pain in his shoulder, Bjorn rose and moved behind a tree. The Wildman was now silent, still working at the bindings around his legs. Bjorn could see the thin wisp of rising smoke and the flicker of fire through the trees only a stone's throw away. The fire looked to be set amongst a small huddle of rocks. He could see figures moving about. He could smell their cooking. He was ravenous. How long since he had last eaten? He turned back to the Wildman. He was now free, squatted low against the ground, watching the huntsman. Bjorn eyed him carefully, waiting for a sudden movement, but the man simply nodded and silently backed into the trees and, within moments, disappeared.

The hunter reached up and gently probed the wound in his shoulder as best as the pain allowed. He could feel the crust of dried blood on his skin, the shaft, still buried in his back was sticky and the puncture still weeping fluid. It must have struck bone for him to be still breathing—he had been lucky. *There is nothing I can do about it now,* thought the hunter.

Bjorn turned his attention back to the fire through the trees for another glimpse of his captors. The sun was almost gone, and the shadows of dusk had crept between the trees. The hunter could see little through the tangle of branches and undergrowth. The rocks and bushes obscured his view, but he spied higher ground overlooking the camp. He must see if he could get to his horse or face a long journey, possibly being pursued through the wilds on foot. He must find his horse if it was here.

He moved away low and silent through the trees, being careful not to make any sound, but the forest was his craft. Bjorn melted into the darkened forest and circled around the camp until he looked down upon the fire below. There were six of them he could see, all huddled around the fire, illuminated from the shadows in a red and orange glow from the flames.

Could it be? They were primitives, clad in skins and appearing to be adorned with bones and skulls—some human.

His captors were armed with little more than sharpened branches. He watched as one of them scraped at a hide near the fire. They were using stones to scrape and cut, and he noticed some of their spears also had heads of sharpened flint. *Stonemen?* Were these the savages of old legend? Bjorn looked on in disbelief. Some were butchering a carcass while others sat around eating and seemed to be daubing their faces and hair with the blood of their kill. He couldn't take his eyes from their food, the large chunks of meat roasting over the fire. It smelt good to the starving huntsman.

It was then he heard the whicker of a horse amongst the bushes, it seemed to be not far from where he had been bound and laid. He must have passed right by and not seen her standing quietly amongst the dark undergrowth. He made his way back. He needed to get to his horse and be quietly away before they next checked the prisoners. He had lingered too long already.

Bjorn made his way back down and through the darkened trees to where the savages had left the prisoners. *They left their other kills by the prisoners. She must be near too? Just another prize from the hunt.*

He searched silently. With each passing moment, a frantic panic built in his stomach. Then, the familiar shape loomed up before him out of the gloom. She was tethered to a low bush with thick branches. The thick foliage had blocked her from view. He let out a held breath in relief.

Bjorn smoothed her nose and spoke a gentle word in her ear. The horse flicked her ears but made no sound. He felt for his saddle and reached into his bags. They were open and had been tipped out, empty. His bow gone, and his axe, too; everything. Then he spotted a torch moving amongst the trees. It was coming towards him. Bjorn swore under his breath and ducked out of sight. They were checking the prisoners.

The bone-clad savage appeared carrying a flaming branch in one hand, and chewing at a hunk of meat with his other. Bjorn had run out of time. He would soon be found to be missing, not enough time to get away. He had only one choice.

The savage tore at the meat, chewing noisily, and didn't notice a dark shape steal from the shadows behind him. The hunter seized his face from behind with his weak arm, covering his mouth, and plunged his small knife into the savage's throat. He drew the knife across his throat in a swift action and felt the blade ease as it pierced his wind pipe. The savage dropped his flaming branch and made a gurgling, wheezing sound while clutching his throat. But he could not cry out. He bit hard onto Bjorn's finger. The hunter had to grit his teeth not to make a sound, but the pressure quickly eased and the man went limp, blood slowly pumping away from his neck. The hunter let him drop to the floor and shot a glance back to the camp. He could see the fire through the trees. Nothing. They had not heard.

Bjorn saw the meat on the floor and stood there horrified. It was an arm, a human arm. Charred and half-eaten, it was unmistakably human. Its fingers twisted and blackened. The hunter felt a wave of sickness come over him. *The smell.*

He held on to a branch and tried to control his gagging stomach. That smell, how good it had smelt. The thought of it now made him retch. They were cooking people! They were *eating* people! He stood frozen and horrified, staring at the blackened arm.

Bjorn couldn't move. He just stood staring at it, but he knew he must go, and go now. He shook himself free of the stare and seized his chance. He untethered his horse and led it quickly into the shadows. He mounted up and rode off between the dark trees.

He rode as fast as he dared between the trees. Clinging low to his horse and holding the reins with his arms around its neck so as to avoid the low branches that came at him out of the darkness. Every hoofbeat seemed to jar his shoulder painfully as he rode, but the elation of his escape seemed to have deadened the pain somewhat.

As he emerged from the trees, he recognised he was back in the rocky pass. Suddenly there was the blast of a horn behind him. They had discovered the dead savage and the missing prisoners. A pang of excitement and fear ran through him. He rode for the mouth of the pass. He would head south and west to make for the border. Then the horn sounded again but this time it was answered. Another horn blew off to the north, and then another somewhere closer. There were more of them, other hunting parties. The horns blew again in pursuit and Bjorn rode on into the night.

CHAPTER FIVE

The Longship

The mist hung low over the rolling waves as the first glow of sun appeared on the far horizon. The prow of the ship surged forward through the low swells. The sail bellied in the strong south wind, a wind to take them home.

At the ships' stern a lone man stood at the tiller watching the sunrise. He looked off starboard, the sky brightened with shades of orange and red as the orange orb of the sun crept up over the seas. The colours of the deep rolling ocean came to life out of the grey of the night. The man at the tiller was Olaf, and he was glad of the sun, it meant they held a northerly course across the Great Sea and must surely sight the southern shores of Arnar soon.

They had sailed on day and night after the first

oarsman had died. He was one of the new ones, a slave the captain bought back in Myhar. Olaf recalled the dry dusty ports full of many strange dark-skinned peoples. It was a place called Otowig, or Atwowic—he really wasn't sure. The peoples of those arid lands spoke in strange tongues and accents like nothing he had ever heard, every merchant and trader seemed to speak differently.

Old Graff and his boys had left the ship at port some months back and the captain was still short of oarsmen. The captain had been directed to the slavers by a merchant he had dealings with. Some local merchants knew an obscure Telik dialect used in trade with foreigners there. Others just gestured and pointed at their wares speaking fast and loud in a local dialect but it allowed the captain to trade. Gold it seemed, spoke in all languages.

There were Telik slaves, who spoke a common tongue, up for sale in the slave pens. Folk captured from the wars that ever raged between the Myhar realm of Syx and the southern Telik lords. However, these seemed a poor choice. The captain made port often in Telis and did not want trouble when he did. It would not look good for a foreign ship to have Telik slaves on the oars.

The slave pens also stocked many men of different races, locals and people from the other lands of Myhar. And so, the captain chose two. Both were men of Myhar, and unlike the existing Cydor oar-slaves on board, they were dark-skinned and much larger in build. The captain kept them chained and placed them at either end of the ship so they had little contact. Neither spoke a language the men aboard could understand, but they seemed to know their purpose and gave little trouble.

The ship had made the unplanned and treacherous two week crossing across the Great Sea at inordinate risk, but the captain was in considerable haste. Fear had sailed from Myhar with them.

It was after a few days had passed when one of the new slaves started to get sick. Olaf and the others first thought it was just sea sickness, but then the slave collapsed and started to bleed.

He died screaming, and the crew quickly threw his body into the murky depths. The loss of a man on a voyage marked it with a bad omen for the crew. And, perhaps, it was a coincidence, or perhaps some bad supplies from a strange land, but Olaf noticed that now, by the sunrise of each day, more men had taken ill. Fear crept amongst the crew. Many feared they had brought something with them from those strange exotic shores. They feared they would catch the sickness and die in the same terrible way as that dark-skinned oarsman had, crying out in terror as dark blood oozed from his eyes and mouth. A grizzly demise, this was not the glorious death in battle or a death undefeated in old age as many men in Arnar strove for.

The crew were eager to throw the dead man overboard. And once they had, and without leave from the captain, the fearful crewmen seized another slave, a man of Cydor, who was feared to be suffering the onset of the same terrible malady. They threw him overboard also. He went kicking and screaming into the waves and disappeared below. Unfriendly stares turned to linger on the remaining

Myhar oar-slave.

He had watched his countryman die and be cast overboard without any response. His solemn, dark eyes gave away nothing. The men called for him to be thrown over also. The captain refused and commanded he remain chained to his oar.

The panic of a sickness aboard spread, and sailors prayed they would live to see their home shores. The captain wished to return home to Arnar with great speed before he lost any more men.

The usual route home would have taken them east through the Telik straights and north, skirting Telik realms bound for the familiar waters of southern Cydor, and then west to Arnar, a voyage of months, through many seasons.

Captain Sheb had sailed for long years and had travelled these distant waters before, but few ever dared attempt the long crossing. And even less can claim they have made it. The Great Sea was a vast expanse of unknown storm racked seas, known to have claimed many brave fools.

The fearful crew would rather take their chances and urged the captain to make the risky, direct crossing. And so, he gave the order to sail north and across the open seas. Never had he heard any tale of lands on the Great Sea between Myhar and Arnar, so he gave the command to make haste and keep going through the night.

That was all many nights past now, days upon days of huge rolling swell and tumultuous skies. Olaf looked down across the deck where the men slept restlessly under the flapping sails. The figure of the captain still stood sentinel at the prow. The captain took many of the watches himself and had again stood all night at the prow looking off into the tenebrous waters, searching for approaching dangers.

Captain Sheb had long sailed his ship *Glyassin* from port to port selling and trading the goods he saw profit to deal in. Olaf had learned in his years of sworn service that *Glyassin* was the name of a water goddess revered in western Arnar where she was built. His most recent venture had taken them far to the distant lands of Myhar to acquire silks and the peculiar horns and beautiful skins of strange beasts. The mottled skins of plain-stalkers and great cats were very fashionable amongst the Telik lords and rarely seen in Arnar, he hoped to return to the northern ports of Cydor and Arnar to trade his lavish cargo and make a considerable profit.

But now, the worry of this dangerous open sea and worse, the sickness that seemed to be spreading through his crew, weighed heavy on him. Profit was far from his thoughts.

The sun had risen now and the red sail flapped in the good wind.

'Sent by the gods,' muttered Olaf.

The prow of *Glyassin* carved through the rolling swells. She was an old longship but sleek and fast. There was an open deck and a lower deck where the oarsmen sat and the cargo was kept. The lower deck could be accessed through a hatch near the stout mast. Eight oars per side when fully manned, the old ship still made fair time at sea without wind and could course along the long rivers that flowed through Arnar and Cydor, rowing against tides and currents as they needed.

The sail, hung on a single wide crossbeam, was patched here and there. It was once a deep crimson but was now fading in the years of sun. Still, a mighty fine sail, it had been acquired at the wondrous port of Telos. The sail always reminded Olaf of those impressive, yet strange foreign Telik cities. Great markets and bazaars lined the waterfronts, a place where many exotic goods from far and distant lands could be found. The greatest harbours and buildings Olaf had ever laid eyes on, whole cities of stone.

The captain drew Olaf's gaze as he shifted his weight. The captain had stood in watchful vigil for many hours now. He wore a sword, known to have been bought at those exotic ports, a fine Telian short sword. It was the captain's badge of rank, yet other than that, his clothes differed little to that of the crew. Olaf could see the sword now at Sheb's waist as the captain stood at the prow, motionless, looking out to sea.

The risen sun lifted the nights mist and as the morning wore on, it was discovered another two of the crew had become sick. One, another oar-slave but the other was one of Sheb's sworn crew. Olaf was afraid. Most of the crew seemed fine, just a cough here and there but others had fevers.

It could have been anything, probably just the food or water from Myhar, or the long rainy nights at sea. Olaf couldn't help remembering the dark man's eyes bulge as the blood trickled from them, dying and in agony.

Even Olaf had a cough, but he had often spent

the recent nights guiding the ship by following the stars through the cold, rough seas. He was weary, but he knew they could rest soon. Land was perhaps only hours away. He longed for it to be the day to sight land, to make port before sunset and sleep in a good bed.

Before the sun had reached noon above them, a thin dark strip could be seen on the horizon. It was land. They were home. The sleek hull of *Glyassin* cut through the rolling swells as Olaf steered them towards the distant shores. The great grey cliffs along the shores, of what must be southern Arnar, soon came into view.

The captain, by then joined by several other excited members of the crew, turned, and made his way to the stern.

'Olaf, turn to starboard and follow the coast. We make for Arn's Anchorage,' ordered the captain.

The tillerman nodded.

He then turned and bellowed orders to the crew to adjust the sail upon the turn. Olaf steered clear of the cliffs and turned to follow them northeast. The waves broke against the tall cliffs. Menacing rocks could be seen in the surf at their base, it would be unwise to stray too close.

Olaf guided the *Glyassin* along the rough coastline until the sail no longer had the wind and had to be furled. The oars put to sea.

The beat of the oar drum was slow and steady below. The cliffs on their port side soon gave way to trees and rocky coves as they crept south west.

The crew dumped the remaining suspect food

and water from Myhar overboard. The sailors refilled the water barrels from a stream flowing down the rocks into one of the small coves that lay along the ships' route.

The spirit of the men improved greatly now the shores of Arnar were in sight. The horror of the slave's gruesome demise already fading, and the menace of the sickness seemed to lift.

Before long, they passed small fishing villages nestled along the coast. And soon, as the sun hung heavy on the western sky, the *Glyassin* was gliding into the mouth of the Bane River, passing the two hulking rocks that stood sentry to the mouth of the harbours' bay. Safe passage between the two colossal pillars was assured by the great beacon fires that blazed at the top of each.

The bay was quiet. The evening hearth fires of the town could be seen smoking on the higher ground above the bay. Bridges built of stone and wood could be seen further along the river marking the sprawling city of Arn.

There were many ships and small boats moored at the maze of wooden jetties jutting out from the banks. Several boats were pulled up onto the pebbly beach and more anchored in the shallow water by the shore line. Most of the boats were longships of the Arnar style but there were others, strangely rigged foreign ships and Telik Barriemes.

Olaf smiled, relieved as he steered the *Glyassin* gently onto the stony beach. Some of the men gave a cheer as they felt the rough gravel scrape against the ships keel from beneath their feet. They had made it.

The sailors scrambled to the open deck awaiting

captain Sheb's command to unload and disembark. Olaf and his shipmates took their promised coin and left the captain and the bosun to command the oar-slaves in unloading the ship and went in search of a tavern and some good Arnarian food.

Olaf made his way along the narrow twisting streets. The town of Anchorage was the main port for the capital, and the largest in the central region of Arnar, and it was a maze of storehouses and merchant shops. The buildings were mostly round, made of wood and thatched. Some however, had a few stone frames and features. A few houses were roofed with turf and others were just large barns, storehouses owned by the various local lords and merchants of the town.

The narrow winding streets were surfaced with layers of dirty straw and hay. There were pens of livestock attached to many of the houses, some of which had obviously escaped to join the chickens and stray dogs wandering the crowded streets at will.

The place had the rank fishy smell of a port, the stench of rotten food and fish mixed with the accumulated waste of people and animals.

He coughed. He noticed he had, indeed, developed a tickly cough, but he was not so bothered by that now. He was home and wandering through the old bustling port he had visited so many times. He had never been sick on-board nor had any of the dysentery or fevers as the other sick men did. He concluded that was probably the effect of the strange food of the last few months. Olaf was sure the cough was just a product of the recent long cold nights steering the longship through the dark and dangerous waters—just a bit of a cough.

The crew went their separate ways but Olaf and a number of other men quickly found a large smoky tavern with a low beamed roof and set to the important business of spending some of their hard-earned coin.

It was a small round hall with a hearth blazing at its centre. The tavern was filled with benches and stools alongside wooden trestle tables. At one side the tavern keeper had a bar made from a thick plank of timber set onto the tapped ale barrels. There was a ladder going up to the tavern's sleeping platforms. The platforms running around the inside wall were held up by thick beams and created a low wooden roof over some of the tables.

The tavern was full of people sitting and drinking. Many were sailors and merchants; others were local folk of the town. The various drunks stooped over their drinks. There were women. His eyes lingered on several of the womenfolk sat nearby. Olaf hadn't seen a good woman in months.

The fat tavern keeper busied about, tending the bar and occasionally sending a small kitchen boy off to bring his customers food.

Olaf approached the bar.

'What can I get you, friend?' greeted the tavern keeper.

'We need food but we don't want fish. Seen far too much fish…and some ale too.'

Some of the men laughed as the sailors occupied a nearby bench.

'Well then, we got bread and some good wheels

of cheese, or there's salted pork, but that's about it, other than some salt fish,' said the fat tavern keeper with a smile.

Olaf gave the man several coins, and when satisfied, he sent the boy off to bring them food. He poured tankards of the pale looking local ale from one of tapped barrels under his bar.

Olaf raised his ale, 'We made port, lads. Now we drink.' They cheered and drank deep.

The sun had long set, and the crew of the *Glyassin* had eaten heartily and sunk many tankards of the local ale. But why not? They had travelled far and captain had said they would not go back out for some days. Captain Sheb needed new oarsmen and time to find buyers for his exotic skins and silks. They had brought many other trinkets and small goods from Myhar to sell, which would take time. So, the crew knew they were not needed.

One of the other men, a young Cydorian named Talad, stood up, swaying drunk, and collapsed on the floor to a great roar of laughter from the tavern's revellers. The tavern keeper shouted some prompt threats from behind the rough wooden bar. Olaf and his remaining crewmates lifted the poor fellow and carried him out, all laughing.

Suddenly, Talad started coughing then emptied his ale-filled belly all over himself and the surrounding floor of the narrow street.

'Little minnow can't take his drink,' shouted one of the men.

'It's not that piss they brew in Cydor here, lad.'

They all laughed at him and left him to finish. He

was sick again. But this time, dark crimson of blood splattered down his face.

The men all stood back stunned. Surprise turned to horror, the lingering fear of the voyage slammed back to them and many turned to run.

Olaf turned, the sudden shock had slightly sobered him, and he found himself running. He made his way down another street as the panic gripped his chest. He didn't know where to go. He had intended to stay at the tavern, but he wouldn't go back there now, and he didn't want to go back to *Glyassin* either.

He followed the street as it twisted and turned around the darkening buildings. He came across other taverns but kept walking onwards until he finally stopped outside a long low building that stretched round to make its own courtyard. A sign swung in the breeze outside its door marking it as another tavern. It was relatively quiet so Olaf made his way in.

Inside the entrance was another ale house, similar to the last but long and thin, with less folk. Those that were there sat in small groups, they glanced at Olaf as he entered, and then continued their quiet discussions. Olaf noticed the antlers of a great forest stag over the ale barrels in the far corner. The tavern keeper here had no bar but was serving from a stack barrels at the back. Olaf approached him, knocking into a table as he went. He was drunk, and his voice was slurred, but he managed to get a room and asked the tavern keeper to bring him ale and a hot meal. They had not eaten much other than cold stale bread and salt meat for weeks, and Olaf wasn't even sure what kind of meat it had been.

After a disapproving glance from the tavern keeper, Olaf made his way through the alehouse and out to the back part of the tavern.

This part was a long building set at a right angle from the alehouse where the guest rooms and kitchens were. The tired tillerman made himself comfortable, the renewed panic of the blood and sickness seemed to be passing.

Although as he lay there, he did wonder if young Talad was still breathing. Did he die or was it all that food and too much ale? Perhaps someone should go back to check him? He coughed and his head was spinning drunk. Perhaps he needed to be sick also. 'Just the ale,' he assured himself

He was glad the lads couldn't see him. He got up and made his way to a pail in the corner to vomit up the nights excess.

Just ale, no blood. He was relieved, and he felt better at once. Yet, he couldn't stop thinking about that dark Myhar oar-slave, his gurgling bloody screams, and of poor Talad, his bulging eyes, full of fear and shock, his chin stained crimson.

He shook himself. Olaf decided he needed a woman to take his mind off this. They had been many weeks at sea, and he had seen nothing but Telik and dark Myhar women for months. Which of course had an exotic appeal, but he craved a good local girl from Arnar. He sat up on the bed.

Yes, a woman, he thought.

There were many whores and free women in the harbour towns of the world. He would find one. He rose, and still his head spun. He steadied himself.

Olaf had drunk stronger brews than this ale in his time.

Gaining his composure, he muttered to himself, 'Now, where would I find myself a good woman? Or a bad one… Ha!' He paused. 'Perhaps that old tavern keeper could point me in the right direction. Yes, let's ask him.'

He felt a trickle on his ale numbed face. He lifted his hand. He stared, his mouth agape. There was blood on his fingers.

His heart froze, and he cried out, 'No… No! Not this way!'

He coughed again, then reached for the last of his ale. Clutching his tankard, he staggered for the door in search of his woman. If Olaf would not see another moon, he would not die without having a woman first, and more ale besides.

So, he wiped the blood from his nose. He could taste it in his mouth. He coughed. A stream of blood ran down his chin, and he fell back against the clay-covered wood that made the wall of his room.

He was stunned with terror and the realization of his encroaching fate. He lay back against the wall. His head felt heavy. He gagged swallowing the blood back down. It made him gag again, he couldn't hold it long. Olaf screamed, and then coughed hard, spraying the floor with crimson gore.

***

The tavern keeper had heard a scream from the room that drunk sailor had taken. He'd best go see.

There was no sound from the other side of the

door now. Cautiously, he slowly opened the door slightly and popped his head round. The man lay dead.

'Gods damn it,' muttered the tavern keeper, swinging the door open wide.

The bleeding eyes bulged from the dead man's face, locked with the terror of his last moments. A terrible dark red seeped from his face and mouth. It seemed to be coming from under his clothes also, leaking from his trousers, staining a crimson pool on the dirty straw of the tavern floor.

The tavern keeper shuddered with revulsion and closed the door hastily. But, for him, it was already too late.

CHAPTER SIX

A Ritual of Bones

The apprentice sat in the back of the wagon. He felt every bump and stone as they rolled along the track through the ruin. The sun had almost set and it was nearly dark. He had begun to regret his choice to come along. His leg was twinging with pain at every jolt on the wheels.

There was a lantern lamp hanging up at the front where Master Logan sat holding the reins, guiding the old horse with commands alone. He chuckled at an outburst of pain from the apprentice as they hit a big bump.

'You OK, lad?' asked Logan.

'Fine, master, just a bit sore.'

The master turned his head, 'I'm not trying to hit the holes but this track has possibly never seen a wagon before we came.' He laughed. 'Not far anyway. Look, you can see old Eld's torches at the stones up there.' He pointed off to one side.

Through the ruins and low trees, the apprentice could indeed make out the flickering glow of many torches atop of a low hill amongst the crumbling ruin. Next to the apprentice, the great hound sat on his haunches, looking about with his head over the side. This was the same wagon Truda had returned in. Indeed the apprentice could make out the smears of blood here and there. A putrid smell still lingered. He wondered how long Truda's corpses had lain there. The apprentice shifted to avoid sitting in the putrid smears, he didn't want another man's drying blood in his robes, and definitely not a dead man's.

They came around a copse of old gnarled trees, growing twisted and bare in the thin soil. The apprentice could see the track was headed up the side of the low hill, weaving between a rough shod ring of barrows and mounds.

The hill was crowned by a ring of great stones looming into the darkening sky over the ruins. The wagon rolled up towards the top of the hill. Amongst the barrows, the sloped sides were dotted with several structures of low crumbling masonry, some of which had been consumed by the grass and earth and appeared as smaller grassy earthworks and ditches.

The apprentice had seen such stones before. Relics left by the ancient peoples who once dwelt in these lands before the rise of Arnar. They could be found littered about known the realms of man in one fashion or another.

Logan gestured towards them. 'The great and ancient monuments to unknown gods, or perhaps great pillars of ancient halls, I know not. But I've seen stones like these left in sacred groves and high places in many realms on my travels. Many peoples have now adopted them into their ways or converted them to be used as tombs or places of worship. Some stories say they were left by the First Sons.' He paused in thought, 'You know, some folk shun them as evil places, too? While they say, others erect new circles or monoliths for their own purposes. It's curious, we've always used them.'

The apprentice did not reply. He was staring up the giant stones in awe. Since their arrival, his amazement of them had not diminished.

Logan rambled on despite the lack of comment. 'My family has buried our dead up in the hills about Forn for centuries now, many generations. There are several ancient stones up there.' Logan paused again and looked up as the wagon rolled into the shadow of the first ancient monolith and fell silent. The shadow felt oppressive, bearing down upon them with the ancient weight of the stones themselves.

This ring was huge, larger than any the young apprentice had seen. The stones towered over the low twisted trees that surrounded the low hill. The apprentice turned too quickly and caused a nasty twinge from his foot. He had been enthralled by the huge dark veined and smooth stones since he first saw them.

The wagon came around the stone and between

another towering stone, entering the great ring of shadowy sentinels. The wagon headed for the centre towards a large amount of ancient stone debris. Some of the walls still stood here and there, but many stones lay scattered about. This was once a great place he suspected, laid to ruin by the passing of years. The apprentice tried to imagine what it would have looked like. Rebuilding the scattered stone in his head, he marvelled at the work of ages past.

Torches flashed and flickered through the ruin, Master Eldrick was already here. Master Logan brought the wagon to a stop with a gentle command.

'Will you be okay through here?'

The short passage through these ancient paths, strewn with fallen stone, had not crossed the apprentice's mind.

It was not far, following the remains of ancient passageways to the centre area at the very pinnacle of the hill.

'I will take my time, master,' said the apprentice, managing a wry smile. The apprentice was getting more apt in his skills at walking with the staff, being careful not to knock the awkward splints and thus send a nasty pain shooting through his ankle.

'If you don't appear shortly, I'll come find you.' Logan laughed and made his way down from the wagon and off into the gloom trailed, as ever, by the great hound.

There were torches set about, some were burning low, but the apprentice knew the way regardless. A matter of a stone's throw through the fallen hallways of this ancient hall, but nevertheless it took many careful and tiring minutes, only knocking his leg once, to emerge on the other side.

He came out into a circular area relatively clear of debris. There were no old walls here, just three standing stones in the centre. These were much smaller than the great monoliths that now enclosed them, still tall against the sky over the ruins. These were more like those he had seen to the south, shorter, perhaps around the size of man.

The apprentice slowly made his way towards them. There was a ring of torches around the stones. The apprentice could make out the large flat stone which lay at the centre.

He could see his hooded colleagues and the movement of their torches. The fires lit the stones in a ruddy light and smoke was sent swirling between the stones by the breeze. As he approached, he saw the flat stone had its macabre decorations and glyphs in place once more—the bones of ancient warriors were on display, once interred in the mounds of the ruin, until Logan's probing's had unearthed them. The apprentice could see great circular arcane symbols marked on the ground around the stone altar. There were many strange markings and writings on the floor and on the surrounding stones, some written in charcoal and some in white chalk. Blackening skulls adorned the torches about the altar. Upon the altar-stone itself laid the slightly mummified skeleton, the bones arranged, complete as it had lain undisturbed for centuries until they had disentombed it from its subterranean sanctuary within one of the nearby barrows.

The smallest hooded figure, who he recognised as his master, hurried over and greeted him. 'Good, good. We're all here, the night is upon us and the moon is not yet rising. We still have time; we will try the ritual before it rises as we have much more work ahead.' His robes seemed stained with the blood of his afternoon's work, but he didn't seem to mind. He beckoned to a small trestle table he had set up off to one side just behind the stones. 'Sit, boy, observe, and take note if you will.' The apprentice was seated as the others began the ritual.

It took time. Eldrick reciting from a text in a droning voice, his words strange, a language from distant lands or perhaps long since forgotten. His master's voice became almost a chant at times, often repeating the same phrase over and over again. Logan and Truda moved about him, carving the arcane symbols of the rite into the living air with the prepared ritual knives.

At the climax of the ritual the master's voice rose in crescendo, repeating the final line of text again and again until he fell silent. All held their breath, waiting—waiting for some stirring from the altar. Moments passed, and then doubt began to set in. Nothing. Still they waited but nothing. The master stood with his arms raised and his eyes seemed blank and glazed. He stood there long after everyone else, he finally turned and started to write in a journal at the table where the apprentice sat looking on.

'I'm sorry master,' said the apprentice quietly.

'No need,' Eldrick replied, still scribbling with a large quill.

'It felt different before, master, when it worked.' The master stopped writing and looked at him. The apprentice went on, 'The darkness, it closed in about us, there was a definite energy, a feeling, but not again since. Only…' He trailed off.

'Speak, boy. Only what?'

The apprentice hesitated, 'Well, perhaps it was just me, but I thought I felt it out in the ruin. The night I fell.'

The master looked at him for a long moment before he spoke, 'Interesting. Perhaps a manifestation of fear. A reaction of your mind to the darkness on either occasion, but indeed interesting. I shall make a record of your observation.' The master began writing again.

Eldrick nodded. 'Indeed, my boy, but never fear. This attempt merely confirmed my suspicion. We will attempt it again shortly, and this time, well, we will see.'

The slim crescent of a waning moon now hung low in the darkening sky as another ritual again neared conclusion. As Eldrick droned and chanted, a darkness seemed to shroud around them. All was pitch black and dark beyond the swirling smoke and fire. A terrible chill descended upon the stone ring as the master chanted the verses of rite. The strange words echoed and seemed to whisper on the breeze. The apprentice felt the power and the presence, that same terrible chill.

The swirling smoke seemed to form terrible faces, surely a trick of light and mind. The apprentice took a sharp breath as the master's voice, almost shouting, repeated the final phrase. His skin prickled as his hair stood up on end, his heart pounded in his chest—it was happening.

A skeletal hand jerked up. It began to rise from its slab like a terrible puppet on invisible strings. The apprentice froze, he could not move, his eyes transfixed upon the rising skeleton. Master Eldrick cackled in triumph. 'Behold,' he shouted. 'Ancient one, you have been summoned.' Its skull slowly swung to regard Eldrick. Ghostly whispers filled the air around them, the voices of many. The skeleton held there a few moments. Then it collapsed with a *crunch,* bones clattering to the ground. Some shattered to dust on impact. Everyone stood silent, eyes on the lifeless bones. An eerie silence descended upon the scene and the air once again became still. The chill passed and the warmth from the torches slowly returned.

Master Eldrick stood, arms still raised. Logan laughed nervously. 'Well, Eld' we did it, again, and it was incredible.' He looked back at the fallen bones. 'Incredible!' He walked to a rock and sat down, shaking his head in disbelief.

'The moon…' muttered the apprentice to himself.

Eldrick seemed distant but slowly lowered his arms. His eyes tired, he looked about at their faces, and then made his way to the table. Eldrick leant next to the apprentice, his breathing was heavy. The apprentice went to speak, but no words came. He was awestruck. Eldrick clasped the apprentice's shoulder and smiled weakly.

'Just one more task now, my friends,' said Eldrick. Logan threw the old master an inquisitive look. Eldrick did not respond but instead made his way to speak with Truda and sent her off, still bewildered, through the ruins. On what errand the apprentice did not know.

'What are you up to now, old friend?' Logan enquired but Eldrick waved his question aside, busying himself in his grimoire and the little journal once more, whilst muttering under his breath.

Truda returned pushing a barrow and as she drew nearer, the apprentice could see, to his horror, the grey cold eyes of a bloody cadaver and what appeared to be some other gruesome remnants of Master Eldrick's anatomical studies. As Truda lifted the dead man onto the altar the apprentice saw the man seemed to have been cut in two and had no legs, just a gory torso, its lower half bound in blood-soaked bandage. The apprentice stared at the corpse unable to avert his eyes for long before a repulsive and morbid urge brought his gaze back.

'Eld! What is this?' demanded Logan as Truda brought forth what appeared to be a severed head, its blank eyes staring off into the smoke. She lifted it by its hair and placed it alongside the torso on the bone adorned altar.

'It is part of my study regarding the ritual, Logan,' replied Eldrick casually.

'You are intending to attempt the ritual on that?' said Logan, appalled as he pointed to the remains occupying the altar.

'Exactly,' replied Eldrick.

'But Eld, we cannot, we should not attempt this,' insisted Logan.

Eldrick grunted and waved a dismissing hand at

him.

Logan persisted, 'The Bone Ritual is done, it is finished,' he paused, 'and upon witnessing it again, I have no doubt it is a mystery of awesome power— It is undeniable. Yet, it is wholly unnatural and…and the very essence of nightmares. This is a fell thing you are toying with, Eldrick. We should not.'

Truda had paused but Master Eldrick waved her on to continue. Master Logan again objected but Eldrick cut in angrily, 'It needs to be tried. I must know.' Eldrick calmed himself and continued, 'I intend to try my variation of the ritual. Using the secret arts of the Bone Ritual I hope to summon a spirit back to its former vessel in much the same manner and revive someone long dead.'

Logan shook his head in disbelief.

'Do you not see, Logan? It would be a great discovery, greater even than the Bone Ritual. This is the power to cheat the gods of death themselves. Imagine the people we could save with this, all that we could learn through this.'

Logan looked troubled, and then spoke, 'Old Night or whatever god commands these spirits, will not appreciate you stealing the souls back to this world. What wrath will you bring upon us?'

Eldrick laughed. 'You do not know that, Logan. And what gods? Truly, if they even exist, I have seen little evidence in all my studies and it is something I have studied in depth.'

Logan did not reply, his was brow furrowed in thought.

'Do you not at least think it should be tried?' exclaimed Eldrick in frustration at what he saw as his colleague's lack of vision. 'If we don't, it is only a matter of time before someone uses my work to try it. I will not have people say I didn't explore every possibility.'

Logan's eyes moved to the grim altar his apprentice was still arranging.

'This is dark meddling, my old friend. Secrets best left to the gods. Do your ritual. I will have no part in it. I will observe with the lad, but I warn you, we should not dabble in such black arts.'

'Do as you will,' said Eldrick with a flash of anger in his voice. Logan turned to Truda. 'You walk in peril, lass, but do as you will. I will not forbid it.' Truda shrugged and continued at her work.

Master Logan scowled and sat down against the standing stone nearest the apprentice, their eyes met, but he didn't speak. Logan sat silently against the old stone, his face perturbed and distant.

The apprentice thought better than to disturb him, instead his eyes were drawn to the grizzly endeavours of his master and Truda around the altar. The master was busy drawing great circular symbols on the floor around the stones, each bearing more of the strange runes and writings familiar to the apprentice from his study of his master's work on the Bone Ritual.

Eldrick then joined Truda at the altar and using the blade of the long twisted ritual dagger, they began carving more strange arcane glyphs into the skin and face of the dismembered dead man.

The markings had been previously made on the bones with charcoals, the apprentice had spent much time over the past weeks at that very task. Eventually the decaying skin was covered in markings which the apprentice recognised as those used to bind a spirit back into its bones so it may rise once again.

Master Logan looked on without word as Eldrick began.

There was much chanting in an eldritch tongue as the master and Truda prepared. The master raised his arms to the sky. The apprentice noted the moon creeping over the great standing stones that encircled the top of the hill. The moon cast little light and was just a thin sliver in the dark sky. The black moon would rise the following night he was sure.

The master's droning voice echoed amongst the stones as that familiar darkness again enveloped them, consuming the diminishing light of the flaming torches. A gust of wind sent the smoke from the torches swirling off into the night. The apprentice felt the hairs of his neck prickle up as a chill draft swept in around the stones. He could hear the return of faint whispers on the wind. The master was calling the dead, and they were here.

The master's voice rose to a commanding shout as again the ritual came to its zenith. The hound started barking and howling. The beast lay low in the grass baring its fangs at the encroaching darkness. They all stood, breath held in anticipation. The apprentice could feel the chill breath of the restless dead turning his skin to gooseflesh, and worse, he could feel their unseen eyes watching him, eyes full of spite.

A malign presence assailed the apprentice. He clutched at the wooden idol hung at his neck, his resolve faltered as the resentful shades stole not only his life's warmth but seemed to draw and devour his very will into the whispering darkness around him.

There was a sudden gasp from Truda. All eyes turned to her. Truda's stare was fixed on the altar. Logan rose and approached but suddenly stopped and took a step back, his attention fixed on what he saw there. The apprentice could not see clearly through the smoke and using Logan's walking staff painfully raised himself to his feet. He steadied himself against the standing stone before slowly limping over to discover what wondrous horror beguiled them. The hound was still howling and barking wildly as the apprentice passed.

A ghastly shriek pierced the gloom and echoed amongst the stones. The apprentice startled, he stumbled and fell as he tried to turn to face the noise that appeared to come from all around him. A great surge of pain exploded from his foot as he lay stricken. He cried out, but Truda and Eldrick just stood there transfixed. The master still stood with his arms raised. His eyes seemed dark and distant. Another blood curdling shriek pierced the night.

***

Logan looked around, his eyes searching for the source of the sound. He froze in terror as he eyes fell onto the disembodied head perched amongst the candles and skulls of the altar. Its dead eyes were staring off away from him, its face was hidden facing the other way towards Eldrick. Yet Eldrick stood with his arms still raised his eyes seemed darkened, almost black. Logan was shocked to notice his fellow master seemed to look through him, his expression was vacant, and he had a twisted smile across his aged face.

Another shrill shriek from the altar. Logan seized the severed head by its blood matted hair and raised it up so he could look into its face. The dead man's pallid skin had been cut deep with the arcane runes that now covered its staring face. The mouth gaped open. Just a dead man's head. Logan had seen worse. The mouth suddenly snapped shut and its dark eyes rolled up at the master. It snapped its exposed teeth at his face and screeched again. Logan dropped it in horror, and kicked it hard. The head tumbled away, still shrieking, falling down into the darkened ruins below. He heard another terrible scream, but not from the dismembered head. This was a voice he knew.

CHAPTER SEVEN

Revenant

The dead man's chest seemed to rise and it slowly turned its head. The lifeless eyes full of malice and sheathed in darkness stared straight at the apprentice. One arm jerked up and slammed down grasping the altar's edge. Not taking its dark eyes off the apprentice, it brought its other arm up and dragged itself onto the ground. Clawing at the earth with its long, animated fingers, it dragged itself towards him.

The apprentice was petrified like the stones that stood silent around him. He could not move or take his eyes off the grasping torso slowly pulling itself ever nearer. The pain in his foot was intense all he could do was scream. The bandage around the dead man's waist slid away as it clawed through the earth. A putrid coil of entrails spilled out and trailed behind it in the dirt, still it drew closer. Its eyes full of malice and intent, snapping its gaping teeth together biting at the swirling smoke.

The apprentice screamed again. Still unable to move a hysteria of fear set in. He looked again for help from his master, but he and Truda still just stood there. The dead man seized his good foot with a terrible vice like grip and tried to drag the apprentice closer. The apprentice wildly kicked and struggled, but he could not release its iron grip. Pain exploded up his broken leg as he thrashed for freedom. The dead man seemed to snarl and wheeze as it snapped its teeth and with a terrible strength slowly pulled the apprentice's leg into its snapping maw.

***

Logan leapt forward and drove the altar dagger into the clawing torso until it bit into the earth underneath it. The dagger had no effect, the thing hardly noticed, it just continued dragging the apprentice closer. He then pulled the shaft free of the rotting muscle and bones, and drove its long twisted blade smoothly through the back of the dead man's skull.

The steel point protruded through the thing's open mouth, reddened with congealed blood and gore. The iron grip lessened and the body trembled and fell limp into the cold earth. Logan pulled the dagger free and looked at the shaking apprentice. The apprentice stared off through the smoke, his eyes seemed lost. He just lay on the floor shaking and whimpering.

Eldrick slowly lowered his arms but still just stood there. Truda had her hands on her face in disbelief but then she ran to Eldrick. 'We did it,' cried Truda. 'You did it master.'

His voice shaky, but excited. The terror somehow already forgotten replaced an almost hysterical excitement. Master Eldrick turned to her and placed an aged hand on the young apprentice's shoulder with that same twisted smile still on his face.

The stricken apprentice did not look so excited, instead he looked cold, unable stop himself shaking; he just lay there his eyes wide, still unable to speak.

'You call that success,' roared Logan.

The smile dropped from Truda's face.

'You summon back fell creatures from the dead. You lost control, it attacked the lad, did you not see?' thundered Logan, his expression full of anger.

'I did not lose control, Master Logan,' snapped Eldrick. 'The boy is unharmed. You dealt with the problem. When exactly did I lose control?'

Logan was taken aback by the sudden spiteful change in his old colleague. 'You're losing your mind if you cannot see the peril of your endeavours, my old friend. Can you not see yourself, this is evil?' Logan looked around at his companions. 'The living should not use the dead as playthings to summon like puppets at your command.'

Master Eldrick turned to Logan his voice calmer.

'My mind is as sound as ever Logan, it was indeed unexpected. Who could have guessed what was going to happen, but the situation did not get too out of hand.'

Logan shook his head, 'Too out of hand…' he muttered. He threw up his hands in frustration and stalked away angrily.

***

The apprentice spoke little on the return journey to the camp. He just lay shaking in the back of the cart and caught himself muttering more than once. After the ritual Logan had walked on ahead to ready the cart, trailed by his great hound, and Truda had busied herself throwing the bodies off into the burial pits with the other remains of the discarded subjects of Eldrick's experiments.

They departed the summit leaving the torches to burn out. The apprentice lay in shock, his mind on the edge of a dark precipice. It took all his remaining will to keep his sanity from forever plunging into that dark abyss, never to return to him. Perhaps it was his stretched and shattered nerves, perhaps not. But as the cart painfully bumped and jolted back down along the winding track towards the camp, the apprentice swore he heard that terrible shriek once again, echoing amongst the stones and gnarled trees of the surrounding ruin. He shuddered and sank down low into the cart.

The following morning the apprentice was still mostly silent and distant. The master let him slowly pack his possessions before his long return journey to the College. He often found himself pausing to stare off into the nearby trees and mossy stones. The apprentice could not stop thinking about the previous night, about the clutching hands and evil black eyes.

Master Logan had spent many hours at council with Master Eldrick upon their return. They spent most of the night shut away in Eldrick's tent. They talked until the morning and at times it had become heated. The apprentice had heard their raised voices in the dark hours while he huddled in his blankets trying to sleep.

Before midday another cart rolled up along the track and into the campsite. At the reins was a grim looking man wearing thick heavy leather over his clothes and wore a long dirk hung at his side—one of the hired-swords. The apprentice had seen little of the hired-swords since their arrival. Even on the long journey here, they had spoken to the hired men very little, only giving them nervous glances as they rode past the carts, and receiving back only icy stares before kicking their horses on ahead. Only Logan seemed at ease in their presence, and it was Logan who strode out to meet him. The man got down from his perch at the reins of the cart and met Logan with a nod. They spoke for a short time, and then the man turned and made his way back down the track disappearing off into the trees.

Truda was given the task of loading the cart for the journey. Logan and the master were checking through the apprentice's work from the previous day. They checked through the reports and finds that they were sending back, ensuring all was to their liking and nothing forgotten. Both masters had other parchments and scrolls, letters, and messages to be delivered by the apprentice upon his return.

The fragile parchments and books were wrapped in waxed linen and stowed in sturdy wooden cases which they tied down and covered in skins to keep the rain off.

Soon all was packed and ready. The apprentice bade his colleagues farewell, it would be another moon—perhaps more—before he saw them again. Master Eldrick gave him his final instructions then made his way back to the work that had so pre-occupied him of late. Master Logan and his apprentice, Truda, helped him into the cart. 'Good luck, see you back at the College I suppose,' said Truda quietly. 'I shall miss you now I have to do all the work,' she said with a smile before jumping down. The apprentice held her gaze for a moment, and then Logan climbed up beside him and took the reins.

***

The great hound bound up into the back of the cart, clambering all over the apprentice as he made his way to curl up behind his master. Logan grinned at his beast's capering, and with a sharp word the horse started forward, pulling the cart back down along the rocky track.

'You okay there, lad?' asked Logan.

No reply. Master Logan turned to look at the apprentice. He was staring off into the ruins, whether he saw them or not Logan could not say. Logan noticed the apprentice looked very weary. Locks of his hair seemed to be grey in places, and he had deep lines in his face around his eyes, it made him look older.

Just as Logan turned back the apprentice answered, 'I'm okay, master.'

Logan did not believe him but laughed. 'Bit late there.'

The apprentice swung his gaze to him. 'I am glad we are leaving this place, master, I can't stand them watching me any longer.'

Logan eyed him strangely. 'Well I'm not leaving yet, Eldrick wants to stay a while yet and Truda seems very keen on Eldrick's *healing* lore so I will also stay a while. Keep an eye on them, and let the girl learn what she can from your master.'

'He is very wise,' said the apprentice absently.

Logan eyed him again and continued, 'I have other studies to continue, anyway. Many minor delvings I can busy myself with, there is much still there to uncover and study—many large mounds, perhaps I may find one of an ancient king or chieftain. Yes, much to stay for…to my peril,' he said with a grin.

The apprentice returned the grin, he seemed slightly more himself. 'But master, does that mean I will journey back with the cart alone?'

Logan laughed again, 'No, lad, that hired-sword you saw earlier will take you and watch over the cart and your good self.'

***

The apprentice did not reply. He did not want to seem afraid of the man in front of a master, but he did not want to spend long nights alone with such a man as his only companion. At least he would be safe on the road the apprentice supposed. The hired-swords in the service of the College would not get paid until their task was done—not often to the liking or usual ways of the mercenaries that wander the realms. But the pay was just good enough to tempt in many men and it was a position that also often worked out for the College if they did not return.

The cart rolled along the grassy track slowly winding down the tree covered hillside. They appeared to be clear of the ruins. On either side he saw nothing but trees fading off into the gloom of the forest. After a while the trees became larger and sparser in places and eventually opened out into clearings full of grasses and heathers, some littered with rocky outcrops.

In places, through the gaps in the trees, the valley below could be seen. They were on the slope of a great valley between high snow-covered peaks which dominated the skyline above them. There were many huge rocks and crags as the track picked its way down through the stony grottos.

Upon one of the rocks alongside the track, the grim man sat waiting for them. Logan hailed him as they drew closer. He called the horse to stop and the mare obediently brought the cart to a halt. Logan got down and again the man greeted him with a nod. As they talked, the apprentice suddenly became aware of several others standing up amongst the rocks above. They stood silent, staring down at him amongst the grey stones. Some bore long spears others had bows or a hilted sheath hung at their side. These men were their grim protectors, watching over the pass to the ruin.

The hired-swords in service to the College were mostly unsworn warriors of Arnar, or men previously of the city guard, but they also sometimes attracted other fighting men, city thugs and cut throats. The apprentice had often tried to mask it in their presence, but he was afraid of them.

He had no love for violence and had avoided the path of the old warrior ways followed by many in the realms of man. He was never a warrior, but a man of books and writing, a man who valued knowledge over valour. The apprentice knew many secrets that these men could not dare fathom but still the fighting men he encountered always seemed to look upon him as weak, and still he feared them.

Logan approached and turning to apprentice he said, 'I bid you farewell. Bronas here will take you back to the town of Eymsford. Speak to the College brother there, give him this.' Logan handed him a folded parchment sealed with wax bearing the College mark. 'He will get you further passage back to the College.'

Logan then went to the back of the cart, unloaded a barrel, and rolled it over to rest upon a big stone nearby. The hound clambered over to sit beside the apprentice wagging its tail. The apprentice scratched its great grey head between the ears and the hound licked at the apprentice's face, covering him in slimy slobber. The apprentice wiped his face and groaned.

Logan laughed. He whistled sharply and called the hound over. The great hound leapt down and ran to his master still wagging its wiry grey tail, and then sat at his side.

The grim hired-sword climbed up onto the cart and with a silent nod to the apprentice took the reins. The apprentice could see one of the men rolling the barrel away as the grim silent man flapped at the reins and the cart started forward.

As the cart rolled past Logan, the master called out, 'Good luck and safe travels, lad. Look after those cases and try to rest that leg.' The apprentice turned to wave him a salute of farewell, and watched as Logan made his way back up the track towards the ruin, as ever followed by the shaggy hound.

The terrain further down the track was rough and steep. The apprentice looked around at the valleys and crags they were descending into. Above, the skyline was dominated by the other great peaks of the highlands. The sun was coming down behind the high ridges above them, the day was getting late it would be dark soon.

The track wove its way along ridges and down the shallower slopes and passes. They appeared from the trees onto the rolling moors of heather and rock that were the foot hills of the great range of peaks men called the Spine of the World. The apprentice looked back to where they had come from. The cart was at the foot of a steep tree covered slope that led up into high rocky peaks. The ruins lay hidden halfway up, nestled on a small plateau. No sign of either ruin or flat ground showed on the high slopes of the highland valley they had descended from, it was tucked from view, hidden out of sight.

It would have been almost impossible to stumble onto if they did not know already of its existence from Logan's local tales.

The cart rolled to a stop by a pile of large granite stones beside the track and not far from the last of the trees. 'We make camp here,' said the grim man named Bronas.

The apprentice sat and watched the darkening sky over the hills – such a magnificent view. He was glad to be away from that cold haunted place. Other than when necessary the hired-sword did not speak to him, and neither did the apprentice try. The apprentice made a bed on the cart, but he could not sleep. He just lay there for long hours watching the clouds and the stars, thinking of his long painful journey back to the College. He could not wait to sleep in a real bed back in the safety of a town. He looked for some twinkling of fire from his colleagues or the hired-swords further back up the track, but saw nothing. They seemed to be alone for miles around although they had probably not yet travelled a full league since leaving the ruin.

Then he felt it again. He was being watched. A shiver ran over his skin and a cold seemed to wrap itself around him. He clutched at the idol hung at his neck. But still that watching menace haunted him. The apprentice wondered how long it would be before he could rest easy once more. After a while the feeling passed, and he drifted off into an uneasy sleep.

He awoke in the night suddenly and looked around. The fire had burned low, and he could see his silent companion asleep on the ground not far from the fire. The night was dark, no moon rose in the sky. Tonight was the black moon.

His leg throbbed with a dull pain. Why could he not stop his hands shaking? He could hear a bell ringing in the distance. The bell chimed steadily. The apprentice was drifting back into sleep. Was it a dream? For how long it had been ringing he did not know. Had it woken him? It must have been a dream.

He remembered the deep tolling of a bell ringing out from high up in the distant hills. The bell echoed down through the valleys and across the shadowy moors, ringing out slow and steady for some time, until suddenly it fell silent.

CHAPTER EIGHT

The Watch Post

'There it is again. Do you hear?'

The wind whistled through the rocky bluffs making the crackling torches fight to stay aflame. Again, a faint toll of a distant bell could be heard rolling through the hills on the winds.

'Aye, lad, I do.' The old guardsman stood looking out into the night. He turned to his young companion with whom he shared this watch, 'Go get Arnulf.'

The young guard hurried along the walkway of the wooden palisade. The weathered old guardsman watched him go. The lad was no soldier, just some boy from the town, barely a man. Sworn to serve his lord and take his turn in the guard before returning to the fields until called upon again. It was the old way. Every man of Arnar earned his honour and defended his lord's lands if called upon. The old guardsman turned back to the night shrouded lands below. Again, the bell tolled.

The watch post perched high on a wind blasted outcrop of the mountain side. The mountain itself was the last great easterly peak in the northern range of Arnar. In the daylight, a snowy summit could be seen towering above them and to the east, the mountain side fell away sharply as tall grey cliffs overlooking the border lands below.

The mighty mountain range, known as the Spine of the World, stretched down hundreds of leagues from the snow blasted wastes of the far unknown north, stretching vast distances to reach the borders of Cydor and Arnar. Great walls of stone made a natural western border of war torn Cydor, before the Spine then ran across Arnar's north eastern territories to the ocean. The mountain range separated these lands from the rest of the realm of Arnar which created a region known as the Borders. The border for which it is named is with that of the ancient realm of Cydor, now in an ever-uneasy peace with Arnar. The region had long been disputed by these two great realms and was watched over vigilantly by the warriors of Arnar as a terrible civil war raged across the border.

The old guardsmen pulled his cloak tight around him to hold off the biting wind. The nights were growing colder, there was frost growing in his beard. The bell chimed again faintly on the wind followed by the sound of approaching footsteps. 'What is it Hagen?' His lord stood next to him wrapped in furs.

***

'Listen, m'lord,' said Hagen. The two of them stood at the palisade staring off into the gloom. Arnulf could hear nothing but the howling wind and the crackling of torches.

Hearing nothing, he turned to speak, then it rang again. He paused, trying to place the direction of the sound.

'Aye I hear it Hagen, a warning bell?'

The old guardsman continued his report, 'Aye, m'lord, that's what I feared. It rings from the west, from the High Passes.'

'From the west? How can that be?' replied Arnulf.

'I have heard no horns or drums, seen no burning, m'lord. The lands below are still,' added Hagen.

'Yet a warning bell rings out for aid? A bad omen,' Arnulf muttered to himself.

There was a silence as Arnulf decided what to do. It rang again. 'There are several small farms and homesteads that could be ringing the bell, m'lord, but I've never heard of anyone round here with a bell? And I've never heard of anybody living up in the passes either, they say the lands up there are too hard, m'lord. And there are the old legends…'

Arnulf heard it again, the bell tolled in the distance. Arnulf had made up his mind. 'Hagen, take a few men and scout out the High Passes to the west, find that bell, and find whoever is ringing it.'

Hagen nodded and the old guardsman turned to

go wake his chosen men. Arnulf placed a hand on the guardsman's shoulder as he made to leave.

'If you find trouble you must return swiftly, or sound a horn. If there's trouble in the passes we must raise the alarm and ride forth to defend Arnar.'

Hagen nodded again and without another word he made his way along the palisade walkway. The bell rang again and Arnulf looked up off towards the dark mass of the night covered mountain looming to the west.

Arnulf stood a while looking out from the palisade, listening for another faint chime of the distant bell as the wind whistled about him. The watch post was high above the night shrouded borderlands below. In daylight the guardsmen of Arnar could see a great distance across the lands below, ever vigilant against an old threat from Cydor.

There had not been open war between Arnar and its mother realm, Cydor, for hundreds of years now, yet the tradition of keeping the watch posts along the border manned had endured. The need was even more so in recent years, since the outbreak of the civil war, those lands were no longer safe. Bands of marauding outlaws roamed free, while the great lords clashed with their king in a war that has now raged long years and had ravaged the ancient and once fair realm of Cydor.

The bell once again tolled, echoing along the valleys.

'Definitely west,' muttered Arnulf.

He doubted the possibility a warband had made its way across the border and somehow found a way up into the High Passes, it was unheard of. The cliffs ran sheer for hundreds of leagues and other than minor raids, no attack had come from Cydor since the wars of forging, but he could not risk it. It was his duty.

He glanced down into the watch post. It was a small huddle of low round stone and wooden buildings, each with conical thatched or turfed roofs, where perhaps twenty men lived while they stood guard.

The lord of each village and town around the borders takes his turn to stand guard at a watch post every year. Arnulf had his lands and the people who lived there were sworn to him, it was now his time to keep the watch manned.

He had maybe twenty good fighting men, but they watched the hall and the town down in the lowlands, there were only ever five at most up at the watch post. The other men were guardsmen from the town and surrounding villages, farm lads mostly who take a watch in turn as part of the oaths to their lords.

In times of war, the great lords summoned all their nobles and each brought his fighting men to their banners. In times of peace, the men of Arnar were farmers and fishermen but, still, the warrior ways were never forgotten.

The bell rang again. Arnulf looked out but could see nothing in the dark night but the inviting flicker of the fires through doors of the watch post's round buildings below. Other doors were quiet and dark, the men asleep. Only the sentries on watch were to be seen, slowly walking along the palisade or standing by the braziers, trying to keep warm.

The wind picked up and made the banners of the watch post below flap wildly. The great banner of Arnar flapped beside his own. He looked at the sigil illuminated on his banner by the flickering torch light, a black axe on a crimson field. The axe and spear had been the preferred weapons of Arnar since ancient times. The people of Arnar learn from a young age to use them alongside a shield. This way was favoured by most of Arnar's warriors. Few men owned a sword, fewer still the great swords. The sword was a symbol of wealth and power, although many still preferred the ancient honoured axes of their fathers.

The greataxe had been the ancient sigil of the Cydor kings for many centuries, since before histories began, before Arnar was forged. Arnulf had an old greataxe himself, inlaid with bronze it was said to be passed down from the days of Arn. And so, like the ancient kings across the border, he took it as his banner sigil also.

His thoughts turned to the old days. He remembered seeing that banner flying alongside the hundreds of others when the armies of Arnar retook Aeginhall, many years ago, far to the west on the coast. He was young then, and Hagen was there. The old warrior must have been around the same age as himself now.

After a short while, a small group of guardsmen had gathered in the compound below. Arnulf watched as the men mounted their horses and prepared to ride out.

Soon, the party of three horsemen rode out from

the watch post. There was no gate–this was no defensive position–just a gap in the embankment that circled the watch post. The low embankment topped by a wooden palisade was the only defence.

The men rode with their round shields slung at their backs, and they carried long spears at their sides. One by one, Arnulf watched them depart from his vantage point on top of the palisade. They were good men, all three his own, local fighting men and warriors sworn to his service. Arnulf remembered when Hagen had served his father, and he was just a young lad. Hagen was old now, his hair and beard more than touched with grey, but Arnulf would still rather have him beside him in the shield wall than many. The three horsemen rode out of sight into the gloom of the quiet night.

That was the moment he noticed; the bell seemed to have fallen silent. He waited a while, nothing. Arnulf looked up into the moonless night, a black moon. He clutched the wooden charm hung around his neck.

'By Old Night himself, a bad omen,' he muttered to himself. After a moment, he then turned and left the remaining sentries on the palisade to their watch and made his way back to the warmth of the fires and huts below.

***

Hagen led his scouting party down the slope following the trail south out of the watch post, and then turned west heading up into the bleak high valleys of the passes. The rocky trail was dark without the moon. The men had to trust to their horses to pick a safe path down the track without stumbling in the dark.

'What is this Hagen? Why are we riding out in the middle of the night?' grumbled one of the men.

'Did you not hear?' said Hagen. 'We heard a warning bell on watch. Arnulf wants us to take a look up in the passes. So here we are.'

The guardsman looked up into the dark sky. 'Riding out on a black moon, too. Varg save us,' he said. 'Aren't we the lucky ones? There are old and evil places up in those passes. The folk about talk of haunted ruins and evil spirits which guide the unwary to their peril.'

The other guardsman riding behind laughed. 'Are you afraid, Branik? How often do we get to ride these poor beasts? Once or twice in a moon? It's a cold night but I think it's good to be out. Standing watch over the border lands for hours on end does start to wear thin—if you can believe that?' he said with a grin.

'Aye, lad,' said Hagen. 'But unless it was Branik's spirits, someone was out there ringing that bell, and it's only the living I'm concerned with. I have never met a ghost that could do me harm but, nonetheless, there's a black moon out, Old Night's time, and it's a dark night at that, so stay alert. We will have reached the High Passes by daybreak at this pace anyway, so keep your eyes open.'

The trail led them west around the high ridges of the great mountain and into a high valley surrounded by looming peaks capped with snow. The terrain about the track was rugged, rolling heathers and rocky gullies choked with thorny gorse bushes. An occasional small, twisted tree grew from amongst the rocks alongside the track, their roots clawing onto the stones seeking patches of earth.

After perhaps an hour or two the trail met another and stopped, leaving the choice, one way heading south east towards the rolling moors of Arnar's Border lands and the other, winding up to the northwest which led through the High Passes. Hagen looked away to the south and east. The horses were now high up in the mountains, and the lands to the south down through the valleys below looked dark and quiet. Hagen turned his horse up towards the High Passes and rode on.

'Hagen, will we not search the track to the Waystone and the farms on the moor to south?'

'No,' replied Hagen. 'If the passes are clear and we find nothing we will ride by there on the way back, if the warning bell had rung from the farms, we would see the burning but I see no glow of flame, the lands are still. Besides I heard it myself. It wasn't coming from the borders it came from up there.' Hagen pointed up towards the dark hills.

Suddenly, the sound of a horse galloping echoed down the pass.

'Quick, lads, let's see who this is. I want arrows on him while I halt him.'

Hagen unslung his shield from behind and held it with his reins to his chest at the ready. His horse stepped about eagerly. The rider emerged from the darkness around a bend up the track ahead of them.

'Halt!' shouted Hagen. Still the rider came. 'Halt in the name of Arnar!' The rider showed no sign of slowing, galloping out of the gloom towards Hagen as he barred the track. 'Halt man!'

The rider was nearly on him.

'Take him down,' bellowed Hagen. The arrows flew. One caught the rider in the shoulder, he was knocked back, but he didn't fall. The rider plunged out of the gloom and past the guardsmen at a full gallop. Hagen wheeled his horse and as he kicked his mount forward to pursue another arrow slammed into the flank of the rider's horse.

The horse screamed out and toppled over, crashing to ground. The rider was hurled to the floor with the arrow still sticking out of his shoulder.

'Watch the pass. Quick, you with me,' barked Hagen.

Hagen rode to the fallen rider and lowered his spear at the crumpled figure. It was a man. He lay twisted in the heather with the now snapped arrow high in his chest. In the fall he had smashed his skull on a rock. His head was bleeding badly. He looked up at Hagen and reached for him.

'They're dead,' he groaned, and then he fell limp.

Hagen did not recognise him. 'He's not a local man, and he is armed, look…' Hagen raised the man's cloak with the tip of his spear to reveal a sheath hung at his side. 'Damn, you got him good, but I wouldn't have minded a word with him.'

'He said, "they're dead?"' said the guardsman behind him. 'Who's dead?'

Hagen shook his head, then replied, 'I don't know, lad, but this doesn't look good.'

The fallen horse screamed again. The guardsman got down and removed an axe from his saddle to put the poor creature with the gods. The blow was quick. The guardsman muttered a word and kissed the pendant around his neck, and the creature soon stilled.

Hagen looked off north into the pass. 'There could be more. Move on, lads. Scout the track, keep your eyes open. We stay quiet, have a look, and get back—got it?'

They rode off cautiously, shadows under the black moon.

A glimmer of light had started to appear on the eastern sky as the horses wound higher up into the passes. There were more trees clustered about as they got higher. The faint light began to reveal the open barren scrublands of the High Passes and the tree covered mountain sides they were winding up through. A mist hung over the wet morning heathers and began to creep through the dark trees about them. It was getting thicker as they climbed.

Hagen whistled and his men reined in, looking at him. He had heard something. He raised his arm and cupped his ear, a signal to his men. They all looked around silently. There it was again—a horse. The men heard it, too. All eyes turned to the direction of the sound coming through the trees. Hagen sent Branik off to look. He was gone a minute or two, and then he appeared again.

'It is horses, Hagen. Up off this way,' he said pointing up off the track. 'There's another track, off this one, going up the hill. Would have ridden straight past it if I wasn't looking.'

Hagen looked off through the misty trees. He

could see some big rocks looming up ahead.

'Would make an easy ambush, so careful,' said Hagen with a frown.

There was indeed another track, nearly hidden amongst the trees and undergrowth. It seemed to lead towards the sound of the horse. They rode carefully until the shape of a horse appeared from the morning mists ahead. It was tethered to a tree amongst the rocks. The beast seemed distressed and was trying to pull itself free.

Hagen signalled to his men and they rode around checking the high rocks and trees about. All seemed clear. They found a campsite back among the rocks. The fire had burned low but was still smoking. There were weapons and belongings strewn about, even a near empty barrel of ale by the burnt-out fire.

'They cannot have gone far, search about. Looks like only a few of 'em, wouldn't mind knowing who they are. So, stay sharp they could return.'

Hagen continued along the track, which led past the big rocks and up into the trees, until his horse suddenly reared and kicked. The other horses seemed restless and nervous. The horses kept neighing and snorting, and the horse tethered to the tree thrashed to get free.

'What is wrong with them?' cried Branik as he struggled to stay in his saddle. His horse kicked and wheeled about, not wanting to go further.

Hagen could not urge his mount on further. The beast just pulled away and walked back. They rode back and dismounted, tethering the horses to trees. Hagen did his best to calm the beast before taking his axe from his saddle and sliding it through a loop in his belt, and then once again took up his spear and shield. Branik did the same, and the other guardsman, a man named Darek, took up his bow and ran to join the others.

'We leave the horses here,' said Hagen, 'and go look along this track. If there is any trouble, we get back to the horses and ride like the wind.'

The others nodded their agreement.

They quietly moved up the track that wound up off into the trees. Staying off the track itself, they cautiously picked their way through the rocks and undergrowth alongside to make their approach harder to spot if someone was watching the track ahead.

'Hagen, look!' Darek pointed as a figure loomed out of the mist on the track ahead. They shrank back into the undergrowth. A lone figure slowly limped towards them.

'There's only one. Let's find out who they are…' whispered Hagen. 'This time, we get answers. Careful now.'

Hagen emerged onto the track and called out, 'You there, halt, for Arnar!'

The figure was closer now. The face cloaked, the figure just kept walking slowly forward. The horses thrashed and neighed wildly from behind them. The guardsmen looked around, fearing the horses would break free.

Hagen called again, 'You there, who are you? We are the guard of Arnar. Show yourself!'

No reply. The figure just kept walking slowly forward one jerky footstep at a time with its arms stretched out towards him.

Darek notched an arrow.

'Do you need help?'

No reply.

The figure was close now. It was an old man.

'What is this?' said Darek.

Still, the silent figure advanced. As he got closer, Hagen could see something on his face—blood. There was blood on his hands, too.

'By the gods,' muttered Hagen. He took a step back and levelled his spear. 'I said halt, old man! Who are you?'

The old man just kept walking towards Branik, with his arms outstretched. The old man groaned.

'What was that, old man? Do you need help?' asked Branik.

The old man stumbled forward and clutched at the guardsman.

It was then Hagen saw the old man's back.

'By the gods, what is this?' repeated Hagen.

He had seen his share of blood in battle, but still, this chilled him. The old man had a great wound on his back, as if his cloak had been torn into by some terrible beast with ripping claws, taking chunks of skin and flesh with it. Bone could be seen through great bleeding hole in the old man's back.

The old man collapsed into Branik's arms. Branik dropped his spear and held the man from falling.

'He is so cold,' muttered Branik as the man clutched at the guardsman fiercely.

'Crone, guide us. What did this?' said Hagen, horrified.

Branik suddenly cried out. Hagen heard his flesh tear as the old man pulled away. The old man snarled and sunk his teeth into Branik's neck again. The hood fell back, and blood sprayed on the old man's face. The guardsman collapsed with a look of horrified surprise as the blood pumped away from his throat. The old man leapt on the fallen guardsman and started trying to tear at his mail armour.

Darek drew back his bow and loosed his arrow. It struck the old man, and he staggered back with the arrow protruding from his chest. He snarled again and lunged at the bowman, leaving Branik stricken on the ground. Darek stepped back, fumbling for another arrow as the old man lunged towards him.

Hagen rushed forward and battered the old man down with his shield. The spear thrust was hard and swift into the man's chest. He twisted it free as the old man fell.

'Crazy bastard. Are you okay, lad? Branik?' said Hagen.

He looked around. Hagen suddenly felt an iron grip seize his ankle. He wheeled, and to his dismay, he saw the old man had more fight yet. He looked down into the old man's blood-smeared face. He had strange dark eyes. He snarled like a beast. *Is it a man?* It snarled again, and Hagen again drove his spear into the old man, surely a killing blow. It let go of his leg. The old man writhed and gargled beneath the spear point, flailing for Hagen's leather boots again with his bloody claws.

'Just die,' roared Hagen, and leaving his spear tip impaled through the old man, he unhooked his axe from his waist and brought it down in a savage strike across his face. He felt the blade of the axe bite through bone, the strike jarring his arm in his sudden fury. The old man lay still.

Hagen ran over to his fallen comrade. Branik lay, blood still oozing from his neck, his eyes blank. He was dead.

'Bastard,' muttered the old guardsman.

Darek knelt next to his fallen friend and pulled Branik's helmet over the staring eyes.

'What was that? He just wouldn't die,' said the younger guardsman.

'I don't know, but we should go,' said Hagen, catching his breath. The horses were neighing frantically. They reared up and thrashed around, trying to break free. One did and ran off through the trees.

It was then that Hagen turned and saw them. They had come lumbering out of the mist, quietly unnoticed. Several other figures now advanced down the track. As they came into view, he saw the one nearest appeared to be naked and had runes carved into his skin. Another dressed much like the rider they had slain in the night. Some had great and terrible wounds and were splattered in blood. Hagen stared in horror. How could a man suffer such wounds and still stand? They looked dead. More came groaning and limping towards them with arms outstretched.

Darek notched another arrow and loosed it at the first man with the carved skin. It struck him, and he fell.

'Come on, lad, to the horses. We ride,' called Hagen. The guardsman loosed another arrow. The arrow struck, and the man staggered but just came forward again, snarling. The naked man began to get up again. The guardsman panicked.

Hagen shouted again, 'Come on, run!'

Darek turned and froze at what he saw before him. Branik stood there, pale and splattered with blood. His eyes, dead and black, like the old man. Branik lunged at the surprised guardsman and sank his teeth deep into his arm. Hagen grabbed the guardsman's shoulder and pulled him free. Branik took a chunk of flesh from his arm, and blood ran down his chin as he chewed at it. Hagen was horrified. He hesitated a moment, then struck Branik hard and low with the axe. It buried deep into his side, and he fell.

Hagen grabbed the stricken guardsman, who stood, holding his arm. 'Run, fool.'

The two guardsmen ran for the horses and mounted up. The dead men limped along slowly in pursuit. They wheeled the panicked horses and rode back down the track.

'He was dead, Hagen. How? He bit me.'

'Just ride,' replied the old guardsman. He trembled. He could not believe what he had just seen. *Those men were dead.*

They rode fast and spoke little. The mists still clung low as they emerged from the tree line into the barren high valley. They passed the body at the crossroads and rode up the track that led to the watch post.

Darek slumped low in his saddle until, finally, he fell from his horse. Hagen dismounted and ran to him. He was bleeding from the bite on his arm and looked pale.

'I'm hungry, Hagen. I need to eat. Now!' He spoke through clenched teeth. The lad seemed angry, from the pain or delirious from the loss of blood perhaps?

'Okay, I'll get you some food. Wait there, rest a few minutes.' Hagen returned to his horse. He hadn't planned to be longer than a day so they brought little food.

Something struck him hard on the back of the head. The world blurred, and he fell to the floor. The guardsman stood over him. He was breathing heavily and had a strange look in his eyes.

'I must eat now,' bellowed Darek.

Hagen could feel something dripping off his ears and down his neck. It was on his face. He touched his cheek and looked at his hand. It was blood.

His head was bleeding badly. The guardsman dropped the rock and bent to pick up another larger one with both hands. He advanced on Hagen. Hagen tried to get up, but he couldn't. His head span.

'No!' cried Hagen.

The guardsman advanced with the rock held high above his head. He laughed hysterically. Hagen took the horn from his belt and blew it as hard as he could. It sounded loud and deep. The guardsman shrieked at him. Hagen blew again but it was cut short as the rock crashed down.

***

Arnulf stood over the body of the old guardsman. The horn lay by his side. He ran his fingers across the engraved patterns that ran along the head of his great axe and looked at the scene in front of him.

The sun had already begun to rise over the peaks and ridges above them. One of his men stood behind him in silence, holding a spear and shield. The other men clustered about, leaning on their spears. Few had mail. They were the townsfolk and men of the villages whose turn it was to stand guard at the watch post.

The crows had got there before them. Rhann circled overhead, the greater kin of crows. The huge black carrion birds soared on thermals rising off the pass, circling the kill below. Their smaller cousins had moved in now, the rhann having had their fill.

The birds flapped away and cawed in anger when the men approached. The body lay at the side of the track and had been torn open, the entrails pulled out and pecked at. The creatures of the pass had been feasting. The torso lay trapped and crushed beneath a large rock. The blood, still wet, was splattered across the nearby rocks. It seemed to be everywhere.

'No way for a man to die,' muttered Arnulf. It looked like Hagen, one of his men.

As they stood there in silence, another horseman rode up and reined in.

'M'lord, there is another up the track. He had an arrow in him, and his head was smashed in but he's not one of us.'

Arnulf looked up at him. 'No sign of the others yet?' he asked.

The horseman shook his head 'We did find two of our horses though, just running free, m'lord?'

'Trouble,' said Arnulf in a grim tone, again turning to the scene at his feet. Arnulf was angry and saddened. This was one of his men, a man he'd known his whole life, the man's son was sworn to him also. *How will I tell Hagen's wife?*

He had no time for that now. They must get a warning to the farms on the moor and raise the guard.

'He is with Old Night now. Cover him in stone, and we move on.'

Arnulf turned back to the man on the horse.

'Erran, take one of the town lads who can ride and ride fast, send word to the Motte, bring my men, and send word to Fergus at Weirdell. Tell them the guard has been attacked, one dead, two missing, no sign of the attackers. Tell them I'm going to find out who did this, and that I will await you and the men at the Waystone, and hurry.' The horseman spurred off back down the track.

He needed more men. He did not want to risk an ambush with so few. He now only had one sworn fighting man with him, Hafgan. The others had gone with Hagen, and Erran rode ahead. Of the other men, he left three men at the watch post with orders to light the beacon if attacked. The watch posts must always be manned, and so Arnulf brought every man he could spare. He had less than a dozen men and only one horse, his own, perhaps more with those loose horses.

Arnulf was troubled. He turned to his band of men who had begun covering the grisly remains of Hagen in rocks. 'Men, we march to the Waystone and check with Hern's Farm. If they've seen nothing, we'll come back and guard the pass around the

Waystone. Whoever is out here must come through there to come down from the passes. When Erran returns with the other men, we will return here and search the passes. Someone will pay for Hagen.' He paused, glancing at the rough stone cairn being piled over his friend.

'Hopefully, if Hart's luck was with them, the others have made it back already but keep your eyes open. We don't want to get caught out.'

Arnulf sent some of his men to fetch the loose horses and watched as the others laid the last stones over Hagen. He shook his head sadly and mounted his horse.

The men started to make their way back down the track. Before long they came to the crossroad where the track met the old trail to the High Passes.

Arnulf could indeed see the limp body of a man laid in the rocks near the path. He rode over, it was as Erran said. The man lay twisted with an arrow in him. He rode back and sat upon his horse as he watched his few men file past and head south towards the Waystone.

Hafgan reined in his horse next to Arnulf's.

'Look, m'lord, up there.' He pointed back off up the hill. The old trail was still steeped in mist. 'There's people up there.'

Arnulf looked, there was indeed someone there. He saw only one at first, a dark shape approaching through the haze, but he soon realised there were several figures slowly limping out of the mist and staggering towards them.

CHAPTER NINE

Pinedelve

Bjorn had ridden on through the night and now the eastern horizon again grew lighter, silhouetting the surrounding hills against a dawn sky. The trees and rocks rushed up from the gloom and then were gone, left behind as the horse cantered onwards.

He had ridden his old horse hard through the night, only ever stopping briefly to rest and water the poor creature before riding on. His horse was sweating and lathering. He must stop a while or he would kill the beast, but he feared to linger long in case they found him.

The horns had been braying in the distance behind him but it had now been several hours since he had last heard one. However, he didn't know if they had tracked him, or if they even had horses, but he didn't want to take any chance.

He reined in by a small creek and dismounted. The water formed a small pool where it bubbled up out of the rocky hillside and flowed away down a narrow channel it had carved through the ground, disappearing into the grass. The water was cold as he splashed the water into his face and drank.

His shoulder throbbed, the wound was swollen. He peeled his shirt away from the skin on his back, careful to avoid the arrow still protruding from his shoulder. The cloth was sticky with blood and puss. He cursed and knelt, fighting back the pain. *I have to keep going.*

He wiped down the sweat from the horse's flanks and neck with a rag as the old nag drank its fill from the pool.

Once she was tethered, the hunter slowly climbed up the hillside and surveyed the country he had ridden through, searching for signs of pursuit. No sign of anything other than the rocky slopes and the clusters of trees that grew here and there.

The forested mountain slopes, crowned with their white and grey peaks dominated the view to the east. The pine forests seemed to spill down from the slopes and stretch away into the now distant hills to the northeast back the way he had come. He looked back down the slope to the pool and could see his horse below.

He looked to the south and scouted the lands ahead. Looming above the rocky valleys that lay ahead, Bjorn could see a landmark he recognised in the distance. The Pine Spire, a lone peak which rose from the forest on Arnar's northern frontier, it marked the border and the lands he knew lay beyond.

He sat a while and rested, always staying watchful of the trees he had ridden through. Suddenly, there was movement. A figure burst from the distant tree line and sprinted across the open ground towards him. Bjorn swore and ducked down. It looked like one of the savages, perhaps a scout or an outrunner. Bjorn watched for a moment.

He was swift and covered the ground quickly, stooped low as he ran. The savage would soon see his horse. If only he had his bow, he could soon make the shot. Bjorn scrambled back down the slope and mounted his horse.

As he wheeled his horse to gallop off south, he saw him. The savage stopped. It was him—the Wildman. He just stood there looking at the horseman. Had the savage followed him? Worse, had he in turn been tracked? Bjorn looked to the distant trees expecting to see a warband of savages burst from the trees in pursuit but there was none, just the savage Wildman staring at him.

He kicked his heels and rode off at a gallop towards the Pine Spire leaving the lone figure stood in the distance behind him.

It was late in the day when he began to approach the lower slopes of the Pine Spire. The lone mountain towered above the surrounding pine forests that covered the lands in these parts. Its high slopes were covered in pine trees, and it could be easily recognised for its distinct twisted looking peak.

It was said that in some time past, a great cataclysm had split the peak asunder and a huge landslide took half the mountain side away, leaving the twisted claw like summit. The great landslide left bare cliffs and rocky slopes on one side of the great mountain but the rest was covered in the thick pine forest.

Bjorn had travelled these slopes before. He remembered hunting mountain cats and stag in these forests while in the employ of local lords some years back. He also recalled visiting a farmstead or two with his hunting party not far from the Spire. And so, he made his way south through the foothills searching for a trail or some sign of the local folk.

He found himself at the foot of a high cliff. The cliff ran in either direction for as far as the eye could see and blocked his path to the south. To his left the cliffs ran off up into the tangle of terraces and ridges that formed the lower slopes of the Pine Spire. To his right the cliffs could be seen above the trees heading off to the west. He could climb it easily, but he could not traverse it with the horse, which would mean he would have to leave the old beast. No, he had to choose a way.

He turned his horse and rode west hoping to find a way up. Bjorn followed the cliffs some miles, carefully picking his way through the trees while searching for a path south.

The day was getting late and the sun was low before he found a way up. West had seemed the best route and the cliffs had indeed got lower, but the cliff had pushed him back north as well as west. He did not desire to return north into the hands of the savages, and was relieved to find the way up in the last light of the day. So, taking his horse by the reins, he led her carefully up a scree slope littered with large rocks until they reached the tree line above.

The hunter paused and looked down into the darkening forest below. Light was nearly gone so he led his horse away from the exposed cliffs south into the trees. He picked his path carefully in the dark, leading his old mare by the reins. He walked for an hour or two in the dark woods before finally, he rested.

Bjorn awoke suddenly. He had fallen asleep. He did not remember going to sleep, it had been days since he had last slept, and he had slept longer than he should. He found himself sitting against a tree with his horse tethered nearby. His back was agony, a throbbing, pulsing pain. He felt the shaft protruding from his shoulder and considered removing it, the pain would be intense. No, he shouldn't. He could not risk bleeding out from removing it or worse, passing out from the pain and being found unconscious by his pursuers. He had risked too much in sleeping already.

He rose shakily and looked about. The sky was already light but it looked like the sun had not long risen. He was hungry. Suddenly a memory of horror struck him, the revulsion at his hunger upon smelling that arm. That charred *human* arm. Images of the savages and their gruesome feast ran through his mind. The memory left him stricken and his stomach heaved. Bjorn had thought of little other than escaping, but now couldn't get the images out of his head. He could almost still smell it.

He shook his head. He knew he had to control himself. He had no food, and he must get word back to Old Stones and tell his gruesome tale to Lord Archeon and his northern lords.

Bjorn mounted his horse and again headed south. He rode south following the cliffs that had blocked him yesterday afternoon. He rode along the cliff top where the trees were sparser until his eyes caught a glimpse of something below. He had himself been down there, following the cliff, only yesterday. He reined in.

His eyes searched the gaps in the trees below. There again, he saw something. It was someone running. He lingered a moment, searching the trees, his heart beating fast, but he saw nothing more and turned and rode on.

Bjorn was troubled, he was being tracked. Was it the strange Wildman? He could easily climb the cliff but had he tracked him and followed on foot? He could be one of them but had not proven to be any danger, yet. Still, he would take no chances.

More worryingly, what if it was the savages? A sudden flicker of fear shivered through him as he thought of the savages running behind him in pursuit. It was not like him to be afraid, but he was unsettled. Yet again Bjorn was being hunted.

Either way, they were on foot, and he on horseback. He was also now close to the safety of the halls and farmsteads of Arnar. Would they follow him into towns? Surely not, but it was not impossible. Bjorn would have to be on his guard. He rode on.

Bjorn stopped at the top of the hill and looked down into the large clearing. Nestled below was small cluster of round wooden buildings with conical roofs, a farmstead.

Smoke gently streamed from the holes at the top of some of the larger buildings. People could be seen moving about. A few had seen the horseman on the hill above and had stopped what they were doing to gaze up at him. Bjorn made his way down. As he approached Bjorn dismounted to show he was a friend, slowly walking amongst the houses. There were a few sheep and some pigs in enclosures woven from willow. Game birds hung along the top beam of one of the houses.

A man approached. 'Greetings, friend,' said the man, although he eyed the hunter warily. 'I am Bennis. This is my farm.' He said gesturing to the surroundings. 'Folk call me Old Ben.'

'I am Bjorn the huntsman, in the service of High Lord Archeon. Well met, friend. I am unarmed but I'm hurt. I am in need of some food and water for me and the horse before I move on.'

The farmer looked him over. 'I have heard of a Bjorn the hunter. Perhaps the same?'

Bjorn smiled. 'Perhaps,' he replied with a nod. The farmer's eyes widened.

'I have heard stories of your hunts and deeds. My home is honoured. Come, sit by the fire and sup with me if you will. Tell me what brings you to my home while I have someone see to your horse.'

The farmer beckoned to one of the watching farm workers to take the huntsman's horse, and then motioned for him to follow.

The farmer, Bennis, was an older man but still broad and strong from his years of farming. He led Bjorn towards the largest house and ducked inside. Two of the farm boys stood staring at the stranger before a woman hurried them off. She threw a nervous glance at the hunter before hastily returning to her work. Bjorn followed Old Ben and ducked under the thatched roof and entered.

The room was well lit from the open shutters built into the timber frame which held the thatch roof. There was a central hearth enclosed by wooden partitions that also divided the round house in two. Colourful hangings and drapes made from stitched hides hung from the walls and partitions. The hearth looked as if it could be opened to the back room also. But now, in the old way of receiving a guest to hearth and hall, the partitions were closed to the back rooms, leaving the hearth open to the door.

Bennis took a seat facing the fire and the door and beckoned Bjorn to sit beside him.

'So, Bjorn, tell old Ben what you will. You are wounded? Indeed, you look pale…'

'I was ambushed north of the border. I took an arrow, I need a healer. I cannot remove it alone.' Bjorn leaned forward and twisted as best he could.

The farmer gasped, 'So much blood. We must get that out of you soon, friend, before a sickness sets in. I dare not let my people touch it—we have not the skill for such a wound. But there is a healer in the village for the lord's men. We should get you there as soon as we can. I will take you myself.'

'Thank you, friend,' said Bjorn.

'It will take a small time to prepare your horse. Perhaps time enough for a drink. I'm sure you're thirsty.'

Bjorn nodded thankfully. The farmer continued 'And perhaps also, you could tell me what brings you to the border? An ambush you say? And I suppose you would like to know the latest on Donal's place?'

'Donal's Place?' asked the hunter with a shrug.

The farmer seemed surprised. 'No? Then never mind. I just thought...' He trailed off then continued, unable to resist the gossip. 'You see, a lot of folk have been talking. Don's place was left deserted. No one knows what happened to them—very strange.' He paused. 'Well then, if not about Donal...' He left it hanging and poured a dark ale into a horn while waiting for Bjorn's response.

Bjorn took the horn and drank deep; it was bitter and heavy but good.

'Well met friend,' he said again, raising the horn to his host. 'No, friend, I was not sent here for your Donal, but the tale is indeed of interest, and perhaps also to the high lord who sent me.'

Bennis raised his eyebrows at the mention of a high lord.

'Tell me what you can,' continued Bjorn. 'Have there been others missing?'

Old Bennis leaned back and scratched his beard. 'Well, there's been talk and rumour coming in from the west road for the last couple of moons, but few believed the stories, and then Don disappeared. Now people are nervous. They fear the stories are true. Neither he nor his boys have been seen since before the last full moon.'

Bjorn listened on. 'Go on,' he said when the farmer stopped.

'There's not much to tell, I only know as much as the next man about these parts but Lord Kervan sent men to search his farm, and the forest, but they didn't find anything. Just empty buildings, no sign of anything or anyone.' Then he shrugged. 'Folk are saying the Beast took them, but the village is full of talk,' said the old farmer before taking a long drink from his horn.

Bjorn sat thoughtfully and the farmer watched him. Then he finally spoke. 'Your lord, Kervan, his hall is in the village we're going to? I must speak with him before I ride west.'

'Aye, his hall is in the village. I can send word ahead for you. I'm sure he would be glad to receive you. I have lived here on his land for years, he collects his dues as any lord, but he is a good man. I have drunk with him in his hall and we've talked many times. Now friend Bjorn, you have yet to tell me of your ambush?'

Bjorn smiled and nodded. 'I do thank you for the ale and the hospitality of your home, friend. But now you must listen,' said Bjorn. The farmer looked suddenly wary. 'I was sent to hunt the beast folk speak of.' The old farmer sat up with interest. 'But if there is such a creature, I have not yet seen or heard any real trace of it. I have searched many of the places where folk have disappeared, and from one such place, I found something.'

The farmer leaned in closer toward his guest. 'What did you find?'

Bjorn smiled. He always enjoyed telling a good tale. Then after a moment, he said, 'Tracks.'

'Tracks?' repeated Bennis. 'What tracks? The beast?'

Bjorn smiled. 'As I said, friend, I have seen nothing of this beast. Instead tracks from some sort of raiding party, and I followed them, tracked them for days out across the border into northern Barrens.'

'Outlaws from the Barrens?' asked Old Ben taking another sip of the dark ale.

'Perhaps,' replied Bjorn. 'But I was ambushed by my quarry and taken, but not by outlaws, but by some sort of Wildmen. It is hard to believe, friend, but they looked like the Stonemen from the old stories. They seemed strange, wild and primitive.'

Old Ben laughed suddenly. 'No, friend, if not outlaws. You must have been attacked by one of the tribes that dwell out there. Well you're safe now friend, they fear Arnar and would not dare come south to face our steel.'

He laughed again but awkwardly stopped as he met Bjorn's gaze. Bjorn sat running his thumb along the blade of his small knife, the knife that aided his escape. The farmer looked at it nervously as Bjorn slipped it away in his boot.

Bjorn leaned forward, his look was deadly serious. 'They are one, perhaps two days to the north. If they found you here friend, and they likely will, I think they would kill you all.' The room became tense, and the farmer looked worried.

'Mother save us,' muttered Bennis.

Bjorn continued, 'I have travelled far and seen the folk up there. These were no border tribe. I have not seen their like. I saw terrible things, friend Bennis. I warn you now, they are a danger to our borders, and to you and your folk. Do not doubt me, friend.'

The big farmer sat back with a deep look of concern on his aged face, and then asked, 'How many?'

'There were many, friend,' answered Bjorn. 'I saw only perhaps a dozen but a day's ride north and I heard the horns of many others. There could be thirty, or fifty, or more. I don't know. But I believe that these Wildmen have been raiding the Barrens and, now, have turned their gaze across the border into our lands, coming from the hills to north. They are taking people. I only tell you all this as I would warn you, move your people until it is safe. This is why I must ride to warn your lord, and then return west to bring word to the lord that sent me.'

Bennis was quiet and thoughtful, and then spoke, 'I have to plough before winter, there is still much to do. I must think, but I will find some food for you, friend Bjorn. Rest as you need, there is ale, and I will send word for you, and as soon as the horse is ready, we will go. If you will excuse me, I must speak with my people, they will have questions, the wife certainly will.' Bennis smiled, and then rose. 'I will return shortly, friend Bjorn, and then we will go.' Bjorn nodded his thanks, and then the farmer disappeared behind a drape into the back room.

Before long he returned with food, some bread and cheese, and then hurried off again leaving Bjorn to watch the fire burning away in the hearth.

Bjorn sat watching the smoke rising up through the roof a while until the farmer, Bennis, returned to tell him his horse was ready when needed. Bjorn rose from his seat next to the fire and turned to the farmer.

'Thank you, but I must be on my way. We should not linger. I need this seeing to,' said Bjorn, indicating the shoulder. 'Do you know yet what you will do?' Bjorn asked.

Old Bennis frowned. 'I do not know yet, perhaps I will show you to Kervan's hall in the village and listen to what he says on it. Perhaps we go to the village for a few nights, perhaps we stay, I do not know but I thank you for the news, and for the warning.' He smiled and placed his hand on Bjorn's good shoulder. 'It was an honour to sup with Bjorn the hunter. Now follow, I will show you the way. It is not far.'

The farmer led Bjorn out to the horses. Once mounted, they rode down away from the farmstead, following a path off into the trees while Old Ben talked.

He talked about the local folk, the local game he had caught, his bad onion crop this year. He seemed to have a tale for every rock and tree along the path. Bjorn rode mostly in silence but listened to his host's tales and rode onwards.

The cart track went on winding through the seemingly endless pine forests that covered most of the northern regions. The track they followed, merely two wheel ruts along a well walked path through the trees.

They had ridden perhaps less than half a league when Bjorn suddenly raised his hand, his talkative companion falling silent.

'There's someone coming. Horses.'

They watched the forest ahead. The farmer began to speak but Bjorn sharply raised his arm again, and he fell silent once more.

'Listen,' said Bjorn.

A small group of horsemen came around a bend ahead and reined in when they saw them. They were warriors but not dressed for war. They wore no mail. They wore plain clothes or leather under their long cloaks, and had shields slung at their backs. One had a coloured pinion hanging from his long spear, his lord's standard.

One rider came forward and raised his open hand. He wore a green cloak trimmed with furs. His fair hair tumbled from beneath his helmet which concealed his face, all but a friendly smile. 'Greetings, old friend,' said the rider to the farmer with a nod, 'and who is your companion?'

Bjorn rode forward. 'I am Bjorn the hunter, in service of High Lord Archeon, and may I also ask yours?'

The warrior laughed. 'I am Kervan Staggat, these forests and the lands about Pinedelve are my own. I heard the famed Bjorn was coming to my hall,' he said with a glance at the farmer. 'So, I rode to meet you myself, well met, friend.'

Bjorn nodded. 'An honour.'

The warrior continued, 'We have met once before Bjorn, some years back. I rode in the hunt you led for Henry Kekburt. I was much younger then, still a lad. I remember you shoot that boar after old Henry missed it, a memorable shot.' He removed his helmet and revealed his face.

Bjorn remembered the boar and Kekburt, but he could not place this man in his memory. He smiled. 'Of course, lord, I thought I knew your face from somewhere. Well met, friend.'

Kervan smiled and kicked his horse back towards his men.

'Come, friends. I have some good ale and mead. I would be honoured to host you. I hear you are wounded? I have a healer, I will send for her on our return.'

Kervan and his men rode them back to the village, which turned out to be not much further along the track. The lord had replaced his helmet and rode up alongside the bedraggled hunter.

'A nasty wound. You were wise not to pull it out,' said Kervan. Bjorn grimaced but gave no reply.

Kervan continued, 'One wonders how such a thing could happen? So, tell me, Bjorn, what has Lord Archeon got you out up here for? You have no bags, no bow. Are you travelling unarmed?'

Bjorn again recounted his recent travels hunting the beast, and of his escape after the ambush. Although, he kept silent about his lone pursuer, he did not want the blame for being followed. The others riding behind all listened in as Bjorn told his tale, and the farmer Bennis nodded and smiled when the hunter spoke of him.

The trees eventually opened out into a rocky valley carved from the ground like some great cleft and nestled at its bottom was the small village of Pinedelve. Little clusters of houses covered the valley floor each with small patches of ploughed land or animal enclosures huddled around them.

'Pinedelve, friend Bjorn, my home,' said Kervan as he led them along the track towards the nearest houses. He and his men shouted greetings to folk who had come out to watch as they rode past.

Pine trees crowned the ridges above them as they rode further into the village. Kervan led the riders towards the long hall that was built on raised land near the centre. There were many buildings here, huddled around the hall forming a couple of crude streets. The folk they passed were mostly woodsmen and hunters. It seems that word had spread that a renowned hunter had come to their village, a small crowd had gathered to catch a glimpse of the man they had heard tales of.

The man they saw however was haggard and dirty. To many, he was much older than they had imagined, his tangled black hair streaked with grey. His cloak was torn and frayed, his once fine clothes and face were covered in filth and he rode a tired dirty horse.

Some of Kervan's men came out to take their horses. The master of Pinedelve led Bjorn up the wooden stairs into the long hall. As soon as he dismounted Bjorn watched the lord giving instructions to various servants, who scurried off about their tasks or trailed behind their lord into the hall. His men followed and closed the door to the curious rabble forming outside.

CHAPTER TEN

Hern's Farm

He stood staring into the water of the babbling creek below. His hands were still shaking. Arnulf couldn't believe what his eyes had seen this day. He heard footsteps approach behind him.

'M'lord, they still haven't returned. I think something might have happened.'

Arnulf shifted his gaze away from the creek below, to the farmstead in the distance. It was barely visible from where he stood, a small huddle of buildings nestled against the far cliffs. His gaze lingered there a while before shifting to fall upon the Waystone before him.

The afternoon was late, the sun already hung heavy in the western sky. The towering ancient stone, known to the local folk as the Waystone, stood alone on a grassy hillock beside the old trail and marked the pass north back into the mountains. The old stone cast a long shadow across the trail that ran beside it—the road they would soon again take.

His eyes traced the road from the small bridge he stood upon, to the Waystone, and beyond as it wound back up through the break in the cliffs and up into the passes of mountains. The huge cliffs of the mountains nearly surrounded them, a great barrier of stone rose to the sky and went for many leagues in either direction. The old Waystone marked the only way up into the old passes, now rarely travelled and treacherous. The passes were said to reach across the Spine of the World, crossing the expansive mountains and into the Barrens bordering the northwestern frontier of Arnar. Arnulf looked again at the farmstead in the distance. It sat upon a terrace of land at the foot of the cliffs to the east.

'Arnulf?'

Arnulf stared off at the distant farmstead without turning.

'Where are they?' he said finally. Arnulf scanned the moorlands and the farm track leading off towards the cliffs, then the distant farmstead, hoping for a glimpse of his returning men.

He sighed. 'Look, Haf, the beacon, it hasn't been lit'.

The big man stepped forward and looked off up into the mountains beyond the Waystone.

'I'm sure the men at the watch post are still safe.

We slew them all, m'lord,' said Hafgan reassuringly.

Arnulf clutched at the wooden charm hung at his neck, and then replied. 'Aye.'

He returned his gaze to the creek below. It frothed over the stones before disappearing under the mossy wooden frame of the old bridge they stood upon. Arnulf placed a shaking hand on his axe head to steady it.

'How's the boy?' asked Arnulf.

'He's hurt bad, m'lord. He and a few of the others who were hurt are heading back for Ravenshold.' He hesitated, 'The lads asked me if we were all heading back?'

Arnulf turned to the big warrior beside him. Hafgan was one of the biggest men Arnulf knew of, one of his own house-warriors, his best. Hafgan stood awaiting an answer. His face looked grim, his mail splattered with dried blood. He had removed his helmet. His head was shaved, and he wore a swirling inked design on his left cheek, hiding an old scar. Arnulf surveyed the big warrior. He alone seemed unshaken. Arnulf felt his spirit bolstered by Hafgan's grim resolute face. He was glad to be in such company.

Arnulf then looked back towards the straggle of men he now led. Several stood watching, leaning on their spears or shields, while others sat amongst the trees beside the road. They looked tired and forlorn. One sat clutching his arm rocking slowly back and forth against a tree. Arnulf nodded towards him and looked enquiringly at Hafgan.

'He was wounded, m'lord, but he says it's not bad. Looks like it hurts like hell though. He could have gone back with the others but…' He hadn't finished when a horn blew from the south.

The horn's call drew Arnulf's gaze to the horizon. He spotted the glint of steel. A small host of men appeared on the brow of the hill to the south.

'It's Erran,' said Hafgan.

'And Fergus has come,' said Arnulf as he spied the blue falcon emblazoned on the shields of the approaching outriders. 'Thank the gods.'

There were horsemen approaching, and amongst them marched warriors; men of the villages and farms who didn't own a mount, but had shield, axe, and spear—Arnar's proud warrior folk. There were a few amongst them, the house-warriors and sons of wealthier farmers and merchants—those who could afford the expense—wearing mail that shimmered in the dying sunlight.

The men turned to look and some cheered as the approaching men spilled down the hill towards them. Arnulf spotted Erran amongst them. The young warrior kicked his horse into a gallop and broke away from the host.

Erran reined in as he reached the bridge.

'Lord Arnulf,' he said with a nod.

Erran was Arnulf's youngest warrior, the horse merchant's lad, but he was strong, and he rode well. His father bought him a sword too, a fine blade for one so young.

'I brought the household men and a dozen others, and I sent word as you said.' Erran turned to the approaching riders, and then dismounted. 'Lord Fergus caught up with us by Bryrebrook, m'lord,' said Erran as he turned back to face them. A look of concern grew on his face as he looked around at the other guardsmen. 'What happened?' asked Erran.

The young warrior turned to Hafgan, 'Where are the others?' he asked. But instead of an answer, Hafgan waved him aside with a grave look as the other horsemen rode up and reined in by the bridge.

'Hail, Lord Arnulf,' called Fergus as he rode up between his outriders. Several women road in his guard, well-armed and in fine armour, Fergus' beautiful but deadly chosen warriors.

Fergus rode with no helmet and had a distinct long mane of thick red hair and a long beard he wore braided.

'I came as soon as I got word, my old friend. My hall is close,' said Fergus with a smile. His smile faded as he looked at Arnulf and his men. 'What happened, Arnulf?' asked Fergus.

Arnulf looked up at his friend Fergus. 'We have been attacked, men are dead. Hagen is dead.' He paused and looked toward the floor to mask his grief before continuing. 'We heard a bell on dead moon watch.'

'A bell?' said Fergus.

Arnulf nodded. 'Hagen took some men out to look. We heard his horn sound, calling for aid. We marched out in force to search for them.' He paused. 'We found him dead this morning. No sign of the others. We found other bodies, but they weren't of our folk, just Hagen. Hagen is dead.' He paused again, still struggling with the thought of it. 'Then we were attacked…' He trailed off.

'I am sorry, my friend,' said Fergus. 'Outlaws?' he asked. But as Fergus looked from Arnulf to his men, he knew this was not so.

'They looked like beggars, or some raving mushroom cult. But it could have been a disguise...or some foul trick.'

Fergus listened on with a now amused face and waited for Arnulf to continue.

'They were ghosts, dead men walking. We filled them with arrows, but they just came on. They tore him apart.' Fergus looked shocked at this last statement. Arnulf looked away again trying to push the gruesome memory to the back of his head, and then went on. 'The poor lad, one of *my* men, they tore him to pieces. We slew them all, but there could be more.' The men nearby looked at one another warily.

Fergus shook his head in disbelief, 'Dead men.' He laughed. 'You sound like you are the one who has joined the mushroom cults, Arnulf.'

Arnulf studied the floor. He didn't like feeling foolish.

'Is he leading me down the path, Haf?' asked Fergus, turning to the big warrior.

Hafgan shook his head slowly.

Fergus looked at them both, and then off toward the Waystone and the hills beyond.

There was a sudden commotion erupting behind Fergus and his horsemen. The men were shouting. One of Arnulf's guardsmen, the man who had been gently rocking back and forth, had leapt up and sprinted off onto the moor and into the maze-like tangle of briar.

'Thom you cowardly bastard,' bellowed Hafgan but to no avail.

Erran went to mount his horse, but Arnulf placed a restraining hand on his shoulder.

'Not now.' Arnulf shook his head, 'No, let him run. Stupid bastard dishonours himself. His father's will feel his shame. I will deal with him, don't you worry.'

Arnulf watched him run and disappear into the trees. Some of the men grumbled disapprovingly but Arnulf paid no heed. Instead he turned to Fergus, still sitting on his horse, and said 'I will ride back and search the passes. Will you ride with me?'

Fergus nodded. 'I will ride with you, Arnulf. You are the Lord of the Watch until winter. It would be my duty.' Fergus bowed mockingly from his saddle with a mischievous grin, and then said, 'Lead on, old friend. I would see your ghosts and dead men for myself.'

Behind the great tangle of beard and red hair Arnulf could see the Fergus he had known as a boy. He had that same look in his eye he had worn since they were young. Arnulf felt a smile creep onto his face. 'It is good you are here, Fergus,' said Arnulf.

Arnulf looked back thoughtfully toward the Waystone again and the mountains beyond, and then traced the cliffs to the distant farmstead at the end of the meandering farm track across the moor.

'First, I must check at Hern's Farm over the moor,' said Arnulf. He beckoned for his horse. 'I sent men there who should have returned hours ago.'

Fergus looked to the farmstead.

'Less than an hour's ride I'd say. You think they are besieged by ghosts and grebins?' laughed Fergus.

Arnulf feigned a smile. 'Well, perhaps we will find out.'

They rode up to Hern's Farm in the dusk light carrying torches to light their way as the light faded. Most of Arnulf's men made camp by the Waystone, to guard the way to the pass and await the wagons. Those who could ride accompanied Arnulf and the horsemen of Weirdell to investigate the farm.

They followed the muddy farm track across the gorse tangled moors. Arnulf rode alongside Lord Fergus, followed by their sworn house-warriors who rode dressed for war.

Fergus's fierce shield-maidens rode behind him. Some had flowing locks of long hair whilst others wore their hair tightly braided and had paint on their faces. All finely armed, they were women it was wise not to anger.

The warriors rode all armoured in mail and wore the sigils of their lords emblazoned on their round shields, Arnulf's black axe on crimson and Fergus's white falcon on blue. The sworn warriors wore swords and fine axes at their belts. They carried long spears tipped with coloured pennons; Arnar's finest warriors. Arnulf and Fergus led twenty well-armed warriors on horseback. The small force moved in a loose straggled column along the track as they followed their lords across the moor.

Hern's Farm sat on a wide terrace of low cliffs that thrust up over the moorland below but still lay in the shadow of the great grey cliffs above. Those cliffs marked the southern ridges of the Spine of the

World.

The path wound its way across the moor, running between thick patches of gorse and briar, before falling into the shadow of the cliffs. Even in the evening gloom, they felt the darkness of the cliffs above bearing down on them, like riding in the shadow of a stone colossus towering above them. With their shields slung on their backs, and while carrying their torches in the failing light, they rode swiftly and soon reached the rocky path that led up onto the farm's terrace.

The folk who dwell at Hern's Farm had allowed and even encouraged the gorse to grow in a thick hedge that enclosed the farmstead like a natural palisade of thorns and yellow blooms. The horsemen rode through the gap in the gorse wall and entered the farm's wide courtyard.

There are few sizable trees on the north moor so the houses were made of piled stone and had turf roofs. They were still mostly round, but some had an odd shape to them. The animals had broken loose, the enclosures were empty. The buildings were dark, there was no smoke. None of the hearths had been lit.

The men dismounted and moved about, peering into the gloomy doorways with their torches raised.

'Where are they all?' demanded Fergus.

Arnulf felt troubled. Where were his men?

'Arnulf!' came a shout. One of the men was beckoning from a dark doorway. As Arnulf approached he saw the man shaking.

'Lord Arnulf,' he said again, his voice breaking. He pointed into the dark doorway.

Arnulf took his torch and illuminated the inside of the house. An axe lay near the door, both handle and blade smeared in blood. Arnulf looked from the axe to the shaken warrior, and then stepped inside.

The room was in disarray. Tables had been knocked over and furniture broken. There was blood everywhere. The floor was slick and glistening with gore. It was even splattered on the roof beams. Slumped against a wall sat the remains of a guardsman. He had a hatchet through his skull, and his chest and stomach had been flayed open, his innards spilled from the terrible wound. Great chunks of him were missing, some of his limbs stripped to the bone and his face mangled.

Arnulf ducked back out of the doorway and resisted the urge to heave.

'What?' exclaimed Fergus.

Arnulf shook his head and waved him away. Fergus went in himself. He emerged with a pale look of horror on his face.

Arnulf's eyes were drawn to a great dark smear on the ground. He moved his torch nearer; blood. The torchlight revealed the blood streaking off towards the darkened doorway of a nearby building. Something heavy and bloody had been dragged inside.

With a glance from their lord the nearby warriors levelled their spears towards the door. They looked nervously at one another as they slowly edged closer to the gaping darkness of the doorway.

Hafgan strode forward and held his torch low and looked inside.

'It's empty,' he said with some relief.

'Search it,' commanded Arnulf. 'Search everywhere.'

The men moved amongst the houses, their torches flickering light and shadows on the eaves and walls of the squat stonewalled houses. Then came shouts of alarm. Men searching the huts had found another set of gruesome remains, again disembowelled and in places stripped to the bone, like the leavings of wolves or some great hill cat. One of the men ran out and vomited as the others watched in silence. Arnulf ordered the bodies to be covered with stones and dirt. No one wanted to move them so they were covered where they lay and left there to rest in the dark houses of the farmstead.

'This place has become a graveyard,' said Arnulf.

'There has been a great slaughter here, how many were there?' asked Fergus.

Arnulf scratched his beard, 'Well, when Old Hern died, his two lads took over together, so with their women and children, and perhaps a few hands, nine, perhaps ten?' His face flickered with shadows in the torchlight.

'Some beast has been set on this place, Arnulf. They have been slaughtered and butchered like sheep, perhaps wolves or dogs, or some evil beast trained for war.' Fergus threw a glance at one of his nearby shield-maidens who stood protectively close. She looked around nervously watching for a lurking danger.

'I fear for the rest of them,' said Fergus. 'If any live they must have fled onto the moor,' he said gesturing out into the dark shapes of the gorse bushes beyond the torchlight.

Arnulf's face was grim. He could see the distant torches and fires of the other men camped at the Waystone. The fires flickered away in the distance beyond the gap in the thorny palisade as his warriors and guardsmen sat about awaiting their return. They were no doubt resting and drinking, oblivious of the carnage over the moor.

Arnulf felt a shudder. It felt as if he was being watched with unfriendly eyes. His eyes searched the tops of the buildings in the farmstead, then the nearby gorse thickets and up at the shadowy cliffs that were illuminated by their flickering torches. He was half-expecting to see some nightmare creature skulking, watching them; but nothing.

The warriors were hasty to leave, Arnulf had no desire to linger in this charnel house with its watching eyes either. They were mounting their horses when a young girl dressed in a linen shift appeared from the darkness and ran through the gap in the gorse.

Her white shift was easy to see in the gloom. She stopped in the middle of the track as she saw the warriors and their horses and stared at them. She stood a moment, then turned and fled back into the shadows.

'Quick catch her,' shouted Fergus to his horsemen. They cantered after her carrying their torches. Arnulf could hear them shouting for her to stop.

The riders returned carrying the struggling girl and placed her before the mounted lords. She was covered in blood, all over her hands and face, the linen of her clothes stained a deep crimson.

'She tried to fight me when we caught her, lord.

Nearly bit my finger off when I grabbed her, too, but we got her,' said the horseman, shaking his hand. The girl lay on the ground groaning, clutching her arm.

'I think she is hurt,' said the warrior as he dismounted. He pulled the girls arm away and revealed a deep wound on her arm. It looked like teeth marks but the wounds had become rotten. Black veins ran away from the wound, it oozed with puss and blood.

She screamed at him and pulled her arm away, trying to run again, but the warrior caught hold of her. Kicking and screaming he again brought her before the lords.

Arnulf got down from his horse and looked at the girl. 'We will not hurt you,' he said gently. 'We will help you if you don't run. Who hurt you?'

She looked up at him, and then around at the mounted men and warriors standing by their horses. She looked terrified.

He didn't think she would speak, and then, after a long moment, she spoke.

'It was my brother. He is after me,' she said then looked away.

'You're safe now,' said Arnulf. 'Where is he? Tell me what happened.'

'A man came, a warrior like you. He was hurt, we tried to help but when he came close, he attacked my brother and we ran home. I got my da, and they got him and took him home. But he was mad. He tried to hurt my ma, and Brin said I should run away and hide. People were fighting each other. My da and Brin were fighting. I was scared, so I ran onto the moor. I don't understand.' She looked around fearfully. 'I saw other men coming, like the bad man, so, I hid. I saw Brin attack them. I could hear my ma screaming and people shouting, but I dare not come out. Everyone was fighting each other, my da, Brin, my ma.' She started crying. 'Why were they hurting each other?'

'It will be okay, lass,' said Fergus. 'You're safe now. What happened then?'

Through her sobs she continued, 'I hid a long time, 'til it was dark. When I came out, I saw my brother, Brin, but he was different—scary. He said it was safe, but he chased me. He was mad like the first man. He was too fast, he bit me and wouldn't let go 'til I hit him with a stone. Then I ran away and saw your lights coming. Please don't let him get me.' She broke down again and wept on the floor.

'Where did they all go, lass?' said Arnulf. There was no reply.

'We saw none on the road here, they must have fled,' said Fergus quietly.

Arnulf signalled his men. 'Bring her, see to her wound. We can't search the moor in the dark. We could ride right past them and not know.'

The warrior picked her up and carried her away. Arnulf turned and looked at Fergus, who said nothing but returned a troubled look, and then mounted his horse. The girl rode with the warrior who had caught her, a man named Olad, a man sworn to Fergus. She rode slumped in the saddle in front of him. He had to hold her from falling most of the way. She said nothing more on their return journey. The warriors left Hern's Farm behind them and rode back along the dark farm track across the moor. The others awaited their return at the Waystone.

CHAPTER ELEVEN

An Arrow of Stone

Bjorn found himself led through to a sheltered corner of Pinedelve's hall. A young girl led the way, and spoke only to ask him to sit. The hunter sat down in a wooden chair as the girl left him, pulling across a hanging as she departed. She returned carrying a bowl of water and was followed by another, an elderly woman.

'Wounded? An arrow I hear?' said the elderly woman. Her face was wrinkled. She had stern eyes that looked him over from head to toe as she walked about him. She wore a scarf over her greying hair, tying it back to trail down her back.

'Well, we'll need that shirt off. Quickly now, off with it, don't be shy,' she said with a wry smile.

Bjorn unclasped his wool cloak and carefully removed his open leather tunic with the aid of the girl, gently sliding it over the exposed shaft. The shirt below had to be peeled away from his skin. The sticky blood had dried and encrusted around the wound.

'What a mess, man. How long has this been left?'

'Long enough,' grunted Bjorn. 'I couldn't take it out alone.'

She gave him a steady frown, and then moved behind him to clean around the shaft with a damp cloth. The hunter winced as pain shot through him. She eased the arrow back and forth slightly.

'It glanced the bone over your shoulder blade. Lucky, any lower it could have punched through to your lungs. I will need my things, lass.' The young girl nodded and went to fetch a satchel from the floor and brought it to the woman.

'There will be pain. But I will be as swift as I can, dear. Bite this,' said the old woman, placing a roll of leather in his mouth.

He did not cry out as the pain tore through his chest, but he couldn't help a heavy grunt as she pulled the arrow free. He felt fresh blood spill down his back. Another burst of numbing agony as she probed the wound with her finger, before washing the wound out, and then covering it with blood moss and binding his shoulder with tight linen.

She handed him a small flask. 'Drink, it will help.'

The liquid appeared to be some local fiery spirit. He drank deep.

'This will, no doubt, need seeing to again. Keep it clean,' said the elderly woman. She took back the flask and drank herself, and then dropped the bloody arrowhead into his hand.

'I wish you blessings of the Mother and the Crone. You have my thanks,' said Bjorn looking up at her.

She returned a smile that filled her face with lines.

'Safe travels, hunter,' she replied.

She ducked through the hanging and left Bjorn to get dressed with the aid of the young girl. The girl gave him a blushing smile, opened the hanging, and scurried off quickly without word.

Bjorn rose from the chair. His shoulder throbbed still, but despite the pain, with the arrow gone and his wound bound tightly, it felt somewhat more comfortable than before.

He looked down at the bloody arrow in his hand and lifted it to examine it closer. Set upon the broken shaft with pine resin, an arrowhead of flint stone.

As he strode back into the main hall Kervan beckoned for him to sit at one of the chairs around his great table. Bjorn pulled out a chair and sat. Some of his men stood by the door while others sat down. He called for food and ale as Bjorn looked about at the lord's hall.

Kervan's banner was hung behind a fine oak chair on a raised dais. His banner showed a black stag on a green field top left and black bottom right, the same as shown on the shields of his warriors. There were furs and cushions adorning the furniture, and hunting trophies lined the roof beams.

Bjorn thought it a fine hall.

'How is your shoulder?' asked Kervan. 'I hear Maud removed the arrow and dressed your wound. She is skilled at such.'

'It's been better,' said Bjorn as he seated himself.

'Good, good,' said Kervan. 'So, the great Bjorn has come to hunt the beast,' said Kervan, addressing the others at the table. 'But instead, he tells me there is no beast. He says it is a hill tribe of savages from the north trespassing in our lands?' At hearing this, the other men muttered amongst one another.

'And you're certain they have been crossing the borders to raid?' asked Kervan as he poured himself and his guest ale.

'I believe so, I will report as much to the high lord when I ride west,' said Bjorn.

'Savages... Stonemen?' said Kervan bemused.

The hunter produced the broken arrow. It clattered across the table as Bjorn tossed it towards Kervan. The lord picked it up and examined it.

'A stone arrowhead,' observed Kervan with a frown.

Bjorn nodded, and then after a moment said, 'Will you hear my council, lord?' Kervan nodded and gestured for him to continue.

'Send word to the other lords nearby. Summon a force and ride north and stop them. It is in your power to pursue those who would threaten your lands.'

Bjorn paused as several servants, the young girl amongst them, appeared with food which they laid out on the table, cured meats, cheeses, bread, and fruit. There was cooked meat. The other men including farmer Bennis sat eating and listening. Kervan took a steaming leg of padridge, a local wild fowl, and took a bite.

'You want me to muster a force,' said Kervan with a full mouth, 'and ride north to attack these savages? On your word alone...and leave my folk unprotected?'

Kervan frowned, and then said 'Eat, friend. You look like you need it. It is good,' while offering the hunter a bowl of bread.

Bjorn felt pale, his appetite had dissolved. That smell—it was the meat. It made the blood drain from the hunter's face.

'They are eating them, m'lord,' said Bjorn, his voice low. 'They are slaughtering the folk they take like pigs and eating them. I saw it with my own eyes.'

The others stopped chewing and stared. Kervan looked at his padridge leg and put it down.

'I saw it with my own eyes,' declared Bjorn. 'They were not men. They moved like animals and were feasting on men's flesh. They were savages, cannibal Stonemen, like in the old stories, but more terrible than I could have imagined. I saw it. On my honour, I swear.'

The men looked shocked at Bjorn's unexpected words. They looked from one another nervously, and then to their lord.

'You swear this is true?' said Kervan, not quite sure if he believed it himself.

'On my honour, m'lord,' answered Bjorn.

'Then evil things do indeed haunt the forests,' said Kervan quietly. He shuddered. 'I will give your council some thought, friend Bjorn. May the Crone guide me. But now, what will you do?' He sat staring at the steaming pork on the table, a horrified look upon his face.

'I was sent to hunt the beast and get answers, if there are any to be found,' replied Bjorn. 'So now I will ride back west and speak with the high lord at Old Stones. I will advise Archeon to send men north to stop them if he will listen. These savages need the steel of warriors to end this, not the bow of a single hunter.' Bjorn paused. 'If he commands it, the northern lords may ride in force but this place, the farms, the folk here, are under threat now. These savages must be stopped.'

Kervan rose and paced about the hall, being followed by his hounds; they were dashing between the chairs looking for scraps.

'So, you will ride west for Old Stones?' said Kervan. 'You will need a fresh horse, that old mare won't make it much further. Leave her here, she will be cared for. I can give you another.'

'Thank you, m'lord,' said Bjorn with a gracious nod. 'And could I ask a favour of you before I ride out?'

'For this grim news I would grant you perhaps a favour at least. What do you ask?' Bjorn did not like to ask and lowered his eyes.

'They took my axe, my bow…'

'Of course,' cut in Lord Kervan. 'Kell! Come, show Bjorn.' One of the warriors stepped forward. 'Kell, give him your axe, I'll get you another and show him to the fletcher, get him what he needs. Good man.'

The warrior hesitantly laid an axe on the table beside Bjorn. It had a thick handle, the blade was slightly bearded and was inlaid with a rune mark.

Bjorn picked up the axe.

'Thank you. I will return to repay you, on my honour I will.' The hunter nodded to the Lord of Pinedelve, and to the warrior named Kell. Then draining the last of his ale, he rose to follow the young warrior to get the provisions he needed.

The lord watched him leave and called after him, 'Repay me by returning for a hunt friend Bjorn.' He laughed, and then sank into a chair deep in thought.

Bjorn was soon mounted and ready to leave. Kervan stood at the top of the wooden steps that led to his hall.

'Safe travels, friend Bjorn,' said Kervan. 'As I said, return when your tasks are done. I would use your services for a hunt. I would see you make another shot like I saw those years ago. I'll pay you well.'

Bjorn ran a finger along his bow. He had chosen a sturdy looking long bow from the lord's stockpile, and the fletcher gave him a good-sized quiver. The arrows were fletched with black feathers, rhann perhaps, and they were well made.

Bjorn nodded slowly to Lord Kervan and smiled at his host before turning his horse toward the west road and urged it onwards. He rode a young bay horse, well broken, it rode well. Bjorn felt a sudden pang of sorrow for the old mare he was leaving behind, his only companion for many weeks. She had been a good horse. He patted his new steed on the neck, and it flicked its head as if sensing Bjorn's thoughts.

The hunter turned back at the small crowd that had gathered at his coming to the hall. They watched and waved. He raised an arm in farewell.

A flock of mountain geese appeared over the pine trees above and flew across the open sky. Bjorn grinned, despite his shoulder, he could not resist. He swung suddenly round in his saddle, notching an arrow, he aimed high. He found his mark and loosed.

The crowd cheered as the goose fell from the sky and tumbled to the ground. He wheeled his horse and bowed from the saddle extravagantly. He grinned at Lord Kervan as the lord clapped amongst his men, and then the hunter cantered off down the west road, leaving the cheering woodsmen of Pinedelve behind him.

CHAPTER TWELVE

A Night for Valour

Word of their encounter with the dead men that morning had already spread about the camp and was believed by few of the newcomers. But now, upon the riders return, word of the gruesome discoveries at the farm were soon known to all. The men watched curiously as the girl was carried away and put down to sleep. She was placed under guard in case she spoke any more.

Tales that had been dismissed and laughed at were now listened to earnestly, and the men sat about their fires listening again to the grim tales of Arnulf's guardsmen.

They heard of how the dead men had limped forward out of the mist like beggars reaching for help. They heard how some of the guardsmen approached to help the strange beggars and how they were then mauled.

One of the guardsmen, an older man from the village told them how young Tarbart from Glen Farm was literally torn limb from limb screaming as the guardsmen rained arrows into them with no effect. The others nodded when asked to corroborate the seemingly impossible story. The men were all talking amongst each other nervously, some of them laughed and called it absurd, but others looked worried. Another of the guardsmen was telling the others how the dead men gripped the rims of their shields and tore them away. They seemed heedless of axe or spear, taking many thrusts and blows before they fell twitching.

Talk turned to the bodies left up in the pass and to the missing men. When Arnulf heard Hagen's name whispered, he turned and glared at them across the campfires.

Hafgan shouted, 'That's enough. We killed the bastards before, and if there are more, we will find them and kill them too.'

The group quietened down at his rebuke.

Hafgan stood. 'They will be driven from our lands and we will find our men. They had no armour or shields, and we do. We won't be caught off guard again,' said Hafgan defiantly.

Arnulf turned back to the wide fire pit as Hafgan sat back down. He touched the wooden charm at his neck. He hoped the big warrior was right.

Turning to Fergus beside him, Arnulf said, 'I hope the gods are watching over us, my old friend.'

'Of course the gods are watching us,' said Fergus

loudly so the nearby men stopped to listen. 'The gods are testing us, my friends. I for one will not fail them. I swear it to Varg.' Fergus stood up and raised his horn of ale. 'They test us,' he said, 'because here dwell men who will fight, and we should be honoured that they have chosen us—perhaps the finest warriors of Arnar—as their champions. Old Night will be denied my spirit this night.' He raised his ale as he said the last part, and the men cheered and laughed.

'Well said, Lord Fergus,' said Arnulf drily. 'Very inspiring.' Fergus grinned and sat down.

'Aye, if tales be told, I say a man makes his own luck,' said Fergus quietly. 'But here's to the gods. May Varg watch over us.' He raised his horn to Hafgan beside him and drank deep, spilling ale over his beard.

***

He laughed and drank but the lord of Weirdell masked a terrible feeling that his old friend, Arnulf, had been playing no joke, in fact he was almost certain now. Yet, how could these stories be true? He worried; what did that to those people back at the farmstead?

***

The warrior Olad came and joined them at the fire and began chewing on a strip of saltpork.

'Has she spoken, friend?' asked Arnulf over the flames.

The warrior coughed, and then said, 'Only to demand food Lord Arnulf. We gave her some, but she says she is still hungry.' He shrugged and coughing, continued with his saltpork.

Hafgan noticed the man looked pale.

'Olad, friend, you look tired. Make sure you keep that hand clean,' said Fergus nodding at his roughly bound hand. Before adding, 'A scratch like that can go bad out here.'

The warrior shrugged again, 'She sank her teeth in good when I grabbed her. I must have put the fear of the gods in her, bearing down like that.'

'Aye,' said Hafgan. 'But your Lord Fergus is right. I've seen it. A dirty wound festers. I remember long ago, during the war, we marched to fight the rebellion out west. Old Graffwulf lost half his fingers on one hand.' Hafgan raised his right hand to demonstrate. 'It went bad, and eventually, sent him to meet Old Night too. He was sick for days before he went. Not a good death, friend.'

Olad stopped eating and waved a strip of half-chewed pork at Hafgan.

'Don't tell me that,' said Olad. 'You were at Aeginhall?' he asked changing the subject.

'Aye, that we were. With Arnulf and Fergus, we were just lads then. Was a hard fight.'

Olad's eyes widened, then he grinned.

'My lord has mentioned it,' said Olad with a grin at his nearby comrades.

'I doubt we'll ever hear the end of it,' said one of the shield-maidens as she strode past.

Fergus looked up at her and grinned broadly. The men nearby laughed.

She smirked and walked on to her companions at a nearby fire. She was dressed for war. She wore a carved leather cuirass over a plain mail shirt and fine sword scabbarded at her waist. A falcon emblem was carved into the leather on her chest, the sigil of her lord. Her brown hair hung down her back and was tightly braided against her scalp at the top. Her face and arms were covered in swirling designs of blue paint, and she wore two gold arm rings on one arm.

'Who is she?' asked Erran. Young Erran had been sat quietly beside Hafgan, listening to the talk.

'She, lad, is the Death Nymph,' replied Hafgan. 'Astrid is her name.'

'She's one of Fergus's warriors, isn't she? I saw her as we rode in.' Erran eyed the gold rings on her arm. 'He has rewarded her well. What else do you know of her?' said Erran with interested eyes on the shield-maiden.

'Ha,' laughed Hafgan. He lowered his voice, 'You're a brave lad, but I'd keep away from that one. She's a killer,' said Hafgan, although he could see what drew the young man's attention. While formidable to behold, her face had a stern beauty. Her tight breeches certainly would tempt any man's gaze as she walked away.

'Why do you say that?' replied the young warrior.

Hafgan pulled his eyes away and looked at Erran. 'She is in service to Fergus now—she and her shield-maidens are never far away—but before that… You've not heard the tale?' asked Hafgan.

Erran shook his head.

'Well, the story goes, she was not always a warrior. She was once a servant at a great hall in the south to some lord. And she killed him.'

Erran shook his head. 'Really, why?'

'Well, from what I've heard he was…not kind to his womenfolk. He was known for his cruel punishments. If he was displeased with one of his servant girls, he would be severe. Sometimes, he would use them, force himself upon them. The stories I've heard say he was a right bastard.

'One night, he tried to rape the young lass,' indicating Astrid, 'and she put a knife across his throat.'

Erran nodded grimly.

'But then, and this is the good part, well, she killed his guards, too, one by one it's said. She freed many of the slave-girls and servants, she bade them to come with her and fight for their freedom.

'The story goes she stole a ship and escaped leaving a corpse of any who stood in her way. She and her warriors raided and robbed, and their reputation grew. She became known as the Death Nymph. Other women joined her, looking for a chance at glory. Her warband grew fearsome.

'The dead lord's son sent many folk after her, but few ever returned. She slew any man that was sent after her. She was once declared an outlaw by many lords.'

'But she is no longer?' asked Erran.

'No. It was then the king took notice, besieged by his lords, he put a large bounty on her head and declared her wanted for the murder of her lord.

He laughed. 'I'll give her this, she knew she could not stand free forever, so she turned up in the capital and docked her ship at the royal wharf and demanded to see the king.

'Some say she demanded to collect her own bounty, and others say she offered her sword in vassalage, claiming the lordship over the dead lord's lands.

'Anyway, they say, protected by her shield-maidens, she marched up to the palace halls and none stood in her way.

'The king is said to have been impressed by her, but he could not allow one of his lords to be murdered by a servant girl, and for her to raid his lands as bandits. She is said to have pleaded to the king for him to hear her, she told him what that lord had done to her, to many others among her warriors. It is said, she declared, "She only ever wanted rightful vengeance, and now, their chance at glory among men."

'He was moved by her. Look at her, it is not hard to imagine, and he offered her trial by combat.

'She, of course, won. A fight worthy of songs, they say. He pardoned her and her warriors. They became feared mercenaries in more recent times. There are other tales of her deeds I've heard also, but in each, men fall bloody and dead at her hand. Her name is well deserved. And now, she is sworn into Fergus's service.

'Lucky him. Why Fergus,' asked Erran glancing over at the red-haired lord.

Hafgan regarded Fergus also. He now sat across on the other side of the crackling hearth speaking quietly with Arnulf.

Hafgan lowered his voice. 'If the talk is true, her

service to Fergus is at his father's request, and likely expense also. It pays to have the best and most well-known warriors under your banners.'

Erran nodded.

Hafgan scratched his shaved head and continued, 'Angus is high lord of all lands north of the Spine, of the borders and all the Old Lands. The head of the most prominent noble family in the north; all others were sworn to him and him to the king himself. They are old friends, but even Arnulf is sworn to Fergus' father. And his fathers before him had been sworn to them. One of Angus' sons would likely one day take his place. So, the high lord sees to it, he and his sons have a fierce body of men, some of the finest and well equipped of all the northlands.

'The Death Nymph has become a warrior of high renown, a truly feared shield-maiden.' Hafgan nodded over at Astrid, 'Warriors like her need to swear service to such lineages also of high renown. She wants to further her deeds legitimately. Warriors like her bring many warriors to their lord's banners, and are often richly rewarded for it.

'Despite her pardon from the king, if she stayed unsworn she could be declared a bandit or a marauder by some lord and eventually hunted down. I'm sure she has a lot of enemies. I imagine she was tired of always looking over her shoulder. So, why not choose to come here.'

Hafgan smiled. 'You know, lad. We border-men rival amongst the best warriors in all Arnar. As I say, Fergus is the son of a high lord, his father holds the borders. Why not come here to earn her place.

'These are old lands, lands from which men once of mighty Cydor first sailed south to forge a kingdom. Lands which stood firm against the kings of Cydor, ravaged and yet held through the old rebellion and the wars of forging. We the proud, a people of warriors,' recited Hafgan.

'Ever ready to hold these lands for ever more,' finished Erran. The lad knew the words of the Saga of Arn—they all did—these were the proud words of all the border-men.

'I think, I would like to meet her,' said Erran moving to rise.

'Don't be a fool, boy,' grunted Hafgan, tugging him back down. 'She will probably cut your cock off and feed it to you.'

'Aye, lad,' chimed in Olad, who had been sitting listening, 'It's true, one of our men took a shine to her in the hall. He's got a scar down half his face now. I would listen to your friend and stay well away.' He leaned in, 'You know, she says she ain't never met a man worthy of her anyway. Word is she only enjoys the company of women. She'd rather a woman with honour than any man. So, I'd stay well away.'

Erran looked over all the more enthused.

'She is a match for any man, Erran,' warned Hafgan.

Erran laughed. 'Just like me then.'

Hafgan shook his head as the young warrior rose to his feet.

Arnulf and Fergus looked over inquiringly.

Hafgan shrugged, 'He's a bloody fool,' he said.

They watched him approach the shield-maiden's campfire.

'He isn't?' asked Fergus with amusement.

Olad and the others nodded.

'Ha, this will be good,' laughed Fergus.

Hafgan had to give respect where respect was due, for the lad withstood their plainly icy reception to his intrusion of their hearth for several awkward minutes. The big warrior was out of earshot but saw Astrid initially dismiss the young Erran which was followed by the cruel mocking laughter of the other shield-maidens. The young lad seemed to persist a while, and then returned—surprisingly without incident—to the campfire. He resumed his seat beside Hafgan.

'Well, she didn't put a knife in you,' said Hafgan. 'What did you say to her?'

'I told her; You all told me to come and speak to her, but that I sensed it was a cruel and perilous joke played on me by mean old men.' He smiled at them. 'I asked her name and told her mine. I asked if she was actually a mighty warrior. And then, they laughed at me. So, I asked her for the honour of sparring with such a mighty warrior, to learn what I can from her.'

'And?' asked Fergus eagerly.

'Well, she didn't kill me,' said Erran with a grin. 'She said, "Perhaps," and then I thought I'd best leave. So, I'll take that.'

They laughed. Hafgan shook his head in disbelief and handed the young man his ale. 'You challenged the Death Nymph to spar. You're a fool.'

***

The men talked and drank, but the humour and good cheer soon subsided into the gloom. The events of the past day weighed heavy on their minds. They slept an uneasy sleep as the sentries stood about talking quietly while looking off into the dark moorland about them.

Arnulf sat and watched the fire burn low, listening to the crackling wood and the sounds of the moor at night. Some of his house-warriors slept around the fire. He felt as if he was being watched. That same dull nervous feeling in his stomach grew until he forced himself to look around.

Most of his men were asleep, he could see one of the other fires still burned, a few men sat around it still awake and talking quietly. A sentry stood nearby the fire involved in the talk and another walked slowly around.

He looked off into the darkness but saw nothing but the gloom and shadow of night. Still he could sense something out there staring back at him, watching him from a dark place. Arnulf carefully placed some small pieces of the twisted thornwood onto the dying fire—the best firewood and kindling the men could find nearby. The fire slowly burnt back into life.

He caught a flicker of movement from the corner of his eye. He sat up sharply, and looked off into the night.

Arnulf saw a dark shadow moving quickly out of the darkness towards the camp. He shouted out to the sentry. The sentry turned to look where the shout came from, but in doing so, turned away from the dark form hurtling towards him out of the darkness. It was too late.

There was nothing Arnulf could do. He watched as the dark thing leapt onto the sentry and tackled him to the ground, the man cried out in surprised alarm.

Arnulf jumped to his feet and picked up his greataxe as others awoke around him. He ran towards the shadowy figure as it mauled the surprised sentry. Arnulf heard the man scream out in pain, the scream turned to a sickening gurgle as his throat was torn out.

Blood gushed from the sentry's neck. His arms flailed and legs kicked weakly before he fell limp. The dark figure stooped low over the dying man as his life ebbed away. Arnulf and the nearby men were horrified to a standstill by the abrupt and chilling end to the scream. Arnulf stopped just feet away from the dark figure. He was met by a fierce glare, its eyes glinting in the night on its shadowy face, a human face.

It had the form of a man and but the figure before him seemed black as if it were a man made of ebony. It crouched low on all fours and glared up at him and a moment passed where no one seemed able to move. Its stare suddenly broke and its black head jerked away as the girls scream pierced the night air.

She had awoken with the others at the cries of alarm and seeing the dead man and the black skulking form above him, she screamed.

The dark man-shape darted towards the scream and was upon her in seconds. In the firelight its body glistened black and wet. It seized her in one arm and carried her away using its other arm to lope away.

The men ran forward in pursuit. An arrow whistled past it and another overhead into the night. The creature shrunk to the ground momentarily then continued. Another arrow flew, it caught it just as it sprang forward again, and it screamed out in pain. It dropped the girl and tried to crawl away but Arnulf was upon it quickly.

He stood over the crawling black man shape and hefted his axe. It was breathing heavily, the arrow had caught it in the chest.

'Careful, lads,' shouted Arnulf.

The warriors quickly surrounded it and levelled their spears. Some had snatched up torches and the flickering light revealed it was indeed a man. His clothes and hair were slick with bog mud. The mud stank of stagnant water.

Arnulf kicked him over with his thick leather boot. The man cried out in pain.

'Who are you?' shouted Arnulf.

The man shrieked at him and clawed at him like a wild beast. The mud-man leapt towards him shrieking but was soon checked as the greataxe buried deep into his shoulder. Arnulf swung low and felt the blade smash bone before he drew it back with a grunt.

The girl lay weeping on the ground.

'You killed him,' she wailed. 'You killed my brother.'

Arnulf looked at her pitifully. 'Take her back,' he commanded.

Arnulf kicked the man over onto his back. There

was a gasp from a warrior standing nearby. The man was smeared in black stinking bog mud, probably fell in one on the dark moor, but the torch light revealed a crimson ichor glistening over everything and dripping from his hands. His fingers had been chewed to reveal a sharp tip of bone. Blood dripped from his gaping mouth, it was smeared all over him. No skin showed through the gore and rancid mud.

When Arnulf turned, he saw Hafgan behind him. Fergus stood by also shaken out of his drunken sleep by the sudden violence. He stood with his shield and an axe in hand; he had a fur draped about him. Fergus was flanked by two grim faced women, armour glinting beneath their furs.

The other warriors warily lowered their spears.

'That was no dead man,' said Fergus.

'No,' said Arnulf in a grim voice. 'He bled and died just fine.'

Fergus laughed. 'Ha, you're a grim bastard.'

'He followed us from Hern's Farm,' said Arnulf. 'I knew someone was out there, watching us in the dark.'

'Do you think he killed them?' asked Fergus.

'Perhaps.' Arnulf paused, 'What evil has spilled from these passes? The dead walk and now men are driven mad, killing their kin like beasts.'

'Old Night lets his evil spirits free around a black moon, lord,' said one of the men.

Arnulf looked at him. 'The dead moon has passed now, the new one is born,' said Arnulf, 'it is as Lord Fergus says, the gods are testing us, friend.'

They threw the body off behind some rocks away from the camp; they would cover it perhaps in the morning. They covered the dead sentry in a cloak and moved his body to lie near the wagon; the body would have to wait until morning.

The men made their way back to the campfires. Arnulf ordered the guards to be doubled. The men built back up their fires and relit the torches thrust into the ground about the camp. Uneasy, they settled back down around their fires. Fergus sat down and seemed to fall asleep immediately. Arnulf placed his axe at his feet as he sat down before the fire and began to clean the blood off the blade.

The warrior Olad came back to the fire and looked at Fergus.

'What is it, friend?' asked Arnulf.

'It's the girl, Lord Arnulf. She is sick. Her wound, her whole arm, has gone bad. It rots. She will probably die from it.'

A cry of alarm roused the camp once again. Arnulf stood up and once again stared off across the torches. Fergus awoke and sat up.

'What is it now?' demanded Fergus and picked up his sheath and removed his sword. He discarded his sheath on his cloak beside the fire and walked off through the burning torches.

***

Fergus stopped as his eyes fell across the nightmare before him. The girl looked up at him, blood dripping down her chin and staining her white shift with fresh blood. She pulled her hand from the dead sentry's throat. She held a globdule of flesh in her hands and took a bite. She looked up at Fergus and chewed slowly. He saw her eyes roll back in her head. Blood squirted across her face and ran down her chin as she bit into it again. She snarled and ran towards him, with her eyes blazing. He stood frozen in disbelief, watching her speed towards him. She was mere paces away when one of the warriors sprang forward and buffeted her with his shield.

It was young Erran.

***

'Kill her! She is a demon,' shouted one of the warriors.

Hafgan saw Erran standing over the girl. He drew his sword but hesitated. The girl stood up and ran, but Erran dropped his shield and sprang forward to seize her. She swung around and tried to sink her bloody teeth into his arm, but he shrank back just in time. He went to lunge with his sword but hit her hard with his fist instead and sent her reeling back. He stood over her with his sword but was unable to strike. He saw before him not a monster but a young girl.

Hafgan strode forward, the boy couldn't do it, but as Hafgan approached, the girl leapt toward young Erran, and then suddenly stiffened. Hafgan watched the girl hurl herself heedlessly at Erran's levelled blade. It ran through her with her own momentum. Hafgan stopped as the young girl slid to the floor, coughing mouthfuls of blood down her chin.

'Finish her,' said Hafgan in a low tone.

Erran twisted the sword and pulled it free, but after standing over her a long moment, he just turned and walked away shaking his head. Hafgan looked down at the poor girl dying before him he drew his knife and stepped forward to end her suffering, but she was dead within moments. Hafgan sighed with relief; the grim deed was not needed.

The horses all around suddenly seemed restless. They began to rear up on their tethers and neigh loudly. One of them broke free and galloped off into the gloom.

'Men, calm these horses,' shouted Arnulf.

Horsemen galloped off carrying torches to find the horses while men tried desperately to calm the remaining beasts.

Hafgan helped Olad carry the girl away into the darkness when a fierce grip seized Hafgan's arm. He turned to see the blackened and blood smeared face of the girl's brother bite down hard on his arm.

The man's teeth shattered on Hafgan's mail sleeve. The men dropped the girl, and Hafgan drew his sword. He hacked at the man's shoulder and severed his arm with several savage blows. The man fell to the floor, the arrow still stuck in his back and the deep axe wound his lord had just inflicted gaped open. He could not be alive, yet he rose again and reached towards them with his remaining arm as the men backed away. Hafgan knocked the hand away with his blade and swung hard. The mighty blow sent the dead man's head rolling along the floor, and his mangled body fell to the ground. Hafgan picked up the head by the slick muddy hair and held it up.

Its dead mouth suddenly let loose an unearthly

shriek. The big warrior nearly dropped the thing. Instead, he jammed it hard onto a nearby torch that thrust from the ground. The torch hissed as it was extinguished. The head silenced and sat quietly on its macabre mounting. All eyes were on Hafgan and the fallen dead man. All but Fergus'.

***

Fergus was fixed on the girl, who now stood again before him. Her head lolled disturbingly to one side as she slowly shuffled forward. Dead blank eyes fixed into his very soul.

'This must be a nightmare,' said Fergus as he stood stricken, watching the frail looking figure limp towards him. He heard Arnulf gasp in horror as he turned and saw the girl.

The girl limped slowly forward between the torches her eyes fixed on Fergus. With each step, her punctured abdomen oozed congealing fluid, further staining her white shift to a ghastly deep shade of crimson.

The men stood back in terror, watching as the girl limped amongst them with no heed to their presence, her dead eyes fixed on Fergus.

Chaos was breaking loose, shouts coming from the wagons, the horses rearing and screaming.

'Kill it,' shouted Arnulf from nearby. 'Kill it.'

Fergus's warriors drew in beside him, and the women raised a wall of blue painted shields. It was Astrid who seized her courage and ran up behind the girl. With an awkward, yet firm, thrust, she ran her spear into the girl's back.

The girl screeched and writhed. Astrid pulled it free, and the girl turned on her. Astrid's spear shook, betraying her trembling hands as she tried to keep her weapon level. She thrust it again and drove its point into the girl's hissing mouth. The dead girl hung suspended and impaled a moment, and then the renowned shield-maiden dropped the spear shaft and let them both flop to the floor.

***

Arnulf watched the girl fall limp, then his attention was drawn to the commotion by the wagons. It was over before he got there. The dead sentry lay sprawled on the floor, speared and covered in axe wounds. A lone warrior stood by the body, his eyes haunted.

'Get rid of it,' said Arnulf to a group of men stood watching. 'And those,' he said gesturing at the severed head and the other bodies.

Fergus dismissed his warriors and sat down next to a fire and gazed into the flames. Arnulf turned to the young warrior. He looked shaken and stared down at the body of the sentry at his feet.

'You were brave, friend,' said Arnulf, and then looked over at Fergus, who still sat watching the flames dance in disbelief.

'Thank you, lord,' said the young warrior, his voice quavering.

'What is your name?' asked Arnulf.

'Malachi, lord,' said the young man nervously.

'Malachi,' repeated Arnulf. 'Well met, friend. From Weirdell?'

'Yes, lord.'

'What happened, lad?'

'He came back to life. He tried to attack the horses. I defended them.'

'Alone?' asked Arnulf.

The young warrior nodded. Arnulf clasped the man on the shoulder and led him away, towards a nearby campfire.

'Brave indeed. I will make sure your lord hears of it.'

Malachi nodded, his hands still shaking.

'You do the men of Weirdell proud. Were you wounded?' asked Arnulf, looking back at the sentry's body.

Malachi shook his head and sat, staring into the fire.

'Brave indeed. Try to sleep,' said Arnulf, and then he made his way back to his own fire.

The dead were taken away from the camp and piled with stones so they could not rise again. The men would not wait until morning and toiled in the dark as others stood about with torches.

Arnulf found Fergus sat down next to the fire.

'This must be a nightmare,' said Fergus again, shaking his head. Arnulf sat down and laid his axe beside him. There was no sleep to be had now, and so they sat, as did many, awaiting the dawn, nervously peering off into the gloom, fearing another lurking danger.

CHAPTER THIRTEEN

The Wharfs of Anchorage

The brawl erupted from a tavern door along the wharf front. Two men grappled each other on the floor, throwing punches and kicking wildly as they tried to gain advantage over the other. A third emerged from the gloomy entrance at a run and delivered a savage kick to the face of one of the downed men.

The shouts and sounds of crashing furniture from within the tavern, and the brawl unfolding in the street, attracted a small crowd of onlookers. Folk rushed over to watch from the busy avenue leading to the fish market. The crowd jeered and laughed, eager for blood and gossip to pass on.

The wharf front of Anchorage saw its fair share of fist fights. Numerous taverns populated the wharf front district and drew a healthy clientele of drunks, sailors, and fishermen fresh in off the water, often spoiling for a fight after too much ale and the boredom of being stuck on ship.

Another kick sent a man sprawling to the floor. He rolled about blinded, blood running from a broken nose, which he clutched at with both hands. The crowd cheered.

***

'Little bastard did it again,' exclaimed the trader. 'Ran off down there,' he continued, pointing down the narrow side alley between a storehouse and a merchant's shop.

Wilhelm surveyed the stall before him. Baskets of fish were on display along with a selection of large individual fish, each one different. He noted some kind of thrasher eel, its grey scales flecked with red. A large brown-fin lay beside that, its mouth gaping up at him. Strips of dried salted fish hung from a frame beside the stall.

'He sneaks up and grabs it,' said the trader angrily gesturing at the hanging strips. 'I've tried to have 'im, but I can hardly chase the little bugger. Can't leave all this,' he said, waving at his wares. 'I'll be robbed blind.'

Wilhelm listened on and nodded distractedly, his eyes following a man who was stumbling along the street and had stopped to lean over a barrel, coughing and spluttering. He vomited behind the barrel. Wilhelm looked away in disgust.

'Damn drunks,' muttered the warrior under his breath.

His eyes then fell, more pleasingly, upon a lithe young woman as she walked up the street.

The trader sighed loudly. Agitated, he said, 'Are you even listening to me?'

'Um, yes, of course,' said Wilhelm, pulling his attention back to the trader.

'Please, can you and your lot just collar the little shit. He's a filthy scrawny little bugger, so big,' said the trader levelling his hand in the air. 'Black hair, real scruffy. He's been back three times this week already—the little bastard.'

'Don't worry, we'll do what we can, friend,' replied Wilhelm, turning to his fellow guard, who nodded in agreement.

'We'll keep an eye out, aye,' said Wilhelm.

The trader scowled and turned to tend his wares. Wilhelm caught the eye of the guard beside him once more, who grinned back.

Sworn to the Huscarl Warrick, Wilhelm and the others were on guard. The huscarls were the finest warriors, often men of great renown, all sworn to the king himself. They commanded scores of their own men each and provided between them a personal army serving the king. When not marching under the king's banner, his huscarls were tasked with keeping the king's peace around the great town of Arn and in the surrounding towns, which the king governed directly. The port of Anchorage was one such town, and the great honour of its stewardship had been trusted to Warrick. Now as powerful as any lord, he had a good mind for such administration.

Wilhelm caught the eye of the warrior beside him and nodded towards the alley. The twisting alley appeared empty. The thief would need to be caught red handed or pointed out by the trader. And even then, still have the stolen goods on him if the patrol were to throw him in the gaol. Wilhelm had his doubts about apprehending the young thief. Still, he thought he had better search the alley and take a look in the street beyond to satisfy the angry fish trader.

He threw another look at his fellow warrior. The man named Ox returned a sardonic smirk, complete with an arching brow and a slight shake of his head.

Ox was not a tall man, nor was he particularly broad. In fact, he was the smallest of Warrick's men. His lean face had a pronounced angular nose. His hauberk hung from his wiry frame like it would from a scarecrow.

The amusing name had stuck after a night of heavy drinking. His good natured humour had laughed off what many would have heard as a slight, and the name just seemed to stick, as names sometimes do. Despite his stature, he had time and time again proved himself a formidable warrior. Wilhelm liked his company, as quick to scrap as he was quick to laugh, was Ox.

'We'll never find the bastard,' said Ox, obviously sharing Wilhelm's doubts.

Wilhelm sighed. 'Aye.'

Adjusting his chain hauberk and belt, he then moved to enter the alley.

A sudden commotion caught his attention. A

crowd had formed down the busy street. Shouts could be heard over the bustle of the fish market. Ox also stared off through the crowded street towards the wharf front. With a blend of curiosity and concern, both men abandoned the futile search of the narrow alley and made their way towards the growing crowd.

***

The door closed and the man turned to face her. His blood shot eyes flashed with desire. His jerkin looked stained with beer and spilled food, his face unkempt. She awkwardly forced a smile as his leering gaze ran across her body. His attentions brought an uncomfortable self-consciousness that swept over her, and she wrapped her arms around herself. He moved towards her. Drawing up close in front of her, he pushed a chunk of hacked silver into her hands. His stale breath stank of ale. She tried not to recoil from his touch as he stroked her cheek with a finger. His calloused hands felt rough on her skin.

'Come now, lass. Let's see you.'

She stepped back and let her shift slip over her shoulders and fall to the floor, revealing the slim lithe curves of her body. Her skin prickled with goose pimples in the chill air.

He guided her backwards, lecherously groping at her breasts. She felt the straw bale against her legs and could retreat no further. He pushed her down on to her back. The straw scratched against her bare skin, dozens of tiny spines spiking into her before giving way as she settled her weight.

Climbing over her, he fumbled inside his trousers and forced her legs apart with his knees. She closed her eyes as she felt his hand slide down between her legs. She braced herself, aware of what was coming. She winced as he pushed himself inside her.

It was over quickly. He grunted and groaned as he spilled his seed inside her. She shuddered and lay motionless, still clutching the silver tightly in her hand. He breathed heavily, stale breath hot against her face.

His breathing slowed, and he pushed himself off her. She remained still, not meeting his eyes.

'Ah, a drink now, I think,' he said as he buckled his trousers.

She made no reply.

'I'll come find you again sometime, lass.'

He turned to leave.

'Until then,' he said as he slipped out of the storeroom door.

She lay there, still staring up at the rafters, clutching the silver in her hand. After he had left, she began sobbing quietly. She felt sick. After a moment, she rose slowly and retrieved her shift from the floor. It looked filthy and frayed. Nym sighed as she pulled it over her head.

She looked down at the chunk of hacked silver in her palm, perhaps part of a bracelet or arm ring. She would at least eat today. She composed herself, and with a glance back at the bales at the back of the storeroom, Nym slipped out of the door into the street beyond.

***

The crowd had gathered at the intersection of the east market street and the wharf front row. The clamour and shouting confirmed Wilhelm's suspicions, a brawl.

'And it's still early,' joked Ox.

Wilhelm grunted in reply and said, 'Aye, one of those days it seems.'

The two warriors pushed their way through the crowd. The bystanders, flinching away on contact with the cold steel of their mail as the warriors pushed past them.

Three men stood surrounded by half a dozen others. Two more lay on the floor, one writhing in pain, the other seemingly unconscious. They looked like sailors.

The trio were headed by a large set man who was bleeding from his nose and hefting a broken table leg in his hands. His two companions flanked him, eyeing the encircling attackers whilst jeering and shouting.

The lead man bellowed defiantly, 'Come on, you dogs. Not one of you got the balls to take me.'

He swung the table leg wildly at the nearest man facing him. The sailor dodged back out of reach.

'As piss wet as Jarlson himself,' bellowed the big man. 'Ya fuckin' traitors.'

'Cydors,' muttered Wilhelm.

'Their civil war is now spilling out here, too, by the looks of it,' replied Ox.

'Not in Anchorage, I won't have it. We've got to move.'

Wilhelm spotted more men running from a ship

on the wharf. The newcomers looked armed with an assortment of weapons, fish knives, hatchets, one had a heavy gaff. It was not immediately clear whose side the newcomers were on, but it appeared like this was about to get messy.

Wilhelm could see more of his fellow warriors amongst the crowd across from him, also drawn from their patrols by the commotion. They needed to act and quickly. Warrick would be most displeased with such a breach of the king's peace. A mass brawl and blood on the streets would not be overlooked. They would be cleaning the piss trench and scraping vomit from the floor of the mead hall for weeks if this went sour.

He caught the attention of one of the warriors opposite and after an exchange of gestures between them, the patrols pushed out of the crowd and moved in to separate the brawlers. Only a fool would attack the king's men.

The flood of armed Cydor sailors running down the wharf, and the sudden appearance of the king's men threw the scene into confusion. The trio in the centre seemed emboldened by the arrival of more sailors and began lashing out trying to break through to their arriving comrades.

Wilhelm and the king's men struggled against the brawling mob, pushing them back with the shafts of their spears. A handful of warriors with spears levelled, blocked the gangway of the wharf, halting the onrushing sailors and barring their path.

Ox had several of the opposing crew pinned behind his spear as they shouted threateningly and taunted the remaining combatants. One of the battling trio, seeing an opening, took advantage of the restrained enemy and lunged.

There was a flash of steel. The sailor buried a knife into an adversary's neck. Blood gushed from the wound, the crimson ichor splattering over Ox and the nearest bystanders as the knife was pulled free. The stricken man made a terrible gurgling sound and fell to floor. A pool of his own blood slowly spread across the ground as the dying man convulsed, his life ebbing away. The crowd gasped and fell silent.

***

'Hold it steady, you fool,' said the old tavern keeper as he hammered the spile through the shive of the keg.

'I may only have half an arm, but I can still stave your skull in if you don't hold it steady,' shouted Jor once more as he hammered the spile with his good hand.

The poor drunk assisting him, who had only helped for a free draught of ale, had begun to wish he had not bothered.

'Ha, there it is,' said the tavern keeper, 'Now, who wants a drink? Yes, yes, you'll get yours. I already said as much, aye. Anyone else?'

The tavern was occupied by the usual daytime crowd, a handful of regulars and the odd sailor. Most sat quietly on the benches around the central hearth, talking amongst themselves. A few others sat alone in silence nursing their earthenware tankards of dark ale. One man, plagued with a racking cough, sat trying to drink his ails away. It was quiet. Business in the taverns had been quiet the last few days, since that cursed ship had sailed in, scared off all the customers.

The tavern air was musty and smelt of stale ale. The floor was covered in mildewing straw that was in need of changing. Wisps of smoke wound up from the hearth and out through the central hole in the roof, which other than the door, were the tavern's only source of natural light.

Jor struggled with a tray of tankards, his arm severed at the forearm. It made the job trickier than it once was. Although, over the years, he had become adept at balancing the tray on his stump and steadying it with his remaining hand.

'Where has that lass got to?' said Jor to no one in particular. He hadn't seen the young waif all day. She certainly could be doing this for him, earning her keep.

One of his regular patrons ran in and excitedly spoke to some of the men around the hearth. Several of them rose and made for the door.

'What's up, Seb? Something going on?' enquired Jor as he watched his patrons leaving with purses heavier than he would like.

'Proper scrap going on over the way, Jor. Come see. The guard is out sorting it and everything,' said the man before he disappeared into the street.

Jor had heard the growing commotion occurring outside. Fights were nothing new along the wharf front. But curious, he delicately placed the tray down on the bar and went to the door to watch from the doorway.

It was all but over from what the tavern keeper could see. The king's men were out, dispersing the watching crowd. The wharf had been closed off, but sailors crowded the jetties. A gaggle of men sat detained at spear point bound up in ropes. Others were being dragged away unconscious or wounded. There was still shouting as the king's warriors struggled with a couple of the men, fighting on as they struggled against being bound.

Jor suddenly noticed the body on the floor. Blood could be plainly seen, even from his vantage point. The door of his tavern was raised off the street slightly, it allowed him to see over the heads of the remaining crowd.

'Oh, gods, the poor soul,' muttered Jor.

'Aye,' said one of his patrons beside him as he too watched on.

'Word is, they are all Cydors,' said another, 'Stupid fools.'

Jor watched as the king's warriors dragged the dead man off to one side and threw a sack over the body. One of the sailors had been shackled in irons and was being led away.

'Seems we missed the best of it,' said the man beside him, and then he turned and went back inside to his ale by the hearth.

***

The street seemed busier than usual. She threaded her way amongst the passing folk, stepping aside for a man struggling with armfuls of fishing nets, followed then by a finely dressed woman carrying a basket. She stood to the side and watched the dozens coming and going, still clutching tightly, the chunk of silver in her hand.

Another woman stood opposite, watching her intently. One of the witch-seers by the look. Her hair was adorned in trinkets, and the seer's eyes were smeared with a dark paint, making her eyes bright and intense as she stared over at her. Such women were found here and there in every town, plying their trade in divination and selling strange potions for this and that. Nym had been to one once. The seer had read her fate from wooden cards she dealt out on the table before her. The woman's attention made her uneasy, so Nym hurried on.

Something was going on up the street a crowd had formed ahead. A man knocked into her, his face ashen and pale. He coughed hoarsely and stumbled on through the passing throng. Nym watched him disappear then ducked into a narrow side street, which backed onto the waterfront. She passed storehouses and small houses, and then came to a dishevelled hovel and pushed the door open. The door creaked as it swung open, spilling light inside.

'Sister,' came a young voice in greeting as she entered.

A young boy sat to one side trying to sharpen a rusty knife on a rough stone. Her brother's face had grown thin, his black hair hung greasy and matted over his eyes.

She came and knelt beside him.

'Look what I found,' he said, brandishing the old knife, obviously discarded and blunted.

'You be careful with that, Finn. Don't cut yourself.

'It's not sharp yet, still working on it. But I think I can get it good. Got us some food, too.'

He gestured at some dried fish strips laid on a piece of filthy cloth and grinned.

She frowned. 'You be careful, little brother. They will catch you before long. It wasn't the same one again?'

Her brother laughed. 'He can't catch me, Nym. He's too fat and stupid.'

'What if he points you out to the king's men and they catch you? They will take your hands, or brand your face and sell you. Please don't. I can't lose you, too.'

His face fell, her young brother looking crestfallen. He thought she would have been happy with his prize. She seemed angry.

In truth, she was angry, at all that she had sacrificed this day for the lump of hacked silver she clutched still in her hand.

'I could have bought us some food,' she said as she slowly opened her palm to reveal the silver to her brother.

'Where did you get that?' he asked accusingly. 'You tell me not to steal, yet it's okay for you.'

'I earned it,' she said ruefully.

'How? The old man never pays us.'

'Never you mind, little brother, but I didn't steal it.'

Finn eyed his sister suspiciously.

Nym thought it best to change the subject. She stared up at the hovel. The roof had large holes in the reed thatching. In fact, the entire place was in great disrepair. The beams were rotten. One had fallen and rested an end in the dirt, the entire roof sagged on that side. The low walls had crumbled, the woven wicker frame exposed. It failed to keep the rain and filth from flowing in from outside and vermin scampered in and out at will. It would not be long before someone pulled it down and built a newer building in its place.

'It will be cold tonight. It will likely rain later, too,' she said. 'We should go to the tavern tonight. Old Jor will give us something hot to eat, and it will be dry. I really would like a bath if he will let me,' said Nym.

'No, Nym. Do we have to? I don't like going there. The old man doesn't like me,' whined Finn.

'Doesn't trust you, more like,' replied Nym. 'No, we're going. I don't want to stay here again tonight.'

Nym looked thoughtfully at the knife in her brother's hands.

'Do you think you could get it sharp enough to slice a few slivers off this?' she said gesturing with the silver.

'I'll try,' replied Finn.

The challenge set, he returned to sharpening his knife in earnest.

'Good. Will be better in slivers, will go further. We're heading by the weaver's stalls first, I need something else to wear, this is ruined,' she said brushing off her filthy shift. 'And I could pay for a bath if the old man's being off. You could do with one too little brother,' reflected Nym.

Finn pulled a face and returned to his knife.

***

A warrior approached the group of men watching the aftermath of the brawl from outside a tavern's door.

'Move along, lads. Get back to your business,' said the warrior as he approached.

'Aye, we just came out to see,' said Jor.

'Nasty business, now inside you go,' said the warrior.

'Aye, looks it,' said Jor waving his patrons back inside. 'Just curious, Wilhelm. They won't cause you no bother.'

Jor moved up beside the warrior, and they both watched as the tavern's customers filed back inside to retrieve their ales. Wilhelm eyed the men menacingly as they disappeared one by one.

'Haven't seen you for a while,' said Jor, turning to the warrior. 'Are you well?'

'Aye, as good as I can ask for,' replied Wilhelm, removing his helmet.

'The gods have had fun these last few days, it seems. More death for the wharf front,' mused Jor. 'Perhaps it *is* cursed?'

The pair both turned to look at the lone longship berthed at one of the docks.

'Aye, so it seems,' replied the warrior as he made a warding gesture towards the ship. 'It's called *Glyassin*. We think they brought the sickness with them.'

'Folk are saying that it is cursed, that it sailed from Old Night's own waters,' said Jor in a low voice. 'Death's own ship they say.'

'Aye, folk shun it. The harbour master said no other ship is willing to take a mooring at that dock. Nobody goes near it except the guards, but none are too happy about that duty.'

'Aye, I bet. Is it true not one survived?' asked Jor. 'That's the word here about.'

'Not quite. All but one. We found the others scattered about, dead, blood everywhere. Not a pleasant sight, Jor, I promise you. Poor bastards.'

'I don't doubt it, friend.'

Something catching his eye, Jor leaned inside the tavern door and shouted, 'You! Touch that keg and I'll nail you to it.'

Shouts and curses were thrown back at him.

'Nail him to it? Ha, which you gonna hold? The nail or the hammer?' came a slurred shout.

Laughs followed.

He turned back to Wilhelm. 'Bastards,' he muttered, itching at his stump.

'One survived, you say,' continued Jor, his interest piqued. 'Who was he? Word about is all aboard died.'

Wilhelm leaned close. 'Aye, there was one,' he said quietly looking about. 'A foreigner, one of the rowing slaves.'

'You don't say,' said Jor, rubbing his stubbled chin. 'Did he say what happened? Where they'd been?'

'No, not one of us can understand him,' said Wilhelm, spreading his hands. 'And I'll tell you this, you must see him, not like any man I've ever laid eyes on, Jor. His skin is dark as tar. Never seen anything like it.'

Jor, hanging off his every word, asked, 'What happened to him?'

'Well, he's been carted off to the College. They hope someone up there will know more. Perhaps one of them can speak his tongue.'

'A dark man, you say, on Old Night's death ship. Gods, I don't know if I like the sound of that.'

Wilhelm nodded gravely.

'So, what they gonna do with it? The ship?' asked Jor nodding at the cursed longship. 'I imagine the harbour master wants it gone.'

'I don't know, Jor. I've heard nothing. But you're right, folk want it rid of.'

'Should cast it off as the tide's going out. Set it alight, I say,' said Jor.

'Maybe they'll do just that.'

'Ahh, here she is,' exclaimed Jor as he sighted the young waif returning through the milling crowd.

'Where did you get to, lass? Got ale that needs serving. They might want food, too.'

'Get that ale soaked up and get more in 'em, I say,' he muttered to Wilhelm.

Wilhelm shook his head and threw the tavern keeper a sly grin. Jor chuckled.

'Get on in there, girl. I'll take their coin, though. I won't be long.'

Nym ducked inside, trailed by her brother. Jor grabbed Fin's shoulder as he passed. 'You stay out of trouble, lad, if you're sleeping under my roof, you hear me?'

Wilhelm eyed young Finn suspiciously as he quickly scurried in after his sister.

Jor shrugged after they had gone inside. 'I tell

you Wilhelm, she's a good help, does her bit. But I gotta keep my eye on him. A dead weight that one, another mouth to feed. Does half the work of young Nym there.'

Wilhelm raised his eyebrow questioningly.

'Knew their pa,' explained Jor. 'They come and go. I wouldn't see 'em out on the street. Besides, it's just me here, and I need the help in the tavern. They don't need paying, just feeding and a roof to sleep under from time to time.'

'Ha, you don't need to explain, Jor. She's a pretty lass, aye,' laughed Wilhelm.

Jor felt slightly awkward and abashed at the suggestion. He was about to object but his attention was drawn to the street in front of him.

A man pushed through the milling crowd and staggered towards them. People backed away as he approached them. He coughed hard, spluttering. He fell to his knees. There was a scream.

The scream brought all eyes to fall upon the kneeling man. There were gasps of revulsion rippling through the street as people finally saw him. He seemed to be staring at Wilhelm and Jor, it was impossible to tell whether the man saw them. His eyes streamed with blood. He coughed again, dark blood frothed from his mouth, and he groped the air frantically before collapsing into the dirt.

The crowd backed away. Even the remaining king's men were reluctant to approach him, standing alongside the locals watching in horror.

The man coughed and vomited and began convulsing violently, splattering blood about as he writhed. He froze in grotesque poses for a few moments before fitting once more.

The street had grown quiet, all watching silently aghast as the man died. The dying man's grunts and death throes were terribly audible in the shocked silence.

Except neither Wilhelm nor Jor could not help but notice another sound amongst the crowd. They found themselves examining the onlookers. Looking nervously from face to face, neither could help but notice the pale drawn faces mixed throughout the crowd. The hacking coughs, which had once gone unnoticed, now barked throughout the eerie silence of the throng assembled before them. Were they sick, too?

Another terrible scream pierced the air from somewhere nearby. Panic rippled through the crowd. There were shouts of alarm. People began running, hurrying away from the death laid before them.

Jor cast a glance at the sinister longship moored at the dock, its mast rocking slightly back and forth. He shuddered. The aging tavern keeper could almost feel Old Night's cold breath as he stalked unseen amongst them. Cold and silent strode the god of death, a grim smile upon his chill lips.

CHAPTER FOURTEEN

The Hound in the Mists

The dawn light brought another mist. It crept over the rocks and scrub with its swirling and seemingly ghostly tendrils. Other than a few nearby gorse bushes, only the Waystone could be seen. The great stone, looming faintly into view as the moorland about lay shrouded in the white haze.

The slopes in front of them were still barely visible. The trail ahead, winding back up into the passes, weaving between huge rocks and outcrops, as it disappeared up into the mists of the hidden peaks above.

The torches had burned out. Some were still smoking as sentries stood nearby gazing out into mists. Arnulf sat before a dwindling fire with his fur cloak wrapped about him. He pondered the day ahead with apprehension.

He had not slept. Few had, for fear of dreams of staggering dead men and the lurking things of the night. He had a fear that he would return to the pass only to find the bodies of those they had slain, only one day past, had gone. He feared, too, that the bodies of the men slain in the night, or of the girl, were to be found gone with the morning light. He shuddered. So many fears gnawed at him, stealing his sleep. What terrible thing had the gods sent him into?

Dawn came, and with it was discovered the bodies of the dead. Still laid behind the rocks, buried in the shallow pit topped with stones, still dead. Arnulf was relieved. Old Night had claimed their spirits back into his cold realm.

Although with the dawn light, Arnulf was now troubled by a new sinister tiding. The warrior, Olad, had mysteriously disappeared without trace. The sentries claimed to have not seen him go. None amongst them had seen him leave or seen anything else. Arnulf was troubled.

The reinforcements who came with Erran had brought fresh bread in the wagons from home. Some of the warriors sat around a rekindled cook fire and shared a loaf. Arnulf and Fergus talked quietly of the passes that lay ahead.

'None among us have ever ventured further along the trail than where the path forks off up to the watch post,' said Arnulf.

Fergus nodded slowly. 'The trail into the passes beyond is seldom trodden, only by those few brave explorers or mad men seeking adventure. I have never spoken with anyone who claims to have been up there. But I bet some of the locals may have ventured into it, even if not far.'

'Aye. Shame there is none to be found,' said Arnulf with a frown. 'The ancient trail has been unused for centuries. If what the folk say is true, it allegedly passes through the treacherous high valleys that lie amongst the peaks of the Spine. It is said a path through can be found.'

'Aye, I have heard of it, through to the frontier and the western Mark of Arnar. But it is also said that the trail is littered with bones and the ghosts of those who failed,' said Fergus with a grimace. He continued, 'I know of no man in living memory who has dared to travel too far along the trail past the path to the watch post. The ways are lost. But still, the stories have endured, haven't they? In truth, who knows what we will find up there?'

Casting a long glance up through the mists, Arnulf said, 'There are tales, still lingering, I have heard them myself. Tales of snowy high caves where giants and spirits dwell, of crumbling ruins and evil things stalking the night. You know—the local folktales we heard as children whilst sat around the fires on cold winter dead moons. I have heard the men tell those same stories around the fires up at the watch post. It is all we have to go by.'

Fergus smiled weakly. 'Well, we will be famous upon our return, my friend. The great adventurers. Arnulf and Fergus, and their brave warriors.'

'I thought you were already famous, the great Fergus of Weirdell,' said Arnulf mockingly, managing a smile.

Fergus grunted in amusement and smiled.

They sat in silence a moment until Fergus went on. He frowned. 'This matter of my man, Olad, is quite unsettling. Where is he?'

'I wish I knew, Fergus. But indeed, it is troubling.'

Astrid stood nearby their fire, not intruding but protectively close. 'Still no sign of him, lord,' she reported after obviously overhearing them. 'I'll send out some riders to search nearby.'

'And still no one saw anything?' enquired Fergus.

She shook her head. 'They're all talking about it, though,' she said with a nod to the encamped warriors around them. 'There's talk of him being snatched as we slept. Heard just as much of him sneaking off and running for it, too. But no one saw for sure.'

'I didn't know him,' said Arnulf, 'but he did not seem the man to desert.'

Fergus grunted. 'No, he isn't,' he agreed. 'At least...I wouldn't have thought so.'

'If he has been taken...'

'Don't,' said Fergus, waving Arnulf off. 'After yesterday, I don't know what to think.' He shook his head. 'He has probably run to save his skin.'

'He saw terrible things in the darkness last night, as did we all,' ventured Arnulf, 'but he spent time with that little girl. Perhaps seeing what he saw drove him to flee, to break his oath to you. Perhaps he had seen enough, or the fear made his mind slip. If he is found, will you punish him?'

'I must. Wouldn't you?'

Arnulf nodded but said nothing, thinking of the wounded guardsman who he let run at the Waystone.

'I cannot let that go, breaking his oath,' growled Fergus. 'It is not good to look weak in front of my warriors. He must be punished…' He looked off into the misty passes. 'I have a feeling we will find him…but I dare not think how,' said Fergus grimly.

The men had begun to make ready before dawn broke. They were all eager to leave after the night's events, even if that meant heading up the old watch path and into the unknown of the High Passes.

The outriders spurred off in front to scout the path ahead and the others trudged up the trail in their wake. Some of the men led their horses and walked alongside the others. Erran and two of the men rode off with the scouts.

Arnulf watched them ride off with their round shields slung, each painted crimson and with the great axe of his sigil. His hand found the head of his great axe which hung from the side of his horse's saddle, and he absently ran his fingers over the engraved steel as he rode. He looked up into the sky; the sun was but a low glow coming through the swirling mists above.

Fergus rode beside him, laughing and talking, the events of the night forgotten in the dawn hue. He felt better. In the daylight, it now seemed as if the night had all been a terrible dream from all the ale. He shuddered to remember it.

The watch path twisted up through the great misty cliffs and into the bleak scrub of the high valleys that led to the passes.

Arnulf felt strangely relieved when he reined in his horse over the pile of twisted dismembered bodies that his men had left at the roadside the morning before, still where he had left them. The crows flapped around cawing angrily at the horsemen, waiting to return to their grim feast. A single rhann took flight from amongst the hopping crows. The great black wings flapped effortlessly as the rhann circled its way into the sky, followed by its smaller crow brethren, to await their return to their feast of the dead.

Fergus took a spear from a nearby guardsman and used it to push one of bodies off the pile so it lay sprawled on the ground.

'So, these are your dead men, Arnulf?' said Fergus as he poked the corpse with the spear point. 'They are certainly dead,' he said with a smile. 'Not a local man that I've ever seen. And what is this?' he said, prodding at another. Fergus looked closer. He saw strange symbols and glyphs carved deep into the dead flesh. Fergus shuddered. 'Are these runes? I don't recognise the markings.'

Arnulf shrugged and shook his head.

Fergus drew back from the stench of rot that hung heavy around them.

'I don't know but the markings have not healed. Look here, they are open and fresh but they have not bled,' said Arnulf. 'And I swear to you, these men were walking until we hew them down yesterday. But look, some of these men look dead a week...and that smell.'

He gave Fergus a grave look. 'Come, let's move on. I cannot bear that stench much longer.'

Arnulf kicked his horse away from the gruesome monument left at side of the trail.

Arnulf sent men back to the watch post with orders to report back with any news, while others rode off in small groups cautiously searching the trails ahead. Some brave few rode as far as the high snowy peaks before turning back. They reported finding nothing other than the glimpse of a strange carved stone, which they dared not approach too closely for it was surely haunted. They rode back triumphantly, having gone farther than any other man in memory. But all seemed quiet. None wished to linger long in the passes, and so the warriors urged their lords to make their way back down the trail to the familiar ways below.

The two lords sat upon their horses beside the trail, surrounded by their warriors, deciding the best course of action. To venture further, or whether to turn back, and again make camp below.

The talk was cut short as an eerie howl sounded from the depths of the shadowy trees nearby. The men wheeled about to face the noise. Those nearest the trees from which it came, backed away slowly with their spears levelled at the shadows beyond. The mournful howl seemed to last a long time and was followed by an equally long eerie silence.

Only the leaves could be heard rustling in the trees. None wanted to break the silence, all awaiting some terrible creature of legend to come bounding towards them. But none came.

Fergus finally broke the silence.

'You men,' he said, beckoning towards some of his warriors. 'Search the trees a way, scare off that beast, was probably a wolf.' The warriors looked nervously at one another. 'What! Are you afraid?' snarled Fergus. 'Do most of you not give thanks to the wolf god, Varg?' he said looking at their nervous faces. He laughed. 'Fine. With me, Astrid. We search the trees.' Fergus nudged his horse off the trail and into the trees. He drew his sword and shook his head at his men as he led the Death Nymph and her warriors into the undergrowth.

Arnulf concealed a smile, and then kicked his horse after Fergus with a nod to Hafgan. Hafgan gestured to the other men to follow and so they also filed between the twisted trees after the others.

Arnulf heard a shout ahead. He urged his horse onwards, followed closely by Hafgan. The horses picked their way nimbly through the trees and shortly came out into the open. He found himself in a small clearing that was dominated by large craggy rocks, many of them taller than the surrounding trees.

Fergus and some of his men were already there, dismounted and stood about something on the floor. As Arnulf drew nearer he saw there were two bodies laid there. One appeared to be a terribly wounded old man, impaled by the shaft of a long spear. The other had the familiar looking harness of a guardsman.

'Branik, lord,' said Hafgan from behind, confirming Arnulf's fears.

'He's one of mine,' said Arnulf gravely as Fergus turned towards him. 'He rode out with Hagen, and now they're both dead.' Arnulf frowned, 'And still no sign of the other.'

'He took the miller's boy, lord. The lad named Darek,' said Hafgan.

Arnulf looked at Hafgan and saw young Erran had reined in beside him and stared down at Branik.

'He might be about somewhere, Arnulf…or taken?' said the young warrior.

'Look here!' shouted a warrior across the clearing. The man was pointing towards the corpse of a horse that appeared to have been slain while still tethered to a tree and had been torn open, its grisly innards strewn about.

Arnulf started to walk his horse towards the grim discovery, but the beast would not budge. He tugged at the reins, but his horse simply snorted and stamped its hooves, backing away.

'The horses are spooked, lord. They don't like seeing one of their own laid dead,' ventured Erran. 'My Pa's horses were the same. I seen it before, won't go near a dead one.'

They tethered their horses to one of the nearby trees and proceeded on foot to fulfil their morbid curiosity.

Other men were emerging from the trees, drawn by the shouts of those in the clearing. The newcomers joined the rest as they stood staring down at the fallen guardsman and the mysterious old man. The warriors had already begun to search about amongst the rocks. It was not long before they came upon the remains of a small deserted encampment, and what seemed to be a path winding off still further into the trees.

'This track has been recently travelled,' said Hafgan, noting the wheel ruts and the broken foliage beside the track.

Arnulf dismounted and bent over the fire pit. It was cold but had been used recently.

'Whoever was here left in a hurry, lord,' said Hafgan. 'They didn't take anything with them. Perhaps they are nearby?'

Fergus strode over. 'Or, perhaps they are slain and piled beside the trail back there,' he said.

Arnulf looked about. 'I don't know, old friend. It is possible, but what of young Darek's fate? And still no sign of Olad.'

'Olad probably fled back to Weirdell, Arnulf,' snapped Fergus. 'We will not find him here high in the passes. He knew nothing of this place, this I assure you.'

Another howl came through the trees, this time seeming much closer. The men, picking through the campsite for anything of worth, were brought to a standstill. They all stood watching the trees, searching for the source of the eerie howling. Arnulf stared off down the shadowy track that led further into the trees. He thought he saw movement, or were his eyes tricked by the gloom.

A large dark form appeared from the undergrowth along the track ahead. It stopped and turned to face them, its eyes glinting as they caught daylight amongst the shadows.

A murmur ran through the warriors as it slowly started moving towards them. The great shaggy beast moved on all fours and sniffed the ground cautiously with its long nose. It was some sort of huge hound, bigger than any he had seen.

Arnulf's young house warrior, Erran, stepped forward, notching an arrow. Several others did the same but Arnulf raised his arm.

'Wait. Only loose if it attacks,' commanded Arnulf as he waved the bowmen down.

'What are you doing, Arnulf?' exclaimed Fergus. 'It is a monster. We should kill it.'

'Perhaps,' said Arnulf, 'but look, it fears us.'

The hound was slinking around the tree line eyeing them warily. It did not seem to wish to enter the open ground of the clearing, or approach the cluster of men and their levelled spears.

Arnulf slowly walked forward and carefully knelt, not taking his eyes off the beast, and extended his open hand.

'Be careful, Arnulf, it could savage you,' said Fergus.

But Arnulf appeared not to heed his friend's warnings. Instead, he slowly edged closer. The great hound sat on its haunches and watched him curiously. Arnulf saw no malice in its eyes, it seemed wary. But still, he did not let his guard down.

He moved closer but the great hound backed away and bared its teeth.

'Look out, Arnulf,' shouted Erran.

Arnulf's hand moved towards the hilt of his knife, sheathed at his belt. But as he did, the hound responded with a low growl from its throat, and he moved his hand away. The great beast seemed satisfied and silenced, instead sat watching Arnulf intently.

Man and beast sat watching each other for a moment as the others looked on in silence. Arnulf extended his open hand towards the beast. The hound sniffed at it cautiously, before retreating a few steps back, and then slowly creeping back for another sniff.

'Good dog,' said Arnulf softly as the hound nuzzled at his hand and allowed him to scratch between its big shaggy ears.

Satisfied the hound would not attack, he took a moment to examine the beast. It was a big dog. Its coat, a tangle of matted grey hair. It had a long snout set with smouldering yellow eyes, framed by bushy brows and long shaggy ears.

The great dog took to sniffing about the floor. And so, Arnulf slowly rose and turned to the throng of men gathered behind watching.

'I have never seen a beast like it,' said Arnulf.

'Indeed friend,' replied Fergus watching the huge hound warily.

'I don't think he means us harm,' said Arnulf. 'He seems tame.'

The beast began to take an interest in his boots, sniffing at them intently.

'How can we be sure?' said Fergus.

'We can't,' replied Arnulf, 'but he seems friendly enough.'

'I wonder what he's doing up here?' he said to himself.

'Perhaps he belongs to one of the camp here,' ventured Erran.

'Belonged, lad,' corrected Fergus with a dark laugh. 'I'd wager his owner helped make your lord's trailside monument back there.' Fergus chuckled to himself.

'So, what now, Arnulf?' asked Fergus. 'We found their camp and there can't have been many of them, whoever they were, I'm fairly sure they are all piled back there beside the track down the pass.'

Arnulf looked troubled 'Perhaps? But if so, still no sign of my man Darek or the other folk from Hern's farmstead. Where are they?'

Fergus shrugged and spent a moment in thought.

'You men! Keep searching the woods if there's anyone left out here, I want them found,' said Fergus, with a gesture to the surrounding trees that enclosed them.

'I say we scour these woods for any sign of your man, and then find him or not, ride back for the Waystone and check at the other farms, perhaps they saw something. This track has been travelled. Someone must have seen the cart or something.'

Arnulf noticed the hound had gone. He looked about to find it sitting on his haunches amid the track where it first appeared.

'And what of this track? It continues into the trees,' said Arnulf. 'It must lead somewhere.'

Fergus looked off up the gloomy cart track that wound off deeper into the trees. The hound turned and padded further down the track before stopping and turning his shaggy head back towards them. It's piercing yellow eyes shining bright in the dim light coming through the trees.

'Perhaps he has somewhere better to be?' said Fergus.

'We should follow and see what is up there,' said

Arnulf. After a pause he said, 'Perhaps he is leading us somewhere?'

Fergus's cheerful face turned suddenly serious.

'It could be some trick, a foul creature in disguise, trying to lure us to where it wants us.'

Arnulf looked at his old friend.

'Only the gods know?' replied Arnulf. 'Perhaps it is as you say and we are here to be tested.' He smiled. 'I don't fancy coming back up here again if I don't have to. I mean to follow that track and see where it leads,' said Arnulf before steeling himself, and then tracing the wheel ruts that led into the trees, he followed after the great hound.

The track led them deeper into the woods. It was overgrown and littered with stones hidden in the undergrowth. The hound padded gently between the two wheel ruts which were often the only sign that they were following a track at all.

The trees grew squat and twisted. Arnulf ducked low looking under the foliage. He could see little more than the expanse of thin tree trunks disappearing into the thick tangle of branches above, like the columns of a low vaulted hall. He could see little else before the gloom of the forest beyond obscured his view.

Behind, Hafgan walked beside Fergus and they were talking quietly of the horse's refusal to follow with Erran. The young lad was the son of a horse breeder, he knew his horses. Other than their quiet mutterings all was silent, not even the call of birds which Arnulf noted with some unease.

Before long the trees began to thin out slightly to reveal glimpses of ancient crumbling masonry amongst the undergrowth. Strange carved stones lay in ruin, weathered by countless years of wind and rain. Ancient vistas of paved stone now overgrown and covered by moss could be made out between the thickets of brambles and twisted trees.

The hound padded on, occasionally turning back and awaiting his wary followers before again moving off ahead once more, following the wheel ruts that wove through the mysterious emerging ruins.

'Arnulf, we must tread lightly,' called Fergus. Fergus walked behind and peered around at the strange crumbling walls that were now visible, giving only a hint of their former design.

'This place has a grim feel. I think we would do well not to awaken the spirits that slumber in this place,' continued Fergus.

'Indeed, m'lord, old spirits must certainly haunt this place,' added Hafgan.

Arnulf clutched at the charm hung at his neck.

'Aye, we will not linger, but I must know where this great beast is leading us,' said Arnulf, nodding at the hound ahead.

The great grey dog was again sitting on his haunches ahead of them. His tongue lolled from his mouth, panting, seemingly awaiting their approach. No doubt waiting to again slink off ahead, leading them deeper into the ruin. The hound instead left the cart track and disappeared off between the crumbling masonry.

'Arnulf!' exclaimed Fergus. 'Where has it gone? I don't like this. It feels like we are being watched. This creature is leading us to our doom. Haf, tell him.'

Hafgan stepped forward so the others could not hear. Warily looking around, he said, 'Lord Fergus is right, Arnulf. There are unfriendly eyes on us. I can feel it. They could spring their ambush at any moment.'

'Lord, we will follow you—you know that—but I advise we turn back and leave this place or at least prepare ourselves. They could be hiding anywhere amongst this,' said Hafgan, with a gesture to the overgrown walls that now surrounded them. He eyed the nearby stones suspiciously and held the hilt of his sheathed sword in readiness.

'Sound council, Haf,' said Arnulf clasping the big warrior's shoulder. He turned to the others behind who had followed the track with them.

'Men, unsling your shields, arm yourselves, be ready in case…' His words trailed off as the hound appeared once more on the track.

The great hound sat beside a fallen down section of wall that seemed to form an entrance to a derelict enclosure beyond. The hound turned and disappeared back out of sight.

Arnulf motioned his warriors forward. They moved quietly, shields on arms and with axe or spear in hand. Astrid and her formidable women formed up around their lord, alert and ready. Fergus had only a handful of warriors now, the others, guarding the deserted camp or scouring the nearby woods, only a horn blast away.

Astrid stood at the front of her warriors, her shield on one arm, an axe hanging in the other. She swept a fierce gaze into the gloom of the ruins.

Erran stole a lingering glance at the famous shield-maiden. Hafgan clasped the young warrior by the shoulder.

'Stay sharp,' he whispered harshly in Erran's ear.

Hafgan led the guardsmen forward and cautiously approached the crumbling gap into which the hound had disappeared. Erran took one last glance at the forbidding warrior woman and followed.

The young warrior moved past and ranged ahead of Hafgan. He waved the guardsmen back and approached the gap alone. Hafgan shook his head at the young warrior. The youthful display of his mettle was obvious to his older eyes. Hafgan wondered if the lad would be so brazen if the Death Nymph were not watching on.

Arnulf watched as the young warrior peered over the tumbled stone after the hound. Erran turned back bewildered.

'Lord,' he called in a hushed voice, 'come and see this.'

CHAPTER FIFTEEN

The Cursed Ones

He found himself in a low wooded hollow within the thicket. The branches gnarled and twisted around him, the undergrowth grew thickly amongst them. A large flat rock created the space he now occupied. He perched upon it, peering from his hiding place. The air smelt of earth and dead leaves. A beetle scampered away across the grainy rock. His hand shot out, and then the hapless beetle crunched between his teeth.

He emerged from the thicket crouching low, and clambered up onto another rock laid between the boles of tall trees that stretched up high above.

He sniffed the air. He could smell it again. He sniffed again—blood—and something else now, something strangely familiar, yet nothing he had ever smelt before. His focus was ensnared by the strange new scent, his mind wrenched on a tether by a terrible urge, there was no resisting it. That new smell, he would find it.

A dull rage still seethed within him. He had found himself pounding the floor or smashing the boles of trees until his hands were bloody, unable to vent his inexplicable spiteful malice. He felt calmer now, but still the anger simmered within him.

His arm no longer felt any pain. The wound—the bite—had blackened. The dark discolouration was spreading up his arm in dark tendrils beneath his skin.

He couldn't remember things. He had killed; a face he knew. He had been a friend once, perhaps? The man's name escaped him now, but he remembered the taste, and his mouth watered.

His memories had been slowly consumed by the darkness. Each time he fed, less and less remained. His own name had even become hard to recall, it seemed now a distant memory. His very being, leached away by the hungry whispering blackness that had seized him. Now a wretched creature remained in his place, a grotesque mockery of the one once known as Darek.

He flinched at a sound. She was following him, he knew. He caught her scent a while back. He would have killed her. But, her eyes, he saw it had her too. The darkness, hidden deep inside her eyes within the glare she transfixed on him at the farm. She smelt of it—smelt of the darkness. And now, she followed, her scent growing stronger as she slunk closer along his trail.

Yet this strange new scent…was not hers. It was different to the scent he was now catching on the breeze. Could there be another one?

He had left none alive, just her and the boy at the farm, and they had fed with him. Until the dead ones had awakened, and disturbed the feed. Then the dead followed on to the moor, but were easily lost behind him now. They were slow. She seemed to have slipped away from them, too.

He knew the moor was not safe. He had seen the flickering torches in the dark, caught the scent of horse. Men were on the moor, too many. It was not safe there.

Skulking across the gorse strewn moor in the night, he had now descended into the woodlands beyond as the sunlight of dawn began to break through the trees. He would be safer here, many places to hide.

She emerged from the undergrowth behind him and sniffed the air before fixing her gaze upon him. Her hair bedraggled. The stink of blood wafted from her, she stank of death. Her hands and tattered clothes stained with blood and covered in filth. She crouched low, resting her hands on the ground. Her face, smeared with crusting gore. They regarded each other in silence.

He caught whispers murmuring inside his head, fragments of her thoughts leaking in to his own through the darkness. It had her too. He had watched as she fed on her own kin, unable to stop herself. It had taken them both.

She approached and sniffed at him. Her eyes were dead, the darkness dwelt within. It had taken hold. He bared his teeth with a deep growl from his throat, and she sank lower submissively. Yes, he was the biggest, the strongest, he would lead. He would accept this one.

He watched her as she sniffed around him submissively. He surveyed her with an impulsive carnal eye. Her clothing was torn and dishevelled, revealing her exposed skin beneath. Her shapely figure, the curves, the glimpse of breast, filled him with a sudden bestial lust. He would mount her and take her. She would be his now.

She looked up suddenly and seemed to catch a scent on the breeze. She sniffed the air. Yes, she smelt it too. The scent of blood. And yes, she could likely smell that strange scent mingled with it—the other. But it could wait. He would have her first, here and now.

Grey clouds rolled overhead and a heavy rain lashed down. The rain hammered on the rocky ground in a thunderous cacophony. The thinning canopy of ruddy coloured leaves clung to the trees in earnest overhead and dripped streams of water to the floor.

Two skulking figures emerged over the crest of the ridge. Creeping close to the ground and slinking over rocks, they walked using their hands, a gait more ape than man. Defiled and now only echoing the form they once held.

A scatter of thin grey trees grew perched on narrow ledges and thrusting out from fissures in the rock of the steep terrace that fell off into a basin below. The pair moved between the trees, clinging to boles and branches in their descent. The scent was strong, even through the rain. Peering over a ledge they beheld the one they had been stalking.

A dripping figure crouched below in the basin. A prostrate form of another sprawled out on the ground before it. The basin had become a charnel scene of ghastly slaughter. The rain had done little to dilute the cruor of the butchery. The ground splattered with blood, a pool of crimson leaking out from the body on the floor.

The crouching figure suddenly looked up from its victim and at the pair watching overhead. Whispers of frenzied engorgement and blood lust pervaded their thoughts as they stared down upon the figure. He had sensed their presence, their scent, as they had his. They had found the other one.

The lurking watcher, once known as Darek, knew this face. It was the one they called Thom, a guardsman once like him. The man-creature below hissed and snarled up at them. This was his kill. He would challenge these newcomers.

The two males regarded each other for some time, gauging each other, low growls rumbling from their throats. Suddenly without warning Darek leapt into the basin, landing deftly into a crouch. He screamed a roar of defiance in answer to the bold challenge of this pitiful creature.

With a bounding lunge he slammed into the one known once as Thom. The overwhelming strength of the impact sent the guardsman reeling into the rocks. Thom yelped, and then slowly rose, hissing and circling on all fours but made no move of reprisal. Darek roared again, baring his teeth. He was the strongest, the first one.

The smaller creature, once known as Thom, moved away to allow the larger fiend to feed. Darek voraciously tore into the mangled corpse. The body was once a farmer, or a woodsman perhaps, it mattered not.

***

Thom had been unable to stop as he stalked his prey through the trees, overwhelmed by a dark hunger. He had struck from behind with callous fury. The man never saw it coming. Thom had watched, trapped behind his own eyes, powerless to stop himself as he killed the stranger with his bare hands. And then, horrified by his own deeds and still watching on helpless, he dragged his kill to this secluded place where a gruesome urge had overtaken him, and he had begun to feed.

***

She watched from the ledge above as the two clashed below in the basin. Her mate had easily driven the smaller one away and usurped the kill. She watched the other as it slowly circled and cowered. It was still very much man, the change still fresh. It had killed and fed, and so he would soon begin to forget, as she had.

Her other life was already fading. Her memories, clouded in her mind. She had watched on as her loved ones fell around her to this malevolence. She had a husband, and children, all gone now. She had other names, Wife, Ma…she had been called Mother—all gone now.

The guilt of what she had done consumed her. She had murdered them. She watched as they fell lifeless to the floor. Her instincts torn asunder, her children, who looked to her for protection, for love, betrayed. Killed by her own hands. She had eaten them. Trapped watching, screaming in her mind, trapped in a living nightmare, watching it all unfold. She had eaten them. Her love, replaced with a terrible rage as her spiralling descent into madness consumed all that she was. Perhaps it was easier to forget, to fall deeper into the darkness, to leave guilt and grief behind.

This other one was no threat but it was like her, one of them. She watched her mate feed. The hunger once again overwhelmed her. Her mouth watered in anticipation. She descended the slope and crouched close to the body waiting her turn. Her mate turned, his mouth dripping with gore and having taken his fill, he motioned for the others to feed.

She sprang forward and tore into an arm lying limp on the ground. Tearing chucks of dripping flesh free with her teeth, she gorged herself. The flesh was going stale, no longer warm, but it was bloody and tasted good nonetheless.

***

The trio flinched back as the body began to twitch. It was awakening. To its snarls and growls, they backed away, watching as the corpse slowly rose to its feet. Its entrails spilled from the cavity they had torn into its soft belly and coiled to the floor with a wet splatter.

The dead man suddenly lurched towards them. The three turned and fled, scrabbling up the slope to escape its grasping dead hands. Darek paused and turned around, staring back at the dead one as it struggled to gain a purchase on the steep slope. The dead man stumbled and fell snarling, before awkwardly rising to try again. The basin would hold it for some time.

The creature, known once as Darek, turned to see the other two awaiting him. They squatted motionless in the rain. He looked them over—his pack. He was the leader, the strongest, the first one amongst them.

They would need to feed again soon. They needed prey. Perhaps they would create more of their own from the ones who were not killed, expand their pack—become stronger.

He stared up at the heavy sky. He felt the rain against his face, and then regarded the other two once more.

Then it came to him. Yes, Darek knew just the place. A place he once knew well, a rich hunting ground full of prey.

A place he once called home.

CHAPTER SIXTEEN

A Watcher in the Dark

Arnulf prepared himself for another grisly discovery but what he saw was quite unexpected. Rising from amongst the ancient masonry stood a large dishevelled marquee.

It was well hidden and seemed to have been built using the decayed walls of the enclosure as a shell, over which a canvas structure had been erected with timbers and rope. Before the marquee, the rest of the enclosure formed a crude courtyard in which Arnulf could see a tangle of cart tracks in the churned mud ahead. The marquee loomed up dark and foreboding. Its entrance gaped open, just a flap that hung and swayed in the cold breeze being blown down from the craggy peaks above.

Arnulf's gaze could not penetrate the shadow

beyond the gaping entrance, but instead his eyes flicked about, surveying the surrounding rocks for any sign of trouble. It seemed quiet. His warriors crouched around him, nervously peering over the old stones into the strange compound before them.

Arnulf nodded his men forward. Together they crept into the muddy courtyard and drew closer to the sinister gloom of the marquee entrance. Arnulf could see the canvas was mildewed and water marked, a sign of many weeks of rain and foul weather. The sides had been closely pegged to the ground and the canvas had been patched in places.

The afternoon had grown late, the sun slowly disappearing behind the high crags to the west. There was still yet light enough to investigate. Hafgan pulled the tent open, spilling light inside. Nothing stirred. Arnulf threw a glance at Hafgan, and then without word, they stepped inside.

It smelt damp. Arnulf could see shafts of light perforating the gloom. Light spilled inside as other warriors entered, cautiously peering around. There were separate tents within the marquee clustered around a fire pit. Beside the fire was a large table, upon which were several burnt out candles.

Beside the fire pit sat the hound on a rug awaiting them. To his surprise Arnulf noticed there were thick rugs upon the straw floor. Hafgan opened one of the smaller tents with the tip of his spear and peered inside. He shook his head and moved to the next. Other than the hound, the marquee seemed deserted.

The warriors began rummaging through the barrels and provisions as Arnulf examined the curious trinkets of one of the larger tents. The tent was lavishly decorated. It seemed quite out of place in such a remote place. The rugs were fine and expensive, there were shelves full of curious things and there was a bed. A small table covered in many burnt candles sat in the corner, stacked with scrolls and bound books. Ink and a set of quills sat in a small wooden rack. Arnulf noted the chair, it was ornately carved and its seat had a fine fur skin draped over it.

He leafed through a large open book on the table.

'The College,' said Arnulf to himself.

The pages were full of drawings of limbs and bones with text written in a spidery script. The sketches and diagrams were incredible, like none he had ever seen. Fascinating yet disturbing to look upon. The innards of men depicted on paper.

He had seen the dusty old skeletal remains of ancient men—long dead—laid in the holy places, and Arnulf had seen battle. He knew men were made of hearts and lungs, and a belly of guts. He had seen them spilled and pierced amongst the battlefield dead. These drawings were chillingly reminiscent of those bloody memories.

He flicked to the last page, marked by a faded green ribbon. These pictures were different, strange symbols and glyphs. He shuddered to look upon them. Strangely he felt he had seen them before although he knew he never had. His eyes were drawn to an old parchment unrolled beneath the great tome. It was full of strange markings and glyphs.

The last pages of the book seemed to be devoted to strange religious rites and practices. Many of the writings he could not read, written in a strange foreign hand, but he could make out the spidery notes scrawled beside them. Strange statements and chilling translations, all too fragmented to make any sense. He shuddered, closing the heavy book.

'Arnulf, you should see this,' said Hafgan, appearing behind him. He stopped as he entered and stared at the rich furnishings.

'Uh, but I think this beats mine,' said Hafgan with a bewildered look. 'What is this?' he muttered.

Arnulf turned to the big warrior. 'Looks like College men, Haf. But only gods know what they're doing up here. What did you find?'

Hafgan's eyes ran over the table. 'The other tent has many books and papers. But not like this. It is plainer. Perhaps you should look, none of the others can make much of it and I have no eye for script either.'

Arnulf smiled. 'I only know a little, old friend, but show me.'

The other tent was indeed much plainer. A simple cot adorned one side and there was another table. But, unlike the other tent, it had little decoration other than a pile of furs on the floor at the foot of the cot.

There were shelves full of scrolls and books here also and a fine large chest. Arnulf opened the chest. He saw just clothes and personal belongings. He reached inside and plucked out a feather brooch, a symbol of the College.

'The College indeed,' he muttered.

Hafgan eyed the brooch in his lord's hand and nodded a silent agreement.

He made his way to the table and looked at the scrolls left out. Unrolling and scanning each one in turn.

'They're maps. I think it's the ruins and here about. Have they been mapping the ruin? Sounds like the sort of pointless study the College would undertake.'

Hafgan grunted humorously.

The great hound joined them. It padded in and lay down on the furs, watching them with curious eyes.

A foul stench pervaded his nostrils.

'That smell,' said Fergus as he ducked into the marquee's main entrance. 'This whole place stinks of death.' Fergus blinked as his eyes adjusted and found Arnulf. 'Find anything?' he asked.

Arnulf tossed the brooch over.

'College,' exclaimed Fergus. 'What in the gods are they doing up here?'

Arnulf shrugged and shook his head.

'Still no sign of the folk here?' asked Fergus.

'Nobody here. It's deserted,' said Arnulf.

'Well, we found some,' said Fergus grinning through his red platted beard.

Lowering the parchment he held, Arnulf threw him an enquiring glance.

'Come,' beckoned Fergus.

Arnulf placed the parchment down on the table and followed Fergus outside, trailed by Hafgan and the hound.

'I sent some of the boys up there to look around,' said Fergus, pointing to a bluff rising from the scattered masonry a hundred or so paces away. 'They found something you might be interested in.'

'What?'

Fergus shrugged.

'Have they found Darek?' demanded Arnulf.

Fergus didn't reply and continued towards the outcrop, picking his way through strewn rocks.

Arnulf cursed his old friend under his breath, damn Fergus and his taxing humour.

Fergus obviously hearing, turned and flashed him a grin. 'Not sure, Arnulf, I haven't seen it, could be. But I don't think so from what they said. Come see for yourself.'

Fergus was following, what seemed to be, a travelled path leading up to the outcrop, winding its way through the ancient crumbling walls and stones. Arnulf followed him, still trailed by the hound and the ever near Hafgan, who eyed the surrounding rocks suspiciously as he past amongst them.

'Here, Arnulf, the first one,' said Fergus.

As Arnulf moved closer, he saw a man sprawled on the floor. The man was dead and naked, all but a dirty cloth undergarment.

'Is he yours?' asked Fergus.

Hafgan kicked the corpse over, unleashing a cloud of flies and a terrible stench of rot.

'No,' said Arnulf, covering his nose with his hand. 'You said the first one? There's more?'

'Aye, there's more,' replied Fergus. 'I only saw this one before I came to show you, but my men said there is another.'

Arnulf cast another disgusted look at the sprawled corpse. The man's skull had been caved in by a mighty blow from an edged weapon, nearly cleaving his head in two. He moved onwards, leaving the flies to settle once more.

As he walked, Hafgan felt a crunch beneath his feet. The others turned at the sound. The big warrior plucked the mangled, twisted remains of an old lantern from his boot. Hafgan shrugged and casting it aside, he followed his lord as they approached the looming hill ahead.

The hill, composed of earth over huge boulders that thrust from an outcrop of bedrock, now rose up high in front of them as they drew closer. The trail Fergus followed seemed to wind up around the side of the outcrop. Arnulf presumed it led to the summit.

There, at the foot of the outcrop, amongst the tall grass, lay another body. This one face up, its eyes and mouth buzzed with a miasma of flies. The corpse's leg had been hewn off and laid a few paces away. It looked as if the man had clawed himself onwards to where he now rested and had rolled over to lie facing upwards as he died.

Fergus threw an enquiring glance at Arnulf, who shook his head.

'Who are they all?' said Fergus.

'These men have been dead maybe a week or more,' said Hafgan.

'Aye,' said Arnulf. 'And going on the marquee back there, I'd say the College have had a hand in all this.'

Fergus stroked his beard thoughtfully. 'What in the gods are the College doing up here? And without our leave. My father must hear of this.'

Arnulf eyed the path hewn into the rock itself, in comparison to the rough track they had followed to the outcrop, this carved walkway seemed as ancient as the crumbling ruin surrounding them.

'What do you think is at the top?' said Arnulf.

'Let's find out. These men seemed to have died getting here,' said Fergus.

They ascended. The path carved from the hillside rounded a corner near the hills summit. It opened up from the carved path into a similarly fashioned square cut room. The room was open to the darkening sky and only enclosed by the outcrops of bedrock on three sides, the fourth was open and looked out over the ruins below.

The first thing Arnulf's eyes fell upon was a huge cylinder of burnished bronze set into a wooden frame. A pedestal carved from a single stone sat in the middle of the room.

Arnulf approached the cylinder and ran his hand across the smooth surface.

'Crone's sight! What is this thing?' said Arnulf, awed by the strange cylinder.

Fergus studied it a moment. 'Is it a bracer? Belonging to some giant perhaps? Gods it's huge.'

'I've seen the Teliks with armour of bronze like that over their arms...Vambrace, I think they call them,' replied Arnulf. 'It can't be though... giants?'

'There are old tales of giants but...' Fergus trailed off.

Hafgan chuckled. Both lords swung round to face him.

'I believe, lords, this is a bell. I have seen them at Arn and another at Peren, in the sea tower.'

'I have heard of the bell at Peren,' said Arnulf. 'If I had known it was like this, I would have gone to see it long before now.'

'They are only to be rung in warning. Few these days have ever seen one or heard one toll,' said Hafgan.

'Yet, we did,' said Arnulf with grim expression.

Fergus rapped the cylinder with the pommel of his sword. A deep chime, almost seeming to shake the very rock, rang out and rolled across the ruins below.

'Ha, I couldn't wait any longer. It appears we have found your bell, Arnulf,' laughed Fergus. He raised his hand to strike the bell again when Hafgan seized his arm.

'Stay your hand, lord,' rasped Hafgan.

A flicker of anger showed on Fergus's face before he forced a smile. 'You forget yourself, friend Haf,' he said through his clenched grin, a sharp look in his eye.

'I am sorry, Fergus…lord. But you just announced our presence to any foes who might still be lurking in wait for us.'

They locked eyes for an awkward moment as Hafgan released his arm and stepped back.

It was then the two men noticed Arnulf. He stood at the open side of the room looking out into the ruin, a low wall of old piled stone was all that separated him from the steep drop below.

'What is it, Arnulf?' asked Fergus, joining him at the low wall. Fergus immediately noted the marquee, now clearly visible amongst the tangle of ruined stone below.

'What is that?' said Arnulf, pointing out over the ruins. His gaze drawn by the circling of rhann and crows over the shadowy silhouettes of stone in the fading dusk light. Silhouettes, of what looked like monoliths, rising from the crown of a circular hill.

'An old circle?' said Fergus.

'Have you ever seen one so huge?' replied Arnulf.

'Perhaps part of the ruin, or a strange gathering of stones. Well they do say there were giants in these passes, a giant's hall perhaps?' said Fergus with a grin.

Watching the dark shapes circle in the distance, Arnulf stretched a hand out to lean on the carved wall of the hillside. He recoiled suddenly. A crimson ichor glistened on his hand. 'Blood!'

They had not noticed in the dim light, but now their attention was drawn to the walls and the floor. There was blood splashed about, on the floor and walls around them. A grisly handprint here and there, one smeared the wall, as its maker had lent out a supporting hand upon the cold stone, perhaps their last steps.

'Come, let us leave this place,' said Arnulf with a frown. 'There are no more answers here.'

'Yet, more questions,' muttered Hafgan, as he turned to carefully pick his way back along the winding path to below.

They were greeted at the bottom by two of Fergus's warriors. The two shield-maidens, bearing flaming torches in the growing darkness, stood over the corpse at the foot of the outcrop, their faces grim.

***

Hafgan followed the two lords as they made their way back carefully to the enclosure of the marquee, escorted by the two warriors. He continued to scan the dark surroundings with suspicion as he walked. He had a strange feeling of being watched, it was an unsettling feeling. Why had Fergus rung that bell? It was foolish.

Hafgan suddenly sensed movement to his left. He whirled to meet it, sword in hand. The hound appeared from the dark undergrowth, cowering low. It growled up at him, baring yellow teeth.

'Damn dog,' muttered Hafgan, lowering his weapon as the hound backed away.

'Ha! Snuck up on you, Haf,' laughed Fergus.

The big warrior grunted and watched as the great hound slunk after Arnulf.

The shadows of derelict walls loomed up in their path as they picked their way through rubble, back to the marquee. Smoke from spluttering torches swirled about them and spiralled off into the evening sky. The hound padded at Arnulf's side.

Hafgan was bemused by Arnulf's strange new companion. He wondered what his lord would do with the beast if it continued to follow him.

The hound suddenly cowered again, low to the floor, its hackles raised. Growling at the shadows, it backed off and hid amongst the rubble behind Arnulf.

Hafgan stared into the darkness as Arnulf tried to coax the beast out. It finally emerged, looking about warily.

'Ha, the beast is afraid of shadows,' laughed Fergus, and slapping Hafgan on the back, said, 'Will teach the damn thing to have startled you, Haf.'

Hafgan grunted and continued staring at the shadows amongst which the hound had perceived a threat. There was nothing.

The hound began barking suddenly and bolted. Startled, Hafgan turned as the hound fled. He caught the flicker of movement in the edge of his vision while his head was turned.

He wheeled and side stepped as a dark shape plunged past, missing him by a hand's width. His axe flashed into his left hand, and he struck the lunging shape in a swift arcing motion as it flew past.

A dark figure sprawled on the floor. Quickly recovering, it loped off on all fours before Hafgan could swing a killing blow.

The figure wheeled and stood facing them.

Hafgan drew his sword with his free right hand, his axe still hung in his left, its head bloodied.

'By the gods,' gasped Fergus. 'Olad?'

The warrior Olad stood before them. His stance, slightly hunched. His face slightly lowered but with glinting eyes glaring up at them. Fergus's two guards leapt to flank their lord, levelling their spears with shields raised.

'Olad,' bellowed Fergus.

There was no reply. Shadows danced across Olad's features in the flickering torchlight. A sick smile spread across the warrior's face. Blood seemed to be trickling down off one hand, Hafgan's strike had been swift, but Olad seemed not to have even noticed the wound. He stood staring. And then, he lunged.

Deftly avoiding the spear of the first woman, Olad crashed against her shield, with what must have been great strength, as she was sent sprawling to the floor.

Olad then seized the spear shaft of the other woman, closed, and struck her down with his other fist before she had time to react. She was no match for such blinding speed.

***

Arnulf watched in horror as the events unfolded. Fergus seemed frozen is disbelief as the warrior Olad now stood before him.

Hafgan leapt forward as soon as Olad had initially lunged, pushing past Arnulf, he threw himself at the crazed warrior just as he took down the second of Fergus's guardswomen. Hafgan struck hard with the pommel of his sword, aiming for the warrior's head. Olad was knocked senseless by the mighty blow and fell to the floor.

Blinking, Fergus turned to Hafgan. He said nothing for a moment, and then said, 'Haf, by the gods, I don't even know how that happened.'

'So fast…,' muttered Arnulf, trailing off as he stared at the limp figure of Olad in disbelief. 'I barely had time to raise my axe.'

'You have my thanks, Haf,' said Fergus.

Hafgan hooked his axe back into his belt and helped the two women to their feet. They were not wounded but for a few bruises.

The ferocity and unnerving malice of the sudden attack imposed a short silence upon them.

The hound reappeared and slunk about sniffing the air cautiously. It emitted a low growl as it sniffed at the unconscious warrior.

'I have never seen someone move so fast,' said Arnulf, still looking at the senseless warrior. 'And you, Haf, well done. That was swift thinking. You didn't kill him?'

'No, lord, I didn't kill him,' replied Hafgan. He then grunted, adding, 'I could have hit him with the other end. But we need answers.'

Arnulf nodded. 'Answers,' he repeated. 'Indeed, Haf. Such a blow could have killed him. You judged well.'

'If it hadn't have felled him, I would have indeed killed him, lord,' replied Hafgan.

Arnulf grimaced and nodded.

Carrying the unconscious form of the warrior Olad, they returned to the marquee compound. Arnulf could see the other warriors had lit torches. The ruddy firelight flickered amongst the ruins nearby as the warriors cautiously searched about the compound and stood sentry, vigilantly watching the darkness.

After depositing the unconscious warrior in the marquee, leaving Hafgan to see that he was restrained and put under a suitable guard, Arnulf and Fergus stepped outside into the dusk light. Arnulf sighed heavily and rubbed his face. *What is happening here? What is happening to these people?*

Hafgan soon returned, stepping out of the marquee to find Arnulf and Fergus talking, the conversation rising heatedly as they discussed their next course of action.

'The rhann were circling something,' said Arnulf.

'Perhaps? And then again, perhaps not, Arnulf,' said Fergus.

'We should take a look. There could be more.'

'You plan to go up there in the dark. After that,' said Fergus, gesturing at the now bound and guarded form of Olad. 'It's foolish.'

'I do,' replied Arnulf.

'The men do not want to linger here at night. We should make for the low lands and make camp.'

'Stay then, old friend. I will take some men to look. It will not take long. Some will need to stay here and watch our crazed friend.'

'He must have followed us up here,' said Fergus looking back into the marquee.

'Aye, I felt watchful eyes upon me out in the ruins,' said Arnulf, his voice low. 'He was hunting us, hunting you, perhaps?' He paused. 'Something is very wrong here. What happened to him? I must know. Stay if you will.'

Fergus sighed angrily. 'No, I will join you. I will not have it said that Fergus baulked at the darkness of the High Passes. Besides, I would see this giant's hall we saw from the high overlook. But it could wait till morning.'

'You would spend the night in this place? The men would not be happy,' said Arnulf.

'I propose we leave now and make camp in the pass and return in the daylight.'

'No. This will not take long. I will go now, get it done. I want to leave this place as much as the next man. We look, and then return to the lowlands as soon as possible. I have no desire to return here a second time, it feels cursed.'

'You're a stubborn fool, Arnulf. So be it, I will ready my warriors. Let's get this done quickly and leave,' said Fergus with a sigh.

'Agreed,' said Arnulf. He turned to Hafgan. 'Haf, ready some men, those who are willing. The others will wait here for our return and guard Olad. Tell them it will not be long and to stay vigilant.'

Hafgan nodded and moved off to speak with the others. He returned shortly and said, 'I will follow you, Lord Arnulf, and I have eight men ready.'

Arnulf surveyed the grim faces before him in the flickering torch light—good men. He nodded and turning to Fergus he said, 'Let's get this done.'

CHAPTER SEVENTEEN

The Ravine

The ravine looked perfect for an ambush. The sides were steep and high, inescapable from the road traversing through it. The ravine itself, cut through the terraces of cliffs, which rose from the surrounding pine forest, slicing the cliffs like lightning splitting the sky. It seemed to be the only route from the valley floor up into the high ground ahead without taking a substantial detour through dense forest.

Bjorn paused at the mouth of the ravine and surveyed the road ahead. He could not see far, only to the first bend before the road disappeared behind the facade of rock.

Bjorn ventured in, leading his horse by the reins. The hunter planned to stake out a suitable section of the ravine and await his pursuer, to confront him to whatever end. Bjorn was now tired of this unexplainable pursuit.

For the past two nights, since setting out from Pinedelve, his journey had been tracked. His footsteps haunted by the stalking Wildman. Each night as he made camp, Bjorn had spotted him. He crouched at a distance, peering through the undergrowth or from behind a tree, watching. Each time the hunter rose to challenge him, the Wildman would melt away into the forest without trace.

Bjorn had barely slept these past nights, unable to rest with that lurking menace so close, forcing him to remain awake in a watchful vigil. He had once or twice succumbed to his weary, heavy eyes and fallen asleep. This morning he awoke, to his dismay, to find signs that the Wildman had prowled through his camp as he had slept and had even rifled through his possessions. Nothing, however, was missing.

The road from Pinedelve had brought him deeper into the safety of Arnar, now a good distance from the border. Yet still the Wildman pursued. Such gall, to walk so freely within the lands of Arnar. Perhaps he was indeed no stranger to these forests. Was he a local wanderer after all?

Bjorn was mounted, and although not pushing his horse hard, Bjorn was amazed at the pace and stamina of the man. The Wildman must have run tirelessly throughout each day. How else could he keep such a pace?

Bjorn had once again caught sight of him the previous day. As he stopped to rest and water his horse, he saw the running form hurtling along the road behind him. The Wildman skidded to a standstill upon catching sight of the hunter and squatted down into a crouch, watching intently. Bjorn had made a move towards the squatting figure and at that, the Wildman fled once more into the trees. The hunter searched for tracks and sign to follow but his pursuer had left little, disappearing into the undergrowth like a ghost.

Bjorn regarded the sheer rock face of the ravine now enclosing him. It was composed of a dark grainy rock that glistened wet and was streaked with tiny seams of some kind of mineral. Moss and small stringy plants grew from crevices wherever they could get a hold.

Running beside the track he walked upon, a tiny stream trickled over the stones. Bjorn marvelled at the countless years that tiny stream had been eating its way through the bedrock, the years taken to have carved itself a mighty legacy through the mountainside. How long had it taken to cut its way through, perhaps twenty-span of rock? He could not even guess. A testament, Bjorn thought, to the unbreakable will of the water spirit dwelling in the stream.

It was known such spirits shaped all of the vast wilderness through which men roamed. The spirits of trees displacing mighty stones with only their roots, stones that no man could lift alone. The spirits of rivers, which like this small trickling brook beside him, carved through the rock of great mountains. The gods of winter, waging an eternal war against the sun, sheathing the world in ice, and blanketing the lands with snow as for a time, they prevailed.

But only for a time, as the Lords of Summer would soon return to reclaim the world. And so, the years each come to pass. Hart, the great god of the hunt, the great stag who is said to be uncatchable, in turn, ever pursued by mighty Varg and his wolves of war. All of these things, Bjorn knew, dwelt in balance, and had a great power over the lands of man.

Humbled by these thoughts he smiled and looked about him, he was indeed at his most content whilst amongst the primal majesty of the wilderness.

He felt like Hart himself at this moment, pursued and hunted, but he must also now be uncatchable, and to do this, it was to the cunning of Varg he would now look, to turn his pursuer into the hunted.

Bjorn the master huntsman, against him his quarry would not prove as elusive as the mighty Hart. No, not for Bjorn. The gods had always smiled upon him.

The hunter smiled but no longer in contemplative content. Now, his visage took on a widening smirk of a more cunning malice. His eyes sharp, the hungry eyes of a hunter. Bjorn would soon spring his trap.

The ravine turned a dogleg before running uphill straight for maybe a hundred or more paces. At its far end the ravine turned again out of sight. There had been rock slides, small piles of rocks lay here and there. The rock face enclosing him looked high and steep, climbable perhaps, but no quick escape could be made.

This place seemed suitable. His plan, to hide his

horse from view around the bend ahead and conceal himself amongst the rock piles at the far end. To escape, his pursuer would have to come through him or turn and flee along a straight avenue, easily coverable with his bow. If the Wildman was fool enough to rush him, he would discover the hard way the hunter had some skill with an axe.

Bjorn checked the weapon hung at his belt. The bearded hand-axe, gifted to him in Pinedelve, had a good weight. He then surveyed the avenue stretching out before him. Indeed, here he would make his stand.

Ensuring his horse was tethered securely and out of sight, he secreted himself behind a fair-sized boulder. He laid his bow out on the ground before him within easy reach. Then, he drove half a dozen of the black fletched arrows into the earth in a shallow crescent shape so they could be fired in quick succession if required.

Bjorn nodded, his preparations satisfactory. The hunter then settled back against the rocks with a water skin beside him to wait.

The hunters gaze was drawn by the light pattering sound of moccasin covered footfalls. The faint sound, echoed up the ravine towards him. A shadow loomed up the rock wall before a figure appeared. Bjorn sank low against the rocks, peering through a gap between two large stones.

The figure halted to carefully survey the stretch of ravine ahead. The Wildman. He carried what looked like a crude fire hardened spear. He was mostly naked except a filthy pelt around his waist.

He had daubed strange markings on his skin with ash.

Bjorn watched motionless as the man's eyes passed over his hiding place. He held his breath as the Wildman stared for a few long moments. The Wildman continued onwards. He seemed cautious, moving slowly at first, scanning the ridge above. Obviously satisfied nothing lurked overhead, the man sped up into a jog. He seemed to be searching the floor now as he went, searching for sign of his quarries passing.

The Wildman drew closer. Bjorn silently notched an arrow. Not once taking his eyes off the man as he moved near. The hunter's heart pounded in his chest with anticipation. Closer now…closer. He had him.

Bjorn sprang up and levelled his bow at the Wildman. The man froze, his surprised expression turning to panic. He turned to flee but was again frozen still as an arrow thudded into the earth at his feet. The Wildman dropped his spear and slowly turned to face the hunter once more. Seeing another arrow notched and the bow string drawn, the arrow levelled straight at him this time. He raised his hands in a helpless plea as Bjorn stepped out and round the boulder. The man fell to his knees.

'Why do you follow me, Wildman?' demanded Bjorn.

The man babbled nonsense and made strange cooing sounds, his eyes wild and full of fear.

'Not so bold now, are you?' said Bjorn, 'Will you not answer me?'

The Wildman made no reply but continued his

pitiful cooing.

'Can you answer me?' muttered Bjorn under his breath.

'Listen, Wildman, and listen well. Follow me no longer or I *will* kill you...'

Still no reply from the grovelling figure knelt before him.

'Speak damn you,' roared the hunter.

The Wildman shrank back in fear but made no move to leave.

The hunter stood, arrow notched, for a long moment, watching the Wildman scrabble in the dirt before him. The pain in his shoulder was becoming intense. The wound would prevent him from holding the bow drawn for much longer.

Bjorn became uncertain. Was he to kill this wretched creature? The man had become a pest, but could he really justify killing the man? He had in truth not caused the hunter any harm. But would the Wildman return and exact vengeance upon him if he let him go? Or was this show of force and cunning enough to rid the hunter of the menace for good?

Unsure of what to do, Bjorn just stood there. It did not seem the Wildman would reply or that he even understood what was being said to him. He just babbled on, it was no language Bjorn knew, just noises. *No*, Bjorn could not kill him. There was no honour in it.

The hunter lowered his bow and gestured the Wildman off to one side. The man cautiously moved on all fours. Bjorn kicked the spear away from the Wildman and motioned him back off down the ravine with his bow. The Wildman bobbed his head and slowly climbed to his feet, making a strange hooting.

'Go on, go,' said Bjorn pointing out of the ravine. 'But trouble me no more, Wildman.'

The Wildman backed away slowly, still strangely bobbing his head, and then he turned and fled.

Bjorn watched him disappear round the bend heading for the mouth of the ravine. He waited to make sure the Wildman had truly gone, and then collected his things and returned to his horse.

The hunter rode on, leaving the ravine and his encounter with the Wildman far behind him. The land opened up as he rode but was still dominated largely by forest. Large clearings and meadows became more frequent between the stretches of pine forest.

He rode past a farmstead nestled in amongst one such clearing. He rode on, not desiring to stop. He passed others, until Bjorn came upon a lone tavern at a crossroad amongst a sparsely treed wood, its windows and entrance leaking a warm inviting glow and the sounds of revelry. The main building was circular with a low conical roof and had a clutter of smaller outbuildings and a stable. It appeared to have been built around the boles of several trees, their branches carefully encompassed into the roof. It struck the hunter as a very wide, large building to be out here in the middle of nowhere.

Perhaps not so desolate a region as the hunter had first thought, for it seemed the crossroad was well travelled and the tavern certainly didn't lack the clientele judging by the noise floating off through the wood. It seemed the land was becoming more populated. Although he didn't recognise this place from his travels, Bjorn was fairly sure his destination, Old Stones, should not be much further. A few days at most.

He rode on past, leaving the tavern behind him, searching for a more secluded place to camp the night. After all, he didn't need to stop yet, and he had ample provisions and water. And besides, he felt much more at ease alone in the wilds anyway.

The hunter soon came across a suitable place, a hollow beneath the crest of a wooded hill overlooking the road.

He would sleep under the stars this night.

CHAPTER EIGHTEEN

A Hall of Giants

Arnulf followed the cart track which led from the marquee compound in the direction of the the strange hill. The track wound through vistas produced by husks of decaying masonry, and wove around the fallen and crumbled edifices of another age. They reached the slopes of an ancient mound crowned with what appeared to be huge dark monoliths.

The hound took the lead, padding between the wheel ruts of the track. The beast seemed to know where he was going. Arnulf looked up at the strange stones ringing the summit and followed.

The warriors trailed behind him in silence, scanning their flanks with wary eyes. The tale of the sudden attack on their lords had spread quickly amongst the warriors. Each expecting another ambush at any moment, but none came.

The track ran between two of the great stones. The ruddy torchlight flickered shadows across the smooth surface of the great sentinel stones.

Arnulf looked up in awe as he passed and laid a hand on the surface of one of the standing stones. He flinched back. The smooth cold stone felt full of watchful malice. He shuddered, and then looked both stones up and down once more, before continuing onwards.

A complex of ruins lay within the circle of great stones. The remains of walls and crude arches formed a network of crumbled corridors.

The hound looked around warily and sniffed at the ground. Arnulf watched as it left the cart track and made its way into one of the collapsed corridors.

Arnulf took a torch from one of his men and peered after the hound.

'Your giant's hall,' said Arnulf as Fergus moved up beside him.

The two men stood a moment looking into the gloomy corridor. Then, Arnulf followed after the hound.

The shattered walls of the corridor gave way to open space at the summit of the hill. The bare earth underfoot, carpeted in places by patches of thin grass. The air had a thick fetid stench, the smell of death and decay.

The hound moved ahead still sniffing the floor. At the centre of the enclosed space, a stone slab emerged from the gloom. As Arnulf moved nearer, closely followed by the ever present Hafgan and the others, he could see it appeared to be some kind of ghastly altar.

Adorned with bones and strange glyphs, the altar stone had a dread feel emanating from it. Upon the altar sat several skulls, grinning through the gloom at Arnulf as he approached.

An ornate dagger lay upon the altar and was largely unsoiled, its twisted blade still polished. A small tattered journal rested beside it. Arnulf picked it up.

It was blood splattered. He leafed through the pages. It appeared to be field notes of some sort, an eclectic collection of notes and sketches. He saw rough sketches similar to those he found back in the marquee. Sketches of anatomy and body parts interspersed with passages of scrawled text.

He flipped to the most recent notes. More sketches of the body, but these were unnervingly covered in strange glyphs. He realised he had seen this firsthand, on the corpses left in the valley. Some had similar glyphs carved into their flesh. Arnulf was left in no doubt, there was certainly some connection between the College's work here and the dead they had encountered. He took the dagger and the journal and tucked them away into his cloak.

The ground beneath his feet seemed to crunch as he walked away from the altar. As his attention was drawn to the ground, he noticed it also felt sticky on his boots. Arnulf lowered his torch. The ground seemed to seethe with dark beetles. The tiny beasts were feasting upon a dried gore that plastered the ground about the altar. Arnulf stepped back with revulsion, only to crunch upon more of them as he did.

The warriors moved about the summit inspecting shadowed avenues and stonework at the edges of the enclosed space, few wished to venture too close to the terrible altar at its centre.

Hafgan called out and beckoned Arnulf over.

'What is it, Haf?'

'Listen, what is that?'

A low sound of hoarse moaning, rising to the occasional muffled snarl, could be heard from somewhere nearby. The strange sound seemed to be coming from outside the summit's enclosure, through the ruins of stone.

'It's coming from over there,' said Hafgan, pointing off into the darkness of a ruined corridor that led down the slope of the hill.

'Let's take a look but be careful, I don't want any surprises.'

'Aye, always, lord.'

They stood aghast in silence at the horror they now found before them. The pit appeared to be the source of the sound. It had been recently dug and had mostly steep sides. Its occupants clawed the mud, snarling up at them to no avail. They were trapped.

The hound cowered low to the ground behind them, whimpering and barking, it would not approach any closer. It was afraid. Even the hound knew, what was in that pit was terrifyingly unnatural.

Arnulf stood wrapped in his fur cloak, flanked by Hafgan and Fergus. The other chosen men stood around them. All eyes fixed on the pit before them.

The pit had been filled with the dead, a mass grave of mutilated corpses. Unnaturally, impossibly reanimated, brought back from Old Night's cold embrace, but not alive. The occupants had been long dead. Indeed, some had limbs missing and trailed their stinking innards as they clawed their way through the wet mud, reaching towards the living observers above.

Arnulf's thoughts took him back to the pictures within the great tome in the marquee. These wretched creatures, the subject of some dire experimentation, this the foul work of the College.

The mud swarmed with the beetles that feasted on the blood drenched soil. Black feathers of scavenging birds lay about. It seemed one or two had ventured too close to the more mobile dead, to their end.

The side of the pit furthest down the slope was shallower. Drag marks through the mud on that side, showed that many of the previous occupants had clawed their way free.

Another shallower trench lay nearby, empty, but again signs of escape showed on the ground.

How many bodies had been dumped here? It was impossible to tell. How many of these shambling corpses still roamed the area?

One of the dead clutched at Arnulf. It's snarling maw snapping and biting the air. Its eyes had been pecked away, the skin of its legs peeled back and removed in sections. Its legs too damaged, it was unable to rise to its feet, as were the other remaining occupants, trapped here to rot away into oblivion.

'Haf!' said Arnulf, breaking the silence amongst the living. 'Destroy them. End this!'

With a gesture from Hafgan, several of the warriors notched arrows and began to feather the occupants of the pit. The light, but normally withering, torrent of arrows gradually subsided. It quickly became apparent the arrows had little effect. Several of the bowmen lowered their weapons. Quivers near empty, they had wasted many arrows. One or two of the corpses had stopped moving, but others still grasped at them.

'It's as it was at the pass, Arnulf. Our arrows are near useless,' said Hafgan quietly.

Arnulf frowned. 'Then we burn them.' Gesturing to several of the men, he said, 'Go gather what branches and dry grass you can, anything that burns. Quickly and don't go far!'

The warriors dumped what they could onto the struggling corpses; there was not much, mostly thorny branches and dead grass. Arnulf threw his torch down to ignite the grass. A few others followed suit, their torches pitching into the pit.

As the flames grew higher, an orange light was cast upon the ruins about. The figures below seemed oblivious of the fire as it consumed them, hands still writhing and clutching upwards through the branches as the dead flesh seared and burnt. A sweet sickly smelling smoke rose and swirled off into the night. The warriors of Arnar stood watching in silence.

'We return to the marquee, lads,' said Arnulf after a while. 'And make haste.'

The warriors turned and returned to the cart track. Arnulf stood a moment watching the blackening hands still clutching up at him. His hands shook, and he again steadied them upon the familiar comfort of his old axe. Fergus appeared beside him.

'Poor bastards,' said Fergus. 'Old night take them. No spirit deserves such a curse. It's a shame, though.'

Arnulf turned, his expression questioning. He noticed Astrid and two shield-maidens nearby. Hafgan awaited them a few paces behind.

'A shame?' he asked.

'No giants,' said Fergus.

Arnulf forced a grim smile, both men trying not to think of the horrors within the burning pit behind them.

'Imagine the tales if we had found giants,' mused Fergus.

'I'd rather not. My eyes have seen enough terrible things these last nights, old friend. Will I ever sleep again?'

'Aye, Arnulf, the gods have stretched my nerves, too, but if I don't laugh, I fear I may never again. Come, let us leave this place.'

Arnulf strode away from the pit, trying his best to keep his reserve in front of the other warriors. The hound padded along nervously beside him, staying close. His shaking hands, clutched tightly to his axe as he walked. His legs felt weak, yet he kept his stride steady, leaving the orange glow of the fire, flickering behind him.

As the group returned to the marquee compound, a small group of warriors came out to greet them.

'We saw a fire, lord,' said the lead man as they approached.

'Aye, nothing to worry about,' said Arnulf.

The returning warriors behind Arnulf exchanged glances but said nothing.

'The warrior, I fear he has lost his mind,' said the lead man.

'He is awake?' asked Arnulf.

'Aye, but we have not been able to get near him. He was thrashing at his ropes, trying to get free.'

'His arm is bad, we think he is blood sick from his wound,' said one of the warriors.

'That's not all, lord. He became so violent in his rage, even bound, he began smashing his head against the walls in fury. He smashed his head in pretty good, lord.'

Fergus cursed.

'How is he now?' asked Fergus.

'We tied him down. He is weak, and he hasn't stopped bleeding. He's making little sense, but he is still struggling in fits of anger, screaming at us. We have left him tied down.'

'He is insane, lord,' said another warrior darkly.

'Show us,' said Arnulf.

They followed the warrior back into the marquee. Olad lay on the table. He had been lashed down with rope but still he struggled violently, his eyes wild and dark. Blood smeared his mouth and his chest. Dried blood stained his hands. A foul putrid smell of decay hung about him. It appeared he had recently feasted on raw putrefied flesh. His face was bruised and bloody. His nose and ears bled. There was blood in his hair, and it had begun to pool around his head. Arnulf was shocked at the repeated force it would have taken to inflict this upon himself.

Arnulf looked down in disgust and seized the man's arm to look. Olad roared in pain and fury, but was too weak to resist.

There was fresh blood on his clothes. Hafgan's axe had not cut deep. The glancing blow made a shallow cut into his side and sliced up to his armpit. It bled still, the table slick with his blood.

Arnulf also quickly noticed the arm, it had blackened. He lifted it. It smelt of rot. The bite wound on the girl at the farmstead had festered just like this. Dark tissue had spread around the teeth marks and the darkened flesh had moved up his arm onto his shoulder.

Hafgan stepped close and spoke quietly into his lord's ear. 'Arnulf, that wound,' whispered Hafgan. 'I have not seen it's like, except…the girl.'

Arnulf dropped the arm and threw Hafgan a grave stare. Olad seemed to have passed out.

'Did he wound anyone while you restrained him?' Hafgan asked of the warrior who had led them.

'No, Haf. None,' replied the warrior.

Hafgan nodded. He frowned thoughtfully.

'Lord,' said one of the warriors suddenly. 'He's not breathing.'

'Are you sure?' said Fergus as everyone turned their attention to the bound warrior.

'His chest no longer rises or falls,' replied the

warrior. He moved closer.

'Careful, lad, don't let him bite you,' cautioned Hafgan.

The warrior reached forward and warily checked for breath with his hand, his eyes locked on Olad's face. He shook his head.

Hafgan moved closer and picked up Olad's limp arm. It was growing cold. He let it flop back down.

Hafgan shook his head. 'It looks like he is with the gods, Fergus.'

Fergus cursed and sighed over the body his fallen warrior. 'Poor bastard,' he muttered.

There was a sudden snarl as Olad jerked into a violent fit, thrashing against the ropes once more.

'Varg's balls,' cursed Fergus in shock.

Hafgan jumped back in alarm.

'Is he dead?' exclaimed Fergus.

'I would have sworn he was,' replied Hafgan darkly.

All in the room backed away from the table.

'One way to be sure,' said Astrid in a grim tone. She approached the bound warrior. He thrashed wildly and snarled up at her, but the ropes were too strong. She unsheathed a seax from its scabbard at her waist and held the blade over him, ready to stab Olad's chest.

She looked at Fergus, waiting for his command.

After a moment of uncertainty, staring into Olad's dark wild eyes, Fergus sighed heavily and gestured for her to continue.

She plunged the blade into his heart. It made no effect. Still, Olad snarled and struggled. She pulled the seax free and stabbed again. She looked up bewildered. She must have pierced his heart, yet still, he was not still. She growled angrily. Olad screeched in reply and snapped his jaws. His eyes had discoloured and darkened. The black of his pupils held a dark malice and stared fixedly at her.

Astrid took a step back, and then drew her sword. With a cry of frustration, she cleaved a heavy blow into the dead man's head. And then another. After a third Olad flopped down still.

Astrid's breathing was heavy. 'Mother save us,' she gasped. 'How in Varg's name was he still alive?'

'I'm not sure that he was,' added Hafgan after a moment.

The shocked wordlessness once again returned to smother all in the marquee into a fear tinted silence. Arnulf's hands were shaking. He made a fist and collected himself. He turned to Fergus. 'Whatever transpired here,' said Arnulf, 'it is done.' Arnulf turned to the big warrior beside him. 'Haf, prepare the men to leave immediately. We return to the lowlands, I will not spend a night amongst these cursed ruins. We take what we can back with us.' He strode over to the great tome, still upon the table inside the more lavish tent. He took out the twisted dagger from his cloak, and the tattered journal, and placed them on the books cover. 'We take these,' he said, resting his hand upon the tome. 'And get the men to gather as many of these other books and scrolls as can be carried. The scholars will take a look on our return. We will find out what they have been up to. And your father must hear of this,' the latter said to Fergus.

'And what of him?' asked Hafgan, nodding to the

warrior laid cold upon on the table.

'We take him,' said Fergus. 'My warriors will prepare some means of carrying him.'

'We should burn him,' said Arnulf suddenly, 'like we did the others.'

They all looked at him aghast.

'I should return him to his family, Arnulf,' said Fergus.

'No,' replied Arnulf. 'We should not risk it. We take him back to the mound of dead in the valley and burn them, him with them. We cannot risk them coming back again.'

Fergus was silent a long moment, then he nodded.

Arnulf strode from the marquee with the hound trailing at his heals. He shook his head.

'Still no answers, only questions,' said Arnulf to himself.

'Aye, questions for the College men I think,' said Fergus, as he joined Arnulf. 'Perhaps our scholars can shed some light on that tome upon our return. Answers to all this.'

The torchlight flickered shadows on his face, Arnulf gave a bitter laugh.

'Indeed,' said Arnulf dryly. 'Scholars? They're all College scholars…' He shook his head. 'I've never trusted their like. No honour, no desire for renown.' He spat. 'As meek as lambs, yet still cunning and full of deceit.'

'You think they will lie to us? To my father?' said Fergus.

'To hide the folly of their brothers? Perhaps, I could see that,' said Arnulf, frowning. He sighed and threw a long searching look into the dark ruins about them, his gaze settling on the direction of the monoliths crowning the hill. Shrouded now in darkness, he could not make them out. But still his eyes lingered there a moment. He suddenly laughed.

Fergus looked at him bewildered. 'Something funny?' asked Fergus.

'A giant's hall,' laughed Arnulf grimly.

Fergus chuckled also, and then, as the oppressive darkness stole his mirth, he said, 'Come, old friend. Let's leave this accursed place. I don't like the way the shadows watch us.'

CHAPTER NINETEEN

A Gift of Stone

They came swiftly from the darkness without warning. Faces painted in ghastly white skulls. There was no sound, the scene unfolding in silence. They seized his legs and dragged him away. Bjorn cried out in terror, but no sound would come forth. Clawing the ground, he desperately tried to escape their grasp. They were too strong. He dug his fingers into the soft earth leaving deep furrows in his wake. He reached out for branches but everything was out of reach.

He could see their bare feet, the skulls adorning their waists and the bone fetishes they wore in their hair. He couldn't make out any of them clearly. Spears of sharpened branches jabbed towards his face as he was dragged along like the helpless prey of a hill cat. The scene seemed to be unfolding in a dreadful slow motion.

A ruddy glow appeared ahead through the trees, he seemed to be heading towards it. Then came the flicker of flames. Bjorn could make out silhouettes of manic savages dancing and wheeling around the fire. He could hear their whoops and shouts.

A loud horn blew. That same horn he had heard north of the border whilst making his escape. That same terrifying sound of pursuit, that which had spurred him onwards in terror, leaving his stomach in his mouth, those terrible horns of the hunt. The sound was appallingly loud, filling his skull with its mocking braying.

He was dumped on the floor beside the fire. A familiar face stared down at him from above the flames. A mocking grin upon his face, the Wildman did not even writhe or struggle as the flames licked over his skin.

Burly hands seized him once more. Bjorn fought and kicked but to no avail. He was bound to a pole and hoisted over the fire. He began screaming. Still he could hear no sound, just the crackling of the flames and the manic celebrations of the Stonemen as they danced around him. He wept, helpless and terrified. They had him, there was no escape this time, and they would eat him.

He sensed a dull thud which shook his body. A shrieking skull painted face suddenly thrust itself into his vision. The savage's features were strange and heavy set. Her brow ridge and chin were pronounced. Her teeth filed sharp. She raised a charred arm and took a bite, tearing off flesh to the bone. She shrieked again and waved the arm in his face. The arm he knew. It was his own.

He shrieked again, panic and terror overcoming him as he watched her chewing his flesh. She raised a stone axe and screeched something at him.

The world around him slowed as she brandished the axe over him. The flames licked around him. The savages slowly dancing and wheeling in the flickering light. He turned to the Wildman, still alive, still grinning back at him through the consuming flames.

He looked into the darkness between the surrounding trees. Figures stood there watching, faces he knew, dozens peering from the darkness amongst the trees. He picked out the face of his father, stood watching solemnly. The Wildman stood watching also. And beside them, her face, a face he often longed to see again. The axe descended.

***

Bjorn awoke with a start, his heart pounding. A dream… Such a terrible dream.

He glanced over at the fire. He expected it to have burnt low to mere embers but, instead, the flame still flickered. The dawn was still some time off and the birds hadn't yet awakened. His shoulder ached painfully.

There was an odd smell. He sat up suddenly as he saw the fire. A spitted rabbit sat over the flames, slowly dripping juices which hissed into the hearth. He had company.

His hand reached for his axe, it still lay beside him where he had left it. Looking about, his eyes fell on the intruder.

Calmly sat by the fire, the Wildman watched him intently. Bjorn cursed. Anger flared behind the hunter's eyes. Bjorn sprang into a low crouch, his axe readied.

The Wildman made no move. He simply regarded the hunter calmly over the flames. The fire cast an orange radiance over the Wildman's face. He then reached over the hearth and tore off a leg from the rabbit. The bones snapped as he tore it lose. The Wildman tossed the cooked meat at Bjorn's feet and motioned for him to eat. The Wildman turned his attention back to turning the spit.

Bjorn remained on his feet, his eyes fixed on the Wildman. He had thought to attack the intruder.

Then he cursed again and slumped back down with a long sigh, retrieving the meat from the floor. He sniffed at the Wildman's offering and brushed off the dirt as best he could.

He had always enjoyed rabbit, and it smelt good. Yet, something in that smell repulsed him. He stared long at the rabbit leg until the grease began to run down his fingers. The hunter then threw his gaze at the rest of the rabbit cooking over the fire, its flesh charred and red, grease dripping into the flames with a hiss. The entire scene echoed his dream—his nightmare. He shuddered. His imagination placed himself on that spit, slowly turning over the flames.

Was he still dreaming?

Bjorn could not bring himself to take a bite, his stomach felt uneasy. He delicately handed the leg back to the Wildman and shook his head. The

Wildman looked confused but took the meat from him and took a bite himself.

Bjorn sat back and regarded the Wildman. The Wildman stared back as he chewed, the grease running down his chin. Then the Wildman reached into his furs and drew out a crude knife. Bjorn started at the sight of it but before he could react, the Wildman threw the knife at the hunter's feet. He then nodded and motioned for the hunter to pick it up.

The hunter picked up the knife and examined it, turning it in his hands. It was made of stone. A worked stone blade as long the palm of his hand, made from a long shard of flint. The handle was made of wrapped bark and bound tightly with sinew and strips of the same malleable bark, silver accai pine he judged.

Although crude, it was a thing of breath-taking beauty and made with great skill.

'You made this?' asked the hunter shaking the knife.

The Wildman tilted his head and looked confused. He did not understand Bjorn's words. The hunter sighed in frustration. He then gathered up separate hands full of dirt and twigs, and closed them together in front of him.

'You…make?' asked the hunter slowly while pointing at the Wildman and pressing the dirt and twigs together, and then winding is hand around as if binding it all together. He then held the knife up, hoping the strange Wildman would understand.

The Wildman simply laughed.

Bjorn cursed under his breath.

'This is pointless,' muttered the hunter his frustration growing.

'It's very nice,' said Bjorn as he handed the knife back to the Wildman with a forced smile. He would talk at the savage anyway, even if he received no answer in return.

The Wildman shook his head and pushed the knife back into the hunter's hands.

'You want me to have this?'

The Wildman stared back blankly.

Bjorn laughed, bemused at the gesture. He shook his head. He turned the knife over in his hands once more, indeed a thing of crude beauty. The firelight flickered and danced across the faceted surface of the worked flint.

'A fine gift. Thank you, Wildman,' said Bjorn sincerely. Bjorn regarded the stone knife one last time before tucking it into his belt.

The hunter cradled his axe in his lap, ever ready for some sudden move. None came. Bjorn felt ever more certain the Wildman did not intend to harm him. After all, he had the chance, whilst the hunter had slept. Instead the Wildman had stolen silently into the camp and made himself at home. The hunter sat bewildered by the situation.

The Wildman turned the rabbit once more and then, satisfied with the meat, lifted the spit off the fire and sniffed it. He offered the spit over to the hunter but the hunter waved it away. The Wildman began breaking off pieces of cooked meat and eating it.

'So, Wildman, here we are again,' said Bjorn conversationally.

The Wildman, engrossed in his food, seemed to

be mostly ignoring the hunter's presence as he ate.

'You are a strange one,' continued the hunter. 'Why do you follow me? Why track me for leagues when you could have simply slipped away? And then,' said Bjorn shaking his head in disbelief, 'still not fearing me, even after I had you staring down the shaft of an arrow, bow drawn, ready to kill you.

'Do you feel you owe me some debt? After I helped you escape the others of your kind. After I showed you mercy? Twice now delivering you from Old Night's grasp. You owe me nothing, Wildman.'

The Wildman ate his rabbit as the hunter talked on.

'Wildman...' said Bjorn in thought. 'You must have a name? Some title?'

But how could he make this savage understand him? The hunter thought a moment, before rising to his feet and drawing the Wildman's curious gaze.

The hunter gestured to himself, pointing.

'Bjorn. I am Bjorn,' he said slowly, placing a hand on his chest.

He then pointed at the Wildman, inviting the savage to respond.

The Wildman stared back, cocking his head.

'Bjorn,' tried the hunter again, again pointing to himself, and then back at the Wildman.

He awaited a reply, but none came, just a blank level stare.

Bjorn sank back down and sighed.

'Pointless,' muttered the hunter.

'*Tung...*'

Bjorn looked up startled. The Wildman had spoken. It was the first time he had heard him speak.

'Tung,' repeated the Wildman, now bobbing his head.

'Et acha ay imeeuw,' continued the Wildman. The savage then gestured at himself and repeated, *'Tung.'*

'I don't understand you, friend. But now at least we are getting somewhere,' said Bjorn.

The hunter pointed at the Wildman and repeated the word, 'Tung?'

The Wildman bobbed his head frantically and repeated the word himself.

'Tung,' said the savage with a sharp rap on his own chest.

Then the Wildman gestured towards the hunter and said *'Jorn.'*

'Aye, yes,' replied Bjorn nodding. 'Bjorn,' he repeated with his hand on his chest.

'So, I will call you, Tung,' said the hunter, settling back against a tree. 'Perhaps, in time, you can tell me what you want with me, Wildman...Tung, even.'

The Wildman cocked his head not understanding the hunter's words and now remained silent. After a few moments of silence, the Wildman again returned to his food.

Finishing his handful of dripping rabbit, Tung rose to his feet, wiping his hands on his furs. He calmly walked off into the shadows of the hill's summit. The hunter heard him scrabbling around in the rocks that had fallen from the hollow's sides.

'Where are you going, Tung?' called Bjorn.

The Wildman returned without attempting a reply, carrying an armful of stones, and dumped them beside the fire.

Bjorn looked on curiously as the Wildman picked out two rocks and began hammering the two stones together, smashing a large piece with a smaller one. The sharp, rhythmic *clicks* rang out loudly from the hollow and echoed off into the darkness.

Bjorn watched on, curious.

'What are you doing now, Wildman?'

There came no reply. The Wildman, he now knew as Tung, continued working on the stone, ignoring the hunter.

With a loud *crack,* the Wildman split the large stone along some hidden seam. With another few skilful strikes, Tung shattered one of the pieces into splinters of stone shards. The savage held one up to the flickering light of the fire.

Flint, he is working flint.

The hunter watched as Tung worked the stone, skillfully chipping away at the edges, making another blade of stone. He was making another knife. Bjorn began to see the Wildman in another light, impressed by his apparent knowledge and skill.

The pair sat for some time in silence facing each other over the fire, Bjorn watching the Wildman work on his knife. The Wildman hardly acknowledged the hunter as he worked. Except only occasionally offering more of the rabbit, to which Bjorn again shook his head.

The silence stretched on, and Bjorn's thoughts turned to his nightmare, still fresh in his mind. Those faces staring back at him out of the darkness. He thought of his father. A quiet man, he was a hunter like himself. He let his thoughts drift back to memories of younger times, hunting with his father in the southern woods.

He remembered the first time his father had let him take the opening shot on a deer they had stalked all morning. How he had begged for the chance, and when the day came, he had missed his mark. His father was not angry, ever calm and patient. But Bjorn never forgot that shot, vowing to never miss another. Of course he did. He missed many times back then, but never once did his father get angry, even after many slow hours of stalking a target.

The hunter smiled as he sat before the dwindling fire. Still he never forgot that first attempt, the disappointment, he was so desperate to make his father proud. That memory had always spurred him on to learn, to be the best, to eventually gain the deadly proficiency he was now widely known for.

The hunter couldn't fathom why his father's face had been in the dream, perhaps witnessing the shame of his failure, his final and most fatal failure. Would his father be watching the day he finally went to meet Old Night? Would he have made him proud in the end?

Sat watching the Wildman but barely seeing, another face haunted him more than any other, her face. Her sad eyes staring out from the gloom as he burned, as vivid as the day they had last fixed upon his. Those sharp knowing eyes that saw right through him, saw straight through to his heart truer than any arrow he could aim. He often thought of that face. Her enchanting beauty had ensnared him all those years ago, those seductive looks she gave him, how could he resist her.

And was she still waiting for him? Would she wait all this time for him? He remembered the promise he made. He had not been to her. How long had it been? Years, too many years. He would have done anything for her it seemed. Anything but stay. He sighed. He knew he had been a fool every time he cast his mind back to her face. The face of a love that haunted his dreams once more.

After some time of staring into the flames lost in thought Bjorn slowly began to notice once more the steady sound of the Wildman, still delicately chipping at the flint. Then the sound ceased. Bjorn looked up, his eyes heavy and weary. Tung held the flint blade up to the fire and nodded, making an excited whooping, the first sound he had made for some time.

Then, taking up a discarded flake of the shattered flint the Wildman began scraping the rabbits pelt that lay spread before the fire. Fighting his fatigue, Bjorn sat up. Although he felt in no danger, he did not think it prudent to descend back in to sleep with this strange intruder sharing his camp. So, he watched, too tired to continue his questioning monologue with his seemingly taciturn guest.

The hunter watched as the Wildman scraped at the discarded rabbit pelt. Bjorn was more than familiar with this practice himself and was curious to watch the technique the savage employed. The hunter would have taken the process much further, drying and stretching, a process that can take days if done properly. But after crudely scraping away the tissue off the hide Tung seemed satisfied and began to cut the hide into strips with the flint blade.

He wrapped the stone blade and fashioned a rough fur hide handle. He then began binding parts of the handle with short strips of sinew he had obviously removed from the butchered rabbit carcass before spitting the animal over the fire. All done in silence as Bjorn had slept. How long had he sat there? Quietly sharing the hunter's camp as he slept.

The light of dawn had begun to show on the horizon when the Wildman finally set the newly made knife down beside the waning embers of the fire to dry out the handle. It had not taken long but still a good while to make—Bjorn was not certain exactly how long he had sat there watching the Wildman work. In that time, the Wildman he now called Tung had fashioned a tool, possibly a half-decent weapon, in the matter of only hours. The hunter watched on impressed, fighting off the encroaching weariness to remain awake and vigilant.

Bjorn awoke with a start. He had dozed off, unable to fight sleep any longer. The fire had burnt down. The sun had risen, but it was still early. He had not slept long. The Wildman slept opposite the smoking remains of his fire. Not a dream then.

Quietly gathering his things, Bjorn prepared to leave. He intended to leave alone, leaving the Wildman to his slumber and quietly slipping away before he woke. The hunter had no doubt the Wildman would follow, but he intended to put some distance between them.

As Bjorn crept to his horse, which was tethered to a nearby tree, he heard a strange hoot. Sighing, the hunter slowly turned. Tung was now sat up and regarding him curiously. Bjorn seemed to feel the shame of a child caught in the act of some naughty deed.

Hastily gathering his knife and the remnants of the rabbit, the Wildman scrabbled around making ready to leave. He rose to retrieve his spear leaning against a tree, obviously recovered from the ravine.

Bjorn had been quiet, not quite silent, but still, the hunter could move like a ghost through the brush. Still he had woken the Wildman. The movement of his passing shadow had perhaps woken him? Bjorn could not say but something had obviously stirred the Wildman's senses and alerted him to the hunter's departure.

Sighing, the hunter turned and untethered his horse. Reaching into a pouch hung off the saddle, he brought forth a handful of oats. He held out the oats to his horse and stroked the beast's muzzle, talking gently as it quickly devoured the offering.

He surveyed the road ahead. The muddy track carved through the hillside and wound through the low valley lying below to the southwest, disappearing into the distant trees. Another few days ride, and he would reach Old Stones and the waiting lord, Archeon.

He swung himself into the saddle and looked back at the camp. Tung stood, leaning on his spear with his head cocked quizzically, studying the hunter.

Bjorn nudged the horse forward down the slope and made for the track below. The Wildman followed.

The hunter kicked his horse into a canter as he reached the track.

The Wildman ran along behind the hunter's horse, easily keeping pace. Bjorn was impressed. Tung then moved up to the hunter's offside, running nearly parallel beside him, but remaining slightly behind.

Bjorn found himself bemused by his strange and unexpected companion.

Turning in his saddle, Bjorn called out, 'So Wildman, if you intend to keep following me, you had best keep up.'

Bjorn kicked his horse onwards. The Wildman made no response, his face focused and resolute. He did not falter. The Wildman simply adjusted his pace to match the horse and inexorably ran on.

CHAPTER TWENTY

Fear and Smoke

'Fear.'

'Fear?' repeated Fergus questioningly.

'Aye, Fear,' replied Arnulf.

'What did you feel when you first laid eyes on him? Were you not afraid?' asked Arnulf as the pair rode at the head of the stretched column of weary warriors, all eager to return to their homes.

'Of course not…'

Arnulf glanced sideways at his old friend and snorted in amused derision.

'And it was his fear that likely kept him alive when his masters died. He fled from those things like any sane creature would—perhaps from his own dead master—and lurked afraid in those woods awaiting the arrival of someone...alive. Imagine it, the poor beast. His fear kept him alive.'

Arnulf threw a glance at the hound as it padded along beside his horse. The great shaggy beast was wagging its tail and sniffing around, no doubt excited by the many different scents of the moor.

Arnulf smiled as he watched the beast, it seemed calm, content.

The weary straggle of warriors had descended the pass and now moved away from the Waystone, heading back over the moor. Each step away from the ruins and the eerie slopes of the High Passes noticeably lifted the spirits of the tired warriors as they trudged along the moor trail.

They had left the remnants of the grisly pyre far behind. The pyre now marked Arnulf's legacy of his first encounter with the dead ones. The body of the warrior, Olad, had burned along with the rest. The grim monument of twisted, charred limbs and desiccated black faces now stood sentry over the path up into the High Passes. The pyre stood as a dire reminder to the passing warriors of their nightmarish foe. Many amongst them hoped it had perhaps just been a terrible dream, a dream of insanity and murder, and of dead men that walked.

The last of the warriors and guardsmen filed past the ancient Waystone. The monolith cast its ethereal shadows over the warriors as they marched past. The great carved stone, an ancient marker for the route up into the mountains, laid by the forgotten people of millennia past. It was now said amongst the weary warriors that the old stone was perhaps even an ancient ward from the evil that dwelt in those high forgotten places. All these years, the Waystone had protected these lands, preventing the sleeping evil from spilling down into the lands of Arnar. That tale would surely prevail given the recent events of the past nights.

'So, you will name the beast, Fear?' asked Fergus.

'Aye, it seems an apt name, don't you think?'

'I suppose, as good as any. And as you're naming the miserable beast, you intend to keep it?'

'Aye, I think I will.'

The great grey hound lifted its shaggy head to regard his new master. Its tongue lolled out as it panted, before running off to sniff at the base of a gorse thicket.

'Rabbits,' commented Fergus. 'Perhaps it will make a good hunting dog.'

The flame haired lord steered his mount around another thicket of gorse in his path. The thorned-bush had encroached over one half of the seldom travelled track. Its spiny, yellow flowered branches forming a formidable obstacle which Fergus did not desire to risk his horse's hooves near. It was known, one of those long thorns could make a horse lame if it pierced the softer sole of its hoof.

Returning to the track, Fergus reined in his horse beside Arnulf once more. Arnulf stared off ahead. Fergus noted his friends weathered face; he seemed worn, older somehow. It had not been long since the summer feasts in which they had drunk and revelled as they always had. Fergus had not noticed it then but now Arnulf's once rich dark brown hair had become streaked with flecks of grey. His eyes were cracked with lines and they hung heavy in his weariness.

After a moment Fergus spoke, 'You seem distant, Arnulf?'

'Aye…I was thinking about Hagen and the others.'

A moment of silence passed between them.

'Hagen was a fine warrior. I still can't believe he is dead,' said Fergus finally. 'I remember training with him when we were lads. Do you remember?'

'Aye, I remember,' replied Arnulf with a faint smile.

'You never could parry that strike, remember? That rising strike would smash you in the guts every time,' said Fergus with a grin. The red-haired warrior settled back in his saddle and stroked his long beard as he cast his mind back to his youth.

Arnulf laughed. 'Aye. The bastard was always so quick.'

'And he could drink,' mused Fergus, 'was always a good laugh at the feasts.'

'He was one of my best,' continued Arnulf. 'We fought together under my father's banner at Aeginhall. He fought beside me. It was our first proper battle if you think back. He always kept an eye out for us,' said Arnulf.

'Aye, that was a good fight,' replied Fergus. 'He kept you from pissing your breeches you mean.' Fergus laughed, leaning over and slapping Arnulf on the back.

Arnulf smirked and threw a fist into his friend's arm.

'You're a funny piece of shit.'

They laughed.

Fergus's face became solemn. 'I will not forget old Hagen. I know my father will be saddened to hear of it.'

'Aye,' said Arnulf, thinking of his own father before going on, 'Well, my father awaits him in the Halls of Night. He will keep him in good company. They can drink together again, and we will see them all again one day.'

'Not too soon, though,' said Fergus.

'Aye,' agreed Arnulf.

He turned to look at the warriors trailing behind them. Hafgan rode close behind, his face grim yet ever resolute. Erran rode further back beside one of Fergus's maiden guard, the two appeared to be bickering and disputing some proposed contest of skill. It seemed she would have him prove himself against one of their own before having the honour of sparring with their renowned leader. The young lad was no match for the fierce faced warrior, she had him flustered. She wore an amused look as she taunted him. Astrid's other warriors laughed with her.

The Death Nymph rode sombrely at the head of the group. She didn't join her comrades in their sport, instead riding hard faced. Arnulf thought, either purposefully ignoring the exchange behind her or genuinely lost in hard distant thoughts, he could not tell.

Arnulf smirked and shook his head. The young warrior made him laugh. Erran was a cocky shit sometimes and funny with it. It was hard not to like the boy. But he was no match for the wit of these renowned vipers. These were not young soft girls who had never left their town; these women had become seasoned weather-worn killers. The particular warrior Erran was bandying words with, looked to be one of their best. A weathered woman with tightly woven dark hair, her leather armour looked worn and knowingly modified with patches of mail. She looked like a warrior who knew her business. Arnulf did not doubt she could best the young lad.

Beyond them and the other riders, the remaining warriors and guardsmen trudged in the wake of the horses, tired and drained yet glad to be marching away from the now dreaded passes and their nightmare encounters with the stumbling dead.

Some way behind the loose column, a pair of riders rode as a rear guard. Every now and again glimpses of the other outriders could be seen, galloping between the thickets of gorse and rocky outcrops as they scouted the flanks and the moorlands ahead.

Arnulf sighed and with a grimace turned back to the track ahead.

'I do not look forward to telling Eadith, the poor woman. It will break her heart,' said Arnulf.

'Hagen was good to her. She loved him dearly, a good old maid indeed.' Fergus sighed. 'It's sad, aye.'

Thinking it best to change the subject, Fergus asked, 'Still, I bet you look forward to getting back to the Motte.'

'Aye. It's been a long few months stuck up there,' replied Arnulf. 'I've only been back what two, maybe three times, since last winter. Last time was…'

'Summer feasts,' Fergus cut in, 'we drank that whole barrel and Ewolf punched your man Erran for beating him in that arm wrestle. Good night that,' laughed Fergus.

'He's a good lad, Ewolf. He's grown so fast, becoming a man. Still, he shouldn't have done that, regardless how funny it was. They will be his men one day, I hope.'

'I wonder where he gets that from, ha. You've got a good boy there, Arnulf. He will do well.'

Arnulf smiled.

'Like his father,' added Fergus with a smile at his childhood friend.

'It will be good to see my girls again,' said Arnulf.

'Idony is a sweet little maid too, full of mischief. I think I'd like a daughter,' mused Fergus.

'Well, you know what to do,' said Arnulf with a sly grin.

Fergus laughed.

'Aeslin will be glad I'm back. A wife needs her lord…I hope,' said Arnulf with a grin. 'I hear she's done well with the Motte too, although she's probably used to it by now though, all those disputes and petitions—pain in the arse as I'm sure you've discovered by now—and Ewolf, I'm sure, has helped her in my stead.'

Fergus nodded in agreement.

'Aye, it will be good to get back to her. I've missed her on those cold nights up there,' said Arnulf.

'I bet, you old dog,' laughed Fergus. 'She's a pretty one, your Aeslin.'

'Eyes off, old man, she's mine,' laughed Arnulf, 'Besides she wouldn't be interested in fat old ginger bastard like you.'

'Fat!' exclaimed Fergus. 'You should speak for yourself.'

They laughed again.

'Aye, I look forward to getting home. I'll send someone else up to finish the watch I think, not long now—'til the snows come anyway—then it's some other poor buggers turn to command next year's watch.'

'Aye, good choice,' agreed Fergus.

'I will ride for Eymsford, perhaps tomorrow,' said Arnulf thoughtfully. 'I will need to speak to your father. He will need to be told what has happened here,' said Arnulf. He hesitated. 'I fear he won't believe me. Would you in his place? If you had not seen what we saw with your own eyes?'

Fergus frowned and scratched his beard. 'Probably not. He has ever been a serious man…so serious. If you swore on your honour…'

'Still, he would probably think me a madman.'

'I will vouch for you, my friend. I was there. Our tale is hard to believe, true, but two of his lords—one his own son and the other, Lord of the Watch—both swearing the tale to be true, he would have to believe us, Arnulf.'

'Aye,' agreed Arnulf his voice, full of uncertainty. 'I still fear this could damage us, friend. Damage our reputation, our honour. I will not be mocked or called a liar.'

'They can ride to the damn pass themselves and the word of the men, our warriors. Too many of us saw it. I will kill any man who calls me a liar,' shouted Fergus in defiance.

Arnulf grunted, and then turned in his saddle. All eyes were upon them, having heard Fergus's outburst. He caught Hafgan's eye behind him, the big warrior nodded. Arnulf knew his warriors would stand by him. The tale would spread. Perhaps, they would all indeed become heroes of legend? Still, his doubts plagued him.

Arnulf looked down to his hound, Fear, as the great grey beast padded along beside him once more. It looked up at him with big yellow eyes framed by a shaggy grey fringe. Arnulf wondered at what lay behind those eyes, what had the beast seen these last days? How had it come to be now padding at his horse's flanks? He would likely never find out, but the beast seemed content with its new master, content to trail after him as he led it back to the safety of the lowlands. The hound's attention was suddenly drawn to something in front of them.

Arnulf scanned the land ahead. A thin band of forest could be seen in the distance. They neared the edge of the moors. He caught sight of a distant horseman thundering along the track towards them. As the rider drew closer it looked to be one of their outriders. The woman, her mail glinting beneath her cloak, rode up and reined in.

'Lord.'

'What is it?' asked Fergus, startled by her apparent urgency.

'Smoke, lord. Somewhere is burning.'

'Where?'

She hesitated, her eyes flicked to Arnulf.

'I think it's coming from Ravenshold way, lord.'

Arnulf gasped and kicked his horse forward.

Fergus called after him, but Arnulf spurred his horse into a gallop.

His heart was in his stomach as he rode frantically towards the trees, searching for the smear of smoke on the horizon. He could hear the thunder of hooves pursuing him. With a glance over his shoulder, he saw Hafgan, Fergus, and several others riding hard to catch up. The hound, Fear, chased him also, hurtling through the undergrowth in his wake.

He plunged into the woodlands that marked the edge of the moors. His horse expertly cantering through the undergrowth, avoiding roots and branches as it picked its path through the trees. Arnulf made for a rise in the woods ahead, knowing it marked the ridge that could be seen from the trail rising over the trees.

He reined in upon the ridge and beheld the wide vista of wooded landscape which lay before him. He could see for leagues over the tree tops, he could see the rise and fall of the wooded valleys and dales, the surrounding hills shadowed against the horizon. And to the southeast, a dark plume of inky smoke that stained the grey skies.

'No, it can't be,' muttered Arnulf.

There was the odd farmstead in that direction but it did indeed appear to be coming from the Motte, from Ravenshold, his home.

CHAPTER TWENTY-ONE

Ashes and Embers

The ancient hill fort, which folk now called the Motte, sat high over the settlement below and commanded the sky line above the large town of Ravenshold. The hill upon which it sat thrust up unnaturally from the floor of a stony valley. The town sprawled at its feet, occupying the remainder of the valley's floor. Animal pens and tilled allotments were scattered across the town, the people had fitted them here and there in between the round buildings with their low piled stone walls and thatched roofs.

The Motte appeared over the crest of the last valley which obscured the view. Arnulf's heart sank as laid eyes on his home.

The old fort had once stood as only decayed banks of earth and ditches atop the hill for hundreds, perhaps thousands of years, since long before the people of Arnar had made this land their home. The fort had been improved since the old times, the old ditches had been deepened and the earth banks had been raised and built upon. A formidable palisade now enclosed the hills' summit, built upon those ancient earthworks. This place had kept men safe, a refuge and a fortress for millennia past.

Huge plumes of black smoke rose from behind the Motte's palisade. The houses of the town seemed intact, although several seemed to smoke ominously. What had happened here?

Tears welled up in his eyes as he kicked his horse into a gallop, racked with panic.

'Wait, Arnulf,' called Hafgan's voice from behind. 'If we have been raided, the enemy could still be close. We should wait for the others.'

Arnulf took no heed of his chief warrior's warning and rode off. He could see the houses below had not been razed. This was no raid, a freak fire perhaps? But what of his hall? What of the Motte?

His thoughts were of the faces of his wife and daughter, of his son, as he rode to find answers, praying to the gods they were safe behind the high palisade.

Arnulf's ancestors had built the old hall within and the reinforced the old hill fort's defences. His fathers had managed to keep it for generations, since the wars of forging it had never fallen or changed hands. It had become known as Ravens Motte, due to the town of Ravenshold nestled beneath it. Others called it the old name Anvil Motte.

He had been told as a lad, it was the anvil upon which men were hammered and armies smashed, he was told it was un-takeable and that the gods had given its keeping to his bloodline. Arnulf, however, noticed the name may have been also as likely to do with the many smiths that populated the village below. Arnulf simply always called it the Motte, as his father did.

Ravenshold was a mining town. The mines thereabout brought up iron, copper and tin. It had always been an important place, a village of miners and smiths, of forging and delving. The town's market and traders supplied metalwork to much of the border lands. An important site guarded over by an important and well-placed fort. The great fort guarding over the northwest of the border region. Chieftains of old had no doubt held their seat here and now Arnulf was lord of these lands.

He could see no flames rising above the palisade on the hill, just portentous thick clouds of billowing black smoke. The land about seemed deserted, no men working the fields. The buildings around the outlying mine heads seemed devoid of movement as he passed. Where had they all gone?

As he rode amongst the squat round thatched houses, followed by the others, there was no ringing of anvils, no clamour of street traders, the avenues leading to the foot of the Motte were near deserted. Livestock had broken free and roamed around aimlessly. Arnulf watched a pig rooting through the mire of churned damp earth as he rode past. Fowl strutted about, bobbing their heads, but fled in a wild panic as the horses approached. The hound chased them, snapping at them as they flapped away. Here and there the wet mud was stained with slick black pools of blood. Tools and possessions lay discarded in the street. A handful of townfolk were emerging from their hiding places, spooked by the arrival of the horsemen.

'You there,' shouted Arnulf at a man skulking at the side of the street, 'what has happened here?'

Seeing his lord, the man ran over and fell to his knees. 'Oh, Lord Arnulf, you have returned,' he babbled. 'It's too late, too late.' He began weeping.

'What happened, man?' demanded Arnulf.

Hafgan reined in beside him. 'It's Hale, lord, one of the smithies.'

Hafgan addressed the weeping blacksmith, 'Hale, you're safe now. Tell us, what has happened? Were we attacked?'

'Aye, Haf,' managed the man. 'Lord,' he then said with a nod to Arnulf. 'Demons, the dead…'

The man was interrupted by the arrival of armed men. Half a dozen men cautiously emerged into the muddy street, all equipped and dressed for war, their shields raised at the ready. They wore mail and leathers, some wrapped in furs. Most had helmets and they carried long spears. Upon their red shields they bore Arnulf's own axe. These were his own warriors. The man in the lead, Arnulf recognised instantly. His castellan.

The castellan wore fine armour, a mail coat trimmed with stamped leather. His helmet had cheek guards and was engraved with matching designs to his leather trim. His scabbard was adorned with steel plates and wrapped in red ribbon.

'Arnulf,' he said not quite believing his eyes, 'You have come. We sent a rider.'

Arnulf looked at Hafgan puzzled. The big warrior shook his head.

'We passed no rider,' said Fergus from his horse. He and the other riders had now reined in behind Arnulf and sat looking about at the dishevelled street, Erran amongst them, his face shocked.

'What has happened?' demanded Arnulf.

The castellan was named Engle, a good man. He generally assisted in the day to day governing of Ravenshold and the Motte. Not a great warrior, but a man of letters with a good mind for logistics. Arnulf was surprised to see him dressed for war and leading his men. He looked strange in the clearly ceremonial armour.

'We were attacked, lord,' replied Engle, eyeing Fear nervously.

'And…who did this?' demanded Arnulf, his anger flaring.

Engle hesitated.

'Folk are saying say they were demons, Arnulf. I think they were. They wore the skin of our own kin. They looked like people we knew, but they were not. They killed our own. The slaughter had already begun before anyone realised what was happening.' He paused, 'Folk ran to the Motte, they sheltered in your hall. But…'

'What?' demanded Arnulf, his voice wavering.

'Some of them got past the guards. They looked like kin, they just let them in with the others, and before we knew it, they had killed the men inside and the high gates were barred.

'We were holding the lower gate. We couldn't get in. We don't know what happened up in there, lord. They must have killed the guards, and then they fired the hall, with the doors barred, or maybe our folk locked themselves in. I don't know.

'So many were trapped inside, women, the young 'uns... I am sorry Arnulf, we failed you. We failed them all.'

He began to weep.

'No,' muttered Arnulf, shaking his head in disbelief.

'They were like beasts. They tore people to pieces like animals,' continued Engle. 'And the madness...it spread.

'And that's not all, lord. Then...please believe me, Arnulf, I have men who will swear to it. The dead began to walk.'

Hafgan gasped and looked sharply at Arnulf. But his lord was silent. He could not comprehend what he was hearing.

'Someone trapped some of them in a barn and set it alight,' said Engle as he pointed at a smoking building. 'There were people in there with them. We heard them screaming.'

Arnulf cut in, 'Where is Aeslin? Where is my wife, my daughter?'

Engle looked gravely at the floor, not meeting Arnulf's eye. He sobbed. 'I'm so sorry, Arnulf... They were... They were all in the hall.'

Arnulf sank to his knees and cried out in despair. The long forlorn cry broke the silence of the deserted town.

The men were silent and sombre-faced.

Arnulf looked up, tears streamed down his cheeks.

'Where is Ewolf, does he live?'

'He does, lord. He holds the palisade and the Motte now,' replied Engle, his voice grave. 'He tried to cut through the gate with axes. We eventually did, but he couldn't save them. None could get near. The heat, it was too great. None were left alive, everyone was dead or changed. We cleared the Motte and searched but no one survived the flames in the hall, lord. I'm sorry. We lost so many.'

Arnulf knelt on the floor, grief stricken.

***

The castellan turned to Hafgan. 'Please believe me, Haf. The dead walked, I swear it.'

'We believe you, Engle.' Hafgan sighed. 'We have already seen them. We were attacked in the passes. It is true, the dead are walking. The gods have sent a great evil upon us.'

Hafgan placed his hand on the lord's shoulder. Arnulf rose to his feet.

'We must go up there, now,' said Arnulf looking up at the smoke pluming out from the Motte. He pushed his way past and made his way urgently uphill.

Arnulf gestured for Engle and his men to follow after.

'More warriors are coming, the rest of the men are on foot behind us,' said Hafgan to the castellan as Arnulf stalked off uphill. 'They will not be far behind. Lord Fergus and his warriors rode with us, but many are still walking. We rode ahead of the rest. Lord Arnulf would not wait once we sighted the smoke.'

Engle nodded.

'Now, tell me all that happened,' asked Hafgan, quietly nodding at the smoke rising from the fort above.

'We held a shield wall at the lower gate,' said Engle, 'and let our folk through. But it spread. Some changed quickly, others slowly. The wounded…they changed. Families and friends turning on each other, biting, clawing…killing. There has been talk of folk eating people.

'They threw themselves at us, and many died on our spears. They were our kin. I see now they were cursed, they had become demons themselves.'

Hafgan nodded gravely.

Engle went on, 'But we held the low gate and then…the dead rose. The demons scattered. We barred the low gate to stop the dead getting in, folk sheltered on the slopes of the Motte through the night. Thank the gods for the lower palisade. Many more would have died without it.

'The hall burned through the night. By the dawn, the remaining demons seemed to have long fled or hidden, only the dead remained, they crowded the gates trying to get in. We used spears from the fighting platforms at the gates to bring them down.' He held up his hands helplessly. 'They were already dead. How could they walk again?'

Hafgan heard a strange *thud*. He turned to see where it came from. The smith named Hale had returned to salvaging what he could from a nearby house, it wasn't his house either noted Hafgan. There was blood on the floor mingling with the wet mud beside the darkened doorway. Hale had made a pile of possessions on the floor near the door and scurried back inside to gather what he could of use.

Fergus rode up from behind and passed them to catch up with Arnulf. He dismounted beside his old friend. He spoke to him, seemingly trying to offer some consolation. Arnulf gave a sharp reply and continued up the hill.

Hafgan and Engle approached Fergus. The fire haired lord stood with his hands raised and shrugged as they approached.

There was another loud *thud,* Hafgan's eyes flicked to the smithy. Both he and Engle obviously heard it as they both turned searching for its source. Hafgan seemed sure now, it was not Hale the smith as he first thought. He watched the smith as he now turned and approached a nearby house. The nearby horses became uneasy, tossing their heads pulling their reins. Their riders suddenly fought for control of the spooked beasts.

'Have these houses been searched?' the big warrior asked Engle urgently.

'I am not sure, Haf. As I say, I did not come out this morning.'

Hafgan turned back to the smith just as he tried the door.

'No,' cried Hafgan suddenly, running to stop the smith, but it was too late. Hale opened the door and a figure burst out upon him.

The dead man mauled the screaming smith as he

thrashed in the mud. Hafgan skidded to a halt in the wet mud of the street and stood momentarily shocked to a standstill watching the gruesome scene unfold.

***

Arnulf calmly strode back towards his horse. The horse shied away and seemed to want to rear up but changed its mind, its eyes frantic and panicked. Arnulf, paying the distressed creature no heed, unslung his axe from his horse's saddle and turned.

He strode towards the dead man. All except himself, seemed to Arnulf to be frozen and not moving, as if petrified to stone. All stood with their eyes fixed upon the blood drenched wreck of the smith. The dead man stooped above, with its head buried into the smith's torn open abdomen.

Arnulf halted over the creature, his axe hanging down at his side in one hand. It snapped its head up and snarled at the mailed warrior-lord towering over it. The dead man shot out a surprisingly quick arm to grasp at Arnulf's leg.

With a primal roar, Arnulf swung the axe up over his head, and down in a savage blow to check the dead man's snarling maw. The axe crunched through bone, it drove deep into the dead man's shoulder and tore into its chest. Another swing to the neck parted its head from its shoulders, sending the head spinning away into the muddy street.

The axe rose and fell again, and again. A spray of blood leapt from the scything axe. Arnulf's roar intensified with each blow, a rage filled him. Arnulf chopped and hacked with the axe, screaming defiance until raw emotion began to show through in his cry.

The bodies lay in ruin, savaged by the big axe, crushed and mingled into a single mass of pulped and sundered flesh. The two corpses were difficult to tell apart.

The severed head of the dead man suddenly snarled up at Arnulf, this mouth snapping at him, still somehow alive. Arnulf brought the axe down and cleaved the terrible thing in two.

Arnulf slowed. He began to sob with each laboured blow.

'Why?' screamed Arnulf as he struck another blow. 'Why is this happening to us?' The axe descended once more and lifted in a spray of crimson. He broke down, sobbing and cursing, occasionally striking another half-hearted, squelching blow into the remains at his feet.

A hand touched his shoulder.

'Lord.'

Arnulf ceased his onslaught.

'Arnulf, it is…gone,' spoke Hafgan's voice from behind.

***

'Are all the houses cleared, have they been checked?' asked Hafgan, turning back to the castellan.

'Aye, I think so, well most. There has been the odd dead one lurking. The changed ones have fled. Some have been found and most of those were cornered and killed. Ewolf led some men out earlier, to check for any others lurking in the town and return them to Old Night.'

'Are you sure?'

'I think so, Haf, but I wasn't with them so I can't be sure.'

'We must destroy all of the dead if any remain. And any who have been bitten or wounded, chain them. They could be dangerous.'

Engle nodded gravely.

'Aye, some of our wounded turned on us,' explained Engle, 'they became changed and cursed. The madness seemed to spread.' He paused thoughtfully, then said, 'Yet, some have been wounded and appear to still be okay.'

'What of the wounded men we sent back?' demanded Hafgan. 'Would have been the same day young Erran returned to bring more men to the passes.'

'Aye, they returned. We thought them crazy, laughed at their tale. Then…then, we saw for ourselves, saw the dead. They were in the hall…'

Engle trailed off as he realised.

'By the gods, they were in the hall! Lady Aeslin was up there. They went to her as soon as they got here. They were already in there with them all. I did not know at the time. Some of your guardsmen claimed they had been bitten… And we let them up there. I remember, we had to lock up Marsden's boy after he got back. He fell into a rage. By the gods, I didn't know. All hell began breaking loose when the gate guards were attacked. It all just seemed to be happening at the same time.'

'Was it our wounded men who attacked?' asked Hafgan.

'No, no, Haf. Word is, the demons attacked the west guard house, and then just started attacking folk in the streets. I hadn't thought about the wounded being up there in the hall. Was it a trick? Were they with the others all along? What is happening, Haf?'

'I don't know, Engle. I wish I knew.'

'What happened then? Tell me, is there anything else?' asked Hafgan sternly.

'Then, when it seemed clear, Ewolf led men out to check the village. That was this morning, then you arrived.'

Hafgan nodded. He looked over at Arnulf. His lord had risen to his feet but stared into the mangled ruin of the smith and the dead man. He must show strength in front of his people, Fergus had no doubt reminded him of this, but still, he was silent, visibly distraught.

'We're going up to the hall,' said Arnulf suddenly. His face splattered with blood, he held an almost vacant expression. Deep behind his lord's eyes Hafgan saw a terrible despair, and something else, a cold rage which made the big warrior apprehensive, a look he had not seen before. Hafgan simply nodded to his lord, not knowing how to reply.

Engle hurried over. 'Are you sure, Arnulf?'

Arnulf threw him a withering look.

'We are still searching for the bodies,' continued Engle. 'It's grim, lord.'

'Take me to my damn hall, and where is Ewolf?' demanded Arnulf harshly, his voice breaking, obviously knowing well what lay up there in wait for him.

Lord Arnulf mounted his horse and cast a long gaze uphill to the palisade of the Motte, the smoke clouds rising from beyond its stout walls. He then kicked his horse forward.

The hound he had named Fear padded beside his new master. Lord Fergus threw a forlorn glance at Hafgan as he rode past him to follow Arnulf, riding to catch up with his old friend and no doubt to offer what comfort and counsel he could. Hafgan led his horse and walked beside Engle as they followed the two riders up to the Motte.

Engle lead his small group of warriors back to the safety of the gates. The warriors peered fearfully into the shadows for any sign of a lingering foe. They moved carefully and alert but still swiftly, with their shields raised up and ready.

***

Arnulf approached the lower gates of the Motte's palisade. There were two palisades enclosing the Motte, one palisade ringing the base of the Motte, entered through the low gate, the other at its summit, entered by the high gate. The high palisade enclosed Arnulf's hall and the other buildings of the fort behind its high wooden ramparts.

Once inside the safety of the lower gate, they saw the townsfolk of Ravenshold huddled together fearfully on the slopes of the old hill fort. Villagers crowded around the returning warriors. Arnulf scanned their tired faces as he rode past, some wore a look of relief in their eyes, but few cheered. Forlorn faces also stood staring amongst the crowd, their expressions, filled with loss, their loved ones slain or devoured in the flames of the hall above. Arnulf's gaze lingered on those sad, lost faces as he rode past. Others came close reaching out to him, seeking the protective presence of their returned lord. Folk were trying to talk and shout out to him. Arnulf caught snatches of babbling voices but the words faded away from him, he felt wrapped in a veil of grief. He kicked his horse towards the high gate.

Two of Arnulf's warriors stood sentry at the ruined gate, their shields red with Arnulf's axe painted in black upon them. Men stood watching from the palisades fighting platform, looking down from the ramparts upon on the horsemen who were ascending the track to the high gate. The damage to the gate was evident. Arnulf could plainly see where they had chopped a gaping hole through with felling axes.

Arnulf caught a glimpse of his hall, and then with his eyes fixed upon the smoking, charred ruin of his home, he kicked his horse past the sentries and through the gate.

The hall had been reduced to a pile of blackened timber; the nearby buildings were scorched and blackened. The adjoining buildings that made up the rear quarters of the hall had caught also and had mostly burned to the floor.

Yet, the stables stood untouched beside the gates, as did a handfull of minor dwellings clustered across the courtyard, those given to his more important people and warriors. The Master Smith's forge still stood intact, not far from the gates and indeed many of the buildings and storerooms built up against the palisade seemed intact if not slightly blackened.

Thick plumes of dark smoke rose from the wreckage of the hall's frame, some of the timber still blooming with embers. The heat could still be felt emanating from the ruins, but it was becoming bearable. Ash smeared servants picked amongst the cooler areas, searching through the wreckage for the remains of the poor souls who had been trapped inside.

Arnulf slid down from his horse and approached. Wading in amongst the ashes, he stared down at withered and burnt bones. He saw bodies, blackened and withered, shrunken to the size of mere children by the inferno's fury.

He approached what was once the centre of his hall, imagining it as it had been. He came to the place where he judged his seat upon the dais would have been. At his feet, two shrivelled forms huddled together. One, much smaller than the other, that of a child, still clutched in the blackened withered arms of the larger figure. It was impossible to recognise the remains, but he knew. Arnulf was overcome. He knew he had found them. He gently knelt and tried to lift the pair.

'Aeslin,' he sobbed gently.

The figures crumbled. Falling to ash and bones, the pair fell from his arms and tumbled to the floor. Arnulf placed his cloak down and began piling on the bones and ashes. Tears streamed down his cheeks as he held the small bones of the child.

He wept.

Arnulf covered the charred bones with the remainder of his cloak and carried it slowly out of the wreckage.

Fergus strode over and placed a comforting hand upon his old friend's shoulder.

'I…I am sorry, Arnulf,' said Fergus quietly with a gesture towards the wrapped cloak on the floor. He then sighed heavily and stared off into the smouldering embers. 'This is a terrible thing,' concluded Fergus.

Arnulf sighed. 'I need to think…to take all this in. I cannot…' He fell silent and stared into the wrapped cloak clutched to his chest.

'Father,' called a voice.

Arnulf turned, Ewolf appeared through the gate. He hurried to join his father. He wore his mail but had no helmet. Ewolf looked at his father, but something he saw in his eyes brought him to a halt.

He had the same brown hair as Arnulf, wearing it long past his shoulders. He looked so much like his mother. Arnulf was struck by how old he looked, a man now. Arnulf fought back his sorrow as his gaze fixed on his son, his only family now.

Ewolf stared, his eyes wide with grief, at the bundle of fur his father carried. Arnulf placed the bundle carefully on the floor.

'I am sorry, Father…we tried,' cried Ewolf, 'we tried…' Ewolf fell silent unable to find the words.

'Son,' Arnulf exclaimed emotionally and embraced his boy fiercely. Arnulf held his son and looked at him for a long moment. 'This will be avenged, I swear it,' declared Arnulf. 'I swear it.'

He turned to Engle. 'I cannot think,' gasped Arnulf, releasing his son. Visibly forcing back a breaking wave of anguish, he fought to maintain his composure, but his eyes betrayed his leaking sorrow. 'I must do this first. I will put them to rest and then…' Arnulf's desperate eyes twisted any man's heart who met them. His men stood sombre, unable to hold his gaze. He turned to Ewolf. 'Come son.' He clutched the ashen bundle tight into his chest and slowly carried it away.

'Shall I send for the priests?' ventured Engle.

'No,' replied Arnulf without turning. 'We must do this now. Leave us a short while.'

'Haf, Engle, begin bringing them out…' said Arnulf with a gesture to the hall. 'Start having the bodies cleared. We will not be long, but I must do this first.'

Hafgan nodded.

Ewolf joined his father and placed a hand on his back.

The hound growled. Arnulf turned to the beast. 'Fear, what is it?'

'It does not seem to like me,' said Ewolf nervously.

'He's alright,' said Arnulf. The pair made to leave.

Fear barked at the young warrior and growled.

'You best stay here, boy,' said Arnulf speaking to the hound. 'It's okay, I will not be long.'

He turned to Fergus. 'Watch the hound, will you?' he asked almost absently.

Fergus nodded.

'Don't worry,' said Arnulf to his son, 'the beast has barely left my side since we found him. He will get used to you.' He sighed heavily, and then led Ewolf off through the sundered high gate.

***

Fear continued barking and growling as they walked away. Ewolf threw a concerned look back at the agitated hound and waved it away with a vague shooing motion.

Hafgan could not help but notice Ewolf's hand. It had been bandaged. Hafgan and Fergus exchanged concerned glances.

Hafgan grabbed Engle by the arm. 'What of Ewolf? He is wounded?' asked Hafgan quietly in the castellan's ear.

Engle hesitated before answering. 'He was bitten, Haf,' he blurted.

'Quiet, you fool,' snapped Hafgan with a glance at Arnulf. 'Hearing that now could break him.' Arnulf did not appear to have heard. He slowly moved out down from the gates.

'Tell me, now,' demanded the big warrior.

'It was this morning…while they searched the houses. One of the dead, it lurked in the darkness of one of the houses. I'm told it took him by surprise.'

Hafgan cursed and looked towards his lord once more, a look of pity.

'I should follow them and keep an eye on them,' muttered Hafgan.

'Perhaps,' replied Engle. 'Lord Arnulf told us he would be alone. Would you defy him?' He paused.

'I am sure the lad is fine.'

'Don't be so sure,' ventured Fergus, 'Haf is right. I saw it take a man, Olad it was. It was many hours before it took him. I am not sure how many exactly, but he seemed fine well into the evening, but he was gone by dawn, changed. We should not risk it.'

'Aye, lord,' agreed Hafgan. 'I will keep my distance. Arnulf will not see me. He will have his privacy, but I will not be far.' He nodded solemnly. 'I think it is for the best.'

'I feared the madness would take him,' admitted Engle, 'but by the gods, the lad appears to be fine. So do the others.'

'Who?' demanded Hafgan.

'Some were unaffected by their wounds and are back on watch already or are with their families.'

'Is that wise?' said Fergus with a glance at Hafgan.

'They should be watched,' said Fergus. 'No, have them check in again. We will check their wounds. I saw the rot, so did some of the others. If anyone has any sign of it, they will be kept under guard until we can be sure. Go, Haf. We will check Ewolf upon his return.'

Hafgan nodded and made his way out after his lord.

***

Fergus stood watching the big warrior depart after his old friend. As soon as his lord had departed, Engle immediately scurried off to send word to allow the townsfolk up into the Motte. Folk want to search for their loved ones, to bury their dead. Fergus joined his warriors and watched as folk began to ebb through the gate and scrabble through the hot ashes and charred timbers. Fergus shook his head at the harrowing sight. The remains he saw were indistinguishable, shrunken and twisted, charred beyond recognition. Any hope of an individual search for a loved one quickly became a macabre group recovery of any remains they could uncover. The reality of the hopelessness hit the townsfolk hard as they laid eyes on the complete destruction the inferno had left.

He made his way to look out from the gate onto the slopes of the Motte, and down upon the town beyond. Guardsmen and warriors from the watch post were searching for family amongst the huddled crowds on the grassy slopes. Some had not seen their loved ones in months. Fergus stood a while and watched them. The reunions brought some measure of joy to this now forlorn township.

Most of the townspeople were still sheltering within the low palisade, fearing the evil that could still be lurking amongst the quiet buildings of Ravenshold. Some, however, had carefully ventured back out to begin clearing the town. Fergus watched a group of armed townsfolk carefully move along the road towards the market square. Engle seemed to have guardsmen and townsfolk on patrol, cautiously treading through the main avenues of the town, while the brave few returned to their homes. Fergus stood a while watching. The town felt quiet.

The red pennons of Arnulf's banners flapped in the wind over the gates. The sky beyond was a dark backdrop of billowing plumes of thick smoke. Fergus felt a doom had come to Ravenshold.

The hound Arnulf had named Fear crept up next to him and sat down beside Fergus. It seemed anxious for Arnulf's return and looked out down the slopes before trotting off to sniff around at the gates.

A distant horn sounded from beyond the rampart. Faces turned in surprise.

'Lord, men are coming,' called one of the warriors standing on the palisades. 'There are banners.'

Fergus questioningly looked at Engle nearby, and then they ran up on to the platform over the high gate to look out into the valley. Indeed, banners were approaching, carried through the valley by men glinting with steel, men dressed in mail. Warriors of Arnar were coming.

'We sent out riders, lord,' said Engle as Fergus watched the men coming closer, 'to Weirdell and the other villages. I sent a man to Eymsford, too, lord, as I knew you were with Lord Arnulf in the passes. It seems help has come, it's...'

'My father...' finished Fergus bleakly.

CHAPTER TWENTY-TWO

A Plea to the Gods

The water felt barely warm. Jor had only thrown a few pails of hot water into the old tub, the rest made up of cold water drawn from the old well in the courtyard out back. The old man kept a battered black-iron cauldron full of water over part of his big cooking hearth. The heat kept the water piping hot for most of the day while it was alight. But there was never enough water for her to make a bath as warm as she'd like.

Nym sat hunched for warmth in the wide half-barrel Jor had cut to use as his bath. She was nonetheless glad to bathe away all that muck and grime from off the muddy streets of Anchorage. It was one of her few little luxuries—at least there was soap.

She scrubbed and scrubbed with the small lump of soap. She sighed. Still, she could not wash away that feeling. Nym found she could not settle into the calmness the lukewarm bath offered.

Her heart fluttered with a strange feeling. Some dull nagging feeling somewhere in the pit of her stomach. She could not place it, perhaps regret or some guilt? What had she done for a lump of hack silver? Not for love, but for...silver.

But they needed food, her clothes were getting ragged. Her brother looked so shabby he easily passed as some beggar street child these days. *Is that so inaccurate?*

No, she thought in answer. They were not too far from becoming beggars, living on the streets.

Of course, they had always been able to come back to the old tavern keeper. Old Jor let them sleep in the tavern and gave them a meal, so long as she worked for it, serving his customers and cleaning his tavern, sometimes keeping an eye on his cooking hearth while he bustled about. But he did not pay silver, just a place to stay.

He was a good old man though, for the most part. His eyes did linger upon her a little too long sometimes. It would make her feel a little uncomfortable when she caught him at it, and she would make herself busy elsewhere. But she was not concerned. She had noticed many men looked at her that way now she was getting older. It was something she was learning a lot of men just did without even realising. The old man seemed trusty enough to her. He was always well-mannered and mostly cheery.

They did not spend every night in the tavern with Jor though. Her brother Finn was made to work in the back and kept out of the way. The old man didn't trust him, and she knew he was not wrong to distrust her brother. Finn hated being stuck in the back at the tavern, kept away from the drunk folk and the fun. The old keeper didn't want him out stealing from his guests. Jor would cuff him across the ear with a distrustful glare every time he caught him sneaking into the ale room and send him back off to chop vegetables by the hearth, or to roll in the heavy barrels of ale from the storeroom—generally just away from mischief.

So, young Finn spent as little time at the tavern as possible and was often nowhere to be found when Nym awoke for work. Her brother would skulk away when he had the chance and had taken up partial residence in the abandoned hovel down in the alley across the street. It was by the wharfs, and you could see the boats, close enough to hear the waves lapping against the banks of the river. It had become a good place to come this past summer, a place to watch the ships coming and going, a place to escape the old man's chores. But the nights were drawing in. It was getting colder these days, and in the damp of autumn, the collapsing muddy hovel was becoming unpleasant to stay in. They would have to rely more and more on Jor and stay in the tavern.

She looked over at the silver laid on a nearby stool. It lay upon her new dress. She had bought it earlier. She had used her brother's knife to slice a sliver off the lump to pay for it. It was a grey-blue linen shift, and there was a tree pattern sewn into the hems. She had always liked trees, although so few grew near the town now.

She hoped she would look less of a waif in her new clothes. Nym looked back at the silver resting upon the folded linen. She decided she would try to hack it into smaller lumps, she thought it would go much further that way. Nym stared at the silver a long moment.

She had heard it was easy. The girls around the dock, the tavern whores, they had all said it was easy—easy coin. But none had told her she would feel like this. She could not scrub that feeling away. She couldn't push the image of his grunting face out of her mind, the smell of his stale ale breath. It had been different before, with the other boy, a lad she knew by the docks. He was a ship lad. They had fun those few days he was in port. She wondered when he would come back, if she would ever see him again? His ship had long sailed on now.

That once fond memory now soured by the gut-wrenching feeling she now felt at this next experience. She had not even known the stinking drunk. She could not even remember his name, just his face. And how he had looked her up and over, and then led her away.

She had been told by one of the girls it was easy to just whisper your offer into a drunken man's ear and most would likely take it. Silver, a few coins, it was easy, she had said. Nym never imagined, though, that it would be like this.

She shuddered. The water must be growing cold. She rose from the bath to dry off. Pulling the dress over her head, she belted her waist with a purple knot-woven cord. She lifted a bone carved comb from her bag and began to comb her hair, twisting long blonde locks and tying them back behind her head so some still hung loose down her back. A few teeth were missing but it was still a good comb. The comb had been her mother's. It was all she had of her mother now. Both her mother and her father were with the gods, had been for some time now, since she was young.

She missed them. The old tavern keeper had known her father; he never mentioned it much though. She always supposed that was why he kept an eye on them, an old favour, so long as they worked their way of course. It was certainly better than the streets in winter.

Nym opened the door from the back rooms where Jor kept the tub and stepped into the tavern. It was quiet. Jor had closed up till all this trouble blew over. He didn't want folks falling dead in his place, not good for business. Although, as he now often said, neither was closing. The old man sat before his cold central hearth staring into the ashes with a mug of ale in his hands.

'Would you like to come in here with us, Jor? It's warmer,' said Nym with a gesture to the kitchen. 'I'm all done in the back room now, too.'

The old tavern keeper looked towards her.

'You look nice, lass. New dress,' complimented Jor considerately.

'Thank you,' she replied with a smile. 'Are you coming? Don't want folk seeing you sat there by the hearth and banging on the door, thinking we're open.'

Jor grunted.

'It won't help if they see you there,' she added.

Jor slowly rose, steadying himself with his stump of arm. He made his way to join them around the cooking hearth in the backrooms. Young Finn sat by the hearth still trying to sharpen his little knife with one of Jor's stones.

Jor settled with a grunt on a chair next to the hearth.

'Won't do,' grumbled Jor, 'no silver coming in. This best blow over soon. Ain't no good for trade. I bet everyone's suffering.'

'Or dying,' added Finn, not looking up from his knife.

The statement silenced the old man's grumblings. Silence flicked over the room, an unwelcome reminder of the sickness and of the terrible deaths occurring even more frequently across the port town.

They had all heard the talk. The strange sickness was spreading quickly. Its victims meeting a gory and horrible fate as more bodies were being found, convulsed and twisted in final throes of agony, found blood soaked and bleeding from mouths and eyes, and even from below. Folk were describing victims laid bloodied as if battle wounded, thought at first to have been murdered, but then no wounds were found, just blood.

More and more had been found this morning. Talk of sickness rippled a wild panic through the port of Anchorage. Folk were shutting shops and closing taverns early, some not opening back up at all today. Folk were leaving offerings to the gods at the ringed stone shrines on the hills and in the sacred groves. All praying for protection from the stalking gaze of Old Night.

One such ritual was being talked of this evening, a great sacrifice to appease the gods at the great stone circle. The acolytes of the shrines and priests of gods, witches, and holy folk with whom the gods seemed close, were all set to meet together at the great circle as the sunset. The high priests would do as they could, sacrifices and incantations, to try to appease the god of death and stay Old Nights wrath. Such a large and impromptu gathering was a rarity.

'Come, we will be late,' said Nym, pulling a dark woollen cloak over her shoulders.

Her brother's eyes lit up beneath his black mop of loose muddy hair. He jumped up and placed his knife carefully inside his belt, eager to get out and amongst the people. Jor grumbled but also rose, swinging on a heavy brown cloak.

'What are we taking?' asked Nym.

'Ale, lass. What else?' replied the old tavern keeper. 'You will need to help me with it though, boy,' he said, addressing Finn. Fin's face fell, and he frowned up at the old man as Jor began to carefully peer through his shutters onto the street outside. Nym thought the old man looked nervous.

'Is that all? No goat or even a chicken?' asked Nym.

Jor shrugged. 'I ain't got coin for it, lass, not as it's been. I keep ale. My best is what I shall give to the gods.' He paused. 'And what are you giving, lass?' he snapped at her.

She could only open her mouth in reply. She held up her empty hands and looked to the floor, crestfallen.

'That was cruel,' he said with a shake of his head. 'The offering is for all under this roof. Don't you worry, lass.' He forced a smile and looked nervously out into street again. 'Don't like this, not with all this talk of death and plague.' He shuddered. 'Should stay away from it all. Maybe the gods won't notice us.'

'I thought we needed them to notice us, Jor,' replied Nym. 'They will stop it if we honour them.'

Jor grunted. 'Perhaps, but I ain't never seen the gods do anything much but take, lass. They might listen, but they will still take, take our crops, our livestock, our blood, our ale,' he said with a tap on the small barrel of his best dark ale. 'Aye, we will see,' he said with an absent tug on the wolf claw charm about his neck.

They joined the streams of folk making their way to the evening ritual. The people of Anchorage filed through the streets towards the circle of the gods in their hundreds. It seemed most of the town had turned out to honour the gods, to appease the immortal lords in hope they would lift the curse that had befallen their town.

Folk walked cloaked and wrapped against the chill air. Jor guided Finn as he struggled with the wooden barrow loaded with the small, but still heavy, keg of best ale. The street led onto the mud road south. The road led off towards Lord's Grove and the old stone circle.

Two large stones guarded the entrance into the groves. Stood at each side of the road, the ancient worn rocks were topped with a heavy lintel stone to form a great stone arch. It hung low over their heads as they passed below. Nym paused beneath and stared up at the heavy stone nestled above her, its majesty taking her breath away for a moment.

'Move along, girl,' came a gruff voice from behind. Jor nodded in apology to the impatient man and hurried her onwards with a guiding hand on her back.

Walking through that ancient portal felt to Nym as if they had passed into another realm, a realm of the watchful dead, a place where gods strode the between the rocks and the trees. She hoped her parents were somewhere amongst the boughs watching her.

The light of the day was dying, the sun hung low over the horizon in a clouded sky, casting a long gloom amongst the trees. The circle of gods could be seen rising over the old groves and barrow mounds ahead.

The old stones of the gods circle were akin to the ancient rock of the entrance arch. They had all stood since long before the people of Arnar had settled here, an ancient place of reverence to a forgotten people. The folk of Anchorage had adopted the site, had erected new stones. Stones to honour newer gods, cut in their likeness. Others carved with images of ships, of men and heroes, of beasts from legend, with swirling spirals and woven patterns.

Folk had raised cairns and mounds to honour the dead. Burials dotted throughout the groves around the gods circle, the final resting places of the town's ancestors, stone piled tombs of the wealthy and the great.

Crowds were gathering, and many people lined the edges of the outer ditches encircling the stone ring. Bonfires and torches flickered to life amongst the stones. Only just kindled, the flames flickered underneath piles of wood. Soon they would grow to be roaring infernos, lighting the evening gloom, and bathing everything in a ruddy flickering light.

A chorus of drummers pounded out pulsing rhythms accompanied by the low throaty melodies of a lone piper playing the bone flute. Nym took her place amongst the crowd, beside Jor and her brother, to watch the strange assembly of masked figures moving amongst the stones. Horns sporadically sounded out their braying calls, joined with the hypnotic droning, but still strangely melodious voices of the waiting acolytes and priests, their songs reverberated out from the circles centre.

There was an almost carnival atmosphere. Nym peered about the folk stood nearby. The people of Anchorage stood clutching possessions, precious things to be given up to the gods. A wretched looking woman hacked out a cough to her left. The crowd backed away from her half-expecting her to fall to the floor dying. She sneered at the folk stood nearby and wrapped her dirty brown cloak tight around her.

Nym nervously looked at the other faces stood close by. She noticed folk had brought their sick, their afflicted loved ones, hoping the gods would lift their dire maladies and make them well again. She closed her cloak around her protectively, her only shield from their pestilence.

She pulled her brother close, wrapping her arms around his shoulders. He was not best pleased, wanting to be free to mingle among the crowd, most likely looking for mischief, but he did not object to her protective embrace. Perhaps, she thought, he believed her to be scared and thus allowed her to take comfort in his closeness without protest.

A fanfare of horns silenced the murmuring throng. Nym searched the circle's perimeter with curious eyes. It appeared the horns were announcing the arrival of a procession which had appeared along another track coming in from the stone tombs to the west.

The procession passed through the gap in the ditch and made its way towards the brooding majesty of the waiting standing stones. At the procession's head, a group of masked characters wearing skulls as masks. Most notable was one wearing the skull of a stag, its antlers branching out tall and wide from the figure's drawn hood, a high priest representing the god, Hjort, the Hart of Horns—the great stag of the summer forests and the hunt. Beside him the less grandiose and menacing skull of a wolf tucked beneath a hood. This one Nym knew was Varg, the hunter, lord of war and winter.

There were maiden priestesses dancing, said to be the virgins dedicated to The Three. Amongst them shuffled wise aged crones and other priestesses of The Three, some bearing the swollen bellies of those with child.

The manic grinning masks of the trickster god,

the Lord of Fools, bobbed and capered menacingly. There were eagle masks bristling with feathers signifying the lords of the sky. Serpents of the great seas escorted a beautiful woman who walked in the nude, the high priestess of the spiteful sea goddess. As the nude priestess drew nearer, Nym suspected she appeared much younger than she truly was.

A solemn group of black robed priests appeared. They wore human skulls beneath their hoods and each carried a flaming torch. They were known to most, the Keepers of the Dead. In their midst strode the high priest of Old Night, the god of death. Adorned with bones hanging from his robes, he wore a macabre necklace of skulls and carried a twisted elm staff that hung with yet more bone fetishes. Nym was not close enough to hear, but she imagined this terrible figure clattering loudly as he walked with each ominous and measured stride.

These Keepers of the Dead were known to be grim men and women, dedicated to honouring the death god. They kept and revered the bones of the ancestors and were tasked with tending the crypts and barrows that lay scattered throughout the old groves. Carried with them, they had brought the revered bones of the honoured dead, and with these bleached relics they would perform the rituals of the dead at the ancient standing stones of the gods circle.

Dragged behind the procession were chained men and women dressed in white shifts. Nym realised with a twist of horror they were to be sacrificed. They looked to be slaves.

However not all. One amongst them had been

chosen. One, asked to take the honour willingly. That girl who'd accepted the honour, stepped with trembling pride, the dignified fear writ on her face, convinced she would take a revered place in the halls of the dead.

The others fought the chains to escape. Slaves who had no want to die. They were dragged onwards, kicking and fighting until resignation subdued their cries and struggles.

Nym stared at the sacrifices in a morbid fascination. She focused on the girl and tried to imagine what that brave soul was feeling. She looked terrified, thought Nym. But still, what drove each step onwards so calmly? Was it pure resignation, or vigour of belief?

A commotion by the stone arch drew Nym's attention. Horses were approaching; it was the huscarl's men. Warriors made way and cleared space through the crowd. Riding in their midst, a finely dressed man. She recognised him from the festivals. It was Huscarl Warrick, the king's own man.

Warrick wore a decorative leather breastplate hung with plates of steel, or perhaps silver, which glinted in the flickering firelight. He wore a fine helmet and rich-looking clothes beneath his lavish armour. A long fur cloak hung down from his shoulders onto his horse's rump and Nym could see a sword strapped at his belt.

At his side rode a woman Nym had never seen before. Nym was awed by her elegance, wishing instantly she could be like her. Her strong face was pretty, her hair braided and long. The woman held herself with a confidence Nym envied. She heard snatches of murmurs from the folk stood nearby, she picked out the word 'princess.'

The king's daughter had come. Arn was less than half a league along the river from the port, yet she had never seen neither the king nor his sons. She had heard talk of them of course, she had heard of his daughters also. Nym wondered if she truly was the blood of the old kings and if so, which daughter was now approaching the ancient stones. Flanking the woman on each side rode two heavily armoured men.

'Is that the princess?' asked Nym, pulling on Jor's arm.

'Aye, lass. And Lord Warrick, too.'

'Who are those two warriors with her? asked Nym in wonder.

'Huscarls, lass, the king's best men, like Warrick, but likely not lords like him, I'd wager. But who knows? I don't know them.'

'I've never seen a princess,' replied Nym avidly watching the riders as they reined in.

Jor watched the Keepers of the Dead as they busied themselves amongst the stones, arranging the old bones of renowned heroes on stone slabs. The young virgins of The Three danced and dressed ribbons about the ancient stones whilst the masked priests depicting their revered gods took up positions, each before the carved stones dedicated to their sworn god's likeness. Warrick and his riders had dismounted and stood in places of honour before the central pedestal.

The drumming stopped. The crowd fell silent as an unmasked high priest raised his arms from the stone pedestal at the circles centre. He was an elderly man but still maintained a strong vigour, emanating a fierce authority in his demeanour. He wore a cowled white robe, his greying hair and beard both long and wiry.

'Welcome,' he shouted. 'Welcome, brothers, sisters.' He shouted loudly for all to hear. 'Tonight, we honour the gods.' He paused. 'We evoke our ancestors to watch over us, to guide us. There is pestilence, we ask them to drive it away from our lands.'

He beckoned to the drummers and they once again began their rhythmic beat. He signalled for the other priests to begin their rituals. Their chanting and song began as the high priest then began a lengthy oration, the metre of his voice booming in concert with the hammering drums.

There were horses, cattle, and goats all being slaughtered, their blood being collected in earthen bowls and flicked about the stones by the acolytes and priests.

His booming speech drew to a close, and he summoned the sacrifices forwards. There were three in all. Nym had never seen so many, not even at the winter feasts was there rarely more than one sacrifice. He spoke quietly now, Nym could not hear his words. The three were led onto the central stone pedestal and bound to the altar slab. The high priest signalled for the drums to stop. The crowd fell silent and seemed to hold its breath.

The high priest raised a long dagger up to the dusk sky and dedicated it to the gods. He stooped over the first sacrifice. The man struggled but the high priest swiftly drove the dagger across his throat. There was a gout of blood, which splashed crimson across his white gown. The priest moved around the other two, slicing their throats open one by one. The chosen girl accepted her fate silently and with honour. Only one cried out in fear; the last. The shriek of terror was silenced by the dripping dagger.

The blood of the sacrifices flowed over the central pedestal, staining its surface with red ichor. The blood was again gathered up in bowls. The priests moved around each other painting lines of blood on their faces. Then, moving about the watching crowd, they did the same to the observers, daubing a smear of crimson with a finger on foreheads. The high priest himself tended Warrick and the princess, before moving amongst the others in the honoured place within the stones.

***

'It moved,' cried one of the acolytes suddenly. 'It moved!'

Jor strained to see. He could make out the pile of old bones arranged on the flat stone. Acolytes moved about excitedly, obscuring his view from a good look. He had not seen it move, but his eyes had been on the sacrifices. Oh, how he desired to see the bones move himself. *A good omen,* he thought.

'The ancestors are with us,' called the high priest, 'They will protect us from this evil. It is a sign. The gods are pleased.'

The drums began again and a woman began singing, a charged melody that resounded about the ancient stones. The carnival like atmosphere began to return as the sun sank. There would be a celebration about the fires in honour of the gods. A much-needed release from the worry of the sickness that weighed heavy on folks' thoughts. A small feast had been prepared as expected at such a ritual. Folk had also brought food. Ale had been brought from the town. There would be celebration until the fires burnt low. Some began dancing to the drums beat, wheeling and laughing. Possessions began to be thrown into the ditches – gifts to the gods.

Suddenly, people nearby were pointing. Jor craned his neck to see over the crowd. A man climbed from the ring ditch and staggered towards the stones. It seems he had traversed its steep sides and now stumbled towards the priests assembled amongst the ancient rocks, his arms outstretched. The drums dwindled away as all attention fell upon the man. Some of the acolytes moved to intercept him but seemed to recoil as they drew close. The man fell to his knees. Jor assumed he was pleading with them, but he fell to the floor.

The princess walked forward from Huscarl Warrick's assemblage and strode towards the stricken man. Her guards called out, but she ignored their shouts of warning. They hurried after her.

As she reached him, the man had collapsed to the floor, coughing up gouts of blood. She knelt before the dying man and seemed to speak softly to him. The armoured huscarls seemed to be anxiously warning her back to Warrick and his honour guard of warriors.

A gasp and murmur of alarm rippled through the

onlookers. Nym watched the noble lady giving directions to the milling acolytes. They hesitantly lifted the man and began to carry him off as he thrashed in his death throes.

'Another sacrifice to the gods,' shrieked the high priest, trying to maintain order amongst the scared townsfolk.

The princess snapped her head sharply to the high priest. One of her bodyguards placed a careful hand upon her arm and spoke in her ear. She did not take her glare off the high priest. She said something in return to the bodyguard and allowed herself to be led back to Warrick's company, seemingly furious.

More gasps and calls of alarm from the folk nearby. Jor turned to see the crowd jostling. Jor heard a man's voice call out loudly. The man soon staggered forward into view from the parting crowd. Jor could see he carried the limp form of a woman in his arms. From the man's distraught wails, Jor supposed it to be his wife. The limp woman's shawl glistened red in the flickering flames, the crimson of blood still visible in the light of the dying day. He cried out hysterically pleading for help. The huscarls guarding the princess levelled spears at the approaching man, but he just fell to his knees sobbing, clutching the limp form of his beloved. He was hurried away after the fallen man carried by the acolytes.

Panic spread through the crowds. The high priest shrieked out assurances. 'The ancestors have spoken. The gods smile upon us, surely,' he cried. He beseeched them to see the ritual through until its end, cursing those thinking of leaving with warnings and threats of divine umbrage.

'We are forsaken,' someone cried from nearby.

The high priest urged the drummers to reluctantly continue their rhythms. An oppressive chill of fear shrouded the atmosphere and sullied the jovial revelry. Some nervously continued the celebration, trying awkwardly to settle into a festive mood.

***

Nym felt a strange and subtle attention and turned, looking into the crowd around her. She started as her eyes met a staring face, staring not at the ritual amongst the stones but staring straight at her. Nym looked away with a shocked gasp, but then slowly turned to look at her again.

The old woman still had her gaze fixed on young Nym. She held Nym's gaze a long moment before shifting it away. *It's her*. Nym had seen her before. It was the strange woman again—the witch-seer.

She had long wiry black hair contained beneath a dark scarf that draped past her shoulders. Strange trinkets adorned her hair and scarf. The woman's beak nose framed dark shadowed eyes which gave her a slightly exotic look.

Nym had never even spoken with her but still Nym had noticed the woman several times these past days, watching her with an unsettling gaze as she passed. It made Nym nervous. She looked away fearfully.

Nym focussed again on watching the stone circle, afraid to turn in case that strange mystic was still staring at her. The high priest stood upon the altar stone, his feet bathed in blood. He called out urging folk to remain and honour the gods.

Nym let her eyes be once again drawn to the princess. Nym felt an awed admiration for this glamorous woman. She had tried to help that poor dying man regardless of the peril to herself. Nym thought, that in her place she would likely have recoiled away from the sick man in fear.

Nym watched on as the princess now spoke in earnest to Huscarl Warrick. She saw him looking around into the crowds before nodding gravely as he replied. He seemed to be issuing commands to his warriors, motioning to them that they were leaving. The huscarl respectfully nodded to the high priest, and then turned to lead his entourage back to their waiting horses.

A man pushed past her, leading a small boy by the arm. Jor seemed to be looking about uneasily. Nym could see that folk did not know what to do. Jor's gaze lingered upon the sickly old woman coughing nearby. He drew away from her. She saw other folk hastily dumping their sacrifices in the ring ditch and pushing their way out from the watching bystanders.

'We should leave,' said Jor apprehensively, catching the uncertain looks on the young faces of Nym and her brother.

'Boy, break open that cask, pour it into the ditch here,' said Jor with a gesture to the pit before their feet. 'We make our sacrifice now and get away from this. I knew we should not have come.'

Nym turned to see if the eerie mystic were still behind her, staring. There was no sign of her. She scanned the faces of the surrounding crowd. The old woman was no longer anywhere to be seen.

As she searched, her eyes fell upon a familiar face and her stomach suddenly knotted. It was him. He looked in her direction with a blank look. His eyes were reddened, he looked drunk. Nym couldn't look away. Her stomach tied in knots. He was stood with a larger woman of middle years. She had her arm around him. Nym thought either his lover or his wife. She suspected the latter.

Recognition slowly crept across his face as he met her gaze. He looked her over lecherously before his face hardened, and he turned away, pointedly ignoring her. A pang of sickening guilt washed over Nym as she regarded the woman stood with him. The feeling was followed by a flush of anger and humiliation.

Jor seized her arm. 'Come, lass, we're going.'

She was glad to be distracted from her thoughts and escape the uncomfortable proximity of this contemptible man as she allowed herself to be led away by the old tavern keeper.

They pushed through the loitering townsfolk and hurried back towards the stone archway. Other townsfolk scurried back along the track through the darkening groves. The sun had set below the hills and the gloom of night closed in. Behind them, the ring of stones was silhouetted against the orange glow of the bonfires. The drums echoed down through the trees, their timbre becoming hollow in the growing distance.

Nym looked up to a bright crescent of moon, which hung in the encroaching night sky. The sliver of moon looked framed by the illuminated edges of clouds overhead. She noted the first stars had begun faintly twinkling through the breaks of cloud above.

Jor hurried along the track with his cloak wrapped about him. Finn trailed in his wake, throwing longing glances back towards the ruddy glow of bonfires behind him as he wheeled Jor's empty barrow along the stony path. Nym knew he wanted to go back to the excitement of the drums and feasting.

They passed under the ancient stone lintel of the monolithic archway. Nym looked back through the archway into that realm of ghosts and gods. She hoped to catch a final glimpse of her mother's face somewhere in the shadows, looking back at her. Nym knew they were there somewhere and smiled.

Armed men bustled into view and followed through the stone arch behind them. Forcing their way along the path, the warriors were clearing the way so the approaching horses might pass.

***

'Wilhelm,' came a shout from the side of the track. Darkened faces looked out from the gloom. Folk which had stood aside to make way for his lord's horsemen. The other warriors jogged up the trackway bearing spluttering torches.

'Wilhelm,' came the call again. The warrior scanned the faces of the townsfolk he had just urged under the trees. A figure approached with a vague wave.

'Jor! I didn't see it was you,' replied Wilhelm trying to keep his voice down. 'Listen, Jor,' he continued in hushed tones as the old tavern keeper drew near. 'If you have any sense, you will get out of town. This sickness is spreading.'

Jor nodded fearfully.

Wilhelm looked about warily and continued, 'Warrick is going back to Arn with the lady tonight. We're pulling out of Anchorage 'til this blows over. If I were you, old friend, I'd get out too. I must move on, he's coming,' he said with a nod down the track. The sound of horses drew nearer.

Wilhelm clasped his friend's shoulder in farewell. 'Stay safe, Jor,' he said and jogged into the gloom.

***

Nym heard his armour chinking as he moved off. Jor returned to her side as the horses were coming past. Two men moved up carrying torches to light the way. The lord huscarl rode at the front with the princess at his side, her guards close behind. Nym got a much closer look at them as they passed so close.

Warrick looked younger than she expected, perhaps had not yet seen his fortieth year. His chin was shaven, revealing a lean face with sharp features.

The lady's horse trotted next to him. Nym could see the patterns woven and sewn into the princesses' dress. She wore jewellery about her neck. The lady turned her head and seemed to look straight at her. Nym could not be certain, likely all she saw were shadowed figures standing aside for her beneath the trees.

Several of Warrick's men followed their lord, either jogging or riding in his honour guard. The last torches moved past, those carrying them, disappearing into the gloom so only the flame and glare of torches could be seen moving back towards the town.

Jor hurried on, leading them back to the tavern.

'I knew we should not have gone,' said Jor absently as they he fumbled with the chain locking his tavern door. Once inside, he turned to Nym.

'Lass, gather what you need. We're going up into the city for a few days. I think Warrick has the right idea. If he's not staying, then I'm off, too. Maybe he knows somethin' we don't. I know some people in the city. And you, lad,' said Jor pointing a finger at Finn, 'had best keep his hands to himself and keep your nose out of mischief.'

Finn nodded vacantly. He looked concerned by their sudden flight from the town he knew. He had not really been into the city. Nym had a growing apprehension about not knowing where she was going. But still, it was a little exciting.

They gathered a few small possessions and headed back out onto the street. Jor ensured the tavern was locked up, fussing over his chains before they headed off.

Revellers and folk from the ritual had ebbed back through the streets. Some of the taverns they passed were open, spilling light and drunken cheers out into the night, the sickness forgotten with drink.

Jor hurried on, unmindful of the loss of profit, instead driven by the fear of Wilhelm's warning. Jor feared the roads could get closed and they would be trapped amongst the pestilence.

The aging tavern keeper led them towards the old wooden bridge leading to the northern district of Anchorage. It spanned one of the small river channels that flowed through the port town out into the estuary of the great Bane River. The small channels were used as sewers and reeked of fish and foul effluence.

Their route took them into the merchant's quarter. A more prosperous part of Anchorage than the docksides she grew up in, the home of merchants and wealthier folk. They passed workshops and closed up trader stalls, making their way up the main street towards the north gate.

'Where are we going, Jor? asked Finn.

Jor looked at him. 'The north gate, lad. We're heading up into Arn. I know some folk up there where we can keep our heads down.'

'What was that?' said Nym suddenly.

'What?' said Jor still hurrying onward.

Nym stopped and listened. She heard it again. The sound was a pitiful moaning, a call for help. It seemed to come from an alley. She approached apprehensively.

'Jor, I think there's someone down here,' she called out, stepping closer.

He scurried back to usher her onwards. 'Come, lass, leave them. We need to…' His words fell away, and he stood with his mouth agape at what he saw in the alley.

Nym stood frozen shocked by what she saw emerging from the shadow of the alley before her.

A girl clawed at the floor, pulling herself towards

Nym. Her face was in ruin, covered by oozing lesions. Her eyes stared sightlessly, lost behind a two bleeding sores. Blood ran down her chin. She vomited up a stream of gore which splattered on the cobbles. After a fit of coughing, the girl collapsed to the floor, her arms clutching forwards in desperation.

'Move, girl,' barked Jor in terror, unable to take his eyes of the bleeding girl. He pushed Nym roughly onwards as he stared and then, clutching her arm, he fled up the street dragging her onwards.

The gate loomed into view, two torches ensconced at either side, and a lone sentry stood guard. He made no attempt to challenge them as they hurried past him and out into the darkness beyond.

Jor meant to take the road that led to Arn's Marshside, a district of farm slums and warehouses. The road led over drained marshland, now tilled fields, and led into the eastern districts of the city. Still, a scent of stagnant water pervaded the night air. The well-travelled wagon track was a main route for the overland hauling of goods into Arn and was well kept, lined with wooden beams sunk into the soil. Nym tripped and stumbled over a submerged beam. Her toe throbbed where she had stubbed it. It was probably bleeding. She forced back the tears and continued onwards.

They hurried through the fields, careful not to stumble on the dark cart road. Fear still clutched at their hearts as they fled towards the flickering fires in the distance, the lights of the great city-sprawl of Arn.

CHAPTER TWENTY-THREE

Banners from Eymsford

Arnulf staggered along the seldom trodden trail which led from the town and up the hillside of the valley. Hafgan peered over the rocks watching from a distance, before moving up unseen between the trees. Ewolf followed close by his father. They seldom seemed to speak, and when they did, Hafgan was too far to hear the words that passed between them. Arnulf still cradled the ashen bundle of his cloak closely to his chest. Wrapped within the cloak, rested the ashes and charred bones of his loved ones.

The trail led along a ridge overlooking the lake. The slopes above became steep, narrowing the trail and eventually edging the path in with a stony cliff face. Hafgan had to be careful; he would be seen easily on such a narrow approach. He hugged the rocks closely, keeping his distance.

Hafgan remained ever vigilant of some lurking threat to his lord. He constantly checked behind him, all too aware of his lone vulnerability. Aware, he was perhaps more tempting a target for some foul creature than his lord and Ewolf. He remained vigilant, ever watchful.

The stone cliffside had been carved and sculpted as the trail approached its destination. Impressive stone frieze had been carved into the living rock with images of warriors and of horses, of vanquished foes, of his lord's ancestors and their deeds.

Hafgan peered around a shallow bend to see the pair had halted before a dark cleft in the cliff. After a moment, they moved inside. Hafgan had seldom been to this place. It was not his place.

He recalled memories of dutifully awaiting his lord to emerge from the gloom of the catacomb after visiting his ancestors. The opening and passageway to the crypts had also been ornately carved. How far the carvings went, he was not sure, for the passage led quickly into darkness, into the realms of the dead. He would not tread there, not without leave from his lord.

The big warrior waited patiently. He thought he could hear murmuring voices from the dark passageway. As time passed, he grew concerned. Hafgan could not see them and dared not follow. Yet, he feared what could unfold in that dark place if Ewolf suddenly succumbed to the madness.

A carved pedestal sat before the mouth of crypts, it bore the sigil of a great axe and was adorned with carved stone skulls. Hafgan leant upon the old stone and looked off into the lake below. Its surface was still and reflected the clouds above.

He heard footfalls echo up from the darkness. He quickly moved to a hiding place beyond the bend in the trail. How he would escape discovery he was uncertain, they would surely see him along the narrow trail.

Hafgan peered around the bend to watch his lord emerge from the darkness. Arnulf looked emotionally drained, a withered shell of the man he knew. He leant upon the pedestal with both hands, just as Hafgan himself had leant moments before.

Arnulf hung his head and stared down into the lake. His son, Ewolf came up beside him. He spoke gently to his father. Hafgan was too far to hear, but they seemed to be soft words of comfort.

Ewolf raised his arm above his head as he comforted his father. He held something. Hafgan's heart froze. It was a rock. Hafgan sprung forward desperately.

Horns suddenly sounded from across the valley. Hafgan darted bewildered eyes across the valley as he closed frantically upon his lord.

Arnulf's head snapped up as the horns blew. Ewolf's attention suddenly focussed across to the opposing hillsides also. His hand lowered at the sudden distraction. The rock tumbled from his fingers.

'My lord,' called Hafgan as he approached from behind them. His voice startled Ewolf.

Arnulf swung his head.

The big warrior eyed young Ewolf warily, suddenly unsure. Arnulf had seen nothing.

'Banners approach, lord,' managed Hafgan, seizing upon an opportune explanation for his presence. 'Forgive the intrusion, Arnulf,' said Hafgan, his eyes fixed unwavering on Ewolf.

Arnulf did not notice and returned his gaze to the approaching banners.

Ewolf had a strange look to his eyes. His look was anxious. Hafgan suspected the lad knew he had seen what he had been about to do. The young warrior watched him nervously.

'Aye, Haf,' replied Arnulf, his voice hollow.

Horns blew again. An answering call returned from the Motte.

'They approach soon, lord,' said Hafgan.

Hafgan watched the young Ewolf like a hawk as they returned to the Motte. They passed through quiet streets and began the ascent to the gates of the upper palisade.

'Folk have begun searching and clearing, lord,' said Hafgan. Seizing this moment, he said, 'We thought it best to check the wounded again also.'

'Yes, good Haf. It is probably wise,' replied Arnulf, trying to pull his thoughts together.

Hafgan addressed Ewolf, 'Engle told me you took a slight wound, lad?'

As Ewolf turned, he indeed still wore a strange look to his eyes. He was fidgety.

Arnulf gasped.

'His arm,' said Hafgan.

'You are wounded, son?' asked Arnulf urgently.

'Aye, Father, but it is fine. It was not bad,' said Ewolf.

Arnulf turned to Hafgan, a worried look in his eye.

'You will need that seen to,' ventured Hafgan.

'Father, it is fine,' protested Ewolf.

'Is the wound clean?' asked Hafgan as he closed upon Ewolf. 'Here, let me see,' insisted Hafgan. He reached out.

Ewolf snatched his arm away. 'It is fine,' he protested angrily.

'Ewolf,' shouted Arnulf, his voice full of emotion. 'Son, let him look.'

Ewolf allowed Hafgan to pull back his sleeve and reveal a dressing. The wound beneath was small. It did not look bad. Hafgan was however concerned by the dark veins that had begun to appear from the wound like black tendrils reaching up his arm.

'I am fine, Father,' protested the young warrior.

'There are signs of it, Arnulf,' said Hafgan gravely. 'I only hope it is only a rot of the flesh and not of the mind.

'I hope by the gods you are well, lad,' said Hafgan to Ewolf.

'He is well, and he is strong,' ventured Arnulf. 'It has not taken him. I believe he will be alright.'

'I hope so. But lord,' continued the big warrior, turning to Arnulf, 'I fear he still must be watched, just in case, and anyone else showing any signs of it, too. Perhaps, they should be locked securely in a house under guard until we can be sure. We must learn what is happening here.'

Arnulf looked long and hard at his son before nodding slowly in agreement.

Hafgan turned back to Ewolf. 'I am sorry. We

must be certain you are yourself.'

The young warrior began to protest angrily, but Arnulf cut him short.

'Go, Ewolf! Do as I ask. It will not be for long, I promise. You are strong so do not worry, son,' said Arnulf. 'Remain in one of the houses for me. You will be under guard, but I will have them bring you ale and food. Please go, for me, and be well...please.'

Arnulf watched painfully as his son sullenly walked away towards one of the houses. Hafgan gestured for two of the men to follow.

Hafgan did not have the heart to tell his lord what he had seen. He feared the lad was succumbing to the same terrible fate as the others.

'Guard him, do not let him leave,' Hafgan murmured quietly to the guards, and with a glance at Arnulf said, 'and if there are any changes, or he becomes violent, call for us immediately. Do not let him out!'

Ewolf's anger flared as he became flanked by the two warriors. He turned towards Arnulf. 'This is wrong, Father,' he shouted. 'Get away, you bastards,' he cursed, pushing one of the men.

One of the warriors seized his arm. Ewolf fought to break free He roared in sudden fury, but the two men held him firmly and led the struggling warrior into a nearby building.

Hafgan watched on with a worried expression, watching young Ewolf apprehensively as he thrashed and fought to break free. Arnulf watched as his son was led away.

Something behind his eyes seemed to break, and

Arnulf hung his head. Hafgan had no words. All he could do was stand there beside Arnulf in silence.

Hafgan watched the fluttering banners approach. Leaning upon the wooden ramparts of the high palisade's gate tower, he looked down upon the file of men and glinting steel moving through the town below. The big warrior ran a calloused hand over his shaved pate. They were the high lord's men. His banners bore the same swooping white falcon as Fergus wore—their family sigil—but these were red instead of blue.

Hafgan turned to Arnulf. His lord looked down over the rampart also, but he seemed distant, his eyes unseeing. Hafgan felt a deep sorrow for his lord. His family ripped from him, his home destroyed, and now maybe his son. He looked lost in despair. Arnulf fought back a sob and hung his head.

Hafgan placed a supportive arm on his lord's shoulder. The big warrior opened his mouth to speak but could not find the words so he remained silent.

Arnulf took a deep breath and straightened. Hafgan watched his lord's attempts to steel himself, poorly burying his anguish, yet trying to project some manner of solemnity, of lordly authority. Still, he did not speak. He just looked down upon the approaching soldiers.

Hafgan regarded his lord with a grave respect and nodded to himself with a weak smile. Arnulf was strong, Hafgan knew though he would need to grieve in his own way. The big warrior would be relied upon, he knew. As would Engle, the castellan. They would need to be his lord's arm in this terrible time. He would do all he could to return life back to the terrified folk of Ravenshold and leave his lord to his grief.

'Fuck. What is the old bastard doing here?' said Fergus as he laid eyes upon the honour guard.

'We sent riders, lord,' ventured Engle. 'We were under attack. Surely, they are most welcome....' He trailed off as nobody turned.

'Aye,' said Hafgan. 'All that steel will certainly reassure the folk down there that they will be safe now, that their lords will protect them.'

'Aye, Haf,' said Fergus mockingly, 'but you don't have to deal with the old bastard like I do.' He laughed. 'Still, I am glad there are so many.'

Still Arnulf stood, not speaking. Hafgan turned his attention to the approaching warriors once more. The mounted vanguard began to climb the Motte's steep bank towards the keep. Pennons hung from their spears.

'Open the gates,' called Hafgan.

The wooden gates slowly swung open and allowed the riders to spill into the Motte's courtyard. The honour guard rode through in their wake trailing two great red falcon banners.

Angus, High Lord of the Borders, rode from their midst. Fergus's lineage was apparent in his father's face. Fergus shared that same mane of red curls, although Angus had greyed, and his hair was only now touched with auburn streaks. They shared the same nose and eyes. He wore a richly embroidered long brown jerkin over a fine chain hauberk, its rings small and light to not offer much weight. The mail came down to his thighs and the jerkin nearly to his boots. A heavy warm looking cloak hung round his shoulders, it was red with a thin trim of expensive looking fine fur. He reined in his horse.

'Lord,' called Hafgan in greeting as they descended from the fighting platform. The high lord waved him aside and addressed Arnulf.

'Greetings, Arnulf. I have heard terrible things. I am so very sorry.'

Arnulf nodded.

'I did not know if I would find you here, Arnulf. I had word the Watch had been attacked. I trust your post is still manned?'

'Aye, lord,' replied Arnulf, 'the Watch has not been broken.'

Angus nodded.

'A rider met us on the road this morning. He told us the Motte was burning. I have seen the smoke from miles away. I feared the whole town had been razed.'

He dismounted.

'Son,' said Angus with a nod to Fergus as he turned from his saddle.

'I should have guessed you would be here and not back in Weirdell where you belong. Rushing away from your duties when you have much to do, I'm certain. I make you lawgiver and lord of a great holding, and you ride off at the first excuse. Could you not send someone?' He paused. 'Must you always play the fool.' Lord Angus smirked slightly at his son.

Fergus smiled in reply.

'Still, you do your friend a great service, son,' Angus continued. 'You did well to ride for the Lord of the Watch so quickly.'

'Yes, Father. I ever strive for somewhere even close to your wisdom,' replied Fergus sardonically.

'Watch your mouth, boy. You're never too old for a clout 'round the head from me.' He smiled at his son once more. But Fergus looked like he did not doubt it. It was known that his father was ever critical in his affections upon his children and a stern lord in addition.

'Arnulf, come,' said Angus, walking towards the burning embers of the hall. Arnulf followed.

***

'What in the gods has happened here…and up in the passes?' asked Angus.

'My men were attacked, lord,' said Arnulf, his face grim. 'But the watch post is still manned. I lost half a dozen men. We pursued the…enemy into the passes.'

'What enemy?'

'Lord, you would not believe it.'

'Umm we shall see. I did hear some strange words from the last rider we met, Arnulf. The one your man sent out this morning.'

'Engle, lord,' said Arnulf.

'Yes, yes. That rider, whoever sent him. He spoke of the dead…and fell creatures.' He shook his head. 'I thought him to be a madman. Now tell me, Arnulf,' he said, levelling a stern gaze at Arnulf. 'What is the truth of this?'

Arnulf hesitated. 'Lord...I did not believe it myself. My men will vouch, any man would. But...I think we saw the dead walk.'

Arnulf recounted the events of the passes, from the strange bell and of the first patrol failing to return, to the attack in the pass.

'You must have been deceived, Arnulf,' exclaimed Angus. 'The dead don't walk. How do you know they were truly dead? It was some trick.'

'I thought so too, lord. But the wounds they took, no man could take such and stand. They shrugged off mighty blows. They looked to feel no pain and just kept coming. I have never seen anything like it, lord. They were dead, without doubt, rotted, some a long time dead. These were no masks or trickery. I checked some of the bodies myself. They were dead, I swear.'

Arnulf shook his head and looked to Fergus. Angus followed his gaze. 'You saw this, son?'

Fergus nodded as he caught his father's eye, and then looked to the floor. His father's expression was not sure whether it was bemused or furious.

'Seriously, lads, this is no time for stories. You expect me to believe this?'

'I swear it,' said Arnulf. He began to doubt his own memories and hung his head. He could hear the words he spoke. It indeed sounded like the ravings of a madman. Had he been deceived? No, there was no doubt. He had seen it. He looked his high lord in the face. 'I swear it, lord'

The high lord looked to his son. Fergus nodded.

'By the gods,' gasped Angus, 'is there more?'

'Aye, lord,' nodded Arnulf. He spoke of the farm,

of the girl and her brother. Angus's expression became grave as the tale unfolded. Arnulf told of how Olad had changed and turned upon them, of the ruins and the campsite they had discovered. He told his lord the tales they had heard upon their return, of the townsfolk changing, and of the great slaughter that had unfolded.'

'Dear gods,' muttered Angus. The high lord looked around at the charred ruins of the hall. 'Did anyone make it out?' asked Angus gravely.

'No, lord, all perished,' said Arnulf.

'Arnulf, I am so very sorry. The rider…we heard. Many were trapped in the hall.'

Arnulf stared, restraining his grief.

'It is a hard thing,' continued Angus, 'such a terrible thing, to lose them.' Angus paused thoughtfully. He wore an old pain in his eye. 'To lose them… Aye, I know this for myself. They are with Old Night. We will see them all again.' Angus placed a hand upon Arnulf's shoulder. 'Both you, and I also. It is a hard thing, lad, a hard thing.'

They stared into the embers for a short while before moving back to join the others.

'We will hunt these things, Arnulf,' said Angus. 'Kill these dead men, and these cursed ones. Scour these lands. We must. I will not have this evil befall my land, this I swear now before you all.

'Now come, let us find a suitable building and we can get one of your people to find us some ale, and we will talk.'

***

Settled into the guard building beside the gates the lords of Arnar sat around a modest table before a log fire. The guard building sheltered up against the palisade immediately beside the gates. It was a place where the warriors of the Motte often spent time when between duties - or when not at home with their families.

Hafgan sat nursing an ale, regarding the others. Fergus poured himself another ale into a plain pewter cup. Young Erran sat at a table by the door with one of Fergus's men and another from the high lord's retinue playing a game of winds. Fergus hovered around their table looking at their hands before smiling knowingly and returning to the central table.

Engle and Hafgan were still busy discussing the distribution of warriors and defences with Angus as Fergus seated himself. Arnulf had sat mostly in silence nursing his ale, occasionally venturing forth a suggestion or nodding in agreement to the trusted counsel of his advisors. Angus and Fergus had their men billeted in defendable buildings throughout the town as suggested by Hafgan. Barricades and pickets were to be set up on the towns and thoroughfares. All routes would be watched closely, and the town would be heavily guarded. Talk was turning to the pursuit of the enemy. It was being proposed that patrols were to scour the surrounding countryside for any sign of the cursed dead.

Astrid entered the guardhouse followed by two men. The first man was one of Angus's lieutenants. He was mailed and wore an axe and a seax at his waist. He removed the helmet he wore over his straggled dark hair, which tumbled about his shoulders. He was not a big man and had a short untidy beard. For a man of rank amongst the high lord's warriors, he had an unassuming look to him. Hafgan did not know his name.

The second man that entered was not of the warrior's mould. He was balding with a thin face. He wore robes and carried a satchel. He slipped in quietly.

'Lord' said the mailed lieutenant with a nod. 'The men are settled, and we've set a heavy guard out in the town, lord.'

'As are ours,' said Astrid.

Fergus nodded in acknowledgement.

Erran seemed abnormally distracted from his game, his eyes following Astrid. She returned him a stern glance as she surveyed the room.

'Good, good,' said Angus, 'Speak with Engle and Hafgan here. They will direct you with what we have just decided. But first, come. Have a swift drink with us.'

The lieutenant poured ale into a tin mug from a large earthen jug. He poured another and handed it to the shield-maiden.

Angus turned to Astrid as she took the mug. 'You still keeping his arse safe, Astrid?' asked the high lord with a thumb at his son. 'I couldn't put up with his crap. I don't know how you do it,' he added.

She kept a grim face and replied. 'Aye, lord. I do my duties, and he pays us well.' She paused. 'Our lord Fergus needs keeping an eye on, as I am sure you know. And for the sake of the womenfolk, of course,' she added with nothing but a slight smirk at the corner of her mouth. 'They pay us nearly as much as he does to keep him away,' she added with a glance at Fergus.

'Don't listen to her, Father,' Fergus protested. 'She has a viper's tongue. If she wasn't so good with a sword, I'd have her serving in the hall.' Fergus grinned at her. She gave him a wry but stern look.

'Worked out well for the last man that tried that,' muttered Hafgan.

Fergus's father grunted in amusement. 'I can very well believe it,' said Angus as he feigned a disapproving frown at his son.

Hafgan concealed a grin.

'I'll remember that next time I'm handing out silver,' said Fergus directing a glowering smirk at Astrid.

The shield-maiden caught Erran's lingering eye.

'And you, boy, what are you staring at?' she demanded with a scowl suddenly.

The young warrior flushed for an instant but quickly recovered, 'Nothing, forgive me.' He nearly floundered, but then added, 'When you have a moment, I would ask you if you would consider my request.'

'What is this?' enquired Angus.

'The lad asked her to spar, so she can kick his ass,' replied Fergus, still amused.

'It would be an honour,' added Erran.

'And will you?' asked Angus curiously to Astrid.

'If I have to, but don't you think this is not the time for such foolishness, *boy*,' said Astrid harshly, the latter directed at Erran.

Erran looked slightly abashed. He smiled meekly and busied himself in the game before him, not meeting anyone's eye.

Fergus raised his eyebrows. Fergus was about to say something, then thought better of it. She did not look like she would say anymore on the matter, and by her scowl, it did not seem wise to pursue the topic.

'Well,' said Angus cutting the moment of awkward silence that followed, 'how do you like the ale?' He took a deep draught of his mug and nodded with satisfaction. 'Long ride,' he added to no one in particular.

'Lord, if I may…' said the quiet man in the corner.

'Oh yes, of course. Get yourself one, too, man,' barked Angus.

'Ah, no…thank you, lord, but…I didn't mean…' The thin man awkwardly floundered.

'Someone get the man a drink before even the gods hear of his thirst. Ha,' laughed Angus.

'I will, lord, thank you. Uh… But that wasn't why I… Ah…' He stuttered, and then composed himself. 'Sorry, lord. I have been chronicling all I can. There are some strange tales I am hearing. I don't know if I can quite believe it.'

'Believe it,' said Hafgan harshly.

The thin man looked at stern faces surrounding him and pursued the subject no further. When the subject of the dead arose, Hafgan had noticed a certain reservation behind the eyes of those who had not witnessed it themselves. An almost amused disbelief, yet none dared challenge those whose eyes were wrought with grief and terrified by what they had seen.

The thin man addressed Arnulf, 'I am sorry for the fell happenings here, Lord Arnulf.'

Arnulf seemed distant. He sat absently stroking Fear's ears as the hound sat at his feet.

'It is a small gesture,' he went on, 'but with your leave, I can let my apprentice help with work on re-building your hall. He has studied the building craft of some of the greatest artisans in the known world.'

Arnulf looked at the man as if he had only just noticed him for the first time but said nothing.

'Aye, we will rebuild the great hall of your fathers,' promised Angus. 'Do not fear, Arnulf. Life for the folks of Ravenshold will return to as it once was. We will rebuild it all, Arnulf. I will send for what help you may need. And there will be vengeance upon the evil responsible. This I promise.'

'I fear many have lost so much, life will never return. How can it? We lost so many. But you have my thanks, lord,' said Arnulf. 'As do you, friend,' said Arnulf to the thin man.

'Ah, of course. Sorry, Arnulf. This is Calimir, one of my advisors.'

Arnulf nodded a greeting to the man as Angus began introducing him to the others.

Angus continued, 'A fine scholar. His people are already showing their worth in Eymsford. They have made some worthy changes to the running of the harbours, and several of the local farmsteads have been producing much more than last year. Our coffers have certainly noticed the difference, aye. He insisted he come along to... How did you say it? To chronicle events as they unfolded.'

'Indeed lords, an attack on a watch post is unprecedented. Someone should be there to make an account firsthand for the *Great Histories*,' said Calimir eagerly.

'Since we arrived, I have attempted to speak with several of the men who were up in the passes with you but…'

'But what?' demanded Fergus.

'Well, lord, I understand some do not wish to talk but many have become…well, hostile, once I have greeted them. Folk are whispering as I pass, it seems none have any love for a man of the College. I don't understand it.'

Arnulf, Fergus, and Hafgan exchanged glances.

'I do not doubt it,' said Fergus rising. 'The folk with us have returned to their families. I have no doubt word has spread about what we found.'

'What?' asked Angus noticing a sudden change in the atmosphere of the room. Arnulf sat up straight, suddenly animated. He fixed his attention intently on the thin man named Calimir. Fear rose up and looked around warily also sensing the sudden change.

'We found something up at the campsite,' said Arnulf. He leaned over and murmured to Hafgan. The big warrior rose and left the room. He returned shortly and placed a large book and a tattered journal upon the table.

'These are from the campsite up at the ruins,' said Arnulf. He opened the larger book and revealed the seal of the College.

'And we know these fucking bastards had something to do with this,' said Arnulf, prodding the image of the College's seal.

'Now tell me...*friend*,' said Arnulf, the latter dripping with vehemence. 'What were your people doing up in the passes? Tell me all you know.'

'I don't know anything of it, lord. I swear,' said Calimir.

'Don't lie to me,' shouted Arnulf, hammering the table with his fist. He advanced menacingly.

'Please, lord,' squealed the scholar.

Calimir raised his hands and backed away, intimidated.

'I can help. I can tell you who that belonged to if you let me look at it a moment. I may be able to figure out what happened up there, lord.'

'Why should I trust you?' snarled Arnulf.

'Let him look, Arnulf,' commanded Angus, bewildered.

Arnulf paused and levelled an angry glare at the scholar, before relenting unhappily.

'Do not let any of this out of your sight,' fumed Arnulf, indicating the book to Hafgan.

Calimir timidly approached the table under the scrutiny of unfriendly eyes from all present but Angus. It was apparent all who had been up in the passes laid a heavy distrust upon his shoulders.

The scholar quickly scanned the first page.

'It is the grimoire of Master Eldrick, my lords,' said Calimir without meeting their eyes. 'I know of him,' he said as he continued to leaf through the thick vellum pages. 'His work in the lore of healing is well known at the College. It appears he has some expertise in anatomy, herb craft, and ritual healing practices. Remarkable work, lords.'

The last statement elicited an irritated grunt from Arnulf.

'So, what was he doing up there?' asked Fergus as he eyed his old friend. Arnulf seethed beneath a controlled exterior, his eyes fixed hard upon the scholar. Hafgan had never seen such anger in his lord.

'I am not sure, lord,' replied Calimir hesitantly.

'Well, what are the last entries?' asked Engle.

The scholar flicked to the last inscribed pages and began reading. Engle rose and moved to examine the book himself also.

'Well?' demanded Fergus.

'It's…it's some sort of rambling notes from an experiment,' said Calimir. 'It doesn't make much sense. There are detailed anatomical drawings here, and then there is work on some sort of glyphic text—I don't recognise it—he keeps referring to the ritual… And the watching darkness…I can't make sense of it, lord, it's incomplete.'

'These drawings are unsettling,' said Engle. 'This is some grim work. He is drawing the innards of limbs and bodies. How can he know of this? Unless…' Engle trailed off, his face whitened.

'What have you people been doing?' demanded Engle. 'Folk have been butchered for this. People have been *butchered*!' He flicked an appalled gaze around the room. 'What have they done.'

Fergus walked over and looked over the pages. 'And this?' He pointed at the strange text written in eerie looking glyphs. 'What is this, some sort of fell sorcery? Is this what your College does?'

The scholar backed away, shaking his head at the tirade of accusing questions.

'No, the College would not do such things. There are no true sorcerers as you hear in the old tales, they are just stories. There is no truth to it. We are recorders of truth, chroniclers of knowledge.' He appealed to his lord. 'I swear it.'

High Lord Angus nodded but remained uncertain, he obviously trusted this man.

'This is madness,' pleaded Calimir. 'Any of us from the College would be the first to tell you there is no such thing as sorcery. There must be some innocent explanation. I would bet these men were not involved in this.'

'He's lying,' said Arnulf.

The scholar began pleading with Angus.

'Calimir, my friend, you would not lie to me?' said Angus calmly. 'I do not believe you had anything to do with this.'

'Thank you, lord.'

'I hope for your sake you speak the truth,' said Angus. He turned to Arnulf and Fergus. 'Perhaps these College folk met the same evil that befell your men in the passes.'

'I am not so sure, lord,' said Arnulf. 'Why were they up there? And without any leave or word to the Lord of the Watch or, indeed, to any of us. These are our lands. These College men think they can just go where they will, without our say.' Arnulf levelled a finger at Calimir. 'They did this, lord, and he is hiding something.'

Angus sighed. 'Now, swear to me Calimir, you had no knowledge of this Eldrick being in the passes or of any of this.'

'I swear, lord.' The scholar hesitated, 'but I must tell you now, I heard of their passing through Eymsford some moons back. I did not know why, nor did I ask, but I heard they were heading north for Cydor on College business. I did not know what, I swear.'

'Why did you not mention this,' demanded Angus.

'Why would I, lord? Many College folk regularly come and go, all across the realm and beyond. It is no different to reporting a trader had passed through. Why would I?'

'He is hiding something, my lord. I can feel it,' growled Arnulf.

'As far as I have seen, Calimir is a good man, Arnulf. I would see proof before I changed my mind. He has given me nothing but sound counsel' said Angus.

Arnulf scowled and returned to his seat.

'Now, Calimir,' continued the high lord, 'return to the men and keep your head down. The truth of this will come to light.

'But, lord, I can be of help,' protested the scholar. 'If you would let me study this grimoire, or the journal, I can find answers.'

'You will do no such thing,' barked Arnulf. 'These books will not leave Hafgan's possession. Engle can study it. I do not want anything to...accidentally happen to it.'

'But, lord, I would not...'

'Just go, Calimir,' rumbled Angus, 'your presence is not helping here. I will come to you when this is done.'

The scholar backed away towards the door and left.

'The College is to blame for this. Calimir should not be trusted,' said Arnulf once the door closed. 'He will cover for his College.'

'Aye, Father,' ventured Fergus, 'the College is perhaps not what it seems. The evidence is right here before us. They have been practicing a grave evil. This is obvious looking at these portrayals of butchery.'

'Perhaps we should not have that open,' ventured Erran, indicating the open grimoire. 'Who knows what evil could come from it.'

There were nods of agreement and Hafgan closed the grimoire's heavy binding.

'I know this man, and I have met others, they do not appear to be evil men, they are scholars,' objected Angus. 'We here are lords and warriors,' he said with a gesture around the room. 'It is us warriors who spill men's blood in the name of Arnar. Surely we are the butchers here, not these meek men of letters.'

'If you had seen what we saw you would be quicker to damn them for these crimes,' said Fergus. 'I saw pits of dead men, slaughtered, disembowelled, and then somehow risen again. Perhaps Old Night himself sent them back from the grave to avenge this evil wrought upon them. I stand with Arnulf in this, as do us all, they must answer for this.'

'And what would you have me do?' demanded Angus.

'Word should be sent to the king. The men of the watch posts have been attacked. If so by the College's doing, then they should answer for this treason.'

A murmur of agreement rippled through the room.

'And tell him what? That dead men are walking? He will think me a madman,' cried Angus.

'I will go, lord,' offered Arnulf. 'It is my duty as Lord of the Watch.'

'You have your duties here, Arnulf,' replied the high lord. 'The watch posts must be manned. It is your duty 'til after the winter, and you are needed here with your people.'

'I must go, lord,' argued Arnulf. 'As you say, he may not believe the tale from a messenger. And as Lord of the Watch, my sworn word will have weight.'

Angus looked sceptical.

'I will go too, Father,' said Fergus.

'No, no you will not, Son. I will not have our name mocked in the capital for this tale.'

'I must, Father, Arnulf will need that very name to vouch for our tale. I saw this all with my own eyes as did everyone who was with us.'

Angus shook his head in disbelief.

'You still doubt us, Father?' asked Fergus.

'I trust your word, all of you, but…forgive my doubts. Such fantastic claims, I have not seen with my own eyes…'

'I pray you don't have to, lord,' ventured Hafgan. 'But look around, a town full of people make the same claims, dozens lie dead or are missing, trusted warriors swear it upon the honour of Arnar and the gods themselves.' He paused. 'Let my lord ride south and get news to the king. Let him take this before the king and hear what the College have to say on this.'

Angus frowned thoughtfully.

'Please, lord,' said Arnulf, 'I cannot bear to be here. Aeslin, my little girl, Idony, they were in that hall. They are with the gods.' He paused, stricken with grief. 'I cannot bear to be reminded of it every moment of the day. Let me be away for a time. My son will be here, Engle, and Haf also.'

'No, lord, my place is at your side,' cut in Hafgan.

Arnulf nodded gratefully.

'You were not expected to be back here 'til after the snows clear, lord. I can manage,' offered Engle. 'The hall should be rebuilt by your return, and your seat will be waiting. Ewolf will be here in your stead.'

'Aye.' Arnulf nodded.

There was a silence.

'Aye, the king must hear of this,' said Angus finally. 'But the watch posts must remain manned. See to this and I will allow it. You have done your part up there, Arnulf. All of you have. I will do mine and see these lands scoured clean of this evil.'

The door of the guard room crashed open as a warrior rushed in. The sound of commotion outside followed him. A spine-chilling shriek rose over the cacophony.

'Lord Arnulf,' the warrior gasped, 'come quickly. It is your son.'

CHAPTER TWENTY-FOUR

Vengeance

Calimir closed the door to the guardhouse and turned. His normally meek demeanour slowly perturbed by a rising anger. He stormed away towards the gates, barely noticing the commotion erupting across by the far palisade. He was suddenly furious. He fought to contain himself as he walked.

How dare they? Such absurd accusations against him, against his College. For sorcery! Absolutely absurd. There would be no substance to it. He knew the College could prove it, too. Sorcery is a thing of myth.

But the sheer absurdity of it all had him riled. How could these men of power be so superstitious and foolish? He would see one of these dead men for himself and find the truth of the matter.

He felt angry that they would test Angus's trust in him. He had worked hard to prove the worth of the College. Angus sent a lot of gold and silver to the College coffers, and he had paid him well for his services. He worried that the high lord now doubted him.

A pair of soldiers pushed past him in a hurry as he passed through the gates. They hurried towards the raised voices and shouts. It was likely some drunken fight and of no concern to him.

He noticed a small group of townsfolk stared at him as he descended from the gate. He waved but received only icy stares in return. Many of the townsfolk still sheltered on the slopes of the Motte, too scared to return to their homes. They had set up a rambling sprawl of makeshift shelters, built from what they could find. Many folk sat huddled about, swathed in blankets and cloaks. Refugees in their own town.

Folk whispered and watched him with suspicion. A sense of rancour towards the staring townsfolk did nothing to improve his mood. He had done nothing but try to help these people since his arrival. He perhaps had come across slightly condescending, or even mocking, while listening to the accounts of those few townsfolk he had spoken with earlier. They had obviously been fooled by a clever ruse.

The dead don't walk.

The attention on him intensified as he passed amongst the townsfolk. He began to feel uncomfortably self-conscious as he made his way back to Angus's wagons. Folk stopped their conversations to watch him pass. Others were pointing him out and whispering amongst themselves. It was more than the mistrust of a stranger. He was beginning to feel distinctly unwelcome.

He was in no mood for these superstitious fools. The College was the very centre of knowledge and study in these lands. Now these folk stare at him as if knowledge is something not to be trusted—the backward fools.

He found the wagon where he had stowed his belongings. As he rummaged through a bag, some-one knocked into him as they passed and sent him sprawling to the floor.

'Watch where you stand,' came a spiteful voice. 'You're not welcome here, *sorcerer*.' The last word dripping with vehemence.

The two men went on their way and joined an-other group, who all stood nearby, watching him menacingly.

An old woman cackled at him from amongst them. 'You and your College will pay for this, you little bastard.' She pointed an accusing finger at him. 'Murderers,' she shrieked before being bundled away by a younger woman.

He quickly rose to his feet and fumbled in the wagon. He took out a wine skin and his pack and hurried off. He went to join the safety and more fa-miliar company of Angus's warriors. They, at least, treated him no different from normal and offered him a measure of protection from these idiot towns-folk.

He sat on the grass slope not far from the cookfire of some of Angus's weary and foot-sore men. Looking about, he could see unfriendly eyes still lingered upon him.

He twisted the cap off his wine skin and took a deep drink, ignoring the unwanted attention. His anger had subsided into a more anxious fear. These folk truly seemed hostile towards him. Many had lost loved ones, they needed someone to blame.

He sighed and stared into the low flickering flames of the cookfire. The wine was good, from the Telik traders in Eymsford. He took another deep draught.

The gloom of dusk was encroaching. Angus's warriors seemed a little less lively than normal, the dark mood of the town smothering their usual cheer. Most of them paid him no notice and left him to his wine as he tried his best not to be noticed.

The pair of men who had knocked him to the floor at the wagons lingered nearby, trying to intimidate him. They were doing a fine job of it, too. They moved between clusters of townsfolk, talking and throwing spiteful looks in his direction. They pointed him out to some of the Motte's guardsmen. Even they turned to throw hateful glares at him.

Calimir sank low against the grassy bank of the Motte and covered himself in his cloak. He took a long drink from his wineskin and looked up into the clouds. The dark smoke from the burnt hall rose up high into the sky and dispersed into the clouds overhead. The wine helped him slip into a light and uneasy sleep.

A hand clamped suddenly over his mouth. He awoke in shock and tried to call out. His cries were muffled by the tight grip over his face. It was dark.

'You make a sound and I'll slit your throat right here and now,' said a harsh, whispered voice in his ear.

The terrified scholar was pulled to his feet. He struggled to get free. He felt the cold touch of steel press against his throat. He froze in terror.

'He ain't coming quietly,' rasped another hushed voice.

'Aye.'

Calimir felt a sharp blow to the back of his head, and then nothing as he fell into dark unconsciousness.

CHAPTER TWENTY-FIVE

The Dolmen's Eyes

He was roused from his rest by a chill gust of wind. It was dark. He pulled his blanket closer around him. He found himself still laid in the back of the wagon. His eyes slowly adjusted to his dark surroundings. The motionless wagon appeared to be surrounded in a swirling ethereal mist.

He thought it strange and sat up. The wind still gusted against him but it made no disturbance in the peculiar mist. *Strange indeed,* he thought. He pushed himself up with the butt of Logan's staff and looked around the campsite with nervous curiosity.

The fire had burnt down, but he could make out the campsite around the wagon. It was night, and several hours until dawn, yet the white of the mist offered a strange illumination to the gloom.

His companion laid on the floor on a ground sheet. The hired-sword slept motionless, covered in his cloak. The apprentice did not want to wake him.

He stepped down from the wagon. His hair was blown about by the strong gusting wind, yet the wind made no mark on the strange mist that hung thick in the air. The breeze was strangely silent. The surrounding night was shrouded in an eerie quiet.

Looking out into the gloom beyond their cooling hearth-fire, he could make out strange shapes though the mist. He began to curiously wander towards them. Ancient stone menhirs emerged from the rolling fog.

He had not noticed any such stones when they had stopped the wagon to strike camp. Nor had he noticed any trees nearby the road, yet there were evidently trees growing amongst the old stones. It gave him an odd feeling. The menhirs reminded him of those around the mounds and eerie ruins back up in the passes. He felt glad to be away from that cold place.

He wandered further between the stones, every step taking him further from the wagon. He continued onwards, looking into the misty murk between the trees.

He examined the strange old stones as they loomed out at him through the haze. He stopped before one such stone and touched the cold rock of its surface. Up close, he could feel that there seemed to be traces of a faded patterning, which had once been carved into the old menhir.

Oh, how his master, and certainly Logan, too,

would love to see these stones for themselves. He decided he would return to further examine some of the stones in the dawn light. He could perhaps record some of these strange markings. He was certain the masters would appreciate such an endeavour. The hired-sword would grumble at the delay, but despite his intimidating grim nature, he was still in the employ of the College. He would have to indulge the apprentice's work.

As the apprentice absently ran his hand over the faint carvings, his thoughts turned to Truda and his masters. He had enjoyed the company of Master Logan's apprentice. He missed Truda. It would be very good to talk with her again, to see her face, her quick smile and her wry eyes. He thought of her for a lengthy moment and sighed.

He longed for the familiar company of his colleagues. The hired-sword had been solemn company on the road, as if the man resented having him along. The apprentice was not unaware of his burden on the man's workload. He did not feel good for much of anything other than sitting in the bumpy wagon and resting his broken leg.

It was then he suddenly realised, his leg barely felt any pain. He walked for dozens of metres but had not considered his leg once. He still walked using Logan's staff, but he had walked all this way from the wagon with both his legs, almost forgetting the injury. The normally shooting agony of walking had been replaced with only a dull ache. The splint Logan and his master had set was obviously working.

He hoped they were not far behind. After all, the

masters had completed much of their work, otherwise he would not have been sent back ahead of them with a wagon full of reports and findings. The apprentice knew his master, Eldrick, had all but completed his work, as had Logan weeks prior, but still he seemed preoccupied with yet another few rituals. His master had felt something was unfinished yet knew not what it was. The apprentice had often lately heard him mumble how close he was. Almost obsessively his master had insisted on more time, eager to stay a little longer yet to see his work through.

The apprentice hoped his master's work had not been slowed by his own departure. He had not completed several of his studies for Eldrick. He had not finished his moon observations. The very study he had been engaged in when he fell and broke his leg.

Suddenly reminded, he looked up to search the night sky. The silver shimmer of moonlight betrayed its position in the sky through the strange mist.

He had done his best to continue to chart his observations whilst on the road, despite his absence. He hoped the work would perhaps still be useful to his master when he returns. Each night since his departure he had observed the moon. Its shape noted, and its position charted. He recorded his findings as best he could in the back of the bumpy wagon.

With a weird shock that struck the pit of his stomach, he noticed it was the wrong shape. He knew the moon was waxing, the dead moon had been some nights past now. Only yesterday, it had been merely a slim waxing crescent. Through the mists above he became bewildered at how it could look such as strange shape?

A chill ran down his spine. He had never seen such a moon. It felt un-natural and made him apprehensive. The more he stared up at it, the more it resembled a terrible eye, peering down upon him through the mist and wind.

He heard a twig break off in the gloom. He felt a pang of panic and looked into the swirling mist. Dark shapes of what he hoped were other standing stones stood looming through the fog. He could make out the nearby trees growing amongst them.

That dreadful sense of being watched crept over him. It made him shudder. He hoped it was just the buffeting of this strange and silent wind against his face, or perhaps the watchful eye of that strange moon glaring through this eerie mist which had him so spooked.

He thought it best to begin to make his way back to the wagon. He should have known it to be unwise to go venturing off from the wagon at night.

The apprentice turned to retrace his steps through the menhirs and back to the wagon. As he walked, the apprentice worried about what his grim companion could do if he got himself lost. The hired-sword would likely be glad to wash his hands of his crippled burden. He might not even look for him if he found him gone in the morning and quickly move on.

He flicked nervous glances up at the watching moon. The luminous eye watched his every step. It stared down at him. His fearful mind gave it a terrible vulpine quality with definite vertically elliptical pupils. He felt its glare bearing down at him from the sky whilst exuding a spiteful malice, which was unsettling. His imagination played upon him. He thought he saw it blink slowly as he was looking away.

He found himself slightly afraid. Glancing around nervously at every night-time sound he heard through the mist. He quickened his pace.

He walked for several long minutes using Logan's staff to steady himself in the darkness. Surely, he should have come out from amongst the strange stones and found the wagon by now. He felt a sudden surge of panic, and he realised he had likely gotten himself lost.

The apprentice cursed under his breath. How could he have allowed himself to be this stupid? He was certain he had come from this direction. He must have wandered farther than he thought. He continued onwards, hoping the wagon was just up ahead.

A sudden *crack* of a broken twig startled him. It was much closer this time. His heart leapt into his mouth, and he scanned the swirling tendrils of mist where the sound had come from. Nothing.

His panic swelled in his belly, and he hurried onwards. He felt himself shake with fear. He felt very alone. He wished Truda was here. She never seemed afraid, never shaken, even at his master's more grizzly studies or at being sent off across the borders to war torn lands to gather subjects for Eldrick's work. He remembered how she would often laugh at his anxious temperament. It would be a welcome laugh right now in this dark place.

The apprentice stopped as he thought he heard someone call his name. He listened. Nothing, just the eerie silence of the mist.

He heard it again. It was a voice he knew. It was Truda's. Relief and excitement lifted him as his hurried onwards towards the voice.

They have caught up, he thought. The others must have caught up and found the wagon.

He heard his name again. It seemed distant and hard to place.

'Truda, I'm here,' he called out. He knew they must be looking for him. 'I'm here. Where are you?'

He hurried onwards.

He stumbled into an open clearing and found himself amongst a circle of the standing stones. The mist seemed clearer here. At its centre, a huge dolmen loomed out of the gloom.

The ancient structure consisted of several upright stones, which supported a large flat horizontal capstone. The single chamber it created yawned open and was full of a darkness his eyes were unable to penetrate. The apprentice had studied something similar back at the ruins with Logan. He had said they were likely some sort of important tomb. The scope of the engineering required to create such a monument was impressive, thought the apprentice.

He spotted a figure moving slowly by the ancient dolmen. A dark figure in a long flowing robe moved silently through the mist. The apprentice could not see any features through the gloom.

'Truda?' he called and moved closer.

The figure halted, and its hooded face slowly

swung to regard him. A deep darkness from beneath its hood stared back at him.

He gradually slowed to a standstill. It did not look like Truda.

The apprentice's blood froze as he stood staring into the dark hood of the robed figure. It did not move. It just stared in silence, looking strangely hunched and peering up from a near crouch.

The apprentice took a step back. The figure started to move, only slowly, but it began to raise its arm. He froze. The robed figure pointed straight at him.

The apprentice was terrified. He stood petrified, his heart pounding in his chest. His feet would not allow him to move.

Something appeared from fog around him.

He found himself confronted with dozens of glaring eyes staring at him through the mist. He gasped, looking around the menhirs surrounding him. The eyes glowed with a rich malevolence and watched him hungrily. Some seemed only yards away. They surrounded him, lurking in the thick fog beyond the ring of stones, yet whatever bore them seemed obscured by swirling tendrils of mist.

With a feeling of dread, he slowly turned his attention back to the cloaked figure. It stood silent staring at him. His heart jumped as he realised it was closer. It now stood in the open ground between the dolmen and him. He had not seen it move.

It looked motionless and just stood staring intently at him. Still, he could not penetrate the darkness beneath its hood. It had no face. He thought he heard his name whispered from the mist about him. His eyes darted about trying to place it.

Without warning, the dark figure rushed headlong towards him, screeching an awful keening wail. Its robes billowed out as it glided horribly at a terrifying speed.

Beneath the robes, the apprentice glimpsed glistening black limbs which were slender and terrible—inhuman. Its ribs protruded prominently beneath the stretched black skin of its abdomen.

It approached with the skittering determination of some dreadful spider. A pair of those familiar vulpine eyes now glared out from darkness of the hood, boring into his soul and eating what warmth dwelt within him.

A fiendish grotesque skull-like face revealed itself from the darkness of the hood, an awful toothy maw agape. He caught a glimpse of curved horns jutting from beneath the flapping hood as it rushed towards him. The malevolent eyes glowed bright like a burning flame.

The apprentice screamed and tried to run. His limbs seemed to be mired in an infuriating slowness. He felt ensnared in a horrifying slow motion as the dark creature hurtled towards him.

It was upon him. He screamed in terror and levelled a desperate blind kick in hopeless defence as it bore down onto him.

***

With a lurching kick into the side of the wagon, he awoke himself screaming out in agony. The apprentice clutched at his leg trying to suppress the pain by cradling it tightly. The shooting burst of excruciating pain dulled, and then throbbed again with another flash of agony. He gritted his teeth as waves of pain washed over his ankle. He rolled about in the back of the wagon, holding his leg.

He could feel the splint against his leg giving way as he moved. He may have broken it. There was the sharp and ferrous taste of blood in his mouth. He had bitten his tongue as he clamped his teeth down hard and clenched them together during the surges of pain. The apprentice cursed angrily.

He snatched up Logan's staff from where it laid beside him and pushed himself upright. The panic of being chased still had his heart pounding in his chest and his breathing heavy. It had only been a dream. A terrible dream, yet it had felt so real. He felt a cold sweat cooling his skin, it made him shiver. His dream left a lingering sense of unease which he couldn't shake, as if someone was staring at him even now. He looked around.

'Bad dreams again, boy?' asked a derisive voice from the front of the wagon. Bronas turned to regard him with a spiteful smirk.

The feeling of panic slowly subsided. The apparitions of his nightmare were already fading from his memory in the light of day, replaced by a feeling of growing foolishness.

The abashed apprentice felt instantly irritable from the embarrassment and throbbing pain in his leg. He gave no reply to the hired-sword, just returning an angry glare.

The apprentice busied himself examining the

splint reinforcing his broken leg. He had certainly broken it. One of the shafts straightening his leg had splintered, and the binding which lashed it all together seemed loose. He cursed again.

'You were calling out and thrashing about back there. Looked like you were having another bad dream,' continued the hired-sword. 'Must have woke yourself when you kicked the side of the wagon,' said Bronas, amused.

The apprentice was annoyed by this obvious and completely unsympathetic remark from his companion.

'It was probably the pain of my leg disturbing my sleep,' said the apprentice sheepishly. 'I don't remember any dream.'

The hired-sword grunted and turned back to his reins.

'I thought we might have stopped for the night,' continued the apprentice.

'No, lad.' Bronas laughed without turning, 'You haven't been asleep that long.'

'How long was I asleep?' asked the apprentice.

Bronas rubbed his chin. 'I dunno, not long. Only an hour or two.'

The apprentice looked up at the sun in the sky to gauge the time of day.

'When will we stop?' he asked.

'Got a couple of hours of good light left yet,' replied the hired-sword impatiently.

The apprentice looked out from the wagon and surveyed the countryside around them, fearing a glimpse of old menhirs or a strange fog creeping in. There was a long silence as the wagon's wheels rolled along the muddy road. A lone rhann slowly circled high overhead, its presence always an ill-omen. With its ominous dark wings spread wide and with scavenging eyes, it studied the landscape below.

The apprentice turned to search the sky behind them. It was still there. It did not look much further away. But still, it had been on the horizon for two days now. A thin tower of pluming smoke broke the skyline of the western mountains.

'It still looks like it is coming from the mountains,' commented the apprentice, trying to lift the awkward silence. 'Are you sure it is not coming from the passes?'

'I told you, boy, nothing up there. Dunno where that is but that's a big fire. Its somewhere closer than the mountains, a few days behind us now I reckon.'

'What could it be,' asked the apprentice.

Bronas sighed as if he preferred the silence. 'I don't know, I told you, and I don't really care so long as it's behind us and not in front of us.'

'Could it be bandits?' asked the apprentice apprehensively as he searched the roadsides for anything that might be lying in wait for their wagon.

'No, not likely,' said Bronas flatly. 'Whatever's burning is something big. Probably some dispute between lords, and that smoke means one of 'em's losin'. Looks like a village or a hall, maybe some outpost or fort. Then again, could be a lot of bandits,' he said, and with the latter, turned to flash the apprentice a grim smile.

Every bump sent a sharp pain spiking through the apprentice's leg. He would be glad to get off these old roads and onto a ship. He felt exposed, just the two of them on a small wagon. They would make an easy target for lawless men.

'Where are we?' asked the apprentice anxiously. 'How much farther?'

'Still a few days out from Peren,' replied Bronas. 'You will get a ship there.' He turned back to the reins and resumed his silence, ignoring the apprentice.

Despite the hired-sword's assertion, the apprentice still worried for his colleagues. What if they met trouble on the roads? He clutched his necklace and watched the distant column of ominous smoke. He muttered a prayer to Hjort, to keep both himself and the others all as fleet-footed as the uncatchable stag, and one step ahead of trouble. He grunted in grim amusement and it sparked a throb of pain. He would certainly not be fleet of foot, and needed all the help the old gods could send him.

Out of boredom, he idly ran his hands along Logan's walking staff. Such a gracious gift. He did not want to think about how bad this journey would be without it. There were glyphs the apprentice had noticed, carved into the staff's head. The apprentice did not recognise them. He meant to ask Master Logan about it when they next met, and he could return the staff with his most sincere thanks.

The apprentice looked around and sighed. The wagon moved so slowly, barely faster than walking. There were still a few more long, bumpy, and painful days stuck in the back of the wagon. He hoped it would be more comfortable aboard a ship.

He should have no trouble buying passage south

to the capital for himself and his cargo. He had coin enough and documents of payment from the College, if need be. People knew the College paid out on these documents, and so they were as good as gold or silver.

Already, he longed this journey to be over. He much desired for the comfortable and warm surroundings of the College and the city. At least he was thankful for getting away from the cold, damp marquee and the campsite up in the passes, away from those eerie old stones and ancient bones, and soon, this wagon and these terrible wet roads.

That nagging presence still lingered. He had hoped it would diminish the farther away he got from those old passes. Alas, it still haunted him like a fell shadow. It prickled the hairs on the back of his neck, an uncomfortable feeling of something staring at him from some hiding place. It seemed always to lurk just over his shoulder. There was never anything there when he summoned the courage to look. He shuddered and tried to force his thoughts away from the feeling and the surreal memory of his nightmare: That dark inhuman face with its terrible eyes still haunting his thoughts. It seemed to come hurtling towards him every time he closed his eyes.

He tried to keep himself distracted. He tinkered with his splint, trying to reset and tighten the ruined thing. He did what he could to keep his leg healing straight. It was not looking hopeful. He did not have the skill of his masters, and the pain forced him to stop if he moved it too much.

He did not want to have a crippled leg. He had seen the cripples begging in the streets around the

College. They were wretched souls. He feared he could one day share their fate. And now the bindings of his splint were loose, each bump painfully resonated through his ankle even more. He did not know how much more of it he could take. He gritted his teeth and resigned himself to several more painful days, and cold aching nights, stuck in the back of this accursed wagon.

Thought of returning to Arn would have to get him through this. He had a feeling that portentous things awaited him at the College. His apprenticeship must nearly be complete. He and his colleagues would be hailed as most eminent and illustrious scholars upon their return—once the others of the College learned of what they had achieved. What power they had wielded over death in those forlorn and forgotten ruins. He was sure Eldrick could do it again before the council. His masters and, perhaps he himself, could even earn infamy in the pages of the *Great Histories*. He allowed himself a smile.

The hairs prickled up on the back of his neck. He looked around, searching for the lurking watcher. He noticed a strange, gnarled tree growing on the hillside.

For a fleeting moment, he saw a flicker of darkness out of the corner of his eye. A glimpse of a solitary figure, hooded with dark floating robes. It stood, staring menacingly. But when he flicked his eyes back to the tree, there was nothing there.

The young apprentice let out a manic cackle. Bronas threw an inquisitive look towards the back of the wagon, but the apprentice did not acknowledge it.

The apprentice could not understand why this apparition was haunting, not only his sleep, but now his waking moments, ever lurking at the edge of his vision. He wondered if he were simply hallucinating. Perhaps he was slowly driving himself to madness in the back of this wagon? Or was some dark malignant presence truly pursuing him. The apprentice dared not think on it. He sunk low into the wagon and trembled in silent dread.

The wagon's wheels struck another hole in the road. His leg exploded with agony as the wagon jolted his ruined leg. He sat numbly, barely registering the unyielding pain.

He stared unseeing into the wood of the wagons timber frame. His thoughts wandered, his eyes distant. The apprentice thought of dark places while haunted by terrible, malign eyes.

EPILOGUE

The Road to Arn

The morning light brought a heavy downpour. The rain lashed down upon the horses and their hunched riders, cloaks pulled tightly to keep off the weather. A cart rumbled along the road amongst the riders, its cargo lashed down beneath and concealed by a waxed canopy. A troop of armoured warriors rode at its sides as they filed along the east road out of Ravenshold.

Hafgan reined in beneath the lone tree which stood by the roadside on the outskirts of town. Arnulf had glanced up at the tree as he passed, but did not stop. Arnulf rode slightly ahead, alone but for the hound padding along beside his horse. The cart rolled past behind Hafgan as he looked up into the tree.

The rope creaked as the limp body twisted in the wind. They had found him at dawn, hung from the neck with a length of frayed rope. The young warrior, Erran, reined in beside him.

'Poor bastard,' said Erran. 'Haven't cut him down yet then?'

'No,' replied Hafgan. 'The high lord ordered him cut down. But they won't come out 'til this stops I imagine,' he said, holding his hand up to the rain. 'He's not going anywhere.'

'Or will he?' mused Erran grimly. 'I wonder if they will find who did it?'

'Not likely, lad. The guards saw nothing. Likely had a hand in it, too, but nobody is saying nothing.' He paused. 'Word got about, and will likely spread, too. The townsfolk have laid their blame. They've heard what the College has been doing up there. Calimir here has paid that price.'

Erran looked up. 'Do you think he was in with them up there, Haf?' asked the young warrior.

'Who knows? I doubt it. Probably did nothing, but that don't change nothing. The College will still answer for all this. Arnulf will make sure.'

Hafgan threw a glance to his lord. He rode with a heavy head. He had asked to ride alone for a time.

A sudden roar erupted from the wagon. The covering shook wildly, clinking the chains holding its cargo in place. Wild, furious screeching emanated from beneath the heavy covering of the wagon.

Horses escorting the wagon became spooked and shied away. Astrid fought to control her mount. She and Fergus rode at the head of the wagons escort, her shield-maidens forming a majority of the riders.

'I hope he can't get out,' said Erran as he watched. His horse had become nervous at the sudden outburst.

'He can't. That cage is solid and he's chained good,' replied Hafgan. 'We'll get him south to Arn. The king can see for himself.'

The covering thrashed as Ewolf fought against his chains within the cage. He screamed bestially. Hafgan hoped there was some way to reverse this curse. He felt a great sorrow for his broken lord. The College would indeed answer for this, but they could also be the only hope to save the lad, if he could be saved.

Hafgan watched his lord a moment. Arnulf did not turn at the terrible sounds coming from the cart. He rode on solemnly.

Hafgan frowned and turned back to Erran. The young warrior was watching Astrid as she rode past. She frowned at him when she caught his eye. The other shield-maidens riding with her threw him unfriendly glances as they passed.

'I would leave her be, lad. She's a cold one,' muttered Hafgan.

Erran looked at him and grinned. With that, he kicked his horse away from the hanging corpse to follow after the cart.

Hafgan could hear the sound of hooves approaching up ahead. He took one last lingering look at the dead scholar. He grimaced and wheeled his horse away to join his companions.

A patrol appeared ahead. They were returning to the Motte. There were half a dozen riders – the high lord's men. The lead man rode up and hailed as he approached.

'My lords,' he greeted anxiously, 'we just came back. I saw it. By the gods,' he exclaimed.

'What?' demanded Fergus.

The rider looked spooked. 'A dead man, lord, walking.'

'Where?' pressed Fergus.

'We struck it down, lord, but it kept coming. It was back up that way.' He pointed off.

'Did you kill it?' asked Fergus, referring to the dead man.

'I think so, lord. It still shook after several blows but did not rise again. I still cannot believe my eyes,' said the horseman, shocked.

'Anything else?'

'We warned the first farms we came to, as we were supposed to, but some we found completely deserted. Something was not right. We found blood. We got out of there quick, lord. But the folk we saw, we told them to make their way here for the high lord's protection. Many saw the smoke of the Motte and feared the worst.'

'Aye,' said Fergus.

'I must get word to Lord Angus. Safe travels, my lords,' he said before riding off quickly.

'It's spreading,' murmured Hafgan. He clutched a pendant at his neck. 'Gods save us.'

Here ends
A Ritual of Bone

Volume I
of
The Dead Sagas

A NOTE ON THE DEAD SAGAS

A Ritual of Bone will shortly be followed by Volume II: *A Ritual of Flesh* and will continue this epic saga of the struggle between the living and the cursed dead.

Only valour and steel can stand against the rising dead

I would like to thank you for reading.
If you have enjoyed this book, please could I ask if you would be so kind as to leave a review somewhere, in particular on Goodreads, or Amazon. Every review and rating is hugely appreciated.

For more information, and for Lee's mailing list please visit

www.leeconleyauthor.com

ABOUT THE AUTHOR

Lee is a musician and writer in Lincolnshire, UK. He lives with his wife Laura, and daughters, Luna and Anya, in the historic cathedral city of Lincoln. Alongside a lifetime of playing guitar and immersing himself in the study of music and history, Lee is also a practitioner and instructor of historic martial arts and swordsmanship. After writing his successful advanced guitar theory textbook *The Guitar Teachers Grimoire,* Lee turns his hand to writing fiction. Lee is now studying a degree in creative writing and working on his debut fantasy series *The Dead Sagas* as well as also generally writing speculative fiction and horror.

CPSIA information can be obtained
at www.ICGtesting.com
Printed in the USA
BVHW071504231221
624752BV00008B/376